sum

ever

after

ALSO BY JANE CRITTENDEN

Worlds Apart

summer

ever

after

**Jane
CRITTENDEN**

LAKE UNION
PUBLISHING

Text copyright © 2024 by Jane Crittenden
All rights reserved.

Published by Lake Union Publishing, Seattle

www.apub.com

Amazon, the Amazon logo, and Lake Union Publishing are trademarks of Amazon.com, Inc., or its affiliates.

ISBN-13: 9781662509179
eISBN: 9781662509162

Cover design by Emma Rogers
Cover image: © GoodStudio © Natalia Smu / Shutterstock; © jamielawton © Dumitru Ochievschi © Svetlana Aganina / Getty Images

Printed in the United States of America

Mum,
Thank you for teaching me to listen, to ask
questions – and to hold things lightly

Chapter 1

ALICE

Now

Andy Cortez-Hall stares at me. Not in the flesh, but from a photo on a website. His curtains are gone, his smirk is blunted by the business of being important and, even though he's older, there's no mistaking that it's him because he's wearing the black leather Gemini necklace.

Andy?

My fingers touch my throat. I remember how the metal pendant felt cool against my skin when it was all warm and tanned by the Barcelona sun.

Andy's still in Barcelona.

The website tells me he runs a language school over there. Am I surprised? Yes.

I click through the pages and see this is no ordinary school – it's a slick set-up in an impressive glass building with views of Sagrada Familia. As well as teaching English, Catalan and Spanish, they offer German and French lessons, too. I'm nervous, but Janet isn't.

I land back on Andy's photo.

Mum must sense me stiffen as she glances over to where I'm sat on the sofa, her eyes temporarily pulled away from her beloved reality TV show. She leans over the arm of her wingback chair to get a closer look at the photo, but I twist the screen away.

Her round face creases in delight. 'Don't be shy!' she sings out. 'I'm glad you've finally seen sense. As much as I hate to say it, your sister was right – online dating is definitely the way forward for you.'

My gaze is drawn back to Andy's face. Sweat prickles my hairline.

'You know you can do that on your phone.' She nods, as though she's the expert. 'Come on then, show me your hit list.'

This isn't how I planned my conversation with Mum to roll out. *This business* isn't what I expected to find either. I flounder, my mouth dry as I try to gather myself.

A squeal rings out from the huge TV next to the fireplace. A platinum blonde with hair to her waist throws herself into the arms of a bronzed hunk wearing skimpy swim shorts. Mum sniggers, distracted for a moment, and I scroll away from Andy's face. But then my heart jumps again.

Mariana?

Memories cartwheel and then something painful – and obvious – slides into place. Of course. This is why Andy's running a language school.

Mariana's smile dazzles out from the screen, bolder than I remember, her gaze penetrating mine. I drag my eyes away and scan the text below.

Perfecte is run by husband-and-wife team Andrew and Mariana Cortez-Hall.

I don't read any further because now my whole body stings in shock.

They're married?

2

This is going to be impossible.

I look up to find Mum staring at me. 'You okay, petal? Seen an old flame? You've gone a bit pale.' Her gaze drops to the screen and this time I'm too slow to move it away. She catches sight of Mariana and laughs. 'Okay, is there something you're not telling me? You know you can be honest, I'm a very modern parent.' She sighs. 'I've had enough practice with your sister.'

Now's not the time to explain she's got this wrong or dispute her parenting. I shake my head, yanking my thoughts properly back to the present. 'This isn't a dating site,' I say. 'There's something I need to tell you.'

Except now there's a whole load of complications that weren't in the picture before.

Mum frowns and mutes the TV. 'Yes?'

I take a deep breath. Silly really, I've got nothing of great importance to say that will affect her, but I know how much she hates change. I click on to the homepage and turn the laptop towards her so she can see the website.

Mum shifts her body and tries to sit a bit straighter. She loves her plush red wingback armchair and I joke she's like the queen reigning over my sister Charlie and me. But as the years have gone on, she's filling the large chair much more than she used to, and it worries me.

She takes the computer and balances it on her lap. She clicks through some of the pages. Her eyes narrow and then fly back to mine. 'What is this?' she says, her tone dangerous.

Out of the corner of my eye, the TV flashes silent images of the beautiful people cavorting on a sandy beach. A simple life.

'Janet's had an offer: this company want to buy her TESOL school,' I say softly.

Mum reads from the website. 'Perfecte Language School. In Barcelona? I don't understand. Are you leaving me?'

3

'No, of course not! There's nothing for you to worry about. They want to bring their brand to London, not the other way around. I just thought you'd want to know. It's a great opportunity for Janet.'

Mum's face slackens into folds of suspicion and she glances over to the front window where we can see Janet's flat across the road. 'That's all well and good for her but what are you going to get out of it?' she says.

They've never seen eye to eye and I've given up trying to force a neighbourly friendship. 'Perfecte want to expand,' I say. 'We won't just be a TESOL school teaching English as a foreign language, but offer French, Spanish, German – that sort of thing.'

'You don't speak any other languages,' she retorts.

I sigh. 'Look, I'm still going to be doing my normal job, teaching English. Nothing's going to change. I'll still do the same hours and I'll still be here for you.'

Mum clicks the pages again and lands on the photo of Andy. I hold my breath. I'm not going to tell her I know him – that I *knew* him. It's a part of my life I parcelled away ten years ago – and it needs to stay that way.

I watch her read the words already scorched on to my mind.

Perfecte is run by husband-and-wife team Andrew and Mariana Cortez-Hall.

'That Andrew's a looker,' she says, tapping the screen. 'Shame he's taken.'

My laugh comes out wobbly. Perhaps I can avoid seeing them when they swoop in and introduce themselves. Janet's supported my flexible working hours since she first offered me the job at Riverside. It means I can be here for Mum.

Maybe I can plan to be at home that day.

I snap the laptop shut and jump up. 'Cup of tea?'

Mum glances at her watch. 'It's not three o'clock yet,' she says and turns the sound back up on the TV. It's a dismissal, and I'm relieved, because it means we've navigated the change in my job without a drama.

I go through the archway into the kitchen and put the laptop on the dining table. The downstairs of our Edwardian house is mostly open plan these days. Many of the beautiful period features were demolished during the building work, but thankfully I convinced Mum to keep the original front door and living room fireplace.

I glance back at Mum's sticks propped up against her chair. Her decision to renovate made sense, to make it easier for her compromised mobility, though I wish she'd move around a little bit more. But it's hard to insist when she tells me how difficult it is.

I breathe through the familiar waves of guilt and find myself opening the laptop again. I sneak another look at Andy. He's wearing a white shirt, open at the collar, showing a slice of honey-brown skin that I know comes from spending time in the sun.

I stare at the pendant again.

Andy? It's so bizarre. I haven't seen him since we . . .

'It's three now, petal, is the kettle on?' Mum calls. 'I'm dying of thirst. Don't forget it's chocolate digestives today.'

I don't need reminding and I don't need to look at the time. Mum's routines run like clockwork. It's Thursday so of course it's chocolate digestives, just like it's custard creams on Mondays and Jammie Dodgers on Saturdays. I know exactly what she has for breakfast, lunch and dinner every day, too, but there's a list pinned to the fridge with an Eiffel Tower magnet just in case Charlie needs to step in. Though that's a joke. Until her face appears around the house, I never know if she's living here or shacked up with her latest squeeze.

I carry the tray back through to Mum where a woman's face fills the TV, eyes spiked in thick fake lashes, glittery with tears. I nudge at the pile of junk on the table next to her to make space. If I could, I'd sweep the whole lot into recycling but she's precious about her celebrity magazines, catalogues and promotional leaflets that fall through the door, saying, 'They inspire me.' In other words, they fuel her shopping habits. But it's not up to me how she spends her money.

I return to the kitchen on autopilot. It's spag bol night. Sometimes, I try to keep my mind entertained by practising my vegetable-cutting skills but honestly, I perfected this years ago. Plus, I'm only going to blitz them to mush, so what's the point? Instead, I whip through the preparations at high speed and try to ignore Andy creeping back into my thoughts again.

I don't want to tell Janet I know him – and Mariana. Though I suppose I can't keep it a secret forever. I have a feeling she'll delightedly push me to the forefront, with the expectation I'm the lucky talisman to a smooth business transaction when I'm probably a thorn in the Cortez-Halls' plan.

My stomach tilts as the reality of the sale properly starts to sink in. What if Andy and Mariana decide to come over to London for a while? Check out how we work?

I stir the meat sauce. I could make this food blindfolded. Mostly, Mum's menu consists of bland food, so at least with tonight's meal I can hide the pureed vegetables in the sauce. I gave up on the fight to get her to eat healthily years ago because I couldn't hack the teenage temper tantrums. But at the same time, her weight gain is making her mobility worse and it tugs at the seams of my guilt.

Mum laughs at something on the TV and I look up. When she's happy, I can relax a little, but never for long. I stack the dishwasher, wipe down the surfaces and just as I'm about to put pasta on to boil, the doorbell goes. Through the stained glass I see a familiar silhouette.

At the door, Janet bustles inside, her grey hair a nest of frizz that seems to have a life of its own. She pulls me into a bosomy hug. 'I've got some *wonderful* news,' she says, releasing me and settling down on the sofa. She's clasping her hands and looks like she's about to explode with delight.

Warily, I lower myself on to the arm of Mum's chair.

'You're not going to believe this. I had a lovely phone call from Mariana earlier and she wants you to go to Barcelona and do some training with them. Of course I said yes, because no one in their right mind would say no!'

I don't know who's more shocked, me or Mum.

Janet's eyes shine behind tortoiseshell glasses and for a moment her energy sends a sparkle of excitement through me.

'Alice isn't going anywhere,' Mum barks.

The feeling flatlines. I shake my head. 'No, that's not going to be possible.'

Janet forces a bigger smile. 'Alice, you deserve the opportunity! Everyone needs a break from their routine now and then.'

Mum laughs shrilly, shooting a warning signal up my spine.

I place my hand on her shoulder. 'I'm really sorry, but it won't work.'

Janet cocks her head to one side. With her beady gaze, she looks bird-like, which is ironic given her house swarms with cats.

Still, I love Janet dearly.

Mum reaches up and clutches my hand. 'No, it won't,' she says sadly. 'I need Alice here.'

Janet narrows her eyes. 'Do you, Dani? Really?'

'You know how it is, Jan. I'm worse on my feet as I get older.'

'You're younger than me,' she snaps.

Mum's eye twitches. 'You don't need sticks, do you?' She looks up at me and my chest tightens. I slide my eyes away.

Janet exhales noisily. 'It's not really our decision though is it, Dani? I'm not asking Alice to emigrate. Think of going to Barcelona as pressing pause.'

They're both looking at me. For once, I miss the annoying background drivel of Mum's programmes. Suddenly, Andy's cheeky grin flashes into my head, his dancing eyes on mine as he cups my face with his hands.

I swallow. 'No, I can't go.'

'Alice said her job wasn't going to change. Everything works just fine the way things are,' Mum says firmly.

'The school think she's got lots of potential,' Janet pushes back. 'They really like her student food events. They think it's a fantastic idea.'

Mum looks up at me again, eyes flinty. '*What* food events?'

'Oh, it's nothing,' I mutter.

Janet releases a short hiss. She sounds like one of her cats and springs up and streaks over towards the door. For someone small and round, she's remarkably light on her feet. 'Promise me you'll have a think about it, Alice? It's only for a couple of months.'

She manages to sound angry and sad at the same time and my stomach clenches. Torn, I nod, and she slips out of the front door, leaving Mum and I in a cold, empty silence.

'Dinner's ready,' I say eventually.

Mum shuffles to the edge of her chair and I hold out my arm so she can pull herself to standing. I pass her both sticks – like I always do – and she only takes one – like she always does – and threads her other arm through mine. We walk slowly through to the kitchen.

Who'd cook for Mum if I wasn't here? Who'd help her to the table? Still, I feel a tug towards Janet. She's only ever been lovely to me and I don't want to let her down either.

Chapter 2

ALICE

Now

Later that evening I cross the street and knock on Janet's door. She lives on the top floor of a converted Victorian house and greets me holding a tortoiseshell cat that's a perfect match for her glasses.

'Come in, come up,' she says, already turning away to climb the stairs.

I pull on the sleeves of my cardigan and follow, physically feeling the empty space where she'd usually greet me with a squashy hug.

Janet drops the cat in a basket on the landing and goes into her tiny kitchen. I watch at the door for a moment as she bustles about making tea, but the stench of meaty cat food – and the awkwardness of small talk – is overwhelming and I go into the living room instead.

I settle myself into one of the ancient armchairs by the window and pick at the fabric on the arm that has been scratched raw by Janet's cats. From here, I can see Mum's massive TV flickering through the bay opposite. A tabby eyes my lap from the window sill and I cross my legs and look away.

Janet comes in and hands me a mug with a faded kitten photo on the front. She shoos a black cat off her chair, but it springs back on to her lap as soon as she sits down. She strokes its head and I wonder if this one is Mary or Martha. They all look the same to me.

She sighs. 'I owe you an apology.'

I look at her in surprise. 'No, you don't—'

'Oh, I do,' she insists. 'I'm sorry for being short with you earlier. I thought going to Barcelona for training would be fun. I remember how much you loved it over there, and, with your interest in food and so on, I thought you'd leap at the chance to go.'

The leap Janet talks of feels like stepping off a cliff rather than bouncing back into a city I love – *once* loved. A decade is a long time. My life isn't the same. *I'm* not the same. And the thought of working alongside *senyor i senyora Cortez-Hall* makes me feel nauseous.

Out of the corner of my eye, the tabby's still eyeballing me and I angle my body away. But Janet's watching me too, and it's unsettling, so I distract myself by looking around the room. She's taught in some of Africa's poorest countries and the photos that cram the surfaces in here prove it. Kindness blooms in her heart.

'I'll do everything I can to make sure the takeover is smooth,' I say eventually.

Except go to Barcelona for training.

In any normal circumstance, refusing to go would sound petty. But Janet understands my commitments to Mum – at least, I thought she did. She's known every inch of my life since I was twenty. She moved over the road just before my grandma died and steered me through the numb weeks when I didn't know what to do with myself. Charlie, Mum and I had lived with Grandma all our lives. Her house was our home. When Mum had to work, Grandma looked after us, so it was only right I did the same for her in later years – and then she was gone.

Two ginger cats strut into the room and hop up on to Janet's chair. The young one sits across the back and pats her frizz with its paw. The other nudges its head against her arm and she reaches out and tickles its chin. The black one on her lap hisses a warning. 'You're enjoying running the food events, aren't you?' Janet says.

I nod and look down at my tea. It's a stretch to call them 'events' as they're just something I organise on the side if students are interested. Though I enjoy our sociable chats way more than teaching, I can't admit this to Janet. Her suggestion I train as one of her TESOL teachers became my lifeline after Mum's accident. I don't have to work regular hours so I can be home when she needs me. Where would I be without Janet?

I feel like a failure for letting her down.

'Mariana's very interested in what you're doing. She's thinking about making the food events a proper part of the course.'

My head snaps up. 'Really?' I'm surprised – and a bit annoyed.

Janet nods. 'She's looking for ways to diversify. You know, offer something different to students alongside the language teaching.'

And Andy? I want to ask. *What does he think?* An image pops into my head. Walking back from the market, sinking our mouths into sweet, succulent peaches, tasting the sticky juice on his lips as we kissed . . .

'Alice?' Janet's looking at me oddly.

I flush. 'Sorry?'

'Can you put something together for Mariana? To explain how you run the food events?'

I pluck at the armchair threads. I'm uncomfortable that Janet's made a big deal of this when it's personal to me and something that's still evolving. My ideas don't belong to Riverside School, they belong to me. The thought of Mariana sweeping in and taking over . . .

My food events started by accident. I'd made Cornish pasties for myself at home one day and brought the leftovers in for the students to enjoy as there was no way Mum was going to eat them. They went down a storm. In return, some of the young adults told me about a street food curry van they'd discovered over in East London. I went to investigate with Charlie one weekend and the food was so delicious it got me thinking about what other wonderful dishes I might find hidden away in the city.

'Perfecte buying Riverside is a great opportunity for you,' Janet's saying. 'They want you to run the new place.'

'Sorry?' My mind is still floating around food events and I don't notice the tabby spring off the window sill until it thuds on to my lap. I yelp and press myself back into the chair as it needles my thighs.

Janet leans over and nudges the cat to the floor. 'You'll do a fantastic job.'

I'm still gripping the chair arms. I must be gaping, too, because my mouth has gone dry. I reach for my tea and take a gulp. 'What do you mean? Where are you going?'

Janet laughs. 'Don't panic, I'll still be there, but it's time for me to step back. You'll be in charge of day-to-day things. That's why you need to go over to Barcelona. They want to train you up, show you how they do things.'

'But I can't— I mean, I'm not capable . . .' I look down into my tea and run my finger over the chip in the rim. I remember Janet giving me my first cuppa in this mug when the kitten picture still looked fresh and new.

'Of course you are!' Janet flashes me a smile. 'You're my best teacher – and everyone loves your Cornish pasties.'

I smile a little. Word got around after I made the pasties. Now new students arrive having already heard about the 'pasty teacher' and the promise of one on their first day. 'But Mum . . .' I trail off.

Working with *senyor i senyora Cortez-Hall*? No way.

Janet's face drops. I'm disappointing her and I scrabble around for something positive to say, but she's standing up, so I do the same. 'Well, in that case I'll let Mariana know that you can't make the training.'

'It won't cause a problem with the sale, will it?' I say quickly. 'You know I'd go if I could? I can't just waltz away. You know my life doesn't work like that.'

Janet's eyes behind her glasses look glossy, like she might cry. Then she sucks in a sharp breath. 'You know, your mum will be fine if you change your mind.'

I don't like the way she's pushing me. But at the same time, a little voice reminds me this is Janet's life too, her business, and her actions might be about kindness, but they come from a place of survival, too.

It's not just about you.

I sigh. 'I'll think about it.'

Chapter 3

ANDY

Ten years ago

I wasn't supposed to be on a train to Barcelona.

Or a train to anywhere.

But there we were, Jimmy and I, making our way to Ibiza via my uncle's, just as my mum had wanted. We'd trudged on to the train and thrown ourselves across seating for four, hungover from our last night out in Montpellier with one of my brother's mates. Dave had taken us on a bar crawl and paid for all the drinks. Generous. Though the drunker he became the more desperate he was to thank me for helping his sister and, in the end, I had to tell him to stop.

Too much. We both knew there was much more lingering in that conversation than my heroics – and neither of us wanted to go there.

I touched my Gemini pendant and stared up at the world gathering pace outside the window as the train pulled away. I wondered how quickly we could get the fuck out of Barcelona without sending my mum into a spin. Not that I was a mummy's boy and did everything she asked. I was just trying to be a good son – though up until now, I'd made a total hash of it. Agreeing to stop off and see Uncle Enric in Barcelona had put me back in her good books.

'Shift over.'

A girl, similar in age to us, stood in the aisle, grinning. Her blonde hair was shaved down one side and she had piercings in her lip and eyebrow. I'd lay a bet she had tattoos too, probably in places only the privileged would see.

'Charlie!' Jimmy hollered, sitting up.

'Come on, move your arses.' Charlie swung off her rucksack, narrowly avoiding knocking out the girl behind her.

'Careful,' she muttered. She had amazing hair, thick and wavy, and olive skin that probably looked tanned all year around. Wary eyes flitted between Jimmy and me.

I threw her a friendly grin and she responded with a watery smile.

Charlie heaved her rucksack into her arms and tossed it on to the storage rack, causing her T-shirt to ride up. Jimmy lifted thick eyebrows and locked on to her bare, pierced midriff. He ran his hand over his buzz cut. 'You work out?' he asked her.

I could see where this might be heading.

Charlie threw the other girl's bag up top with similar ease and then plopped down next to Jimmy. She flexed her biceps; they were impressive. 'Gym bunny,' she said. She clocked her friend still hovering. 'Jesus, sis, sit *down*.'

Sister?

My gaze hopped between them. Yes, I could see it now. The same broad, heart-shaped face, generous mouth and green eyes, though the dark-haired girl's were a shade more grey. She glanced at me again and I wondered, idly, if she liked blonds. Jimmy and I had spent a week in Montpellier. My hair had gone lighter in the sun and we'd slept off hangovers on the beach so we both had half-decent tans.

I swung my legs around and stood up. 'Which seat would you like, madam?' I said, sweeping my arm out as though she was royalty.

Sister Girl rolled her eyes and sat down opposite Charlie. 'And you know each other – how?' she said, looking at them both.

Her sister laughed, luminous eyes like a window to all the energy bubbling away inside her. Jimmy couldn't peel his gaze away. 'When you were in the loo, I accosted this one on the platform,' she replied, prodding him. 'They're going to Barcelona. I thought it'd be fun if we travelled together.'

Charlie was sitting cross-legged now and close enough for Jimmy to soak up a full view of her cleavage. I turned my attention to Sister Girl. 'Have you been away long?' I asked.

'About a month,' she replied, rooting through her bag. 'How about you?'

'We've spent the last week at my brother's mate's house in Montpellier,' I said. 'We're stopping off at my uncle's in Barcelona on the way to Ibiza.'

'Uh-huh,' she said, and pulled out a pen and postcard. I caught sight of a sandy beach and turquoise sea before she flipped it over.

'How long will you be there?' asked Charlie. 'We're going to Narbonne first.'

'A few days, maybe.'

'His uncle's got a restaurant in Plaça Reial with free digs upstairs,' added Jimmy. 'He said we can stay as long as we want.'

'Except we need to get to Ibiza,' I reminded him.

'Oh yeah – why's that? What's the hurry?' said Charlie.

'I'm DJ-ing,' I muttered. It wasn't strictly true but close enough to the truth.

'For real?' Her eyes shone.

Sister Girl looked up from her postcard. 'What kind of restaurant is it?'

Charlie groaned. 'Do *not* get her talking about food or cooking or restaurants, otherwise you will *never* get off this train.'

'Hey.' She sounded indignant. 'I didn't see you complaining in Amsterdam when you ate a whole bag of *poffertjes* in the market. Or when you insisted on trying a million gelato flavours in that amazing ice-cream place I found in Milan. You've been happy to stuff your gob wherever we've gone.'

Charlie sighed. 'It's true, I'm going to be massive by the time I get home.' She lifted her T-shirt and patted her toned bare stomach, causing Jimmy's eyes to spring out on stalks.

'So?' Sister Girl was still watching me. Her steady gaze was unnerving and my mouth went dry. I was used to dating women more interested in taking selfies than making proper eye contact with me.

I twisted my pendant. 'Erm . . . Spanish food?'

A smile twitched her mouth and she broke into a warm laugh. 'I asked for that.'

'His mum wants us to stick around and help out in the restaurant,' Jimmy continued.

'No chance,' I muttered.

'Really, why?' Sister Girl looked amused.

'No one refuses Sofia,' Blabbermouth continued. 'What was it she said? "You are a disgrace if you think you can go to Ibiza without helping your uncle first."'

His Catalan accent was crap. He made me sound like a kid. I gave him the death stare and his laugh boomed out.

'Sounds like she rules the roost,' said Sister Girl, tapping her pen on the postcard. 'I know how that feels. Mine's the same.' She nudged me. 'You should give it a go. You don't know what you're missing.'

I stretched out my legs and sighed. 'Long hours, high pressure, stress. No, thanks.' I didn't need it; I'd been there before.

Sister Girl's smile softened. 'It's not all stress,' she began. 'What about working the ingredients, making them come alive in your hands, mixing textures and flavours, sharing your pleasure with customers?'

For a moment nobody spoke. Then Jimmy and Charlie both snorted at the same time, causing them to break into laughter.

I grinned. 'Sounds . . . sexy.' I arched my eyebrow to let her know I was teasing.

She rolled her eyes and threw me a smile before going back to her postcard. I leant closer to snatch a glance. She smelt gorgeous, like summer. 'Who are you writing to?'

'My grandma. She's pretty deaf, so instead of phoning I'm sending postcards.' She signed the bottom with a twirl I couldn't make out. 'She likes cooking and wants me to keep her updated on the new food we've tried.'

'So what am I missing out on in Narbonne?' I asked her.

'Weird cheese,' Charlie interjected. 'It's not even made from cow's milk. It sounds disgusting. I told you, she's *obsessed*.'

'Weird cheese, hey?' I repeated. 'Sounds . . . delightful.'

Sister Girl ignored her and addressed me. 'It's a regional cheese that's made in the area. Charlie thinks real cheese can only come from cows, but that's not true, is it?' Her eyes danced but at the same time I felt like her question was a test.

I kept my options open. 'So it's made from . . . ?'

Warm laughter shimmered from her. '*Pélardon,*' she began, exaggerating the French word in what sounded like a pretty good accent to me, 'is made from goat's milk. It's a soft cheese with a fruity flavour and a trace of saltiness.'

Her wide smile removed any hint of pretentiousness and I nodded, hoping I'd come across as cultured as her. But I didn't have a clue. Cheddar, yes. Manchego, even, as my mum was Catalan. I was on Charlie's side; goat's cheese sounded rank.

Clearly I didn't do a good job of disguising my thoughts as Sister Girl laughed. 'Not impressed? Of course, you know manchego's made from sheep's milk, don't you?'

My mouth fell open. How did I not know that? I clamped it shut, scrabbling to bluff my way out of this. 'So is cheese, like, your specialist subject?'

With eyes still on me, she didn't miss a beat. 'Probably.'

'We're not on your regular Interrail trip,' Charlie said. 'My sister has dragged me through Europe purely so she can try out all kinds of weird food. We're on a *culinary tour*, apparently.'

Sister Girl blushed. 'I didn't say that.'

'Sounds posh,' I said, but not unkindly. I liked this girl's mindset. She had a passion. She had a plan. And she was seeing it through.

I had no passions. No plans. Not really.

'Where else have you been?' I asked, genuinely curious.

'We got the ferry to Calais.' Charlie began to count the destinations off with her fingers. 'Then travelled to Amsterdam, Berlin, Munich, Milan, Montpellier.'

'You forgot Prague and Zurich,' Sister Girl added.

Jimmy nodded. 'Impressive. We're getting a ferry to Ibiza from Barcelona.'

Charlie looked at her sister. 'We could go, couldn't we?'

She glanced at me and looked away. 'I thought you wanted to meet up with your mates in Madrid?'

She shrugged. 'Afterwards?'

Sister Girl sighed. 'I'm not sure we'll have time. We'll have to get home soon after that.'

Charlie slumped back in her seat. 'You might, but I don't. I've got no plans.'

'That's my point,' her sister replied sharply.

'It's like being on holiday with my mum,' she muttered.

'Yeah, I'm *just* like Mum.'

They eyed each other and then, to my surprise, giggled.

'You're right. Mum would drag us to Ibiza and tell us to party the night away,' Sister Girl said, rolling her eyes.

'She works in a nightclub,' Charlie added by way of explanation. 'Loves the limelight.'

Sister Girl's gaze dropped to her bag.

'Alice, don't even *think* about calling her,' Charlie said fiercely. 'She's got Grandma. She'll be doing just fine without us.'

Chapter 4

ANDY

Ten years ago

So, her name was Alice.

The TGV sped along the French coast and as it began to curve inland I knew it wouldn't be long before the girls would be getting off. I wondered if we should make a plan to meet up with them in Barcelona before they left.

'How did you get into DJ-ing?' Alice asked me.

I shifted in my seat. My journey was a complicated one and I wasn't ready to reveal the real reason why I was going – to them or anyone. 'It's something I've wanted to do for a while,' I said. 'I turned twenty-one a few months ago. I was bored with my finance job in the City and it felt like time to go to Ibiza.'

Some of this is true. My twenty-first *was* the catalyst – but not because of my milestone age.

Alice looked at me with interest. 'A new start abroad? That's pretty brave.'

'Is it?' I was genuinely perplexed.

She nodded. 'I'd say so. I'm such a home bird.'

'But you're away now – you've visited loads of different countries.'

She leant down and pulled a map out of her bag. 'With this,' she said, waving it at me. 'I couldn't just . . . leave. I always need to know where I'm going.'

'You like to be organised,' I said.

'She can be *so* dull,' Charlie muttered, faking a yawn.

'You'd be hopeless without me,' Alice shot back. She turned her attention on me again. 'Do you know anyone over there?'

'Nah, I've got some contacts though.'

She held my gaze for a moment. 'That doesn't worry you? I mean, living in a strange country, not having a plan?'

I hadn't thought about the move in those terms. All I was thinking about was my brother. Going to Ibiza was something I had to see through. 'Not really.'

She smiled and her face lit up again. 'You like to fly by the seat of your pants.'

I laughed. 'I suppose.'

'Like me!' Charlie said. 'See, sis? Not everyone feels the need to plan out their life in teeny tiny detail.'

'You're in danger of making me sound boring again,' Alice said drily. 'Being organised is a good thing, not a flaw.'

'I'm doing alright, aren't I?' She laughed. 'I made it through sixth-form college,' she said to Jimmy.

'Just about,' Alice muttered.

'What about you? What brought you on your *culinary tour*?' I said lightly.

'I'm starting an apprenticeship in a London restaurant when I get back. I wanted to get some ideas before I start.'

Ah – suddenly our conversation from before clicked into place.

Charlie snorted. 'She's been planning this trip for *years*.'

Alice shot her another look.

'What's on the menu when you come to Barcelona, then?' I said.

'You're Spanish, aren't you?' Charlie said, laughing. 'Why don't *you* tell *us*?'

'Paella,' Alice and I said at the same time.

We locked eyes for a second and I swear I felt something flicker between us.

'You sure *you're* not Spanish?' I retorted quickly to hide the awkwardness. I wafted my hand over Alice. I meant to imply that with her olive complexion and dark hair she looked more Mediterranean than me, but my joke fell flat.

Alice flushed and looked uncomfortable, but my mind had gone blank and I didn't know how to rescue the situation. Charlie snorted and whispered something to Jimmy I didn't catch. His laugh boomed out and I shot him a look but he just grinned.

'You're Catalan,' Alice said suddenly.

She held my gaze with a certainty that was making me realise she didn't seem to care what anyone thought. It was the first time anyone – a girl – had recognised the difference between being Spanish and Catalan. Unimportant to outsiders, but significant to us.

I smiled. 'Half. My dad's Welsh.'

'Why don't we skip on to Barcelona, sis?' said Charlie, staring out the window. High rises were beginning to gather, signalling the outskirts of Narbonne. 'We should stick with these guys. They can help us out if Andy speaks the lingo.'

'Can't help you there.' I crossed my arms.

Jimmy raised thick eyebrows. I could feel Blabbermouth resurrecting itself again.

'Can't remember any Catalan now,' I added quickly, silencing him with a look.

Charlie frowned. 'I thought everyone spoke Spanish in Spain.'

'Darling, you can speak Spanish to me any day.' Jimmy pushed his face close to hers and she swatted him away. 'Aw, come to Barcelona with us,' he said, drooping his expression into a sad face. 'We're going to hit the clubs. We could do with a bit of company.'

I glanced at Alice. 'Do you like music? Clubbing?' I imagined her on the dancefloor, long hair swinging, hips swaying, eyes closed.

She flushed again as though she could read my thoughts. 'Restaurant hours aren't very sociable.'

'She only dates chefs,' Charlie added.

Alice's face flamed in fury. Ouch. I'd lay a bet there was history there.

'We haven't really got the budget to go out while we're away,' she muttered.

'Fun sponge,' Charlie sing-songed back.

Alice shook her head. 'Am I? Where's the money going to come from?'

'Credit card,' she retorted.

'*My* credit card.'

Charlie unfolded her legs and stretched her arms up high. Jimmy's eyes fell to her midriff again and bounced back up. 'It's not my fault I didn't have time to save up. One minute I was finishing college and the next you were dragging me away.'

'Dragging,' Alice muttered. 'Of course I was.'

'You know what I mean – it was all so last minute. How many more times do I have to apologise? I'll pay you back.' She yawned. 'At least I remembered to bring my passport.' She patted her bag. 'Oh, hang on . . .'

Alice sucked in a short, sharp breath. 'Don't tell me you've left it behind,' she hissed.

Charlie rooted around in her bag. 'Got it!'

Alice snatched it from her and hiked up her T-shirt up to reveal a money belt strapped to her waist, just like mine. She fumbled to reach the zip, pulling her T-shirt a little higher and I found myself homing in on a slice of smooth golden skin. She caught me staring and I slid my eyes away. Jesus, I was as bad as Jimmy.

The train shuddered as it began to slow and Jimmy leant into Charlie. 'Well then, cutie, looks like this is goodbye. If I catch you in Barcelona or Ibiza, I'll take you clubbing.'

Alice rolled her eyes. 'Is he always like this?' she said to me.

I laughed, relieved she hadn't dumped me in Jimmy's sleaze category. Though really the idiot was just a try-hard.

Alice jumped up. 'Come on, Charlie, get our bags.'

Charlie sighed and swung the rucksacks down from the rack as easily as she'd thrown them up. This time she clipped the man sitting behind, who muttered *idiota*. Charlie ignored him and Alice apologised.

'Are you the oldest?' I asked her, suddenly curious.

The girls were a similar height and build – curves obviously ran in the family – but in every other way, they were total opposites.

'It's not obvious?' she responded drily, but I could see the smile twitching her mouth. 'Charlie's nearly eighteen and I've just turned twenty.' Her eyes dropped to my pendant.

I touched it. Was she a Gemini too?

'What's the name of the restaurant you're staying at?' Charlie asked.

'Cafè Vermell,' said Jimmy. 'It's in Plaça Reial.' His eyes lit up. 'Hey, if you're skint, come and find us and we'll introduce you to Enric. He'll give you a job.'

'We won't be there long,' I warned.

Jimmy shrugged. 'That doesn't matter. We'll do the intros and then we can bugger off to Ibiza earlier. Your mum won't mind if we've found him some help.'

A silence fell but before I could rescue the situation, Alice's eyes had narrowed. 'Oh, I get it,' she said, hands on her hips. 'Chatting us up so you can please *Mummy*? Getting us to take your jobs so you can swan off to Ibiza?'

I stifled a snort of laughter but then I realised she wasn't joking. 'Bye,' she muttered, lurching up the aisle with her rucksack strapped to her back.

I stood, mouth open, while Jimmy made a show of brushing his lips on Charlie's cheek. 'See you in Barcelona,' he said.

She grinned. 'Maybe – maybe not.'

I watched, frozen, as the girls left and emerged on to the platform. Jimmy banged on the window and blew kisses. Alice shook her head and smiled.

Suddenly Matt's voice sprang into my head – or was it a memory?

Bro, you've got to grab every opportunity that comes your way because you never know what's around the corner.

Wasn't that the truth?

I jogged up the aisle, willing the train to stay put a few more minutes, and stood at the open doors. 'Alice?' I called.

She turned around, her expression smooth and unreadable. Her gaze dropped to my grubby white trainers, travelled up my baggy shorts, over my black T-shirt, pausing briefly at my pendant, and then landed on my face. She looked thoughtful. 'Yes?'

My face stiffened.

Come on, mate, get her number!

I needed to see her smile. I needed to feel that lift of hope. But the ache of missing Matt suddenly became too much. 'Enjoy the weird cheese,' I said, forcing a laugh.

She looked startled for a moment, then she laughed too, and I felt a surge of courage. But just at that moment, the doors began to bleep and close, and all I could do was wave and watch as we pulled away.

I never expected to see Alice again.

Chapter 5

ALICE

Now

The following morning, the front door flies open and Charlie bounces in, hair a faded pink from when she dyed it a while back. She's wearing a denim waistcoat and off-the-shoulder top, revealing a daisy chain tattoo laced across her collarbone – an eighteenth birthday present from Mum.

She dumps a large holdall on to the dining table that's dented and scratched from years of use and reminds me of cooking with my grandma. I'm glad I convinced Mum to keep it when she replaced the kitchen with glossy new cupboards and hi-tech appliances.

I eye the bag. 'Things not worked out with Chloe?'

Charlie met her beauty therapist girlfriend when she went for a Brazilian. On good weeks, she lives in her flat-share above the salon. On bad weeks she reappears back at home, eager to tell me about her latest conquest. I brace myself.

'Yep,' she responds cheerfully. 'She's too possessive.'

'You sure about that? You didn't give her reason to be jealous?'

Charlie smirks. 'I snogged her cousin, but I didn't *know* they were related. He was just a fit bloke in a club who thought I was fit too – what's a girl supposed to do?'

I wince, but my mouth twitches into a smile. 'You're a nightmare.'

'Sis, if this guy had started gyrating with you on the dancefloor you wouldn't have said no. He's gorgeous.'

Thoughts of Andy shimmer into my mind. Mum called him 'a looker'. There's no denying he's handsome – *still* handsome, and if anything, more so now the angles of his face have refined with time. I brush the image away.

'Anyway, I told Chloe it was nothing, just a one-nighter, and she lost it.'

'And that surprises you?' I shake my head, still smiling.

Charlie shrugs. 'It's sex, not marriage, and it's not like I deliberately screw people over, things just . . . happen.'

I raise an eyebrow.

'Come on! I'm not that bad. I like a bit of fun and I'm always upfront about everything. It's not my fault people think they can change me.' She hops up on to the island and grabs an apple from the bowl. 'Anyway, I think Sarah's got the hots for me again.'

'Sarah? As in your ex?' Charlie works behind the bar at The Crown down the road and Sarah's her boss. She's brilliant: quietly in charge, encouraging, and someone Charlie actually listens to. They were a couple for ages but Charlie messed up – surprise – and Sarah was having none of it. 'Are you sure that's a good idea?'

She grins. 'She broke my heart so, yes, I'm all in for another go.'

Poor Sarah.

Charlie crunches down on the apple. 'So tell me, what's happening with the school buy-out?' she says, munching. 'Still got a job?'

Until this moment, I've assumed I'd tell her that Andy and Mariana own Perfecte, but now I'm hesitant. Charlie loves to gossip and cause mischief, and I want to keep this on the lowdown for as long as possible.

She clocks my face. 'Did you lose your job?' She looks concerned, which is very sweet of her.

I laugh. 'No, not at all – the opposite. They want me to run the new school.'

Charlie slides off the counter and pulls me into a hug. 'That's great news, sis! Congratulations!'

'If it pans out,' I say. 'They want me to go to Barcelona to do some training and I've said no, so they might change their mind.'

Confusion crosses Charlie's face. 'You're kidding? Why?' Then her expression clears and she exhales loudly. 'No, no, no. Do *not* let Mum stand in your way. She's held you back for too long.'

Mum's the one thing we still disagree on. Our opposing views about what's right and what's wrong for her have rumbled on since we were young. Charlie has never understood my commitment to Mum.

I've never explained.

There's a complexity to our relationship that's made me who I am today. I'll never reveal the truth to Charlie, to anyone – ever.

How can I when the accident was all my fault?

My atonement is to never let Mum down again.

I have a class scheduled for the afternoon so I make Mum lunch – a doorstep ham and pickle sandwich, no salad – with my own homemade bread. I've got into the habit of baking a white loaf for her and a wholemeal one for me. Charlie refuses both, stating she's on a carb-free diet this week, and heads off to the gym. I make sure Mum's comfortable in front of the TV with a flask of tea and a plate of bourbons for her three o'clock tea break, and head off down the road.

Riverside School is in a building on Richmond's main high street over three floors above a laundrette. The school's name is a stretch. Though in fairness it isn't too far from the river, with plenty of green space and transport links close by, and Janet says the name is a good marketing tool to keep the students coming.

Janet's already here when I go through to our office. Although I'm not her business partner, I've been here for longer than anyone and I'm the only permanent staff member. TESOL teachers don't stick around for long with the lure of jobs in more exotic countries, so Janet employs them on a freelance basis.

This afternoon, I'm teaching my favourite class. They're a mix of young and older students from Spain who work at a local engineering company. I teach them business English and skills to help navigate the social side of work. Although their spoken language is very good now, they're not in a hurry to give up classes. I think they like the meet-up as much as I do, especially since I began organising the pop-up food events.

Today, *señor Paella*'s van is parked out back, feeding students as they depart – and any other hungry souls working in the buildings around us. I've heard good things about the chef, whose real name remains a mystery, and I'm keen to find out if my students think his paella is as good as back home.

I wonder if it will be as good as Sofia's – as Andy's.

I spend the afternoon pushing my class to improve their reading skills, and after the lesson ends, we thump down the stairs to the small car park at the foot of the fire escape. Before we've even exited the building, I can smell the sizzle of garlic and seafood.

The scent stops me in my tracks.

For a moment, I'm not standing on a square of tarmac beneath summer's grey clouds, overshadowed by high, imposing buildings. I'm back in the warm kitchen at Cafè Vermell. I'm sat with Andy in the sunshine, scooping paella from a plastic tub. I'm feeling my heart bloom as he explains how he made the dish – just for me.

'Alice?'

My eyes spring open. One of my students is calling me over to the van. He holds up a box. 'This is very good,' he says, grinning. 'Just like Mamá makes.'

I laugh. It's exactly what I want to hear. And now the speaking part of our lesson begins, and the highlight of my week. My students and I talk about the ingredients, how we'd cook the food, and share stories triggered by the scents and flavours. I share some of mine – but not all.

Some memories are too painful to think about.

Chapter 6

ALICE

Now

'Delivery Leon's here,' Mum calls as the doorbell goes. 'I can see his van.'

I'm in the kitchen making pasties – again – for a new class. As much as I enjoy coming up with new ideas for the fillings, and watching the students' delight when they take their first bite, I'd like an excuse to make something different. Perhaps I will next time. But then they might be disappointed. I'm told some students only sign up to my classes because they've heard good things about my pasties.

At the front door, my heart sinks when I see the enormous box Leon shoves my way. We only know him by name because he comes here so often.

'What have you bought?' I say to Mum, trying to sound cheerful but inwardly bracing myself. I know exactly what to expect. She'll open the box, ooh and ahh over the contents, then ask me to stash it in her wardrobe upstairs with the other stuff. It's wasteful. It's stressful. Her spending is out of control but she refuses to talk about it. What can I do? She inherited her parents' wealth when my grandma died. She's an only child. It isn't my business to tell her how to spend her money.

'It's for you,' says Mum, smiling.

I'm caught off-guard. She isn't one for lavish gifts, telling us she was spoilt rotten as a kid but she'd swap that for love and hugs any day.

'Go on, open it.'

I crouch down on the floor and slit open the tape with Mum's scissors. Inside is something large, round and electronic. I've got no idea what it is.

'It's a robotic hoover!' she says gleefully. 'To help you around the house.'

I smile, half-amused and half-dismayed by her present – if you can call it that. I'd rather she agree to employing a cleaner but she refuses to have strangers 'poking around my home'.

'Erm, thanks,' I manage to say.

Mum's face falls. 'It's not a good idea? I saw it on the shopping channel and I thought, *Alice could really do with one of those*. It does the vacuuming for you.'

I feel mean for not sounding more grateful. 'You're very thoughtful.'

Mum huffs and turns back to the TV. I sense her mood shifting into something darker. 'I'll read the instructions after I've finished cooking,' I say quickly. 'Then we can give it a whirl, okay?'

Once the pasties are done, I give Mum lunch and then start peeling potatoes for the sausage and mash that's on the menu tonight. I'll fry onions later and make a gravy with the sticky residue left at the bottom of the pan. My fresh pesto is waiting in the fridge ready to swirl through my portion of mash, and I'll boil peas for myself and warm baked beans for Mum.

After I'm done, I manage to get the robo-hoover thing going. Mum claps her hands and laughs as it spins around the room. I'm not convinced it's doing a very good job but I don't say anything.

Soon, Mum's got me watching a re-run of *Friends* I've seen a million times before. With one eye on the programme, I message a food van I've heard about on Instagram. Their speciality is Egyptian dishes and I'm curious to know what the food is like. I invite them to park up at our school one lunchtime next week. As I finish, an email pings through.

> *Salutacions Alice,*
>
> Janet says you do not want to come here for training and she is very disappointed. That is no good, disappointing your boss! Do not think we will not pay you. We will, very well, is that a good carrot? Then later we will pay good money to Janet to create Perfecte London – she will be happy then!
>
> Reconsider, Alice?
>
> We are waiting for you.
>
> *Salutacions cordials,*
>
> Mariana and Andrew Cortez-Hall

My stomach knots. I don't like Mariana's tone – and there's no mention of our past connection either. It occurs to me she might not know I am *that* Alice. After all, how many Alice Taylors are there in the world? But I don't believe that for a minute. Mariana had always been ambitious, even if I hadn't realised *how* ambitious, until it was too late. She would have made it her business to know everything about Riverside – including finding out that I came as part of the package. But if she's keeping things quiet that means she's probably not said anything to Janet.

I toss my phone on to the sofa.

'Signed up for online dating yet?' says Mum.

'No.' She's obsessed. But I'm not interested. When exactly does she think I'll have time for a boyfriend?

She huffs. 'Loosen up a bit. You're thirty now, practically on the shelf. You don't want to wake up one day and find yourself still stuck at home and as sad and lonely as me.'

I look at Mum trapped in her wingback chair with only the soaps and reality shows for company. The gradual weight gain over the years, her lack of interest in life outside these four walls, her reliance on the walking sticks – on me.

'It creeps up on you,' she says. 'One day I was swanning about Philippe's nightclub, the next, I couldn't move from this chair.' Her eyes shimmer. 'I was the heart and soul of that place. Everyone knew they'd have a good night with us at the helm. Philippe and I, we were dynamite.'

I swallow. It's not the first time I've heard this story but the burden of my guilt feels as fresh as it did ten years ago.

'Have you thought about getting in touch with him?' I venture. 'If you don't know where he is, I'm sure we could find him online.'

Mum glares at me. 'Why would I do that? He's a married man.'

That hadn't stopped her before. 'Charlie might want to see him.'

Her laugh is brittle. 'Some dad he turned out to be. And anyway, she doesn't need me to make that happen.'

It's true – and Charlie doesn't seem bothered.

Mum's eyes are back on the TV and the clock is inching towards three. I get up and go into the kitchen to retrieve the tin with her Saturday favourites – Jammie Dodgers. It's empty. Bloody Charlie. Sometimes I think she does this to wind me up, to wind Mum up. She knows the rules.

I go over to the pantry and root around for a new packet I've hidden at the back. My hand lands on the biscuits and I tut as I pull them towards me because they've already been opened. Behind, a crumpled-up piece of paper catches my eye and I take this out, too. As I make the tea and put biscuits on a plate, I unravel the ball.

A red warning screams out and my pulse jump-starts. It's an unpaid credit card bill – the kind that only arrives when the company has given up on the soft approach.

Mum and I share a joint account for convenience, as I do all the shopping and pay the household bills, but otherwise she keeps her finances private. I'm not an idiot, though. My grandpa worked for a bank and we live in a five-bedroom house with a gravel drive – the grandest property on our street. Mum's upbringing had been 'charmed', as my grandma liked to put it: a nanny, a pony, a fancy boarding school when my grandparents moved abroad. She'd been surrounded by friends living equally privileged lives, friends who were given trust funds when they turned eighteen.

Mum fell pregnant with me at sixteen. A one-night stand with an 'irresistible Spanish waiter – or he might have been Italian'. Grandpa was furious. Mum told me she could have lived a life without ever working. Instead, she chose *me* over the money her father refused to give her unless she terminated the pregnancy. So she paid her own way, working as a hostess in Philippe's nightclub, and then later had Charlie.

Mum was obsessed with her job, with Philippe, and left our grandma to look after us. She says it was the least her mother could do after her parents dumped her in a boarding school when she was seven. But Charlie and I never felt like a burden to Grandma. Perhaps we gave her a reason to keep going after Grandpa died. Perhaps she *was* making up for the childhood years she lost with my mum?

When Grandma died, Mum inherited everything.

I stare at the angry red bill.

So . . . ?

I stomp through to the living room and shove the junk off Mum's table, not caring that the stack of papers spill on to the floor. I don't need to read the details to know what crap she's been buying because I see it. The doorbell goes and there's Delivery Leon and his happy smile, holding out a box or two addressed to Mum. She rips open the contents like an excited child. I ask her if she *really* wants to keep the freaky dog ornament/Christmas duvet set/massage gun and she nods and sends me scurrying upstairs with her purchases.

'Mum,' I say shakily. 'Why do you owe thousands of pounds?' I stick the piece of paper in front of her so she can't see the TV. The sum is huge and it makes me want to puke. My teaching wage is minimal. Mum pays for everything. I feel dizzy.

Mum snatches up the bill. 'Don't worry about that,' she says, screwing it back into a ball and dropping it on to the table.

'I don't understand how . . . And why haven't you paid it?'

She shrugs. 'Don't worry, petal, I will.'

Fury blazes through my veins. 'You need to pay it *now*.'

She swats her hand at me. 'Stop fussing, it's fine.'

'Mum.' I suck in a breath and try to keep my voice steady. 'Is there a problem? Can't you pay it?'

She shuffles herself straight in her chair. Two red spots circle her pale cheeks. 'Don't be silly, of course I can. My money is *my* business.'

I don't know what to say. Carefully, I smooth the piece of paper back out on the coffee table. 'I'm going to pin this on the fridge where you can see it,' I say, my voice trembling. 'Please can you pay it? Today.'

◆ ◆ ◆

That night I lie in bed, eyes wide in the dark. I can't stop thinking about Mum's debt. Ordinarily I'd speak to Janet – I've been running over the road for her advice since she first moved in. She'd know if Mum was lying and I'm almost certain she is. I can't understand why she wouldn't make the payment if she had the money – or why she'd hide the demand in the pantry.

But our financial affairs are private. I don't want to involve Janet. And there's no point in talking to Charlie. What help can she be?

My stomach rolls. Janet's business might be thriving but I'm not earning the kind of money that could cover the running costs for our home, the weekly food bills, let alone have a chance at chipping away at the debt. Mum might have to sell the house. But where would we live?

I glance around as if I might find answers within these four dark walls. This has been my bedroom for my whole life. I turned thirty last month. I still live at home. I care for my mum.

You don't want to wake up one day and find yourself still stuck at home and as sad and lonely as me.

I'm not able to be financially responsible for myself.

We will pay you well when you are here.

Barcelona? No, it's not possible. I can't.

Your mum will be fine if you change your mind.

Will she? What choice do I have?

Before I talk myself out of it, I grab my mobile and send Janet a message.

I'm going to Barcelona.

Chapter 7

ALICE

Now

The following day, I try to convince Mum to stay home instead of buying Sunday lunch at the pub. Given the awful credit card bill, it's a reasonable suggestion, plus I've been desperate to try out my roast dinner ideas for ages. Since it's Mum's favourite meal, I know mine will win her over. I need to do anything I can to soften the blow when I announce my decision.

I should have known better. Mum's weekly visit to The Crown is as immovable as concrete. I suppose I should rejoice in this regular eating-out experience, but I don't. Frankly, the meals are rubbish. Though it would be disloyal to Sarah and Charlie if I were to voice my views out loud.

The pub is not far from our house at the bottom of the hill. As the road curves to the right, there's a passageway that slips between houses – which only the locals really know about – and it's tucked away down here near the river. Still, it's too far for Mum to walk.

I don't drive anymore. Charlie usually pops back to pick us up in Sarah's car, complaining the whole time. Today, Janet does the honours, humming away with a conspiratorial smile and a promise to collect us later.

Inside, low beams and dark wood panelling give the tiny pub a year-round cosy feel whatever the weather outside. It's rumoured to have once been a drinking den frequented by a king who'd sneak out after dark in disguise and travel here by boat – hence the pub being called The Crown.

Today, the bar hums with regulars but there are also a few faces I've not seen in here before. We discover our usual table has been reserved for someone else.

'Where are we going to sit?' Mum frets, glancing around.

Charlie's laughing with a group at the bar that I remember seeing here earlier in the week. They head in our direction and brush past us to sit at our table.

Mum narrows her eyes.

'Over here!' Charlie calls and points to a smaller table crammed in at the end of the bar.

'What's going on?' Mum says, grasping my arm as we go over.

'New regulars,' says Charlie. 'We don't want to turn them away.'

'You know I like to sit there,' she mutters.

'You'll be fine here.'

The space around the table isn't generous and the chairs don't look that sturdy. I'm worried Mum's going to feel hemmed in.

'Alice?' She looks at me for reassurance. Any confidence I have about leaving her begins to trickle away. I shift the table into a better position and swap out a chair with one from another table.

'Seriously?' Charlie grumbles as Mum, smiling now, settles into the seat. 'It's not like we're asking her to climb bloody Everest.'

As always, I ignore her. Charlie sighs and goes back behind the bar.

'What are you having this week?' I say brightly to Mum. I think it's best we eat before I tell her my news. Plus, I need Charlie by my side because my decision involves her, too.

'It must be beef, petal, because I had chicken last week and pork the week before.'

Our food soon arrives and she tucks in while I push mine around the plate. When Charlie reappears with more drinks and pulls up a chair to take a break, I know it's time to speak up. I take a deep breath. 'So you're living with us again, Charlie?' I'm trying to sound casual, as though we'd started this conversation earlier and got distracted. 'It's ideal as I need you to help with Mum while I'm away.'

Mum's cutting up a roast potato – her second helping – and pauses. 'What? Where are you going?'

'Barcelona,' I say quickly. Better to rip off the plaster than peel away at the edges.

Charlie breaks into a grin. 'Oh my God, that's *amazing*,' she says, getting up and flinging her arms around my neck. 'Of *course* I'll help, no question. Me and Mum will be just fine, won't we?'

Mum looks fearful and she pushes her plate away. Tears gather in her eyes. 'You're leaving me, petal? After all you've said, after all that's gone on, you're going? You promised you wouldn't.'

I gulp and look away. I *had* said I'd never leave her. But that was . . . a decade ago. I meant it then and I hadn't planned on leaving her now. But Mum's debt has given me a shock, reminded me how vulnerable I am if things go wrong. Janet's right: running Perfecte London is a fabulous opportunity. This could be my path to financial freedom, and if it means going to Barcelona to make that happen, then I will.

'It's not forever,' I say lamely. 'Just eight weeks.'

Mum dabs at her eyes with a tissue she's found up her sleeve.

'We'll be fine.' Charlie pats Mum's shoulder. 'Rhubarb crumble?'

'I'm not hungry. I want to go home,' she says quietly. 'Can I have the bill?'

Charlie raises a pierced eyebrow in my direction. She doesn't look anywhere near as concerned as I feel. I've made Mum cry. She's *refusing* her favourite pudding. I feel bloody awful.

We're silent while Charlie goes to collect the card reader. 'What made you change your mind?' she says to me as she returns.

Mum fumbles in her bag for her purse. It flies out and falls on the floor but Charlie makes no move to retrieve it. I throw my sister a look and pick it up myself. 'If I get through the training and wow them enough, then I'll be in charge of Perfecte London.' I don't mention their interest in my fledgling food events because I'm hoping I can find a way to sidestep this bargaining chip with Mariana when I'm over there.

'You're putting Janet before me.' Mum sniffs.

'That's not fair,' Charlie interjects. 'You should be pleased for Alice.'

'Can't you see she's upset?' I snap. 'I don't need you to fight my battles.'

'Someone needs to,' she says, holding out the card reader to Mum. 'You'll go nowhere otherwise.'

I bristle. 'And look how far *you've* come.'

Charlie throws her arm out. 'And what's wrong with my life? Take a look around. I think you'll find I'm doing alright.'

The pub's packed and a group nearby glance over at the sound of our raised voices. Sarah frowns at Charlie who, to my surprise, softens a little. 'Sorry, sis.'

Sorry is not a word I hear from Charlie – ever. Then I see her gaze travel back to the bar where Sarah's pulling a pint. She looks up and they lock eyes. Sarah tucks her long blonde hair behind one ear and smiles slowly, secretively. Charlie glows.

My heart sinks. She warned me something might happen between them but now's not the time. I need her at home, to support Mum, to support me, while I'm gone.

Mum frowns at the card reader. 'Oh, my card's not working. Alice, can you pay?'

Anxiety flutters.

Barcelona – it's the only answer.

Chapter 8

ANDY

Ten years ago

Uncle Enric greeted me with a toothy smile and sad eyes. He pulled me into a tight embrace. I thought he wasn't going to let go, and when he did, I didn't want to acknowledge his glittering tears or the streaks of grey in his bushy moustache, as they reminded me of how long it had been.

'*Cinc anys, nebot,*' he said. '*Quant de temps.*'

I looked blankly at him. Jimmy nudged me. 'What?' I hissed. 'I don't understand.'

'*No ho entens?* Why?' Enric's confusion mirrored my own feelings about the lost language these last five years.

'I don't know.' The words that had filtered into my ears and rolled freely from my lips since I was a kid had disappeared.

Enric patted my cheek. 'Five years is too long away from your country,' he said. 'Give it time. It will come back.'

Sharpness caught my throat. Was Spain really my country? It had never felt that way. Matt was the true Catalan son. He'd been born here, whereas my birth city was London. Our differences still felt raw. Sometimes I felt like we weren't really brothers, and sitting here on the familiar terrace, outside Uncle Enric's restaurant, I felt like that confused little kid again.

Our family had spent summers here. My mum had kept her apartment in Barcelona when she'd moved to England. Back then, the sight of the red parasols meant running into Uncle Enric's arms and demanding ice-cream. Now it meant beer.

'Another?' said Enric, pulling me back to the present.

'Absolutely,' Jimmy replied, lifting his empty glass.

Around us, Cafè Vermell looked the same as it always had. Five tables squeezed on to the small terrace, five red parasols blazing the cafè's name. Despite the bigger, swankier restaurants in the square, the umbrellas were a beacon and Uncle Enric's place had always been popular.

Today was no different – in fact, the whole of Plaça Reial buzzed with activity. Jimmy and I had got off the metro and come through the archway into the famous square with its tall buildings and towering palm trees, and I'd felt a lightness in my step. We'd passed tables of smiling diners and eager waiters, dodged trailing tourists with eyes on the architecture. At the fountain, a crowd had gathered and a cheer rose up for the acrobats performing backflips.

Enric returned with more beers and a platter of cold meats and cheese. 'Sorry, boys, it is the best I can do. The kitchen is *tancada* – shut.'

Jimmy and I got stuck in while Enric went to attend another customer. As the spicy chorizo and tangy manchego hit my mouth, I was reminded of Alice. I felt stupid for losing my nerve and not asking for her number. Okay, it wasn't as though we'd had a deep and meaningful on the train, but I couldn't forget her steady gaze, how she'd understood I was Catalan – half-Catalan – and not Spanish.

I took another bite of the manchego. I laughed softly, remembering how stunned I'd been when she'd told me I'd been enjoying cheese made from sheep's milk all these years.

'What's funny?' said Jimmy, taking another swig of beer.

'Just thinking about the girls,' I said. 'Dumb that I didn't get Alice's number. We could have hung out with them when they got here.'

'Oh yeah? Thought you weren't keen on staying long?' He grinned.

'A few extra days won't matter.'

He winked. 'Good thing I've got Charlie's number.'

I broke into a slow smile. 'Sly dog! When did you manage that?'

'On the platform, before we got on the train.'

I chuckled, but now Alice was within possible reach, I pulled back again. Perhaps better to see how things played out with Jimmy and Charlie first. Alice had been hard to read – and I couldn't remember what Matt's advice had been if a girl blew you out. Had she brushed me off? Perhaps the doors closing and the train leaving had saved me from making a dick of myself.

I didn't want to chance finding out.

Over the days that followed, Enric encouraged us to explore the city both day and night. I couldn't see what my mum was fussing about. Despite the kitchen being closed, there was a steady flow of customers to Cafè Vermell who were happy to sip coffee, have a beer and watch the world go by. He didn't need our help.

Jimmy hadn't heard from Charlie – and he wasn't about to chase her either, it just wasn't his style. He always waited for girls to come to him. Though that didn't stop him from helping his cause, spending the evenings prowling the local bars like a pro. I went along but made my excuses when the night got too heavy and was always first back to our apartment above the cafe. I'd done enough drinking and partying in the City over the years. I was bored by the scene that played on repeat wherever I went – including here, it seemed. I was hoping the Ibiza vibe would be classier: music enthusiasts and dance bunnies. I needed the change.

On our last morning, I perched on a bar stool and sipped an espresso, where once I would have scoffed ice-cream with my brother. The interior hadn't changed since then either. The same black floor tiles sparkled with chips of glittery stone and, above, a disco ball turned lazily in the heat. Red leather booth seating surrounded glossy black tables, with mirrored walls serving to make the small space feel much bigger.

A memory flashed up. Crushing disappointment the year Matt had chosen beer over ice-cream.

'Enric, he is *massa jove*, too young,' my mum had said to her brother.

'Fifteen? No, he can try.'

Sat on the bar stool, about to dive into my bowl of chocolate ice-cream, I glanced at my mum and uncle, relieved my dad wasn't there. I was certain he'd have shouted at Uncle Enric. The three of us watched Matt take his first sip. I saw his face contort but just as quickly he smoothed his expression. 'Great,' he said, licking the foam from his top lip.

I ducked my head to hide my smile. Even at ten, I knew Matt hated the stuff. But he'd always been up for an adventure – and quick with the chat when things fell apart.

He was my hero.

'Liking your ice-cream, squirt?' he'd said, arm on the bar now, beer glass in his hand. He looked like the men we saw gathered in the tavern below our mum's apartment. 'You're going to have to wait five years for your turn.' He raised his glass, took another slurp and my stomach churned as I felt the shift between us.

I'd be having ice-cream alone and he'd be drinking beer with the adults.

But then, of course, time rattled on, and I caught up with him. We were close again – for a time.

'Andy,' said Enric, breaking my thoughts. 'There's someone I'd like you to meet.'

I looked up to see a young woman standing in front of me, tiny and doll-like with huge brown eyes.

'Mariana Cortez, my nephew, Andrew Hall,' said Uncle Enric.

'Pleased to meet you,' she said softly.

I was expecting her to give me the customary kiss on each cheek, but instead, she offered her hand. It felt cool and limp in mine, as though she was only shaking hands for my benefit.

Enric clapped me on the shoulder. 'So! Mariana is one of our best customers. She is also a language teacher. Her school is not far from here and I thought you might want to talk to her about lessons.'

My mind was blank. 'Lessons?'

'Catalan, *nebot*!' He tapped his head. 'Your words are all locked away. They need to come out. Mariana can help you with that.'

My eyes slid over to her and she ducked her head. What had Enric told her? He must have given her some kind of reason to explain why I had once spoken Catalan – but now I didn't.

I folded my arms. 'Don't mean to be rude, uncle, but Jimmy and I are off tomorrow. Remember we said we'd only be here for a few days?'

Enric looked startled. 'Eh? Already? Your *mare* said you would help.'

I shook my head. 'We can't stay. I'll miss the DJ slots if I leave it too late.'

I could see Mariana staring at me out of the corner of my eye. I glanced at her again and she turned away, twirling her hair around her finger.

Uncle's eyes had gone glassy. 'DJ-ing,' he murmured. 'Okay, well, you have decided.' He held out his hands. 'Mariana, sorry for wasting your time.'

The fact he spoke to her in English stung. But it wasn't my fault. I hadn't asked him for language lessons. I hadn't *promised* my mum I'd stick around and help.

'Here is the address of my school,' Mariana said, handing me a card. 'If you change your mind, you will know where to find me.'

I nodded and tucked it into my pocket.

We'd be on the ferry tomorrow, moving on to Ibiza, to pastures new.

Chapter 9

ANDY

Ten years ago

I woke with a start to my mobile's shrill ringtone. I grappled to answer it and muttered a hoarse hello.

My mum laughed down the line. 'You are not up? Enric is too soft. I told him, let the boys have their party, but then they must get to work.'

I sat up and my hangover thumped into my head full force. A shutter screeched open down in the square, tearing through my brain and telling me the hour was still early. I'd hit the bars harder than usual to celebrate our last night. Now I was remembering why I'd decided to cool my partying ways. But I wasn't going to tell my mum I'd been out all hours. That would be like striking a match to kindling.

'We're going to Ibiza today,' I muttered. 'You know we can't hang around – the summer season is well under way and I don't want to miss the last DJ slots.'

My mum made a *tsk* sound. 'You do not know there will be work there, but you have a job being handed to you on a plate by your uncle. I don't understand.'

I flopped back on my pillow. I could feel old criticisms cranking up again. I was a grown man, I didn't need to follow her orders, though she told me I'd lost that right when I lost my finance job. She'd done me a favour by finding me work with Enric, apparently, so why couldn't I see that?

I looked up at the chandelier hanging above my ridiculous four-poster bed. It managed to look both impressive and dusty. I hadn't told my mum the real reason why I'd left my job. It was done. In the past. Time to move on. 'I've told you, I'm not interested in working in the restaurant trade.'

The line buzzed in her silence. *What about family? Does this mean nothing to you?* She wasn't saying it but she'd said it many times before. Now, her saying nothing was worse than the shouting. The emptiness wrapped itself around me, rousing the mess of guilty feelings.

Of course family mattered. It had always mattered. Always.

But I needed to go to Ibiza.

When I'd found the slip of paper tucked inside one of Matt's graphic novels – one of the ones he'd designed and made himself – it had felt like a sign. I'd never be able to draw like him or have the brains to become a hotshot music lawyer, but I could give DJ-ing a go. I'd been messing about with his decks for a while. I had a handle on things, and now I had his list of contacts in Ibiza.

I owed him.

'Enric needs your help,' my mum insisted.

I thought about how my uncle buzzed about the place, smiling and joking with customers. Yes, there were times when people paused to look at the menu but walked on by when Enric rushed to apologise that the kitchen was closed. But that could be fixed.

Just not by me.

'He is not well. He is . . .' My mum sighed. 'It's his heart.'

'Oh.' I jerked upright and my head screamed in protest. I got up and went over to the balcony. Enric had been running the cafe for years. He'd never married. I wasn't even sure if romance had ever been on the cards. I couldn't remember seeing him with anyone. Apart from seasonal staff that came and went, he'd managed the business alone.

Outside, the square was starting to wake up. Some of the bars that doubled as cafes in the daytime had barely closed for the night before reopening again for the morning trade. When you thought about it, Enric ran the bar, served tables and probably couldn't afford to take a day off. A high-pressure job.

I knew all about that.

'Andy, please, do this for me. You don't have to stay all summer, just a few weeks to help out.'

I could hear Ibiza calling.

What would Matt do?

◆ ◆ ◆

Later, I went downstairs to break the news to Jimmy. I found him slumped at the bar, inhaling an espresso, with Enric talking animatedly about the cafe.

'Some evenings the customers like to come inside – we have music and they dance,' he was saying, sweeping his arm around the dark interior. 'Cafè Vermell comes alive!'

Jimmy looked puzzled. 'I don't get it. You're a cafe, right? A restaurant? Not a club?'

Enric laughed. 'When the customers come, we are everything. Catalonians and Spanish join together to party and so do the tourists.' He smiled at us with happy brown eyes like my mum's and pushed an espresso in my direction. 'So you boys like to party? You are enjoying the girls, no?'

Jimmy laughed. 'Too right.'

'Did Andy tell you about the beautiful Mariana?' He threw me a sly glance and his moustache twitched.

'No!' Jimmy laughed again. 'And?'

I shook my head. 'And – nothing.'

Enric flashed a toothy grin. 'She comes here most days, sometimes with her *pare*. He owns many properties in the area, including her language school. I thought she could be Andy's teacher but he tells me you leave today.'

Jimmy yawned. 'Yep, once we get our shit together, we're off.'

I drummed my fingers on the bar. 'About that . . .'

Enric's eyes lit up. 'You spoke to your *mare*, no?' His gaze softened. 'You gonna look after this old guy? For a while? I know, I know, working here is not what you want but, hey, nobody can say no to Sofia.'

Jimmy sprang back to life. 'So we're staying? I'm up for that!'

'Just a few weeks,' I added hurriedly.

'You are both gentlemen,' said Enric with a little bow. 'I am grateful.'

I should have said, 'No problem.' But it wouldn't be true. I couldn't pretend it was okay to be stuck here for the next three weeks. Even if it meant spending time with my uncle who I hadn't seen in five years. Helping him out. Making my mum happy. God knows she'd had enough unhappiness to last a lifetime. Wasn't that what mattered? Making her happy again?

I thought about Matt's list of names folded into the pages of my passport for safekeeping. Mum tugging me one way, Ibiza tugging the other. I needed to prove to Matt I could do it. I'd just have to wait a little longer. I could suck up three weeks. I'd manage the bar with Jimmy. It wouldn't be like real work – we'd have a laugh. We'd tell Enric to put his feet up. The more time he had to rest, the sooner we could leave.

'Andy, come with me,' said Enric, coming out from behind the bar and heading towards the kitchen. I followed him through the door – and then froze.

Alice?

'Surprise! Your friend arrived.' Enric slapped me on the back hard enough to make me stumble.

'Hi, Andy.' Alice looked up from where she was chopping vegetables, a faint smile tracing her face, her voice sounding all casual, as though I should've known she'd turn up eventually. 'What took you so long?'

Chapter 10

ALICE

Now

By the time my flight touches down in Barcelona, it's late and there's already a voice message from Mum. She warns me of pickpockets and sunstroke, and reminds me the niggle in her back has got worse, though I don't remember her complaining about it before. I follow the stream of people to join the queue at passport control, then move on to baggage collection. I've got one anxious eye on the time, wondering when the metro stops running.

As I wait for my suitcase to trundle around on the conveyor belt, I call Mum back. She's absorbed in one of her celeb programmes and keen to keep our conversation short.

'Arrived safely, then?' she says. 'Is your room nice?'

I don't tell her I'm still at the airport, that everyone around me is busy grabbing their stuff, loading up trolleys and disappearing through the exit.

'Yes, all good,' I reply, noting the same black holdall go around again.

'Nice hotel?'

Mum has given me money for the taxi fare and a few nights in a hotel, but I have no intention of spending it. How can I when I don't know what's going on with her finances? She tells me she's sorting out the credit card. But has she? I'm dreading the end of the month when all the bills go out. I've no idea if she's got enough funds to pay them and I need my savings to support this trip.

The burble of the TV filters down the phone, the whistle and wheeze of Mum's breath. My throat constricts. What am I doing here? Barcelona is a big city and, if it's anything like London, it won't be cheap to live here. Mariana wasn't forthcoming about my pay and I didn't like to ask. I don't know how much it costs to rent a room, buy food, pay for travel and all the other costs involved in living alone. I don't know how long my savings need to last.

Then – what if Mum needs me? I might have to hurry home if something happens and how will I afford to buy the airfare?

'Call you tomorrow?' I say when Mum's silence makes it clear she's more interested in the programme than me.

'Bye, petal, miss you already.'

I slide the phone back into my bag and zip it tightly closed. I'd contemplated wearing a money belt like I'd worn travelling with Charlie all those years ago, but she said I was being paranoid. Now, glancing around, I see I'm one of the last few passengers in the baggage hall along with a group of blokes jostling one another at the carousel next to me.

Their laughter is loud and echoey in the empty terminal. One of them wears a large backpack and clocks me. 'Hey, darlin', you lost your gear too?' he calls.

I turn away and realise the conveyor belt has stopped. The holdall still waits to be collected – but there's no sign of my luggage.

'Hey!' the bloke calls again. His voice sounds nearer this time and I stiffen. 'You speaka English?' He's standing in front of me, eyes shot with red, the stench of beer radiating off him.

'Leave her alone,' hollers one of his friends.

'Juss being friendly,' he slurs. 'That dick over there has lost his bag, too. Come with us, we'll sort you out.' He hoots at his own joke, making my skin crawl.

'Thanks, but no thanks,' I say, marching towards the exit, hoping the group aren't heading towards the metro like me. On the way, I google the airline's number but unsurprisingly no one answers my call at this late hour. Around me, the only sign of life is a man pushing a broom around by a shuttered kiosk.

At the station, the ticket machine is broken and won't take cards. I curse, fumbling for Mum's euros, and, after finally managing to purchase a ticket, I head down to the empty platform. Graffiti slashes the wall on the other platform and I clamp my arm down on my bag, mind racing. What the hell am I doing? I try not to think that I haven't got a toothbrush, let alone a clean pair of knickers for tomorrow. Wearing these travel-tired clothes is not the impression I want to make on my first day.

The metro rumbles into the station and I'm relieved to be aboard with the doors closing just as the drunk men stumble on to the platform. The carriage is empty and we rattle along while I hold my breath each time the doors slide open – but nobody gets on.

Soon, I'm striding with purpose towards the hotel, pulse racing, thinking what every woman thinks in the dark, late at night: a confident pace will deter an attacker. I wonder if this has ever been proven. I don't want to know. The furthest I usually venture in the evenings is down the hill to The Crown.

I peer at the numbers, trying to make sense of the address, passing an apartment block and arriving outside a brick building. Confused, I look around. The street is mostly in darkness. I can't see anywhere that looks like a hotel, and the pounding in my chest pricks tears into my eyes. I'm going to have to find somewhere else to stay, but where? I can't face the metro again.

Up ahead, a faint glow frames the blind in a shop's window and, as I approach, the scent of buttery garlic wafts out. I'm comforted by the smell, but I hesitate. Is it someone's house? A restaurant? There's no bell or knocker so I nudge gently at the door and it flies open.

'*Bon vespre!*' cries a short, round lady, gesturing me inside.

Tables glow with candlelight and curious eyes graze over me for a moment before turning back to their conversations and meals. A warm fug of food, wine and laughter spins me momentarily back to the past, to Cafè Vermell, and my spirits lift, a grin creeping over my face.

The lady laughs and waves her hands to get my attention. She chatters a string of something I don't understand; makes a remark to the waiter as he passes. He smiles and nods a greeting, gesturing to an empty table, and although I'm tempted to sink down into this happy place and pretend everything is fine with my evening, I can't.

'English,' I say, pointing at myself. 'Hotel?'

'Here?' She laughs loudly. 'No, no.'

I smile and shake my head, showing her the address.

'Ah!' She gestures for me to follow her back outside and points to a passage between the buildings. A neon pink sign at the top of a metal fire escape flashes *Habitacions Disponibles*. 'There,' she says. 'You come back, *demà*.' She beams again and disappears back into the restaurant.

The alley is dark, and stinks of rubbish and stale urine. *Habitacions Disponibles?* I see nothing that tells me the hotel's name and I'm certain I'm not in the right place. I tread carefully as I hurry through the dark, hoping there's nothing gross underfoot. At the top of the steps, a blank steel door is painted pink like the sign, and I hesitate. Have I been directed around the back?

I glance down into the dark but see no other signs of life. I don't want to return the way I came, so I bang hard, hoping I'll make myself known.

To my surprise, the door flies open and a woman with cropped brown hair and a sulky mouth stares vacantly at me. '*Sí?*'

'I have a booking?' I say timidly.

'*Què?*'

Her puzzled expression makes my stomach drop. I try to peer around her but it's dark inside. I wrestle for another word that she might understand.

'Hotel? Bed?' I say, tipping my head into my palm.

'Ah, *sí, llit,*' she says, pointing at the sign. 'Bedroom. Sleep.'

She steps aside and I've barely closed the door before she's padded off into the darkness. I hear her hand slam the wall and the corridor floods with a harsh fluorescent light. I shield my eyes as I follow her towards a scuffed pink door that she shoves open so hard it smacks into the wall.

'What the fuck?' shouts a male voice from one of the bunks.

My heart jumps into my throat. I turn to the woman, confused. 'Alone? Private? Women only?'

She stares blankly, yawns and walks off.

Street light filters through the thin curtains and I make out three bunks. Bodies occupy the top beds, including that of the man, who grunts and rolls over. I shuffle over to a vacant bunk, take off my trainers and lie down in my clothes, clutching my bag. I just need to forget this day ever happened.

I tug the sheet over my head and catch the scent of washing powder, thank God. I force my eyes shut. I think about home. Mum's reassuring presence in the living room, her parting words earlier: *missing you already.*

What was I *thinking*? What am I doing here? I roll back to the evening in my bedroom when I'd let myself drown in self-pity, scared of being thirty, and thinking my life had idled along for too long. At what point did I think I could do this? I've lost my luggage, I couldn't find my way here, let alone choose a decent hotel.

Tears rush into my eyes but I swallow them down, like I've always done, until they become a hard rock in my stomach.

I'll fix this in the morning.

Chapter 11

ALICE

Now

I have a restless sleep. I dream Mum turns into a lizard creature with tentacles that wrap me into a suffocating hug, and I wake with a start. I slide out of bed, away from strangers' snoring, and go to look for someone who can help me freshen up.

'*Bon dia*, good sleep?' says the woman from last night from behind the reception desk. Her smile is much more welcoming this morning.

I explain about my missing suitcase and, before long, I've hired a towel, showered and cleaned my teeth. 'Can I pay by card?' I say, returning to the desk to settle up.

The lady makes a face. 'No, sorry, cash only.' She looks at her computer. 'But you are here for three nights? You pay when you go.'

I hesitate. My plan was to find somewhere else to stay tonight but, thinking about it in the cold light of day, when am I going to have time to do that? I also need the airline to drop off my suitcase.

'Will you be here when my luggage arrives? Probably after lunch?'

She makes a face again. 'Not sure. You can wait?'

'I'm working,' I say, biting my lip. I can't wear these clothes again tomorrow. 'Is there anyone else who can help?'

She shrugs. 'Sorry.'

I call the airline as I make my way to the metro but after failing to reach them, I jump on a train and soon emerge on to the street near Perfecte. My map tells me the great glass building that stands in front of me is where I'll be working.

I phone the airline again. This time a sing-song customer services advisor answers. She promises my luggage can be delivered this afternoon. 'What's the address of your hotel?' she says.

I think about the difficulties I had finding the place last night. The fact there might not be anyone there to take it. I look up at Perfecte, shielding my eyes from the sun's glare bouncing off the glass. 'Could you send it to my workplace?' I ask.

Once I've made the arrangements, my step feels lighter and I'm about to go inside when my mobile bursts into the gospel-choir chorus I've assigned to Mum's number.

She sounds worried. 'Why didn't you answer? I left a message.'

My shoulders tighten. 'I was on the metro but I thought we'd agreed to talk later?' Before I'd left, Mum had insisted we speak at the same time every day. She'd decided 3.15 p.m. would be best. She'd be settled with her afternoon cuppa and biscuits – and I wouldn't be interrupting any of her programmes.

I must remember it will be 4.15 p.m. in Barcelona.

'I wanted to wish you luck,' she continues. 'Are you nervous?'

My watch tells me time is ticking on. 'Umm, a little. I need to go soon.'

'Why didn't you phone when you got up?'

I sigh. 'We're an hour ahead, remember? It would've been too early. And anyway, I'm speaking to you now.'

'Only because *I* called *you*.'

I feel bad. 'How was your breakfast?' I say, tapping my foot. Monday is cereal and toast – even Charlie can handle that.

'I had to do it myself,' Mum says sadly.

I'm alarmed. 'Why?'

'Charlie said I could manage.'

What the *hell*?

'I spilt the milk. She had to help me change my top.'

I can just imagine how well that went down. If Charlie had simply done what I'd told her, there'd be no dramas.

'I'm sorry. I'll speak to her in a bit.'

'She's going to work.' She sighs. 'I feel really lonely.'

Guilt clenches my stomach. 'Get lost in one of your programmes. The day will pass quickly.'

'I miss you,' she croaks.

'I miss you, too.'

The phone hums and I look inside the building at the lift that will take me up to the top floor – to Perfecte. Mariana and Andy's success makes my head spin. I have no idea what I'm doing here. 'I have to go. I'll call you later.'

As the lift ascends, I brush my hands over the creases in my top and take some deep breaths. I've allowed myself to be so preoccupied this morning, I've not had to think about how I'm going to feel when I come face to face with Andy – with Mariana.

Now it is about to happen.

The doors slide open and a woman springs forward before I've had a chance to step out. 'You must be Alice – I'm Susie!' she chirps in a Scottish accent. Freckles dance across her nose and there's a hint of familiarity about her. Perhaps it's because we're a similar age and she's wearing jeans, like me, though her navy blazer and shirt look smart and business-like compared to the top I slept in.

I reach out to shake her outstretched hand but the lift doors begin to close on me. I jab frantically at the buttons, feeling my cheeks go warm.

Susie laughs. 'Sorry, I'm blocking the way. Come out, come in – welcome!'

Reception is starkly cream with a shiny tiled floor. A weird headless sculpture poses on a pillar next to a desk displaying a vase of cerise pink flowers, and the dim hum of activity floats out from a corridor.

Susie smiles. 'Isn't it an amazing building? Wait until you see Mariana and Andy's offices. This is such a great place to work. They've really looked after me.' She lowers her voice. 'Don't be scared of the big lady boss. She's super-driven, super-ambitious, and you'll learn everything you'll ever need to know about running a successful school.'

A band of pressure tightens the base of my head. I feel a childish urge to run away. But I put one step in front of the other, heart pitter-pattering as Susie takes me past the classrooms and chatters about the years she's worked here. Dimly, I piece together that this new, fresher version of the school came about soon after I left Barcelona.

The news stings more than I expect. I wonder what happened to Andy's Ibiza dream?

'I'm not cut out to teach,' Susie adds. 'Ceramics is my true passion but it doesn't pay the bills.' She pushes open a door to a corridor that runs between two offices. Glass walls either side make it possible for me to see in.

To see Andy – Mariana.

My heart constricts.

'Ta-da!' says Susie.

I blush at her over-the-top announcement, but neither of them hear as the door is shut. Paralysis sets in for a moment as I take in

Mariana leaning over her desk towards Andy, face animated, tight skirt clinging to curves that shout sexy. I touch my shirt, feeling even more rumpled than I did earlier. Then, to my surprise, there's a muffled shout and Andy spins away from her, face contorted.

'Uh-oh, there's trouble in paradise,' Susie murmurs.

I'm hoping we can reverse back out without being seen but it's too late. Andy catches sight of me through the glass, eyes burning with emotion that's unsettling and unwelcoming.

Susie doesn't seem to notice. 'I'll leave you to it,' she says. 'Good luck!'

Chapter 12

ANDY

Ten years ago

'The holiday is over for now, Andy,' said Enric. 'Jimmy is going to run the bar and your friend is going to teach you the important stuff.'

Alice was standing at a long wooden work bench in the kitchen. She was wearing a strappy sundress in a shade of green that showed off her golden skin – and an apron. I watched her slice potatoes with speed and precision. It bordered on irritating. Above, pots and pans hung from a rack fixed to the ceiling and in the corner a fan revolved lazily, doing nothing to lower the sticky temperature in the cramped room. My thoughts jumped briefly to my air-conditioned office in London.

'Is this a joke?' I said, scanning Enric's face for a hint of jest.

'Your *mare* tells me you need to learn some skills and Alice is an expert.'

'Cheers, but if I've got to stick around, I'm working the bar with Jimmy,' I replied, stuffing my hands in my pockets.

My uncle tugged his moustache. 'I need help here,' he said. 'We cannot sell food if no one is making it.'

'Yep, and you have Alice – the *expert*.'

'I see,' he replied, folding his arms and appraising me.

Sweat was fast gathering around my hairline and in my pits. There was no way I could cook for customers. I ate in restaurants, I had take-outs, late-night kebabs or heated my mum's cooking in the microwave. I didn't have a clue – and I wasn't interested.

The sound of Alice's knife hitting the chopping board filled our silence. Jimmy's banter with a customer filtered through from the bar. He had a knack with people. By this evening everyone would think he owned the place.

Lucky bastard.

I inched towards the door. 'Bar work, not kitchen work,' I repeated.

Alice looked up. 'Too hard for you?' she said, smiling and shaking her head.

'No, because I'm a better barman than a chef,' I retorted.

Enric eyed me. 'On which side of the bar?'

Alice snorted.

Then it dawned on me. My mum had told him I had a booze problem. She'd jumped to the conclusion that drink was the reason I lost my job. Okay, so there was some truth to the tale, but it wasn't the full picture. London bars were packed with pissed-up City boys after work, it was part of the territory. But being Catalan, being my *mum*, she didn't get that I wasn't the only one.

I knew she loathed a drunk, but in my twisted reality, getting smashed helped me forget the guilt of remembering that.

I wiped sweat from my forehead. The walls of the kitchen were closing in on me. I'd been set up, thinking I had a choice to work here, but I didn't. Could I really blame my mum? After my dad had left, I'd promised to look after her. In her eyes, I was crawling through life, unemployed, a drunk. I'd hated seeing her face crumple when she heard I'd lost my job.

I couldn't tell her I'd resigned. That the pressure had got to me.

I just needed to be more like Matt. Relaxed, chilled. He'd made our mum happy.

'Alright,' I said, holding up my hands. 'I'll spend one week in the kitchen, learn some new *skills*, then switch to the bar – deal? But you've got to buy a proper fan. It's a sweat box in here.'

Enric laughed, showing big white teeth. 'One week, it is a deal.' He patted me on the back. 'You are a negotiator, just like your *mare*, I like that.' He disappeared into the bar and I went over and stood in front of the fan to cool down.

'Don't hog it, some of us are working,' Alice said, pulling open a drawer. 'Cutlery.' She swept her arm in the same way I had to her on the train when we'd met. Her smirk had me wondering if she'd remembered and her actions were deliberate. 'You know how to use a knife, right?' She held one out to me.

'Didn't your mum tell you it was dangerous to point a knife at someone?' I replied.

'No.' She handed me a chopping board. 'Don't cut the vegetables on the table.'

'I'm not a complete div.'

She smiled. 'That's yet to be proved.' She pushed a handful of red peppers in my direction. 'Slice them, like this.'

I rolled my eyes and got started, sneaking a glance at Alice out of the corner of my eye. Nobody looked good in an apron, especially one sized for a fat chef who liked eating as much as cooking. But Alice had done a good job of tying it tightly around her small waist.

'If you're behind the bar, you'll be working until the early hours,' she said mildly. 'Enric says he's not going to keep the kitchen open all evening. We'll finish up here way before Jimmy does. We'll get more free time.'

'He'll get a lie-in.'

She shrugged. 'If we're organised the day before, we might not have to start so early.'

'Ah yes, I remember now, Little Miss Organised,' I say softly. 'Can't say that's a strong point of mine.'

She smiled and tipped vegetables into a large metal baking tray. 'Oh yeah, that's right, you like to make it up as you go along, don't you?' She poured oil over the top and shook them around. 'Well, sorry, the first rule of cooking is: be organised.'

Alice bent down and opened the oven and I looked away. A week squeezed together in this kitchen wasn't going to work if she thought I was staring at her whenever her back was turned.

I switched up the conversation. 'Go on then. How did you end up coming to work here?' I realised I was genuinely curious.

She pointed at the vegetables. 'They're being griddled, so you need to *slice*, not chop.'

I looked down. 'Same thing, isn't it?'

'No, not at all,' she said. 'Like this.' She ran the knife down the pepper again.

'Tastes the same, doesn't it?'

'Doesn't *look* the same.'

I did what she showed me. 'So what happened?' I pressed.

Alice sighed. 'Let's just say the decision was forced upon me.'

'Oh yeah? How come?'

She plonked a basket of aubergines on to the work bench and plucked one out, slicing it into thick, even rounds. 'You're nosy.'

I laughed. 'This is called a *conversation*.'

Her mouth twitched into a smile.

'This okay, chef?' I pointed the knife at my work.

Alice nodded. 'Charlie lost a chunk of our money. Well, it got stolen. When we arrived in Narbonne, she remembered she'd left it in a locker back in the Montpellier hostel. I mean, honestly.' She stabbed her knife into another aubergine. 'I phoned them,

69

thinking we'd go back to collect it, but they said it wasn't there. Of course it wasn't,' she muttered. 'Not after I'd told them what had happened.'

'That's out of order. Can't you report it to the police?'

She shrugged. 'I can't prove it. All I know is I'm a bloody idiot for trusting Charlie. I thought it was about time she took some kind of responsibility on this trip instead of relying on me. I told her to put the money in her money belt.'

My mind leapt back to the glimpse of Alice's smooth skin as she'd tucked Charlie's passport away on the train. She'd said her little sister was almost eighteen. I gave her a sideways glance. There was no way I'd be able to look after a younger sibling – I could barely look after myself. 'I guess she didn't?'

Alice flattened her mouth. 'You know, I wouldn't put it past her to have done it deliberately. She was very keen to follow you guys. She denied it though.'

'You accused her? Wow, brave words. Bet that didn't go down well.'

'I was probably a bit out of order,' she agreed. 'But I was annoyed.'

'And here you are, stuck in a job you don't want to do, just like me.'

To my surprise, she let out a warm laugh. 'No, not at all! I'm *really* pleased about being here.'

'Seriously? You got a bit upset when Jimmy suggested it on the train.'

Alice shrugged. 'Sorry, for a moment he made it sound like a set-up.'

I released a puff of air. 'Wow, you're trusting. You actually thought him and I had enough brains between us to chat you up so we could convince you to do our jobs for us?'

Alice put down her knife and gave me a long, even look. Just at the point when I felt I should tear myself away from her green-grey eyes, she broke into a grin and burst out laughing. 'Oh my God, Andy, when you say it like that, I sound *insane*.'

I smiled. 'Talking of crazy people, where's Charlie?'

She chuckled. 'Sleeping, probably. Enric doesn't need her to start till later.'

'Oh yeah, what's she doing?' An unpleasant thought occurred to me. 'She's not working behind the bar with Jimmy, is she?'

'Jealous?' she teased.

'Is she?' I persisted.

Alice shook her head. 'Don't panic, she's waitressing, but Enric has asked her to help Jimmy when he needs it. The guy he had before used to do both.'

It was stupid to feel irritated but I couldn't help it. 'He knows she's seventeen, right?'

'No.' She eyed me warily. 'Does that matter? She's finished her education. She's one of those with a late birthday – she'll be eighteen next month.'

I had no idea whether Enric would care. What were the rules here anyway? Socialising was completely different. It was perfectly normal for friends and families across the generations to gather late into the summer evenings to eat and drink. But if Charlie's job was dependent on being able to waitress *and* work behind the bar, and Enric wasn't comfortable with her age, it meant Alice couldn't stay either.

'How long do you think you'll be here?' I asked.

'I don't know. A month, maybe? I'd planned to pick up some shifts in my old job to boost my savings before I started my apprenticeship, but if it works out here, I could stay on a bit longer.'

Alice grabbed a griddle pan from the shelf below the bench and placed it on the hob. 'Can you pass me the peppers, please?' she said. 'What about you? When does your new life begin?'

I handed her the plate and she held it while waiting for my answer. I liked that she viewed Ibiza as my fresh start and I felt an unexpected wash of gratitude. 'A week with you, two weeks in the bar, then we're out of here.'

Chapter 13

ANDY

Ten years ago

At the end of our shift, I practically crawled out of the kitchen and dropped on to a bar stool. Jimmy thrust me a beer. I guzzled back half and sighed. I suppose I should've been grateful Enric didn't expect Alice and I to work all evening, too. I had the rest of the night ahead of me, free to do what I pleased.

'Can you help wash up?' Alice appeared at the kitchen door, hands on her hips. Her hair had worked loose from its ponytail, the heat wisping curls around her forehead.

I took another swig of beer. 'I've done the pots. I thought you were loading the dishwasher?'

'It's broken.'

Jimmy snickered. 'Get to it, boy.'

Alice disappeared and I slid off the stool, taking the beer with me, then grabbing one for her, too. Back in the kitchen, she was bent over the dishwasher, pulling the dirty dishes back out.

I crouched down next to her. 'Beer?' I held out the bottle and my gaze flicked to her mouth momentarily.

She flushed and jumped up, grabbing the beer from my hand. 'Thanks.'

As I began scrubbing the dishes, I wondered when I'd last washed up as much as I had today. Never. Even when I was home long enough to devour one of my mum's amazing meals, I'd chuck my dishes in the dishwasher. All this bollocks from her about needing to learn new skills – what had I learnt today? How to wash up and chop vegetables into fancy shapes. Big deal.

Alice was on her knees again, fiddling with something inside the machine. 'Sorted!' She leapt up and thrust a handful of stinking black muck in front of my face.

'Hey.' I swatted her hand away.

'Food waste, bunging up the filter.' She glanced at the stack of clean dishes on the side. 'Oh well, too late. Not to worry, I'll dry.'

'So *kind* of you,' I said, oozing sarcasm.

She looked incredulous. 'You want me to say thank you for washing up? You should be thanking *me* for fixing the dishwasher. I didn't see you offering to help.'

I didn't bother to say I wouldn't have had a clue where to start. 'That's sexist and, anyway, you told me to wash up.'

'Do you do everything a woman tells you?'

Alice's hands were back on her hips again and irritation burnt her voice. I threw her a knowing smile. 'Of course I do. I'm not *selfish*.'

She pinked again and tutted as she turned away – but not before I caught her smile. Perhaps a week working in the kitchen wasn't going to be such an ordeal after all.

◆ ◆ ◆

'You can't go out,' Alice said to Charlie a little later. 'We're working tomorrow and we need to get back to the hostel.'

We were sat at the bar with Enric while Jimmy and Charlie served. I'd not told my uncle she was only seventeen. Not that it mattered tonight. Business was slow, and despite the early hour, Enric had decided to close after the last customers left.

Charlie made a face. 'I'm young, I can do both!' She'd already had a couple of beers and was halfway through a piña colada. 'Jimmy said he wanted to take me clubbing, remember?' she added slyly. 'He'll make sure I get home safely.'

'Darling, don't bring me into your sisterly dispute,' he said, holding up his hands and laughing.

'Go to Club Barça, it is only over there.' Enric pointed across the square. 'I know Julio, the owner. It is a safe place and easy to walk back.'

Alice's frown deepened. 'Not for us, we have to get the metro to Sants.'

'Eh? Why you stay so far away?'

She shrugged. 'It's cheap.'

Enric looked thoughtful. 'You are working here now and sometimes you will be needed here late or early. You must stay in the apartment upstairs with the boys. They will look after you.'

Charlie punched the air and burst out laughing. 'Result!'

Alice glanced at me and I raised an eyebrow, but she shifted her gaze away. 'I don't think that's going to work,' she said.

Her eyes flitted between Jimmy and me. Perhaps she didn't know what she was agreeing to. For a second, I considered offering to show her around upstairs, but then I remembered my room was a tip and probably had the scent of *Eau du Man* about it.

'The rooms are free,' Enric continued. 'You can work, go party and be home' – he clicked his fingers – 'like that.'

'See?' Charlie beamed at her sister.

'I insist,' Enric pressed. 'It is *boig*, crazy, to travel on the metro late when you do not have to. You must stay.'

His reasoning seemed to strike a chord. 'How many bedrooms are there?' Alice ventured carefully.

'There's a twin room that's not being used,' I said helpfully. I was warming to the idea of the girls moving in. 'We haven't got a living room as that's Jimmy's bedroom, but I've got a balcony we can all use.'

Jimmy pretended to cough. 'He's got a four-poster bed,' he added with a grin. 'Very *romantic*.'

Alice rolled her eyes.

Enric placed his palms on the bar. 'So it is decided. Now I take you to Club Barça, you meet my friend, you shake your hair loose, you stay here tonight and tomorrow we get your bags.'

Charlie bounced out from behind the bar. She pulled her sister into a hug and swung her around. Alice's smile illuminated her face, looking so genuine, so pretty, that a jumble of weird feelings tumbled together in my belly. I pulled my gaze away, a sarcastic remark rushing to the surface to crush my discomfort – but Matt's voice jumped in my head.

Don't screw this up, bro.

Chapter 14

ANDY

Ten years ago

A few days later, I stumbled out of my bedroom and collided with Alice in the hallway. She shoved me away and I banged my shoulder on the wall.

'Oh gosh, sorry!' she said, mouth twitching. 'My self-defence classes kicked in. You okay?' Her cool fingers grazed the heat of the impact. 'You're up early.'

I lurched away from her curious expression and into the bathroom, mumbling something about the market but, by the time I'd emerged from the shower, she'd gone downstairs.

I flung myself back on my bed and stared up at the chandelier. After going to Club Barça the other night, the girls had wasted no time settling in. Charlie slept as late as she could, like Jimmy and me. Alice, on the other hand, liked to be up at some ungodly hour. I was like the rebellious schoolkid sloping in late for class when I finally made it down to the kitchen.

Enric hadn't been impressed. So, today, I'd promised to haul my arse out of bed early and go to the market with Alice.

I yawned. The rough taste of last night's tequilas lingered in my mouth. I hadn't meant to have a big one but just as I was leaving, Charlie appeared with another round of shots. My eyes shuttered closed but a thump on the apartment door jerked them open again. 'Alice is waiting,' Enric hollered.

'Coming,' I shouted back. I rolled off the bed and hopped into some clothes. A part of me hoped my uncle would see how crap I was in the mornings and decide I'd be more useful behind the bar, later in the day. Though I could see waking with a hangover wasn't going to propel me in the direction I wanted.

Downstairs, Alice was sat on a bar stool in a sleeveless red shirt dress pulled in at the waist with a belt. She had big sunglasses propped up on her head and was holding a basket. For some reason I thought of Little Red Riding Hood.

'Going to visit Grandma?' I muttered. 'Don't let the wolf get you.' I scratched my hand through the air and made a snarling noise. Unsurprisingly, she stared at me like I was mad – or still pissed – which was completely plausible given the hour.

She hopped off the stool and came closer. Her eyes travelled over my crumpled T-shirt and landed on my unshaven face. 'Looks like the wolf already got *you*.'

I breathed in her fresh, summery scent and felt a ripple of adolescent excitement. I exhaled. 'Charlie's fault,' I said hoarsely.

Alice laughed and stepped away. 'There's a surprise. You ready?'

'Let me grab an espresso.'

She sighed and nodded.

The first one didn't touch the sides. After the second one and a large glass of water, I felt a little bit of life seeping back into me and I braced myself to face the sharp sunlight. As we headed out across the square towards La Rambla, I pushed hard to lighten my mood. 'What we buying, then?'

'Wait and see,' she replied with a smile. We crossed the boulevard and headed towards La Boqueria, its name etched in stone over the archway. Inside the open market, stalls ran in organised aisles, piled high with produce, looking exactly as I remembered. The place was already bustling with trade.

Alice turned to me. 'What do you like to eat, Andy?'

Her gaze held mine and, for a second, I was caught off-guard. Her eyes had a sea-green tone to them in this light. 'Err . . .' All I could think about was burger and chips. Great for curing a raging hangover but also because that was my default meal. By rights, I should have been a lard-arse but, thankfully, I'd inherited my dad's slim genes – the one and only decent thing about being his offspring.

'I know,' she said. 'Burger and chips.'

I wondered if she was implying my taste buds weren't very sophisticated. It didn't matter as her guess made me laugh, loudly. 'Are you a mind-reader?'

'You've got a hangover.' She smiled and set off between the stalls.

I trailed close behind, watching her expression flicker between delight, pleasure and excitement as she picked up courgettes, tomatoes and avocadoes, inhaling their scent, rolling them over in her hands, examining each one. I remembered what she'd said on the train about working the ingredients to make them come alive. Yesterday, I'd shovelled back one of the meals we'd made, which was good, but I didn't put much thought into what the food *really* tasted like.

Perhaps I should have.

'Stop staring, it's rude,' she said, reaching out for a string of garlic. She pushed the basket into my hand. 'Can you do the talking? You know some Catalan, don't you?'

Els carbassons, els tomàquets, els alvocats. The words shimmered into my consciousness. But I wasn't convinced they'd come out of my mouth. I shook my head.

79

'Your mum never taught you?' She sounded surprised.

'She did, I suppose.' Catalan had filtered into my childhood by osmosis. I remembered words entwining with English, often forming Anglo-Catalan sentences that made sense to the three of us, much to my dad's frustration as he'd never bothered to learn. 'It's just that I've forgotten it all.'

It's weird how a whole language can slide into the crevices of a person's brain in a crisis and become too deeply buried to retrieve.

Alice looked at me like I was insane again. She fumbled with a dog-eared phrasebook and began to splutter out Catalan translations. I winced but admired her efforts and, thankfully, the market trader nodded in encouragement.

At a stall further along, my hungover mouth began to salivate at the sight of freshly squeezed juices stacked in a colourful pyramid on ice. 'Want one?' I said, pointing. 'Which flavour?'

'You choose.'

I ambled over to the stall. Matt had always picked watermelon. I'd always chosen passionfruit and orange. I could have necked mine in one, it totally hit the spot, but I resisted. 'Want to try?' I said, holding my cup out. Alice leant forward and sucked on the straw. Her summery smell wafted into my senses again and I wondered if it was her shampoo.

She beamed. 'This is good. Try mine?'

I declined, still conscious of my stale hangover breath.

She waggled the cup, eyes dancing. 'Come on, this combination of fruit tastes way better than your watermelon.'

A faint memory surfaced. Matt and I having the same argument. In the same place. About the same drinks. 'I know,' I replied distantly. 'You've got the one I always choose.'

Alice paused and looked at her drink. 'You've been here before?'

I grinned. 'Loads of times.'

'And you didn't say?'

'You didn't ask.'

She carried on sucking her drink, her gaze glued to me. The straw shrieked against the empty plastic. 'I suppose I should have guessed. Did you used to spend the summer in Barcelona?'

I nodded and as we carried on walking, I told her about my mum's apartment in the city suburbs, our days spent at the beach or in the cool shade of the parks.

'Isn't this market great?' Alice's eyes shone as they darted over the stalls.

'Yeah, I suppose. It's kind of become a tourist spot, though.'

'Enric told me to come,' she said, sounding a bit defensive.

'Of course,' I replied. 'It's the closest one to the cafe. And anyway, I didn't say the produce wasn't any good. I mean, it's probably more expensive than other, smaller markets you might find in the old town. Plus, if you're on a *culinary tour* . . .' I grinned at her. 'You want to find the best food and the best ingredients, right?'

She smiled. 'Of course.'

'Then, I'm sure you'd find better elsewhere.'

'I wouldn't know where to go.'

I waved my hand. 'Just go exploring.'

She threw me a worried glance. 'I suppose I could get a map from the tourist information centre.'

I couldn't help it; I let out a belly laugh. 'You don't need a map! That's the point – get out there, go and get lost in the streets. That's where you'll find the real Barcelona.'

Alice bit her lip and looked towards the exit. She seemed unsure. I didn't get it. But then I thought about her obsession with being organised. Was she worried about getting lost? The maze of the old town spat you out somewhere familiar eventually.

Except Alice didn't know Barcelona like I did.

My face brightened. 'I'll show you around at the weekend.'

Chapter 15

ANDY

Ten years ago

Alice wanted to explore every inch of the market and my stomach growled as I caught the tantalising scent of baked goods on our way out. 'Over here,' I said, pulling her by the hand. We turned the corner and I was blessed with the sight of a stall laden with moon-shaped pastries. '*Pastissets,*' I said. 'These are amazing.'

We stood looking at them for a moment. Then I became aware I was still holding Alice's hand. We caught eyes and I let go. She dropped her gaze to the basket and fiddled with the vegetables before focusing back on the display.

I wondered if I'd overstepped the mark.

'What are they?' she said as if nothing had happened. 'They look a bit like mini Cornish pasties.'

'They're usually sweet.' My eyes darted greedily over the rows of goodies, trying to decide which one to buy.

Alice nudged me and laughed. 'Alright, I get it, but what *are* they?'

'Fried pastries, like *empanadas*. They're filled with almond paste, jam or sweet potato puree.'

We soon had a bag and began walking back. I watched Alice take a bite of one. 'Oh my, I love the almond, it's divine,' she mumbled, brushing crumbs from her lips. She tried the other two and we began sparring about the best flavour.

Mine was sweet potato. 'Let me have another try,' said Alice, pouncing for the last half in my hand.

I snatched it out of her reach. 'Nope, this one has my name on it. You said nothing could beat the almond one.'

Her eyes danced. 'I might have changed my mind.'

'You said the sweet potato was claggy,' I reminded her. 'And not sweet enough.'

She laughed. 'Come on, give me a bite. I won't know how to improve the recipe otherwise.'

I opened my mouth wide and pretended to pop the last piece in. Alice's hand shot out and, with a grin, she snatched it from me and pushed it into her own mouth. Her cheeks bulged a little as she munched, making me smile, and then she stopped walking and closed her eyes. Her eyelids flickered, her mouth worked. Then she was looking at me again. A sea of green.

'Needs honey and . . . cinnamon, I think.' She spun away, dark hair swinging against her red dress, and I followed, thinking I only had a couple more days in the kitchen left with her – and did I *really* want to work the bar with Jimmy?

◆　◆　◆

Alice was asking me if I'd ever eaten a savoury *pastisset* when we arrived back at the cafe and as I shook my head, I spotted Jimmy on the terrace with Mariana, having coffee. Dressed in a smart suit, she was clearly on her way to work whereas Jimmy, unshaven and half asleep, looked like a hobo she'd taken pity on. After a quick introduction, Alice and I excused ourselves to the kitchen where we got to work.

Alice directed me towards a large sack of potatoes and asked me to peel them. I began hacking with a knife and she squealed. 'Stop! Look at the waste.' She rummaged in a drawer and handed me a peeler. 'You know what this is, right?' she said, laughing.

'Can't I leave the skin on? It'll be much quicker.'

She made a face. 'So lazy.'

'I'll scrub them first. The skin might add flavour?' I had no idea if this was true but anything to make my life easier.

Alice pondered for a moment, and then nodded. 'Yes, let's try that.'

'Are we making *patatas bravas*?'

She flashed me a smile. 'Not today, but do you know the recipe?'

I thought back to being a kid. 'My mum used to make it. I could give it a go sometime. She makes a great paella too – I reckon the best I've ever had.'

'Really? That's my favourite. Be great if you could get the recipe for that, too.' Alice began dropping clumps of meat into a grinder and turning the handle. My *pastisset* rolled over in my stomach as my hangover rose to the surface again. She still hadn't told me what was on the menu.

'You're making a chilli,' I guessed, pointing at the pile of mince.

She shook her head. 'Burgers.'

For me? I nearly said but stopped myself in time. 'Not very Spanish.'

'With a Spanish *twist*,' she added, smiling. 'You're making the chips.'

'Like a Spanish McDonald's? Or a cure for my hangover?'

Alice laughed. 'You flatter yourself.' She rinsed one of the potatoes and sliced it into long, even strips. 'Your turn.' She stood close enough for me to feel the heat from her body, and I messed up my first attempt and cranked up the fan. She showed me again, this time cutting slower so I could see how to make the chips a similar size without having too much waste.

'So what's the twist?' I asked, running the potatoes under the tap.

'A chorizo and manchego burger.'

'With paprika fries?' I suggested over my shoulder.

Alice broke into a smile and nodded. 'I'm liking your idea.'

We fell silent as she carried on mincing the meat. I brought the potatoes back to the bench. 'So Jimmy has a new lady friend, then?' Alice remarked.

'Mariana? She's a language teacher. Enric says she runs a school near here.'

Alice nodded. 'Could be useful. Where did they meet?'

Apart from having post-work drinks in the bar, and the one time we all went to Club Barça, Alice hadn't yet ventured any further.

'Here, I guess. I've not seen her out.'

Alice began shaping the meat into patties. 'Regret not getting your beauty sleep this morning?' she teased.

I raised my eyebrow. 'And there was me thinking you thought I was handsome enough already.'

She rolled her eyes. 'You do like to party.'

'Not all the time,' I replied, suddenly feeling the need to get this point across. 'I'm never out that late. Gets boring.'

'What about Ibiza? DJs aren't known for being tucked up in bed by nine o'clock.'

I smiled. 'That's a different sort of partying.'

'Drugs, not drink?'

'I suppose, but I was thinking more along the lines that it draws a crowd that like decent music and dancing.'

'You're not a fan of the conga, then?'

We smiled at one other.

'How did you go about finding a place to stay in Ibiza?' she asked, putting the grinder in the sink to clean. 'I wouldn't have a clue where to start.'

I shrugged. 'I haven't yet.'

'That doesn't worry you?'

'Not really. It's just details. I'll find somewhere.'

'What will you do in winter? I mean, the club scene must be seasonal, right? Have you got another job lined up?'

My skin prickled and I spun away from her. I hadn't thought beyond the summer. Beyond DJ-ing – and her questions rankled. What was my future? 'What are *you* going to do when your apprenticeship finishes?'

Alice looked startled at my tone. 'Oh. I'm hoping they'll keep me on.'

'And if they don't?' I sounded meaner than I meant to as I genuinely wanted to know. Alice had goals and ambitions. I could learn a thing or two from her.

She stared at me for a moment. 'Then I'll find another job,' she said coolly.

Just at that moment, Enric pushed open the door and clocked the frosty atmosphere between us. He tsked, eyebrows knitted together. 'Andy, are you free for a minute? Mariana is in the bar – she wants to talk to you.'

But before I could follow Enric out, Mariana was nudging past him and coming inside. She glanced around the kitchen and threw Alice a small smile, her gaze landing on me. 'Andrew,' she said, face aglow. 'You are not in Ibiza after all. Would you like to reconsider and join my Catalan class?'

Chapter 16

ALICE

Now

Andy Hall is sitting in front of me.

Sorry, *Andrew Cortez-Hall*, according to Mariana, who glee-fully introduced us moments ago as though he wouldn't remember me.

Apart from greeting me with a nod and a handshake as though we've just met, Andy's face is a mask, like the photo on the website. If I'd passed him on the street I might take a second glance, thinking it was him, but instantly dismiss the idea. All cheek and charm have been sucked out of him.

Does he hold a grudge against me? I should be the one with a grudge against him.

I catch Mariana's eyes rake over my creased top and jeans. I'm about to explain the missing suitcase debacle but she's already saying, 'Alice, it really is *so* nice to see you again,' and throwing me another smile.

She seems warm and genuine – but is she?

Andy's gaze drifts over me and the air conditioning prickles my skin. I notice the gold hoop earring has gone. The black leather of the Gemini necklace has worn grey. My stomach tightens. Now's not the time to fall back to the past.

Mariana eyeballs Andy, who shakes his head a little in the secret language reserved for married couples. I can't tell if either of them is surprised to see me. Did they know it would be me? *That* Alice Taylor?

I let my gaze shift. Mariana's office is substantial with a fuschia-pink sofa and large glass coffee table, as well as the desk. The setting is breathtaking. Behind the happy couple, the view drops away to the city below. It creates a dizzying effect, like flying – or perhaps that's just my state of mind.

'How strange the world works,' Mariana says.

'Strange,' I reply.

She stares openly at me, her eyes artfully made up to look as large and radiant as they did in her younger years. She's wearing a pale pink silky blouse, and gold bangles chime on her wrists as she talks. My eyes land on sparkly earrings, a delicate gold chain at her neck – and a large diamond ring. Confidence had always been her strong point and now vibrates at the highest frequency.

Mariana glances at a piece of paper on the desk. Andy leans over but she pushes it out of his reach. 'Your boss tells me you're a *perfecte* English language teacher.' Her laugh tinkles. There's an uncomfortable pause and, by the way she's still looking at me, I assume I'm supposed to laugh along with her joke.

'Ha, yes, perfect for Perfecte.'

Who calls their language school Perfecte anyway?

Andy grabs the piece of paper – information Janet's given them, I assume – and scans it. Why isn't he speaking?

'You're a teacher and we're teachers.' Mariana states the obvious and gives Andy a side glance beneath long curly lashes. 'How amusing.'

'We don't teach anymore,' he replies coldly. 'And we certainly don't need any staff.'

I'm startled but Mariana's smile doesn't slip.

'We are here to help Alice's career,' she says, tapping her nail on the paper, and I flush. She's making it sound as though I'm a lost cause and desperate for the job.

I'm not – am I?

'You're not making sense,' says Andy, heat creeping into his voice.

I suspect this isn't how they'd normally conduct business. I should feel flattered they feel so comfortable around me.

He presses his lips together. 'Why do you want to teach here?'

I glance at Mariana and it dawns on me that she hasn't told Andy. Her gaze lingers on me while she calculates something in her mind.

Andy pushes his chair back and stalks over to the window. It's weird seeing him in smart trousers and leather shoes. 'Are you going to tell me what's going on?'

'Alice is going to be important in moving Perfecte forward,' she says.

My cheeks go hot. 'Well—'

He spins around. '*What* job, Mariana?' he demands. 'We're partners. You're supposed to discuss this with me. We don't need any more teachers.'

Mariana glides over to him as though she isn't wearing spiky heels and a tight blue skirt. She touches his face and I swear I hear the electricity crackling between them. She gives him a slow, lazy smile. 'Come, listen,' she says softly.

I try not to stare. No wonder Andy married her. He doesn't have a grudge against me. How could I be arrogant enough to think it? Any memories he might have had about us would have instantly evaporated the moment he arrived in Ibiza.

My stomach clenches again.

'Tell us about your food events, Alice,' Mariana says, stepping back to her desk while keeping her gaze on Andy. His head snaps around and her face lights up. 'Andrew, she has lots of ideas, *good* ideas, to help recruit more students.' She turns back to me. 'Tell us more.'

I fidget in my seat. I don't like the glint in her eye. This is personal and despite Janet telling me how interested Mariana had been, this is nothing to do with Riverside. It's a fledging idea and I don't want it stolen and turned into something completely different.

'I organise pop-up food events,' I mutter.

'Yes?' Mariana's smiling and nodding but Andy's got his back to us again.

'It gets the students talking, especially the less confident ones – they're so focused on the food, they forget they're practising English.'

Slowly, Andy turns around and locks eyes with me. I wonder if he's remembering the time he'd been so happy and relaxed he ordered ice-creams for us in Catalan without thinking. The memory stirs a ripple of sadness.

'This all sounds *meravellós*,' says Mariana, her laugh tinkling again. 'Now, Andrew is our mastermind, our *cervell*. You will work with him, learn everything and then take it back to Riverside.'

Andy strides over, face etched in anger. 'What are you talking about?'

'Oh, Andrew,' she says. 'I have always said Perfecte must grow and now is the time. Alice's school is thriving. I have already spoken to her boss, Janet, the owner, about buying Riverside. You will train Alice the Perfecte way and if she is successful, she will run our new school in London.'

A flush blooms in Andy's face. 'That's not possible,' he snaps.

Mariana's eyes widen. 'Why, Andrew? I'm not going to make you share a desk. Susie will bring one in for Alice.'

I look over to Andy's office and see it's a lot smaller than in here. There's a distant view of Sagrada Familia from the window and I pinch myself that I'm *in Barcelona* – and not at Riverside above the laundrette.

'So, Alice, I'm sure you have things to organise,' says Mariana, standing up. 'Come back tomorrow' – she waves her hand over me, bangles chiming – 'but dress like you want to be here, no? Not like one of the students.' She grips my hand. 'I am looking forward to this journey together.'

◆ ◆ ◆

When I let myself back on to the street, I release a huge sigh of relief and a nervous giggle. My head spins at the surreal situation and I hover, turning my head this way and that, deciding where to go, what to do, feeling overwhelmed with the enormity of . . . *life*.

As I strike out along the boulevard, pondering the woman Mariana is now – the Andy of now – I allow the magic of Barcelona to creep into my senses. I gaze up at the palm trees lining the road, the sun filtering through high branches, and roll up my sleeves to feel the warmth on my bare arms.

My suitcase! I dash back to the school and catch Andy striding towards me. For a moment, I forget all that's gone on before – just now – and feel a rush of pleasure.

His face becomes a frown. 'Oh good, I was hoping to catch you before you left.'

'Oh?'

'You know you can't do this,' he says quickly. 'It's just not going to work.'

Any good feelings I have drain away. *He's got a bloody nerve.*

'Really? Why not?' I reply coldly. 'We've worked together before, I'm sure we can do it again.'

Andy's mouth is a line. 'I had no idea about Mariana's plans. I'd no idea' – he throws his arms wide in frustration – 'she wanted to buy a school in London. So when you walked into our offices . . .'

I narrow my eyes. 'What? What did you think?'

He shakes his head; a faint smile appears. 'What the *fuck*?'

I can't help but laugh. 'God, she's got you under her thumb.' I hadn't meant to sound cutting, but Andy's face darkens.

'Tell her your school isn't for sale,' he demands.

I shrug. 'It's not up to me.'

'Why did you come?'

My eyes travel to his throat where his fingers fiddle with the pendant. I decided a decade ago I wouldn't spend any time thinking about what might have been. I've never looked Andy up online. What was the point? He'd made his decision – and I'd made mine.

Why *had* I come?

To help Mum, to help Janet – to help *me*?

'I'm here because . . .' I flounder for a moment. 'I need to see this through.' I don't really know what this means, but I feel a certainty about what I'm doing, and straighten up.

Andy stares wordlessly and I'm about to walk away when I remember. 'The airline is delivering my suitcase today. Could you look out for it, please?'

Chapter 17

ALICE

Now

The following day, Mariana is in reception and welcomes me with a customary kiss to each cheek, which catches me by surprise. Before I get a chance to ask Susie if my suitcase got dropped off yesterday, Mariana's whisking me through to Andy's office.

I'm relieved he's not here yet. There's a temporary desk set up next to his, a fold-out table and chair that looks like something you might see at a church fête or for entertaining visiting family at Christmas. When Mariana said I'd be working with Andy, I didn't expect to be close enough to prod elbows.

'Come, sit down,' she says, settling herself on the edge of Andy's desk and crossing her legs. Her tights are glossy nude and her hair has been blow-dried into loose waves. She wears the same power-hungry skirt suits and heels that she did ten years ago, but I'd never felt threatened by the way she dressed. Perhaps I should have.

Andy appears and scowls at the mashed together seating arrangement. He heads for the window – as far from me as possible. Am I the reason why Mariana didn't tell her husband about her interest in buying Riverside?

'How is your hotel?' says Mariana, eyeing the jeans and trainers I wore yesterday. I fiddle with the collar of my new white shirt.

'Oh, fine. Well, not fine, but I'm sorting that out. Do you know if my suitcase arrived yesterday? From the airline?'

Mariana's brow creases for a moment and then she shakes her head. 'Did you ask Susie?' She glances at my outfit again and her face clears. 'Ah, I see now. You poor thing, you should have said. I could have brought you something to wear.'

I eye her tight skirt. Her frame is still tiny – there's no way I would fit into any of her clothes.

'So, tell me, were your family sad to see you leave?' she asks.

I think about Mum's tears, Janet's joy, Charlie's whoop.

'Your boyfriend, perhaps?' A smile plays around her mouth. 'You have a man, no? Pretty girls always have a man!'

I laugh uncomfortably. 'I don't have a boyfriend.'

'Is that right?' she murmurs. 'Did you know Catalan men are the most romantic in the world?' She sighs and shakes her head. 'In this *ciutat fabulosa* it will not take you long to find company.'

From the corner of my eye, I catch Andy glance my way.

Mariana's smile lengthens. 'Ah, boyfriends, families – we love them, we hate them. I am very close with my family. Susie's boyfriend, Xavier, is *el meu cosí*, my cousin. He works here.' Her smile broadens. 'You will see my *pare* here sometimes, too. He likes to make sure the school is *perfecte*.'

Her laugh rings out and I respond with a faint smile.

'Do you have children?' she says suddenly, looking me up and down as if my body shape or clothes might be a clue to the answer.

The barrage of personal questions feels like a test. 'No, no, I don't.'

'Good girl! We have no time for children either.'

Andy mutters something about getting coffee and walks out.

Mariana watches until the door shuts behind him. She stands and places both hands on the desk in front of me. 'You listen carefully to Andrew,' she says.

I'm embarrassed to find my eyes level with her cleavage and catch a glimpse of a pink lacy bra. I sit back in my chair away from her.

'He's not very good at – how do you say? He is buttoned-down.'

'Buttoned-up?' I suggest.

Mariana cocks her head. 'Mmm, *sí*, closed like a book. But all the information you need is in there.' She taps her head. 'He is our *cervell*. He will teach you everything you need to know.'

Her gaze lingers on me for longer than is comfortable and heat rises in my cheeks. It's like she's drilling into the secrets of the past hidden in my mind. I wonder how much Andy has told her about us. Then the moment passes and she straightens up. 'Don't forget to tell him everything about your food events,' she says, as she heads towards the door. 'He will be *very* interested.'

Mariana leaves and as I wait for Andy to return, imposter feelings clamour in my head. I lean down and scrabble through my bag for a notebook and pen, and when I sit back up, he's placing a coffee in front of me. 'Oh!' I stutter. 'You made me jump.'

'Surprise,' he responds drily. 'Though you're in *my* office, so not that much of a surprise.'

The accusation is annoying. I'm not the one at fault here.

'I told Susie to make yours black but I brought some sugar, just in case.'

He's waiting for a response. Like he wants praise for remembering how I take my coffee *and* praise for predicting correctly that I no longer take sugar. Perhaps he's used to Mariana stroking his ego. But that's not my style. I say thanks and accept the mug, inhaling the scent of good coffee, pleased I'm no longer forced to suffer Janet's chalky Nescafé granules.

'In case you're hungry,' he says shortly, placing a bag on to my desk.

The buttery scent of a croissant wafts out. 'Very Spanish.' My tone is lightly sarcastic, covering my surprise. 'Thanks.'

He shrugs. 'Thank Susie.'

I take a big bite, briefly glancing over to Mariana. I bet she doesn't eat pastries for breakfast. 'You know, I wouldn't normally turn up to work in jeans and trainers,' I say, brushing crumbs from my new shirt.

His eyes graze over my clothes. It's unnerving and I feel my cheeks pinken.

'I did wonder, but each to their own.' His tone is flat and difficult to decipher. Teasing or mocking? I suspect the latter.

I brush hair away from my face, indignant that he thinks I look a mess – even though I know I do. It's humiliating enough to be working here with the successful dream-team, *senyor i senyora Cortez-Hall*, without being lined up and compared to his exquisitely polished wife. Did he expect me to glide into work wearing a pretty sundress like I used to? I'm not that person anymore.

Sitting side by side makes it difficult for me to make eye contact with Andy and I wonder who's going to break the silence first. A part of me wants to dig my heels in, to make the point I can be as obnoxious as him if I want to.

I think back to when we first worked together at Cafè Vermell. When Andy was cheeky, irritating – and flirtatious. Now he's cold, brittle and dry. It seems like the only way to get through the next couple of months is to be efficient and professional – *Little Miss Organised lives on, Andy*. After all, like back then, we have a job to get done.

I turn to face him. 'Where do we start?'

Andy frowns at the computer but he hasn't touched the keyboard yet. 'Where, indeed?' he says, eyes not leaving the screen.

A bubble of annoyance bounces up but I swallow it down.

He sighs. 'Okay, tell me how things operate at . . .' He rifles through some paperwork but clearly it's no help. 'Where you work.'

'Riverside,' I say. It's another stark reminder this plan is all Mariana's. I start talking about how we recruit, the kind of students we attract and the popularity of word of mouth. To Andy's credit, he listens while I ramble on and doesn't ridicule anything I say, but simply nods and makes notes. A heavy weight rests on my shoulders. I'm here to soak up everything I can to inject the Perfecte magic into their new school.

To prove I'm good enough for the job.

Andy taps his pen on the desk. 'Sounds like you have a good business model and it's a bonus there isn't really any competition close by.'

Mariana's giggles spill out of her office and we both glance over. She's stretched out on the pink sofa, mobile in her hand on speaker, and she tips her head back and runs her hand through her hair.

Andy frowns and I look away. Was there trouble in paradise, as Susie had said? It's nothing to do with me. Besides, I'm no expert. My serial short-term relationships are no match for a marriage of – almost ten years?

I swallow.

Andy stands and yanks open a filing cabinet drawer behind him. He slaps leaflets and brochures down on my desk.

'Our current marketing information,' he says. 'We distribute this to schools, universities, and at exhibitions and shows. Take a look.'

He returns to his desk and starts to tap the keyboard.

'Mariana says you want to know more about my food events,' I venture carefully.

He stops typing. 'Do I?' His eyes are flat.

Conversation closed, it seems. I shrug and turn back to the stuff he's given me. I'm happy to keep my ideas to myself.

A little later, I'm still reading when Susie appears in the doorway. 'God, it's like a morgue in here,' she says, laughing. 'Who died?'

I smile, grateful for her sunny presence, because she's right. Soon after Mariana finished her phone call, she waltzed out of her office, throwing us a sparkly smile as she left. Andy's face became like stone but he said nothing.

'Come on, cheer up – it's time for lunch,' Susie continues. 'I thought we'd go to a little place called Cafè Vermell. Honestly, you're going to love it, Alice. The food is to die for.'

Chapter 18

ANDY

Ten years ago

'Come on, Alice, come out with us!' said Charlie one evening as she brought dirty dishes through to the kitchen.

Alice and I had fallen into a rhythm over the last few days but the early starts were taking their toll on me. I got why Alice was too knackered to do anything other than have a few post-work drinks, so I wasn't surprised when she shook her head.

'Well, at least let me make you a Sex on the Beach,' she said. 'Negroni, Andy?'

I nodded.

Charlie disappeared back into the bar and I finished loading the dishwasher. Much as I didn't like to admit it, she was a natural in her dual waitress-bar role. Under Jimmy's tuition/flirting, she already knew how to make some great cocktails and I'd noticed some of the new customers coming back and making a beeline for her at the bar.

'Done?' I asked Alice. She brushed her hand over the work bench and glanced around the kitchen. It looked clean enough to me – and super tidy. She'd rearranged the dishes earlier in the week and had got me to sort out the cutlery.

'I think you missed a bit,' I said, pointing. She swung around and I laughed softly. 'No, *here*.' A piece of hair had worked its way free from her ponytail and I tucked it back behind her ear.

She flushed and jumped away from me.

I held up my palms. 'Sorry.'

'No, it's okay,' she muttered and pulled the band out and shook her hair loose.

I swallowed and spun around, heading for the door. 'Come on, it's cocktail hour.'

In the bar, I was surprised to see Mariana sat on one of the stools all dressed up for a night out. Jimmy had told me nothing was going on between them. He'd just been up early that morning we saw them having coffee together. Enric had done the introductions and she'd invited him to join her.

Mariana was already halfway through her cocktail and giggling at something Charlie said. She gave us a quick smile as we approached.

'Evening,' I said.

'*Bon vespre*, Andrew.'

Alice dropped down on to the stool next to her and released a long sigh.

'Busy day?' Mariana asked her. Alice nodded and yawned, causing her to laugh. 'You are not coming to party with us, then?'

'Nice idea, but no, thanks.'

Charlie placed Alice's drink down and handed me mine.

'I'm having an early one too,' I said.

Jimmy and Charlie exchanged a look and sniggered. 'Joining Alice?' he said.

I thought I detected a hint of pink creep into Alice's cheeks but perhaps that was just wishful thinking. My week with her was nearly over. Though we kind of had a date at the weekend, didn't we? I'd promised to show her around. Perhaps once we weren't working side by side in the kitchen every day, I'd get a sense if she was interested in being more than friends. But then again, I wasn't sure if I liked the idea of spending less time with her either.

Mariana turned to face me. 'Are you sure? Jimmy says you are a party boy. You are a DJ so you must like to dance, no?'

I shook my head. 'Not tonight, I'm knackered. And I need to be fresh for your class tomorrow, don't I?' I smiled, but inwardly I was annoyed with Enric's insistence I go along. 'We both do,' I added, gesturing to Alice.

Charlie sniggered again.

I wasn't interested in sitting in a classroom – that was all behind me. But it was difficult to say no when I so obviously needed help. I was pleased Alice had agreed to come along but, despite the tatty phrasebook she carried everywhere, it had taken some persuading.

'Did you and Jimmy register for my class, too?' Mariana asked the others.

'Nah, I can't be bothered,' said Charlie, spinning around and throwing Jimmy the cloth. 'I've had enough of education. I'm signed up to the school of life now.'

Mariana frowned. 'Where is this school of life? I don't know it.'

The pair burst into laughter and she flushed scarlet.

'It's just a phrase,' I said quickly. 'Charlie means learning stuff from everyday living rather than in a classroom.'

'How long have you run the school, Mariana?' Alice asked.

'Not long,' she said vaguely.

I studied her face. She didn't look much older than us. Being in charge of a school was impressive. *And* she still managed to go out and party?

I thought of Matt's ambitions. Matt the academic. Matt the DJ. Matt the soon-to-be music lawyer. Dreams shattered.

Don't be a waster, bro. Success will get you everything.

'I'm off to bed,' said Alice, standing.

'I'll join you,' I added, without thinking.

Charlie screeched. 'I knew there was something going on!'

Alice and I caught eyes but I looked away first. 'Not like that,' I muttered.

I mumbled my goodbyes and upstairs I made a hasty retreat, but when I plonked myself down on my balcony with a beer, I wondered if I should've asked Alice to join me. But would she think I was making a move on her? Inviting her into my bedroom?

I wondered what my brother would do.

My gaze wandered down to the square where a group of students carrying backpacks spoke in loud voices in a language that might have been German. Waiters whipped tablecloths from tables and stacked chairs away. A couple sat entwined on the edge of the fountain and kissed.

I jumped up and headed towards Alice's bedroom. I hovered, trying to decide whether to knock, when a choir of gospel singers burst into song. The singing continued for a few moments and then I heard Alice say hello.

Interesting choice for a mobile ringtone. I was about to step away when I heard her voice rise.

'I haven't called because I thought it would do us both good if we had some space,' she said. 'You got my messages, though?'

I knew I should walk away. I didn't want to eavesdrop but the strain in her tone held me there.

'You *know* we're away for a couple of months,' she said.

Silence. 'You'll be fine.'

Pause. 'The time will fly.'

'*Please . . .*'

Her desperation tore through me and before I talked myself out of it, I rapped on the door. Then I wished I hadn't. She might realise I'd been listening.

'I've got to go,' she said to the person on the phone.

The door swung open. Alice wore no make-up and her hair lay shiny and loose around her shoulders. She looked like she had the first day I met her. Beautiful.

'Yes?' A tiny frown creased the space between her eyes. 'You okay?'

'Oh,' I said, recovering myself. 'Fancy a beer on my balcony?'

Her face cleared and she smiled a little. 'Thanks, but I need some sleep.'

I nodded and felt a roll of disappointment as she closed the door. Was she talking to her boyfriend? Suddenly the idea of working in the bar didn't seem so appealing. I'd found my feet in the kitchen – Alice was a good teacher.

I would miss her company.

◆ ◆ ◆

The following morning, I woke feeling fresh from my early night, and ambled into the apartment kitchen. My mind was bubbling with ideas for a dish I wanted to make and I wanted to discuss it with Alice. Our Catalan lesson was planned for late morning and we needed to get ahead with our food prep so we could be ready to catch the afternoon trade when we got back.

Charlie was slumped at the table over a cup of tea. Her hair was matted and black make-up smeared the hollows of her eyes.

'Wow, who's the beauty queen?' I murmured, filling the kettle.

Charlie yawned. 'Make me another.' She pushed her mug towards me.

'Big night, then? Did you wake Big Sis?' I'd heard the party pair trample in with the hushed whispers of the inebriated when usually I'd had too many to notice.

'Mother hen sleeps like the dead,' she replied, taking the fresh tea from me. She lifted the cup to her lips and paused. 'Actually, that's wrong. Alice is nothing like my mother. *She* loves to show off about being the life and soul of the party.' She rolled her eyes. 'Apparently, she's *always* the last woman standing.'

'But that's you,' I remarked, sitting down.

Charlie looked surprised, then her mouth went tight. 'Maybe I'm more like *Fun Mum* than I realised.'

Her tone sounded uncharacteristically bitter. I didn't know what to say so I sipped my tea.

'Though I'm not going to end up like her, saddling myself with babies. I'm liking this freedom. No college, no ties, no *Mum*,' she said. 'I'm not going back – but don't go telling Alice that or she'll freak out.'

'Why? You're an adult.'

Charlie let out a bark of laughter. 'Can you remind my lovely sister of that?' She blew on her tea. 'She'll go nuts when she sees my bed hasn't been slept in,' she muttered.

My ears pricked up. 'Oh? I heard you come in—' Something dawned on me and I slapped my forehead. 'No . . . You and Jimmy?'

'Someone mention my name?' The Lothario wandered into the kitchen, running his hand over his buzz cut, yawning. He slumped down next to Charlie and slung his arm around her shoulder. I glanced at them both. Alice was going to go insane.

I pulled myself together. 'Right, mate, get prepared. Today's my last day in the kitchen and then I'm all yours.'

'Hey, don't be taking my job,' said Charlie indignantly. 'I'm brilliant at cocktails now.'

'Time to move on,' I replied with a shrug.

'He can't kick me out, can he?' she said, turning to Jimmy.

He yawned again. 'Nah, we'll sort it.'

She grinned. 'Anyway, you can't let Alice down. She'll be *so* disappointed.'

I snorted.

'But you need to play it cool, okay?' Her tone became coy. 'She'll see right through any bullshit you feed her.'

I smiled. 'Yeah, I've noticed she's a big fan of the eye-roll.'

'Be a nice guy,' Charlie insisted.

'Make me a cuppa,' mumbled Jimmy.

I got up and chucked a teabag into another cup and poured over hot water. 'What do you mean? I *am* a nice guy. I'm making tea for my best mate, aren't I?' I plonked the mug down in front of him.

Charlie turned to Jimmy. 'Is this nice guy really as gorgeous on the inside as he is on the outside? Because, you know, if my sister didn't have her eye on him, I'd give him a go.'

I didn't know whether to blush, laugh or bluster out a comeback. But I noted my mouth hanging open, so I clamped it shut.

'Alice found her boyfriend in bed with someone,' Charlie said bluntly. 'Not long before they were meant to go Interrailing. She thinks all men are losers.'

I winced – harsh. But things were starting to make sense now. 'You're the stand-in?' I said.

She nodded. 'Alice has finally untangled herself from our mum's grip and I want her to stay put.' She nibbled her fingernail. 'Mum's back from New York now. I'd lay a bet she'll be phoning Alice any day and begging her to come home. She's no clue how to look after herself, never has. And when Mum says jump, Alice leaps as high as she can.'

'Why is Alice jumping high?' Mariana stood in the doorway, hair mussed with sleep and in yesterday's dress.

I glanced at Jimmy. He grinned and held up his hands. 'All above board, mate. They had the bed, I had the floor.'

Mariana glided into the seat next to me. Unlike Charlie, there were no traces of last night's make-up left on her face but I detected a hint of sweet perfume. 'It is true. I am not that sort of girl,' she said. 'Jimmy let me stay so I did not have to travel back home alone.' She threw her tiny hand over her mouth to stifle a yawn. 'I can have a shower here, Charlie? I have to go straight to the school to prepare Andrew's lesson.'

Chapter 19

ANDY

Ten years ago

Mariana's language school wasn't far from Cafè Vermell and easy to find with some directions from Enric. I'd been quiet on our way over, ruminating on what Charlie had said, while Alice chattered about the rubbish French lessons she'd had at school. I sensed her reluctance to come today was because she didn't think she was capable of learning Catalan. I tried to pay attention, throw her the odd reassuring word, but Charlie's comment played on repeat.

If my sister didn't have her eye on him . . .

Was it true? Had Alice said something? Or was Charlie making stuff up?

Perfecte Language School was located above a shop selling tourist tat in the old town and the door opened on to a narrow stone staircase. At the top, a landing led to rooms front and back, and we joined a gathering of students outside one of the classrooms, waiting for our lesson to begin.

Mariana threw open the door. '*Benvingut*, welcome,' she said. She was wearing a cream jacket and skirt that drew attention to her bronzed skin. She showed no signs of having had a late night, or that she'd not gone home, and I assumed she kept spare clothes at work.

Mariana strutted to the front of the class in high heels and we all found somewhere to sit. 'Today you all try the lesson,' she said to the class. 'Afterwards, you decide if you want to return.'

I glanced around the room. Her tone didn't sound that friendly and I wondered if it was just me that had noticed, or if it was because her English wasn't too great. 'This is a taster lesson?' I suggested.

Mariana looked at me. She broke into a dazzling smile. 'Yes, a *taster*,' she repeated. 'I like that. Something you try once and see if you want to taste again.'

Someone sniggered and I caught Alice rolling her eyes.

The hour felt long and arduous, and I was surprised by Alice's contributions, which were all spot-on. I made a mental note to ask if she'd been practising. By the time the lesson ended, I'd decided once was enough.

We filed out with the others but Mariana stopped us at the door. 'You did very well, Alice. I think you will suit my Wednesday class.'

Alice smiled and glanced at me. 'Thanks. We'll speak to Enric and see if he can give us the time off.'

Mariana laughed lightly. 'Ah, but Andrew needs something different. He needs lessons alone.'

'Me?' I said surprised. 'I don't know . . .'

'Mariana's right,' Alice said, prodding me. 'One-to-one would be best, don't you think?'

My eyes glazed as I rolled back over the last hour. It all seemed a blur.

'You are *intelligent*, Andrew – *molt intelligent*. I will give you back your words,' said Mariana, curling her hand around my arm.

I shrugged. 'I'll think about it.'

◆ ◆ ◆

Back in the kitchen, I pushed Mariana's suggestion aside and threw myself into the recipe I'd been thinking about over the last couple of days. 'I thought we could roast aubergines with some fat tomatoes, and serve them with mozzarella and basil,' I said to Alice.

'Very Italian,' she said drily.

I smiled. 'Blimey, you're hard to please.'

She laughed. 'It's a great idea, but we'll have to make some adaptions.'

I kicked myself for not thinking about giving Alice a list when she went to the market earlier. She dug through the basket of produce and pulled out some fresh herbs. 'Oregano?' she suggested.

'Would that work?'

She nodded and handed me the aubergines. 'Last day, then? Bet you can't wait to get out of here.'

I picked up a knife and slid it carefully through the flesh. I was beginning to see why the food looking good was as important as how it tasted. The flavours in Alice's chorizo and manchego burger still lingered in my mouth, as did the precision with which she lightly toasted the bun, and layered the cheese and chorizo slice just so on the burger. A mashed-together version from a fast-food chain was never going to hit the spot in the same way. 'Not sure I'll be welcome in the bar now,' I said breezily. 'Charlie's the star of the show.'

'Jealous?' she teased.

'I think I can put up with hanging around here for another two weeks,' I said, keeping my eyes trained on the aubergine. She said nothing and I glanced up.

'Lucky me,' she replied with a smile.

This time our gaze lingered a beat longer than usual. Alice cleared her throat and went over to the fridge. Was I misreading the situation? Looking for something that wasn't there? To hide the awkwardness, I grappled for something to talk about but my mind went blank. The temperature seemed to shoot up in the room. I went over and fiddled with the cranky fan, and then joined Alice back at the work bench.

Her closeness and summery scent did nothing to take the heat out of the moment.

'Mariana's a good teacher, isn't she?' she said, weighing out almond flour to make pastry for *pastissets*.

'I suppose so.'

'How did you find today?' Her voice had become quiet.

My belly tightened. I didn't understand what had gone on in the classroom. I didn't want to talk about it.

She poured sugar into a bowl. 'You going to have private lessons?'

I turned away and dragged a sack of potatoes back to the bench. 'I'm going to make *patatas bravas,* too,' I said, deliberately ignoring her.

Alice was watching me, and then she nodded and turned back to what she was doing.

I clenched my jaw. *Stupid.*

'I'm only here for another two weeks. There's no point,' I muttered. I began cubing the potatoes into even pieces like I recalled my mum doing. Then I remembered I hadn't dealt with the tomatoes for the other dish. I picked one up, slicing it slowly – not too thin, not too thick.

Alice put her hand over mine. 'Hey, slow down. One thing at a time,' she said softly.

For some reason her touch made my throat ache. Then her phone bleeped and she moved away and reached into her apron pocket. She frowned at the message.

'Everything okay?' I said.

'Just my mum, being annoying.'

'Oh yes?' I kept quiet about what I knew, unsure if Charlie might have revealed too much for Alice's liking. 'Mums *are* annoying. Mine won't leave me alone.'

She smiled. 'I remember. You're only here because she insisted, right?'

'Well, apart from her thinking I need to learn some life skills, Enric isn't well. It's his heart. She needs us here to take the pressure off him.'

Alice's face fell. 'I'm sorry to hear that.'

Saying the words out loud and hearing her sympathy made me feel bad that I'd resisted helping my uncle before. 'What's happening with your mum?'

She sighed. 'Nothing really. She's hassling me to come home.'

'Why?'

'We live with our grandma – her mother – and they don't get on. I've always been a bit of a buffer between them. My mum's not very capable without me around.'

'Sounds tough.' Perhaps my own mum wasn't so bad after all. 'Do you have any regrets about coming away?'

This time Alice held my gaze long enough for me to know I wasn't imagining the feelings earlier. 'No, none at all.'

Chapter 20

ANDY

Ten years ago

The day flashed by in a whirl of chat and laughter as we flew around the kitchen. I discovered Alice had worked in restaurants since she'd left school and I told her about my boring finance job in the City where I'd worked my way up over the years. She entertained me with stories of being brought up by her posh grandma, and the clashes between her hopeless mum and Charlie, which were kind of sad as well as amusing.

Alice had cooked her first batch of *pastissets,* made with an almond pastry and a sweet potato, honey and cinnamon filling. They were amazing, and so popular we'd sold out within the hour. She'd also cooked a huge *tortilla* while I'd not only managed my Spanish-Italian hybrid dish on my own, I'd aced *patatas bravas* too.

As we cleared up, we sat on the work bench sharing the last of the *tortilla.* Who knew eggs and potato could taste so good?

'I've been waiting all day for this,' said Alice, picking up my *patatas bravas.* 'No offence, but I was hoping we wouldn't sell out.' She laughed mischievously as she poked her fork into the dish.

'You've already tried it,' I said, hopping off the bench and going over to the sink. Suddenly it mattered what she thought and I felt awkward.

'Slurping the sauce off the spoon doesn't count.'

I kept my back to her and picked up one of the pans from the draining board and ran a tea towel over it. 'You know I made up most of the recipe?'

'You said it was your mum's!'

I turned around, grinning. 'I couldn't remember all the ingredients.'

Alice had her eyes closed. 'Mmm,' she murmured. 'I'm liking the balance of flavours . . . tangy, sweet, a hint of spiciness.'

'Just like me.' I laughed and reached up to hang the pan on the hook above her.

Alice's eyes sprang open and caught me by surprise, causing the pan to slip and clip her on the head. She winced.

'Sorry!' I said, my fingers flying to her temple. 'You okay?' Then I remembered how she'd flinched when I touched her hair. I dropped my hand.

Alice held my gaze and it was like time slowed. I could hear my breath flowing in and out, my senses inhaling the scent of our afternoon, her summery perfume hinting at sunshine and something flowery. Anticipation rippled up my spine.

Her gaze flicked to my mouth and bounced up again.

Go on then, kiss her!

I can't. I shut my eyes to summon the courage but then Alice's lips touched mine. They were firm, insistent, and as sweet as I hoped they would be, flipping my nerves into an adrenaline blast as I tasted a trace of tanginess from the sauce on her tongue.

'*La meva germana!*'

My uncle's voice boomed out in the bar and I sprang away from Alice. She flushed. Immediately, I realised my mistake and floundered, paralysed by what I could hear and unable to find the reassuring words I needed to say to her.

Enric's voice bellowed again. *My sister!* I hurried to the door, throwing a worried glance back at Alice. 'Wait a minute.'

Out in the bar, I found my uncle hugging my mum and I thought he might be crying. When my mum spotted me, she released him and held open her arms. 'Andrew,' she said, squeezing me tight.

'What are you doing here?' I said, confused.

She shrugged. 'Helping. Enric has his operation soon.'

Guilt prickled. I'd been so caught up in my own life that I hadn't even asked how he was feeling.

'So this must be Alice?' she said, looking over my shoulder. 'I am Sofia. Enric tells me you are a very good chef and have been teaching my *fill*, my son, very well.'

Alice's cheeks turned crimson and Jimmy snorted from behind the bar.

My mum spun around and pointed her finger at him. 'I heard that, James.' Then to Alice she added, 'You ignore him – his mind is always in the gutter.'

The timing couldn't have been worse. My mouth still burnt with the impression of Alice's sweet lips.

'We've had a good week,' she stuttered.

'Ah, yes,' Enric began. 'Tomorrow, Andy wants to move on.'

My mum frowned. 'Not to Ibiza, not yet.'

I shook my head. 'I'm not going anywhere.'

Jimmy looked over in surprise.

My mum clapped her hands. 'You're cooking! You're making your *mare* very happy! So, you keep learning from Alice and we will make a chef of you one day.' Then she did that thing where she pinned me with her eyes. 'You are learning good things from Alice, yes? You go to the market every day with her? You do what she tells you? You are working instead of going out dancing? What did you make today?' She folded her arms.

Alice giggled softly.

'A Spanish-Italian dish,' I muttered.

'*Italian?*' My mum looked appalled.

'It tasted great and was very popular,' Alice said quickly. 'It was Andy's own recipe. We sold out.'

I threw her a grateful look.

'We're going to make it more Spanish next time, yes?' My mum looked pointedly at me. 'More *Catalan?*'

I scrabbled for a suggestion. 'With chorizo?'

Her eye was pulled away as Charlie came inside, carrying a tray of dirty glasses. She was wearing a short skirt and pink knee-high socks and had recently dyed her hair blue.

'I'm Charlie, Alice's sister,' she said cheerfully. 'Don't mind how I look, I'm soft as shit underneath. My sister and I are having a great time working here. It was very kind of Enric to give us a job.'

My mum glanced at him.

'*Ells treballen molt,*' he said. 'They all work hard, even this guy.' He pointed to me. 'Alice is – how you say it? – slapping him into shape.' His moustache twitched.

'Whipping,' I muttered.

Jimmy sniggered again and I could feel embarrassment flowing off Alice in hot, excruciating waves. I caught her eye, but she looked away.

I would make it up to her later. Even if she wouldn't join me on my balcony for a beer, I'd knock on her door and say . . . What? What would I say? *Your mouth is incredible. You're a great kisser. I loved your kiss.* I'd sound like a complete twat. Insincere. Pushy. Like the kind of guy who'd cheat on his girlfriend.

In my head, Matt released a loud, noisy exhale. *You properly screwed up, bro.*

'Hey, Mariana,' said Charlie. 'How's things?'

I looked around to see her striding into the bar in a clingy silver dress. She glanced around at us and Enric did the introductions. My mum's face lit up when she heard about the language school.

'Before you suggest it, Alice and I went to Mariana's lesson this morning,' I said, and it felt good to see my mum beam at me.

'Alice is coming back next week,' Mariana added. 'Andrew is not a beginner, so I suggest he has private lessons. That is why I came by tonight, to see if you have decided?'

'Sofia, *Perfecte té bona reputació,*' Enric said. 'The school has a good reputation. Mariana is popular.'

'Will the lessons be with you?' my mum asked hopefully.

Mariana threw me a smile and shrugged. 'I am busy, I am not sure.'

'You are *la millor*, the best!' said Enric. 'That is what your students say when they come here.'

She looked thoughtfully at me. 'Perhaps we have lunch together? What is the phrase? Kill two animals with a stone.'

Charlie screeched with laughter and Mariana flushed.

'Birds,' I said. 'Kill two birds with one stone.'

She flashed me a grateful smile. 'Maybe you can teach me the strange English phrases.'

My mum clapped her hands. 'So it is decided.'

'Mum—' I swallowed down a bubble of annoyance. She'd never have done this to Matt. She'd have let him make his own decisions, not told him what to do.

'But you're moving to Ibiza soon,' Alice said, her gaze level with mine. 'The lessons will help, won't they?'

'Your mobile number, Andrew?' Mariana glided over to the bar. She unclipped a glossy handbag in the same shade of pink as her nails. To my bemusement, she pulled out an old-fashioned fountain pen and notepad and looked questioningly at me. I gave her my number and watched her handwriting swirl on to the paper. She wafted it dry, folded it neatly in two and tucked it in her bag.

'I will call you, Andrew.'

Chapter 21

ANDY

Ten years ago

Later that evening, I paced my bedroom and went out to the balcony, throwing Alice's comment around in my head. I didn't understand. Was she dismissing me? Packing me off to Ibiza because she already regretted our kiss?

I flung myself into one of the chairs and slugged back a mouthful of beer. My brother would have had the answers.

Down below, a bunch of lads staggered into the square, arms slung across each other, singing something loud and incoherent. One of them was wearing a fluorescent green mankini – the stag, I presumed – and I watched them stumble towards Club Barça. They looked to be mid-twenties – Matt's age, perhaps.

Matt will never get married. He'll never have kids. I won't have nieces or nephews. I'll never be an uncle.

I gulped my beer – I'd never considered this before. What kind of woman would my brother have married anyway? Megan had been lovely, but she'd dumped him after he told her he was heading to Ibiza for the summer. He claimed the relationship was long dead anyway. Now I wondered if he'd been heartbroken. The possibility surprised me, but I'd never know. What else would I never find out about my brother?

'Can you DJ at my mate's party?' I'd asked him that fateful day in June as he drove me to my last exam at school. It had been a Thursday morning that still glistened with the finest of details, like watching the same movie on repeat in my head. The sun glowed happiness on a blue sky, a day that should have been enjoyed lounging with friends in the park, not swamped by pressure in a darkened exam hall.

Dance music pumped from the speakers. Matt chomped thick wodges of nicotine gum. He'd not long turned twenty-one and had decided to give up smoking. I remembered him unwrapping a second piece, shoving it in his mouth, guzzling back water and tossing the empty bottle into the footwell to join the others. They rolled around my feet and the breeze lifted the discarded gum wrappers, twirling them like confetti.

I was the cool kid, hanging out with my big bro. We were invincible.

'Will you?' I'd repeated.

Matt glanced over and laughed. 'What? No way.'

I stared out the window. A friend's parents were going away and leaving him home alone. He'd arranged a house party to celebrate the end of our GCSEs. No parents, plenty of booze – and girls. Jimmy and I had leapt at the chance to go.

I'd already told everyone Matt would do a set.

'Please?' I didn't care if I was begging. I was too busy thinking if I could just get him to say yes, my cool status would go stratospheric. I could already picture a bunch of eager girls swarming around me.

Matt laughed and shook his head again. 'Why would I want to DJ at a kids' party?'

'Just this once. I won't ask again,' I promised. 'Please?'

Matt's jaw worked the gum. We pulled up outside school and he whacked up the music, causing heads to turn and me to puff up my chest.

'I'll think about it,' he shouted as I got out. 'I'll see if I can fit it in before I go to Ibiza.'

Now, a cheer soared from the lads in the square, jerking me back to the present. The stag had jumped into the fountain and was splashing the others with water.

A band tightened around my chest and I stood up and gulped in some deep breaths. I gripped the balcony, my knuckles turning white as I watched them. I still had a chance of being the stag in a fluorescent green mankini one day.

That wasn't fair. *Life* wasn't fair. I pushed out a breath and the pain eased a little. Would I ever be able to stay with one woman long enough to holiday together? Let alone find the right one to marry. How did the mankini guy know his fiancée wasn't a mistake?

Restless again, I went back inside with Alice's kiss stuck on repeat in my head. I needed to talk to her. I wandered out to the hall and heard music filtering out from the girls' bedroom. Not the dance tunes I liked to listen to, but something mellow and relaxing.

I listened for a moment and before I bottled out, I knocked sharply. To my surprise, the door flew open as though Alice had been waiting for me on the other side.

Her neutral expression said otherwise. Still, she looked amazing.

'Want a cuppa?' I blurted.

Her face cleared and she smiled. 'Yeah, why not? Thanks.'

I must have been staring a little too long as she threw me a quizzical look before closing the door. I trotted off to the kitchen, trying to work out what was going on. The door to her bedroom was like the door to her mind: ajar now and then, allowing a glimpse of something, then slamming shut with all her thoughts and feelings hidden inside.

I returned with the tea, juggling two hot cups in one hand while I knocked again.

A smile twitched her mouth as she took the cup. 'Thanks.'

I snatched a glance into her room, looking for inspiration to keep her talking. Her bed was made and her Catalan phrasebook lay open next to a postcard. 'How's your grandma?' I said casually.

'My grandma?' Her eyes followed my gaze. 'Oh, I see. Good, thanks.'

'She must be interested in what you're doing?' Our kiss flashed across my mind again and I ducked my head and blew on my tea.

She nodded, amused. 'Yes, of course.'

The mellow tunes continued to roll lazily out into the hallway. 'Good music. Who is it?' I said.

She made a face. 'Not your thing. You won't have heard of her.'

'Try me.'

'Erykah Badu.'

I shook my head.

She smiled. 'Well, thanks again . . .' She began to close the door.

'Do you want to come and sit on my balcony?' I said quickly.

'In your *bedroom*?' She stretched out the word with an amused smile.

I laughed, awkwardly. 'Not like that. I mean, I thought you might be a bit bored of being in your room all the time.'

'You mean *you're* bored.' Her eyes danced.

I wanted to protest that I wasn't making a move. I wanted to say, *you* kissed *me*! What had that been about? It was driving me crazy. 'Well, I am a bit, but that's not—'

'Thank you for the tea, Andy. See you in the morning.' She closed the door.

I stared at the blank, wood surface. The new feelings that had been slowly simmering, building and working their way under my skin were finally becoming as clear as anything.

I really liked Alice and I wanted her to like me, too.

Chapter 22

ALICE

Now

Of all places for Susie to choose – *Café Vermell?*

I steal a look at Andy, half-expecting him to suggest somewhere else, but he mutters that he's finishing something and will get a taxi and catch us up. Excitement starts to fizz as I follow Susie out – I wonder how much has changed?

'Alice?' Andy calls. 'Quick word?'

I pause in the doorway and Susie says she'll meet me in reception.

He doesn't say anything for a moment. I scan his face but can't work out what he's thinking. 'Yes?' I say in the end.

He sighs. 'Can you just . . . I'd rather you didn't tell Susie . . . about when we worked at Café Vermell.'

About *us*.

My enthusiasm flattens. I should ask what the big secret is, but I just nod and say, 'Sure.'

As Susie and I get into the lift, she tells me there's still no sign of my missing luggage. 'Such a nightmare,' she exclaims. 'If your suitcase doesn't turn up later, come over to mine and I'll lend you some clothes.'

Her kindness softens the hard edges of Andy's words. I can't see why our past would be an issue to her. 'If you're sure? Thanks, that would be great.'

Before long, we're making our way through the maze of streets in the old town towards Plaça Reial. As we walk, the sun is high above the tall buildings that flank our route and it casts a pleasing warmth on to my shoulders. Susie chats about how she met her boyfriend, Xavier, who's the IT guy at Perfecte. She points out the street where they live and says I must come over for dinner soon.

Up ahead, the plaza starts to come into view and the excitable fizz returns. Will the square look how I remember or have my memories blurred into a rose-tinted version of reality? I can't help but stop as familiarity assaults my senses. Slowly, I turn a full circle, a smile creeping into my face.

I'm back.

It's like I never left.

Elegant buildings frame the plaza on all sides with porticoes around the perimeter where I imagine the aristocracy once glided in the cool shade of the covered walkway. The square hums with chatter and laughter. The young and the old meander, gather around the fountain, sit at tables eating tapas, drinking wine, and I catch a hint of cinnamon churros in the breeze. My gaze travels up to the palm trees, their leafy branches stroking the blue sky, and drops down to the balcony, to the red parasols – Cafè Vermell.

I feel a squeeze of sadness – and then my stomach butterflies.

Andy's already here – and he's watching me.

'Great, you grabbed the last table,' calls Susie, going over and sitting down.

I'm grateful to be startled back to the present and I follow, taking the seat next to her. 'The plaza's busy, isn't it?' I say, composing myself, yet aware how unnerving it is to be sat here with Andy. He's wearing a navy shirt, the Gemini necklace at his throat, and there's a trace of blond stubble around his jawline.

'Barcelona time.' Susie grins. '*Spanish* time. We love our long lunches, don't we, Andy?'

Now would be the time to say, *I remember*. That I lived in Barcelona for a while, that I bloody well worked here with Andy, but he gives me a tiny shake of his head.

Annoyance stabs. I don't understand.

'Not quite like lunch breaks back home, right?' Susie adds.

Her cheerful manner is a relief and I return her smile. Forget Andy and his stupid secrecy. I'm in Barcelona, it's warm, and I'm not rushing home to make Mum's lunch before dashing back to class.

Susie looks around the terrace. 'Service can be so slow sometimes – you should have a word, Andy.' She stands. 'I'll order at the bar. What do you two want to drink?'

I'm tempted to join her, curious to see if inside still has the red booth seating – the glitterball. Andy must sense what I'm thinking as his eyes drill into me so I give Susie my order and she heads off alone.

'Thanks for not saying anything,' he says quickly.

His evident relief makes my insides lurch. I'm a mistake from the past. A regretful relationship he wants to pretend never happened. He doesn't need Susie to stare in amazement, to compare me to gorgeous, ambitious Mariana. I'm already a reminder to his wife that he lowered himself to my level. How humiliating that must be.

I'm an embarrassment.

I shrug and look around. I swear the tables and chairs are the same. The red parasols must have surely been replaced, but they still make the same cheerful splash of colour in the plaza.

I tip my head upwards, let the warm sunshine stroke my face . . .

. . . I'm sitting with Andy.

My head snaps back. He's watching me again and my stomach turns a somersault. When did he become so *unreadable*? Andy had worn his heart on his sleeve: happy and cheeky, kind and thoughtful . . .

Now he is none of these things.

His eyes jump away. 'Jimmy's not here today but obviously I've not had a chance to tell him you're . . .' His mouth tightens. 'Working with us.'

'*Jimmy?*' I interject. 'What do you mean?'

'He owns Café Vermell.'

My mouth falls open. I've got a million questions, though it's not hard to believe. Customers loved Jimmy from the moment he stepped behind the bar and charmed them with his winning smile. He had a way of making everyone feel like they were at the centre of his universe.

I'm about to ask about Enric but Andy spots Susie making her way back. 'Don't mention Jimmy,' he hisses.

'You're not going to believe it,' she says. 'The kitchen's shut.'

'What?' Andy looks concerned. 'Where's Juliana?'

'Dunno. Carlos isn't sure what's going on.'

'Shit,' Andy mutters, twisting his pendant. 'Jimmy should've told me.' He glances at his watch and jumps up. 'Look, I've got to disappear for a bit. Don't be too long as someone needs to hold the fort and I've no idea when Mariana will be back. I'll see you later.'

Susie and I exchange glances and watch him stride off across the plaza. He used to slope around in no particular hurry to be anywhere. Now his gait is efficient and all business – *more like Mariana's*.

A twist of jealousy surprises me.

'What was all that about?' I say.

She shrugs. 'No idea.'

◆ ◆ ◆

Susie and I decide to grab a takeaway *entrepan* and I'm impressed with her Catalan fluency as she orders our sandwiches. I vow to put the effort in to have some lessons while I'm here – perhaps Mariana will give me a discount at the school. We sit by the fountain to eat and I call the airline only to discover the courier didn't deliver my luggage as they were told no one by my name worked at Perfecte.

While the customer services advisor waits patiently for new instructions, a niggle at the back of my mind has me wondering if Mariana is behind this – but I push it away. Susie jabs a finger at Cafè Vermell. For want of a better suggestion, I confirm the address while she pops over to tell Carlos, the waiter.

I'm excited to see Jimmy again and this is the perfect excuse to come back tomorrow, though I think about what Andy said. Does he want Jimmy and I to pretend we don't know each other? I'll refuse. It's a lie too far.

Back at the school, Susie introduces me to some of the teachers milling about between lessons. They smile distractedly and I assume they've no idea why I'm here. Mariana's in her office with an older man and she calls me in as I pass.

'Alice, meet *el meu pare*, my father, Josep.' Her smile is very wide and very bright, and she's holding herself taut.

Josep is short, about my height, and tilts his head as he assesses me through hooded eyes. A moment passes and as I'm wondering if I should kiss his cheeks or shake his hand, he folds his arms. '*Bona tarda*. Mariana tells me you are the *persona perfecte* to be in charge of Perfecte London.' His tone couldn't sound less convincing. His eyes rake over my clothes.

'Alice has lost her suitcase,' Mariana trills. 'That is why she looks like a student.'

'What do you know about running a school?' he says, ignoring her. 'Do you have experience?'

Mariana goes pink. 'We are training Alice. It is a trial. Nothing has been decided yet.'

'*Silenci*,' he thunders, but his gaze is still on me. 'Alice?'

Alarmed by his tone, I lose my words. 'I'm, well, I'm . . .' I twist my hands together. Then I remember something. 'Mariana is interested in my food events. It's a good way of encouraging students to come back, recommend the school to their friends. We've noticed numbers growing.'

Josep's expression doesn't change. 'Is that so?' he says, eyes swivelling back to his daughter.

She nods vigorously. 'Alice has some good ideas. I am going to bring the food events into the new school as an alternative lesson. Students will pay to learn and enjoy *menjar bé* at the same time.' Her beam looks like it might crack at any moment. 'I hope we can do the same here. *Diversificar, pare,* to grow our business.'

She clasps her hands tight but Josep goes to leave and her face falls. 'Andrew is showing Alice how to run a successful school like us,' she calls out.

Josep pauses at the door. 'And what does your husband think about this idea?'

This time Mariana flushes a deep red. 'He thinks it is great,' she says quietly.

'He loves food,' I chip in.

His eyes tighten their gaze on me.

'I mean, that's what he told me,' I add weakly.

We both watch Josep leave and when the door closes, Mariana releases a big sigh and drops into her chair. 'Thank you, Alice.'

I'm thrown by her gratitude. I didn't mean to help – I hadn't meant to say anything at all. I just don't want Andy to be under scrutiny when Mariana's plans have left him in the dark.

Her eyes light up. 'So Andrew is liking your food events?' she says excitedly. 'Have you two worked out a plan for the new school yet?'

What can I say? That he's shown no interest at all? It's not my place to tell her. 'You'll have to speak to him about that,' I murmur.

Just at that moment, the gospel choir bursts into song on my phone. It's 4.15 p.m. already.

'Can I call you back, Mum?' I say, answering the call. 'I'm just in the middle of something.'

'You promised we'd talk at 3.15 p.m.,' she insists.

I don't remember *promising* but I'm not going to argue. 'I'm in a meeting.'

She sniffs. 'I see. Too important to talk to me now.'

I sigh. 'That's not fair.'

Mariana looks over. I turn away from her. I need to wrap up this conversation. 'Look, I really can't—'

'I know! You've said, you're *too busy* to talk to me.'

'It's not that I don't want—'

'Well, all I was going to say is I've sorted out our *little problem.*' Her voice drops and becomes amplified in my ear as she puts the phone close to her mouth. 'You don't need to worry about money anymore. You can come home.'

A hand lands on my shoulder and I squeak in surprise. Mariana's smiling at me. 'I'll call you later, Mum.'

'*Problema?*' she says as I end the call. 'With your *mare?*'

I try to smile. 'No, everything's fine.'

She's still staring – then nods. '*Bé*. But what have you done with Andrew?' she says, looking over to his empty office.

For some reason, her accusation makes me blush.

She smiles. 'I am having a joke. He works very hard. So now he is not here, you can go too.'

I stiffen. *Leave?*

Her laugh tinkles. 'If Andrew is a closed book, you are an open book, Alice! I mean go back to your hotel. Come back *demà*, tomorrow.'

Chapter 23

ALICE

Now

Susie pushes her bike as we make our way back through the old town to her apartment so I can borrow some clothes. She tells me what it's like living here and how she couldn't ever move home to Scotland now.

'Apart from the fact it's bloody freezing, there's nothing there for me and everything here,' she says. Her smile lights her face and I ask her if she's talking about Xavier. 'Yes, but he's the icing on the cake. I fell in love with Barcelona long before I fell in love with him.'

We come into a square with a church and a small playground beneath the shade of the trees. Mothers gather, eyes on their kids, chatting. Shrieks of play bring a smile to my face. 'Do you think if you have kids you'll go back?' I ask. 'To be closer to your family?'

Susie shakes her head. 'My parents visit all the time – they love it. They've already talked about retiring here one day. And, in the meantime, Xavier's family are like my family.'

I think about Mariana and her father – Xavier's uncle. I wonder if he's as overbearing with the rest of the family as he is with his daughter.

'What about you? Are kids on your agenda?'

I laugh. 'God, *no* – far from it.'

A child tumbles and the mother rushes over and scoops him up in her arms. His cries fill the square and she rocks him. 'It's stressful enough to find the right partner,' I say. 'Let alone allow enough time to get to know one another. Then you've got to make sure they're The One while the pressure of the biological clock ticks on.' I make a face.

'Xavier's keen. He comes from a big family, but we're not ready yet,' says Susie. 'Though the older lot aren't happy that we're "living in sin". They think it's shameful, but for who? Honestly, the gossip that flies between them is intense; they're obsessed with one another.'

The child is back on his feet again, chasing his friend. 'What's your situation?' asks Susie. 'Have you got a boyfriend?'

I shake my head. 'To be honest, I'm rubbish at relationships.'

'How come?'

I hesitate. I haven't had to explain my responsibilities to Mum for a long time. 'My mum isn't great on her feet and needs my help so I don't have a lot of spare time. I feel really bad for leaving her to come here. My sister moved in to take over.'

Susie looks thoughtful. 'Sounds tough on you both.'

Often an explanation doesn't help people understand any better. If anything, they understand less, so I appreciate Susie's empathy. I think about Mum's reliance on me to manage the house, shop, cook and organise paying the bills. It's hard to articulate why she needs me to do this – and why it's important I do it for her.

Atonement.

132

'Still, everyone needs a break, right?' Susie says brightly. 'Don't feel guilty about having some time off.' She nudges me. 'Make the most of it. Xavier has some hot, single friends you might like to meet.'

I smile. 'Thanks, but no thanks. Handling a relationship in the same town is hard enough, let alone in another country.'

'Who said anything about a relationship?' She grins and we both laugh.

The church clock chimes just as we leave the square, reminding me that usually I'd be at home serving tea to Mum in the convenient slot that falls between one soap opera finishing and another one starting. The idea of returning to the hostel and – doing what? – weighs heavy. How am I going to spend my evening? And all the other evenings?

Cooking. *Freedom.*

The thought pops up from nowhere. It's mean of me to think of my time here in those terms, but Susie's right – I should make the most of it. I don't have to cook Mum's bland food to order. Perhaps I should see if I can get a table at the restaurant next to the hostel tonight. Mum said she'd paid the credit card bill. She said I didn't need to worry. I could splash out on one special meal, couldn't I?

Then I must find another place to stay.

'Do you know anyone with a room to rent?' I say as Susie stops outside a thick wooden door and pulls out a key.

'Not off-hand, but I can ask around.' She points up to the balcony where purple flowers tumble over the sides of hanging pots. 'This is our place. Come on, let's find you some clothes for tomorrow.'

◆　◆　◆

I leave Susie's later with a full bag and I can't thank her enough. Soon, I'm trudging back up the street towards the hostel, past the tired apartments and closed-down shops, and a new determination kicks in to get the hell out of here. Outside the restaurant, the fading light shows it to be as scruffy as the other buildings. Paint peels from the walls, someone's sprayed graffiti over the name and the blinds are down like they were before. There's no sign of life and I wonder if the warm welcome I received was all in my imagination.

Looks like I'll be heating soup for my dinner again tonight.

The gospel choir sing-songs from my bag again and I glance at the time. I calculate Mum will be midway through her soap by now.

'Everything okay?' I say anxiously.

'Why are you picking up?' Charlie demands.

'Why are you using Mum's phone?'

'To check you're not taking her calls. Clearly you are.'

'Why wouldn't I? I'm in Spain, not on the moon,' I retort.

'Promise me you won't keep talking to her.'

I sigh. 'Why?'

'Because you're supposed to be switching off from us, from home. You're supposed to be shagging sexy Spanish men, not worrying about her.'

I snort. 'I'm not you.'

'Well, you *should* be more like me. Blimey, sis, let your hair down! When are you going to get this chance again?'

Never.

Loosen up. You're thirty now, practically on the shelf, Mum's voice echoes.

'Where are you? What can you see?' Charlie asks.

I glance down the passage. A stained and ripped mattress slumps over a broken chair exposing its springs, and piles of bin bags and boxes spill their guts beneath the metal staircase. The sign stutters *Dormitori* in neon pink. This place looks more like a sex den than a hostel.

'Barcelona is beautiful,' I lie. 'Just the same as it was before.'

134

'You're going to have *such* a good time. I'm so jealous!'

Mum shouts in the background.

'You sure everything's okay?' I repeat. 'Has something happened?'

'Chill! Everything's fine. Mum's where you'd expect her to be, lodged in front of the TV. Anyway, enough of that – have you been to Café Vermell yet? What's it like? The same?'

It's tempting to tell Charlie that Jimmy's taken over but that would open up the conversation to questions about Andy. 'Umm, yes, but they weren't doing food, so we didn't stay.'

'Oh, shame. Hey, wouldn't it be weird if Andy and Jimmy still worked there?' she muses. 'Good times, hey, sis? Though they're probably still raving in Ibiza.'

Still, I say nothing. I don't need Charlie knowing I sat elbow to elbow with Andy today – and will be for the next couple of months. Her euphoria will fly into overdrive, prodding and pushing me to rekindle the past with him.

I'm not into other people's husbands.

'What about the job?' she asks. 'How was your day?'

My throat constricts as I realise that's why Charlie's called me. She cares enough to ask. Despite my decision to stay quiet about Andy, it would be a relief to admit that working alongside him is excruciating, that I'm an embarrassment to him, and Mariana is as ambitious and beautiful as she always was. But I can't. Charlie will keep raking over the past, teasing me, *annoying* me.

Mum calls out for her again.

'Go on, go see what she wants,' I say. 'There's no point in winding her up by ignoring her.'

'There in a minute!' Charlie yells back. 'God, she's like a stroppy selfish teenager. She needs to learn to wait. I can't be at her beck and call whenever she feels like it.'

I think about the lists I've left pinned to the fridge with the Eiffel Tower magnet, there so long I assume it was a gift from Philippe, Charlie's dad. One details Mum's biscuit routine and the other has the meal plan. Charlie isn't a cook, but Mum's diet doesn't require any kind of culinary skill.

'Don't forget to give Mum vegetables and fruit,' I say.

'I'm not a complete fuckwit. You know I'm a vegan now? Better for weight training. I'll get Mum to try some of my recipes.'

I roll my eyes. 'Vegan? Since when?'

'Since now. I may as well give it a go as I've been meaning to for a while. Mum'll shift the pounds in no time.'

'She won't eat that stuff.'

'She needs to.'

'Like I don't know that? What do you think I've been doing all this time?'

Charlie laughs. 'Feeding her biscuits and white food.'

'Seriously? Is that what you think?' I feel my temper rising as we fall back into our familiar prickly routine. 'You think I haven't tried to help her lose weight?'

'Not hard enough.'

I grip the phone. 'So Mum's weight is *my* fault?'

'She's obese, Alice! No wonder she can't move around without using sticks.'

I shake my head, frustrations with my sister over the last decade as raw as they've always been. 'You know that's not the reason why.'

'You're deluded,' she says quietly. 'Can't you see? Mum takes so much from you and gives you nothing back.'

Mum wouldn't be in this state if it wasn't for me.

'Bloody hell, Charlie, just go and see what she needs and leave me alone.'

Chapter 24

ALICE

Now

The following day I go to work in Susie's denim dress. The sleeves are capped and I've cinched in my waist with a belt, and luckily it looks okay with my trainers. Mariana greets me in reception and looks me up and down but doesn't comment.

Andy glances up as I walk in his office. 'Nice dress,' he says and goes back to his computer.

I go pink. 'Alright, enough of the sarcasm.'

He smirks. 'Who says I was being sarcastic?'

'You know this isn't mine.'

He pretends to look offended. 'I said it was a *nice dress*,' he insists. 'How's that rude?'

We smile at one another and I catch Mariana staring as she strides past and into her office. Andy and I get down to work. Soon I'm discovering a large part of Perfecte's success comes from language and homestay packages they sell to international schools in the Middle East. Before long, Andy's asking what Janet is like and I tell him that she's a friend and neighbour as well as my boss – but stop short of explaining how my job came to be.

I'm half-expecting him to ask why I didn't take up the restaurant apprenticeship all those years ago, but he doesn't. Relief and disappointment uncomfortably collide.

I switch up the conversation and tell Andy about Janet's cats that rule her home and that no amount of hoovering or anti-bac can eradicate their smell. 'She's obsessed – *obsessed*,' I say with a shudder. 'They're mostly rescue cats and I've never liked them, but for some reason they make a beeline for my lap whenever I go over.'

Andy lets out a loud laugh and Mariana's head flips up. 'Sounds like Janet and Mariana will get on like a house on fire,' he says, smiling. 'She worships her Siamese cats and they hate me.'

I don't know if it's the sound of his laughter or the mirth radiating from his face which stirs something familiar inside of me, only that it feels both warming and painful.

Old Andy.

◆ ◆ ◆

The rest of the day passes at a speed that surprises me and when Andy tells me he's got a message from Jimmy to say my suitcase has arrived, he looks confused.

'Susie's idea,' I say quickly. 'I haven't seen him yet. Thank God, he's got my stuff. I kept thinking it was going to end up back at Heathrow.'

Andy taps his pen on the desk. 'It's okay, I explained everything to him yesterday.' He glances over to Mariana.

I think I hear a barbed edge to Andy's remark but I'm distracted when the gospel choir bellows out from my bag. I glance at my watch – where did the day go?

'Your mum?' says Andy in surprise. 'I can't believe you've still got the same ringtone.'

I can't believe he's remembered.

The tune is ingrained in me and usually a comfort as I know I'll always be on hand when Mum needs me. But right now, the commitment to speak every afternoon, at the same time, is starting to feel like a pressure. I wonder if I can talk her out of this routine.

'How are your pink wafers?' I say to her.

Andy snorts.

'Good,' she replies grumpily.

My ears prick up. 'What's the matter?'

'Nothing.'

I can hear her crunching, the sound of the TV. Her silence says she wants me to keep asking. 'Come on, tell me,' I say lightly, though inside my nerves are jangling.

Andy glances at me and shakes his head.

What's any of this got to do with him?

'How was lunch?' I say, changing tack.

'*She* left a sandwich in the fridge,' Mum replies, voice rising. 'I had to do the rest of it myself.' I think back to my phone call with Charlie yesterday. Has she *abandoned* Mum? '*And* I had to make my own tea and biscuits!'

My skin prickles. 'I'll speak to her.'

Something on the TV must catch Mum's eye because she launches into a rant about her favourite actor who's been dumped by the pretty one, who's had a nose job *and* boob job, and never deserved him anyway. I have no idea who or what she's talking about and make appropriate sympathetic noises.

'I'm going to get rid of all my stuff in the wardrobe,' she says suddenly.

I stand and go over to the window.

'Are you still there, petal?' she says.

'Yes, yes, I'm here.' I look out towards Sagrada Familia, the towers still under construction after centuries of building work. The burden to keep carrying on and on, fixing and mending, and never feeling like you're getting anywhere must be huge. Like there's no end in sight.

'So what do you think?'

I sigh. 'If that's what you want to do, it sounds like a good idea. Charlie can help organise a charity shop to come and collect the things.'

In typical Mum style, she switches up the conversation. 'Been to the beach yet?'

'No, I'm working.'

'Lots of sexy Spanish men after you?'

I turn slightly. I catch Andy watching me before his gaze darts away.

'I'm at work,' I whisper. 'I need to get back.'

There's silence again.

'Got to go!' Mum's voice suddenly sings out. '*Celebrity Lives* is about to start!'

My phone goes dead and I stare at the blank screen.

'Everything alright?' says Andy.

I'm certain his question isn't one of curiosity or politeness, but something that simmers a little deeper. 'I'm not about to abandon ship and disappear home, if that's what you think,' I retort.

My words crash land. The blood drains from my face and Andy looks equally pale. Then he looks down and fusses with some papers on his desk. Before I can find a way to resurrect the situation, Mariana sweeps in, jacket on, briefcase in her hand. She comes over and stands behind Andy and begins massaging his shoulders. He shifts uncomfortably but doesn't say anything.

'Perhaps you should take Alice out tonight?' she says. 'Take her to one of your *foodie* restaurants. Show her what our city has to offer. You can exchange ideas for the London food events.'

He twists around and glares at her.

His silence is loaded. I am an embarrassment. He doesn't want to spend any time with me. My gaze falls away and I catch something familiar sticking out from beneath some paperwork. My stomach butterflies. It's the beach ceramic coaster I bought Andy years ago at the market.

My eyes fly up to him again. He *kept* it?

Instinctively, I touch the base of my throat. I'd returned his brother's necklace.

'You both look horrified!' Mariana smiles down at Andy. 'I will come too.'

I spring back to the present. 'Oh, thanks, but I'm picking up my suitcase,' I say quickly.

Andy shoots me a grateful look.

Mariana stares at us for a moment, then shrugs. She gives Andy's shoulders a final squeeze and grabs her briefcase. 'Another time,' she says, marching back out.

As soon as she's gone, he stands and runs his hand through his hair. 'Do you want to go to Café Vermell now? I'll come with you.'

Do I detect a hint of friendliness? I'm about to make a smart remark to remind him that he wants to keep our past a secret. Surely strutting up to Café Vermell together would be a step too far? But acknowledging anything to do with us out loud in his office sits uncomfortably and I'm beginning to come around to his way of thinking. If I can pretend nothing went on between us then . . .

I don't have to explain what *really* happened.

Chapter 25

ALICE

Now

'What's this about foodie restaurants?' I say to Andy as we make our way to Cafè Vermell. I'm amused that Mariana used the word 'foodie'. I wonder if there's a Catalan translation.

'I like eating out,' he says, pushing his hands into his pockets. 'But we're fussy about where we go.'

'Romantic candlelit dinners only?' I respond, trying to sound teasing but there's a slight edge to my tone.

Andy makes a face. 'I meant "we" as in me, Xavier, Susie and Jimmy. Mariana's not into the food scene. She's picky. Only likes food cooked by her aunties or mum.'

I think about the amazing food I've eaten in this city. 'That can't be all bad.'

'No, but it's not very original. We like finding experimental places, new chefs, new restaurants . . . Once they get popular, you can't get a table.'

'An underground foodie scene?' I suggest.

He smiles. 'I suppose so.' We step to the side as a moped putters down the narrow street. 'So how come you're not a chef?' he says. 'What happened to the apprenticeship?'

His question is innocent and understandable. My answer is dark and complicated. It unlocks a piece of my past that I can never share. 'Things didn't work out,' I say breezily. 'I'm enjoying organising the food events though.'

Andy sighs. 'Go on, you'd better tell me about them so I can get Mariana off my back.'

I think about the pop-up food trucks in Riverside's car park. The set-up sounds lame compared to the real restaurants he's uncovered and I give him an overview and vow to get out more when I go back to London. Perhaps one day my food events will become foodie tours to actual restaurants. Then I remember the place near the hostel with the welcoming hostess. The ugly exterior did nothing to promote how warm and alive it had become the other night.

'There's a place near where I'm staying in Sants that's intriguing,' I say. 'You'd walk past without noticing anything special. Someone's sprayed graffiti across the front and there's no name, but when I popped in the other day, it was really busy, and had a lovely, friendly vibe.'

Andy looks at me in surprise. 'Graffiti? You've eaten there?'

I frown. 'Graffiti? Is that what it's called? I don't know if it's the same place.' I explain how I'd got lost on my first night and when I tell him the name of the street, he breaks into a grin.

'Promise me you'll try to get us a table?' Andy's face shines and I see an imprint of the old Andy still there. Then, as we come into Plaça Reial, it's like, if I squint a bit, it could be ten years ago: the square humming, a busker crooning – Andy by my side.

Except he's not really the same Andy I knew.

Am I the same woman?

At that moment, I spot Jimmy emerging from the cafe to serve a customer. His laughter rings out and my chest soars with pleasure. I come to a standstill and grin dumbly at him, at Café Vermell – and before Andy and I have reached the red parasols, he rushes towards us.

'The enigma that is Alice Taylor! What the hell happened to you?' he shouts, pulling me into an expansive hug and swinging me around. Tears prick my eyes. I can't remember the last time someone felt so genuinely pleased to see me. 'Darling, you're *gorgeous – still* so gorgeous, isn't she, mate?'

Andy catches my eye for a second and nods curtly.

Jimmy slings his arm around me and pulls me inside. The cafe's throwing on its evening cloak – the doors have been pushed back and the sun reflects off the shiny black-tiled floor. Andy and I sit at the bar and Jimmy grabs the vodka bottle and cranberry juice. I'm touched he still remembers what I like.

'Hey, not too much.' I laugh nervously as he slugs in vodka. It's been ages since I had a cocktail.

'Still sensible?' he replies, smiling.

Emotion tugs my throat. I can't look at Andy.

'I can't believe you're back,' Jimmy adds, pouring in peach schnapps along with fresh orange juice. He grins and gives everything a theatrical shake to the beat of the music.

I'm floating in that strange parallel world again. Jimmy's lanky frame, shaved head and wide grin are all the same, with a few more laughter lines around his mouth and eyes. His charisma weaves a cocoon around Andy and I – we are the centre of his universe.

'I can't believe *you're* still here,' I retort with a smile.

'Hey, how rude!' he laughs. 'I do own this place, you know?' He puts the glass in front of me, sticks in a paper parasol and a slice of orange.

'Sex on the Beach?' I ask.

'Anytime, darling,' he replies.

We both laugh.

Andy fidgets next to me. His face is closed again. I brace myself, waiting for him to say whatever it is he needs to say to Jimmy about me being here. I'm certain his decision to tag along wasn't out of friendliness, but because he wanted to vet our conversation.

'Want to join Alice in Sex on the Beach?' Jimmy asks Andy, face all innocent.

Laughter pops out but my face goes warm, so I duck my head and prod my drink with the straw.

'Ha, ha,' he replies drily. 'Beer is fine.'

'He used to be such a risk-taker.' Jimmy winks at me. 'Got old and boring.'

I change the subject. 'So how come you haven't splashed your name across the door? I thought that'd be more your style.'

'Jimmy's?' He pretends to muse. 'Doesn't really have the same ring, does it? Sounds like a dodgy bar where you'd eat egg and chips washed down with pint of Guinness. And anyway, everyone knows the red parasols belong to Cafè Vermell – the clue is in the name.'

Little has changed around me other than the banquette seating, which is now black. The disco ball hangs in the middle of the room and the mirrored walls still create the illusion the bar is bigger than it is. 'Not changed the décor then?' I remark. 'It's still moody in here.'

'It's *classy*, darling. Black is pure elegance.'

'Is that right? Or wouldn't Enric and Sofia let you change it?'

'Enric retired,' Andy explains. 'He asked Jimmy if he wanted to take on the cafe. He lives by the beach now with my mum, about an hour away.'

I'm puzzled for a moment. 'You didn't want to run this place?' Then I remember. 'Oh, were you still in Ibiza?'

Jimmy exhales and slides away from us, wiping the bar with a cloth. A waiter appears with a drinks order.

'No, I was here,' Andy says shortly.

I wait for him to elaborate but he doesn't. I think about what Susie told me. 'Did you already have the school with Mariana by then?'

He nods and takes a swig of beer.

'Good thing, too,' Jimmy calls from the other end of the bar. 'Taking over this place has been the making of me.' He places a large bottle of sparkling water on a tray with two glasses and calls the waiter over in a rush of Catalan.

Time's playing tricks. Of course it's not like before. We're a decade on and that's long enough for Jimmy to become a fluent speaker, a local. I wonder how quickly Andy's Catalan came back to him. I'm sure being married to Mariana would have encouraged him along.

My chest burns and I sip my drink.

Jimmy comes back over.

'You still single then?' I ask, noting he's not wearing a wedding ring.

'*Jesus*, don't shout that too loud. The ladies will come running and Juliana will string me up!'

I smile. 'Your latest squeeze?'

He roars with laughter. 'My *wife*, I'll have you know.'

'Juliana's far too good for Jimmy – he's totally punching above his weight,' says Andy. 'She keeps him in line too.'

Jimmy rolls his eyes. 'She does, but I love a powerful woman.' He claps his hands. 'Talking of strong ladies, how's the lovely Charlie? Boy, I had the hots for her but she was having none of it.'

'See? I told you!' I say to Andy, triumphant at being right, as though we're picking up a conversation we had yesterday, not ten years before.

'You know I caught them in bed together?' Andy says slyly.

'What?' I thwack him on the arm. 'And you didn't think to tell me?'

He smiles. 'There was nothing to tell. Don't you remember Charlie told you he was a shit kisser? They had no chemistry.'

Jimmy throws his hand on his chest in mock horror. 'How *dare* she! I've never had any complaints!' He leans closer to me. 'Has Charlie got a boyfriend?' he whispers.

I swat him away. 'You're a married man.'

'I'm messing! I love my wife. She's the *best*.' He beams.

'For the record, there's no boyfriend,' I reply. 'But there might be a girlfriend.' My thoughts fall back to the lingering look shared between Charlie and Sarah in the pub before I left. I hope Charlie doesn't leap back into the relationship too soon. I don't want her moving out while I'm still here.

Jimmy makes a sad face. 'Charlie's gay? Poor me.'

'Pansexual, actually.'

He grins again. 'Only kidding. It'd be great to see her if she visits while you're here.' The waiter appears again with more orders. 'I've got to get to it,' he says. 'I left your suitcase out back, Alice. Help yourself when you've finished your drink.'

'Mate, can I have a quick word?' says Andy, and gestures Jimmy away from me.

I stiffen but take the hint. 'I'll get my stuff,' I mutter, slipping behind the bar, desperate to know what they're talking about. If Andy's embarrassed about me being here then surely I should be involved in that conversation?

I grab my suitcase and hurry back, hoping to catch the tail end of their discussion, but Andy's gone. 'Where is he?' I say, looking around.

Jimmy's eyes slide away from mine. 'He said he'll see you tomorrow. By the way, if you're hungry, I can suggest some places. The kitchen's not open till later.'

I'm tempted to take a look inside, for old times' sake, but my euphoria about the past has wilted into melancholy. Andy and I were getting on okay, weren't we? Yet he couldn't be bothered to hang around to say goodbye. 'You know Andy doesn't want me at Perfecte? It's Mariana's idea to buy my school and bring me on board.'

Jimmy ducks out of sight to get some beers from the fridge. 'So what's the big deal? You think he's still got the hots for you?'

He pops back up, laughing, and I flush. I've assumed I still mean something to Andy. For my presence to matter. 'No, I don't mean . . .' I stumble. 'I think he's embarrassed we were ever an item.'

Jimmy glances at the kitchen as if remembering the past. He leans on the bar and whispers, 'Nah, he cried proper tears when you ditched him. But he's a big boy now, he'll cope.'

I dumped *him*? I suppose things could have looked like that from one end of the telescope – but there's some vital information missing that says otherwise.

'Then again, he's never been one for a heart-to-heart,' says Jimmy. 'But he has *got* a heart. Pure gold is Andy. He'd do anything for anyone.'

I frown. It's hard to remember. 'He told me not to mention the past to Susie. Did he say the same to you?'

Jimmy makes a face. 'Yeah, bloody stupid if you ask me, but I owe him a favour.' He slugs gin into a cocktail shaker and adds some raspberries.

'See! He *is* embarrassed of me.' I fiddle with my straw. 'What are we supposed to do? Pretend we don't know each other?'

'I guess,' he says, shrugging and pouring in orange liqueur. 'So are you staying nearby?'

'No, I'm in a hostel in Sants. It's awful.' I'm already dreading the thought of dragging my suitcase back on the metro and along the skanky alleyway. 'I need to get out of there. Do you know a room I can rent?'

Jimmy looks at me. He puts his finger to his temple. 'Now, let me see, do I *know* anywhere . . .' He pours the pale-pink cocktail into a glass. 'I just *can't* think.'

Despite his sarcasm, my stomach jumps as I sense what he's going to say next.

'Remember the little love nest upstairs?' he croons. 'It's empty – be my guest. You can stay for free. Don't mention it to Andy though. He might go all weird on you again.'

I laugh awkwardly.

Sleeping in Andy's bed.

I give myself a mental kick. I'm being stupid. Really bloody stupid. Jimmy's offering me *free* accommodation.

He clocks my expression. 'Now, now, don't *you* go all weird! What's the problem?' His eyes dance, challenging me to say something I don't want to say because it's just not true.

I shrug. 'There's no problem. The past is in the past.'

'So that's a yes then? Don't you mean to say: thank you *very* much, Jimmy, you're so kind.'

I grin. 'It would be fantastic, thanks.'

'Brilliant. That means we'll get to see loads of each other while you're here and you can meet Juliana.' He plucks a key from a drawer. 'Come on, now's as good a time as any.'

We ascend the stairs I've clattered up and down a thousand times before. At the apartment door, Jimmy presses the key into my hand. 'There you go,' he says with a wink before disappearing.

I turn the key and step inside. It's stuffy and warm like no one has been here for a while. I make my way towards my old bedroom and push open the door, taking in the twin beds where Charlie and I had slept all those years ago. I pass Jimmy's room, now a living room again with a pair of smart sofas framing a floral rug.

Butterflies multiply as I reach the end of the corridor where the kitchen is on the left and Andy's room is on the right. The door's ajar and I prod it open as if something awful might leap out and catch me by surprise.

But everything is the same.

With the balcony doors shuttered closed, the light is dim. My eyes travel over the wooden floorboards, on to the antique wardrobe, then the curved chair that's uncomfortable to sit on and where Andy used to chuck his clothes. They flutter up to the gorgeous chandelier and fall back to the four-poster bed.

My heart aches.

That's the trouble with memories. They have a habit of creeping back into your head when you think you've managed to erase them. It's like the last ten years never happened. And the question that's been demanding my attention since I arrived finally wriggles to the surface.

What would my life have been like if I'd never left?

Chapter 26

ANDY

Ten years ago

Although I'd offered to take Alice on a tour of the old town so we could find some of the smaller local markets, I'd not seen my promise through yet. I'd become distracted with my mum arriving, Enric's hospital visits, and the cafe had been busier than usual, forcing conversation between Alice and I to stay light – and pretend nothing had happened.

Today I'd been forced to take Mariana out to lunch. Apparently she'd popped in for her usual morning coffee, and my mum had decided it was time we begin our lessons. As the time rolled around, she hollered out Mariana's arrival but I didn't rush out. Then when my mum stormed into the kitchen soon after, eyes like lasers, I scuttled out, wiping my sweaty hands on my shorts.

I was mildly surprised to see Mariana wearing a dress, not her usual work suit, which looked long enough to catch on her heeled sandals. Charlie noticed her get-up, too.

'You look nice,' she said as she flew in and slapped a drinks order down on the bar for Jimmy. 'Off on a date?'

Mariana looked at me and heat crept into her cheeks.

I responded with an eye-roll and a small shake of my head to try to dilute her embarrassment. 'We're having a *Catalan lesson*?' I said to Charlie. 'Remember?'

She laughed. 'Call it what you like. Looks like a hot date to me.'

'Come on,' I said, doing the gallant thing and holding my arm out for Mariana to take. The least I could do was make her feel comfortable. Nobody wanted to be the focus of Charlie's piss-take. 'Where are you taking me?'

We walked out into the square and I felt her relax against me. 'My father suggested the seafood restaurant down by the beach. *Ganxa*. It's where he takes all his clients when he wants to strike a deal.'

I smiled. 'Is that what we're doing? Striking a deal?'

Her laugh tinkled. 'Maybe. Do you know this place? You know what this word means?'

I shook my head. '*Ganxa*,' I repeated, searching for some kind of recognition, but nothing came.

'Hook,' Mariana replied. 'You get the joke? Hooking a fish?'

I smiled and let go of her arm to flag a taxi. 'I guess that works. But from now on, we need to speak Catalan, right?'

'*És clar.*'

Lunch with a sea view wasn't a hardship and neither were the *calamars* and *gambetes* – squid and shrimp – fried in a delicate tempura batter that I couldn't wait to tell Alice about.

Mariana spoke slowly throughout the meal so I could catch her words. We switched to English when we veered from our lesson, and she told me how her father owned the building where she runs Perfecte.

'He wants to expand the school so we can teach more languages and find a bigger place that is *més bonic*,' she explained. 'Above a tourist shop is not pretty.'

'Is that what you want? To run a bigger business?'

Mariana looked away and her smile wobbled a little. I wondered what was on her mind, but then her gaze flew back to mine. 'Of course. Everyone wants to be successful, don't they?'

A whooshing sounded in my ears. *Don't be a div, bro, everyone wants to be successful. You've just got to find what you're good at.*

'Money makes the planet move,' Mariana said, nodding.

My mind rushed back to the present again. I forced a smile. 'You mean, money makes the world go around.'

She laughed and patted my hand. 'Andrew, you are going to be such a help to me.'

Later that evening, Alice and I had finished for the day and we were all in the bar with my mum. Alice had been intrigued by my visit to the beachside restaurant and keen to go. But when I'd told her the prices were high – and Mariana had insisted on paying because my lesson was a 'taster' – she'd made a face. 'I'm sure we can find somewhere cheaper to try seafood tempura,' she said.

Now my mum was dishing out the praise and my mood felt light.

'You are doing a good job, *nens*, it is such a relief to have you kids here,' she said. 'Customer numbers are growing and I hear good things from them about your food.' She glanced at the menu in her hand. 'They really like *els entrepans* – the sandwiches with *truita* were a good idea, Alice.'

I fiddled with my beer bottle.

'I can't take the credit,' she said. 'That was Andy. Don't they taste good?'

My mum patted me on the cheek. 'Ah, *fill meu*. I knew you could do it, son.'

'Low cost, too,' Alice continued. 'Bread, eggs, potato. All cheap ingredients.' She smiled at me. 'What did you think of Andy's *gaspatxo?*'

I'd never been a fan of my mum's cold tomato soup, so I'd put my own spin on the idea with a few new ingredients.

'That was yours too?' She sounded surprised.

I didn't know whether to be pleased or offended, but I knew it took a lot to impress her. 'Blimey, I'm not a complete lost cause.'

She nodded. 'Perhaps at last you have found something you are good at.'

For the second time that day, Matt's words came echoing back to me. *You've just got to find what you're good at.*

'Can you teach me how to make paella, Sofia?' asked Alice. 'Andy says no one makes it like you do.'

'Does he now?' My mum appraised me.

'What? You think I said that to get in your good books?' Though I was chuffed Alice had remembered.

My mum patted my cheek again. 'Of course not. But you are not usually so forthcoming with the compliments.'

I frowned. 'But I love your paella. I thought you knew that?'

'Maybe.' She shrugged.

I couldn't remember when she'd last made it for me. Likely, I'd shovelled it in late at night after coming back from the pub. Perhaps I hadn't said thank you – and I should have.

'Of course I will teach you, Alice,' my mum said warmly. 'Perhaps my *fill* wants to learn, too?'

I screwed up my face. 'It looks difficult. Do I have to?'

'You tell me.' She shrugged again. 'So we will do that another time. But first, tomorrow, you two can have the day off. Take Alice to the beach.'

'Oh, I don't mind working. I love cooking,' she said quickly.

My mum smiled. 'I know, you are *apassionada*. But you need to relax as well.'

'I'm up for the beach,' Jimmy interjected.

'Me too,' added Charlie.

Alice glanced at her. 'Sofia might need you here.'

'No, no,' she said, waving her hands. 'We will close the kitchen.'

Charlie and Jimmy high-fived each other.

Alice broke into a gentle smile, her eyes soft, reminding me how my mum looked at me sometimes. 'If you're sure, Sofia?'

'Of course, *carinyo*. Go and have a good time.'

Chapter 27

ANDY

Ten years ago

'Thanks for sticking up for me yesterday,' I said to Alice at the beach. 'Giving me credit for the food, not letting my mum think you'd made everything.'

The four of us had grabbed an empty section of sand on the packed beach and staked out our space with towels. Jimmy and Charlie had already legged it into the sea. I'd whipped off my T-shirt and flopped down, eyes closed, basking in the sun's rays.

'I wasn't going to steal your thunder,' she said, smiling.

Alice had put on a floppy straw hat to shield her face but I noted her eyes flit over me. Was she checking me out? I was glad to be wearing sunglasses. I was doing my best not to stare, but Alice's high-cut black swimsuit showed off her legs and clung to her curves, and it was proving difficult.

I pushed my thoughts back to last night. 'My mum's a tough lady to please.' I thought about how she'd said it was a relief to know I was helping out. 'I like to make her happy,' I added softly.

Alice was still watching me. 'I feel like that too, with my mum. But I wasn't making it up, you know? I really did think your food was good. I loved your *gaspatxo*.'

And our kiss? Alice was rooting in her bag for something. I fiddled with my necklace. 'About the other day . . .'

'Forgotten,' she said, pulling out sunglasses and sticking them on.

I pressed my lips together and looked away, aware of a crushing feeling in my chest. Charlie was mucking about in the sea with Jimmy. They were splashing water at one another and then someone's ball landed nearby. Charlie dived and threw it back to the group, and all of a sudden, they became part of the game.

I clocked Alice's worry lines as she watched them. 'There's nothing going on, you know? They're mates.'

She snorted. 'Right.'

I sat up, feeling a little defensive. 'What's wrong with Jimmy? I know he's got a bit of a mouth on him. And, yes, he's a massive flirt, but he's a good guy.' I thought about how he'd always had my back. 'I've known him since I was eleven.'

Alice looked at me with interest. 'Did you go to school together?'

I nodded and my gaze drifted back to the sea. Charlie jumped into the middle of the group and as the ball flew above her head, she launched herself out of the water and caught it, raising a cheer from the others.

Alice smiled. 'Charlie's been bouncing off the walls since she was a little kid. It was a nightmare trying to get her ready for school in the mornings. She'd run around the house half-dressed, just so I'd chase after her. I gave in with breakfast most days and let her walk to school eating toast because I was worried she'd be hungry.'

I frowned a little. 'Where were your parents?'

'Mum worked at night and slept during the day. Grandma was there, but she wasn't that maternal. I guess she didn't have a lot of practice – my mum was at boarding school for a lot of her childhood. She did her best, but still, I had to help out.'

'What about your dad?'

She smiled. 'I've no idea *who* my dad is, let alone *where* he is.' She glanced around the beach. 'He might be Spanish – or Italian. I'm the result of a one-night stand with a waiter when my mum was sixteen.'

I raised an eyebrow. 'That's a bit intense.' I touched my pendant, thinking for a moment. 'My dad went off a few years ago when he found a younger model. He went back to Wales.'

'Poor Sofia,' Alice murmured. 'Shitty dads and tricky mums, hey? Charlie's not much better off. Her dad, Philippe, is married and my mum's boss. He owns the nightclub where she works and they've been having an on-off thing for *years*. He only comes around when it suits him or he's got an excuse to take her away. The whole situation's a mess.'

I nodded. 'Sounds tough.'

'We weren't, like, *feral* kids,' she said, laughing. 'We were loved. Mum would do mad things like swoop into school and tell them there was an emergency, so she could take us to Thorpe Park or London Zoo. She'd spend the day stuffing us with junk food, sweets and ice-cream – we called her Fun Mum those days.' She smiled at the memory. 'I've always felt protective of Charlie. Don't get me wrong, my grandma is great – she taught me how to cook. I was cooking the family meals by the time I'd started secondary school.'

'Seriously?' Suddenly I felt like a right mummy's boy.

Alice shrugged. 'I love it.' She reached into her bag, pulled out a bottle of sunscreen and began slathering it on her legs. They were already a gorgeous honey colour and I dragged my eyes away.

'Want some?' she said.

I nodded and began to rub the cream on to my arms and chest, then, slowly, I realised *she* was looking at *me*. 'You're a Gemini,' she said, pointing at my pendant. 'Like me.'

For a moment I considered the easy option, which would be to agree. But I didn't want to lie to her. 'No, I'm a Pisces.'

Alice looked puzzled.

'Can't you tell? Pisces are emotionally aware,' I said lightly. 'Kind, creative – quite a catch, don't you think?'

She smiled. 'You seem to know a lot about star signs. So tell me, what are Geminis like?'

I didn't need any star sign bollocks to tell me what my brother had been like. I kept him alive in my mind every day. I had to because if I didn't, I might forget who he was, what he'd been like.

He'd have turned twenty-six last month.

'Gentle, clever, inquisitive, amusing, devoted,' I rattled off breezily.

'Wow.' Alice smiled. 'You really do know your stuff. You've described me to a T.'

Was she like Matt? I didn't really believe in star signs, or God, or heaven. But I needed to believe there was something else on the other side.

'So what's with the Gemini necklace, then? You know you can't change star sign – that's cheating.'

I touched the pendant and my gaze drifted towards the sea. Wearing Matt's necklace made me feel close to him. But I couldn't tell Alice, it was too . . . *much*. 'It belonged to my brother,' I said quietly.

Alice's eyes combed over my face. I sensed her questions hovering, but she stayed silent, waiting for me to carry on.

I wondered if I could say the words out loud.

I took a deep breath and decided to try. 'Matt died.'

Chapter 28

ANDY

Ten years ago

Although I'd described Alice as an inquisitive Gemini, and I knew enough about her to know she genuinely *was* curious, she simply reached out and touched my arm. Perhaps she was gearing up to ask questions, but then Charlie and Jimmy came bounding back, shaking water all over us.

It didn't matter. I'd said enough.

'Guys, you've gotta go in – the water's lovely,' said Charlie, pushing her hair from her face, belly button piercing catching the sun. She was a gym bunny for sure. She'd beat skinny Jimmy in an arm wrestle any day.

'Fancy a dip?' I said to Alice, getting to my feet.

She eyed the sea.

'It's alright, sis, the water's deep but calm. There's no undertow.'

'Aw, come on, I'll look after you,' I said, returning to my usual charming self.

'You'd better – she can't swim,' said Charlie. 'Neither can I.'

'Can't you?' Jimmy looked surprised. 'You didn't say. You looked alright in the water.'

'Throwing a ball isn't swimming, is it?' She flopped on to her towel and stretched herself out, arms flung above her head. 'I *love* the sun. This is *so* good,' she said.

Water glistened on her pale and lightly freckled skin – no tattoo in sight. I was sure that would change the day she turned eighteen.

Jimmy's gaze roved over Charlie and I caught Alice's flinty eyes on him. Not yet ready to relinquish her protective parent role just yet, it seemed.

'Coming in, then?' I repeated.

Alice threw Charlie a bottle of factor fifty. 'Maybe later.'

I took a dip alone and when I returned, Charlie and Jimmy had gone off to get food. Alice's phone chimed again. Messages had been pinging from her bag since we arrived but I'd clocked Charlie throwing Alice dirty looks, which seemed to stop her from checking them. After my eavesdropping, and what I'd heard about Alice's break-up, I wondered whether her ex was keen to put things right, and Charlie didn't approve.

Alice glanced around, then picked up her mobile. She let out a puff of air as she scrolled through the messages.

'Someone's keen,' I said, searching her face. Perhaps that was why she regretted the kiss. She was still caught up with him. I ventured for the truth. 'Charlie said you were supposed to be coming away with your ex?' I braced myself, expecting Alice to be surprised I knew, though I hoped she wouldn't be annoyed. Maybe she'd be sad about what had happened. Angry, even.

Instead she muttered, 'Cheating bastard,' and then brightened. 'It's all turned out for the best. If I'd come away with him then I'd never have ended up working at Cafè Vermell.'

Or met me.

I wondered if the same thought had slid into her mind as she said, 'When are you taking me exploring?'

I liked the way she'd made that sound. Like she was looking forward to going out with me. Like she might consider my suggestion a date. I seized the moment. 'Tomorrow?'

'Will Sofia mind?'

I shrugged. 'We can do the prep before we go.'

She grinned. 'I'd like that.'

Then her face changed, like she was going to ask me something else, but a burst of the gospel choir erupted from her mobile. She flinched and looked over her shoulder, presumably to see if Charlie was on her way back. She sucked in a breath and took the call. 'Hi, Mum, how are you?'

Mum? Not her ex. A warm feeling spread through me.

'I'm on the beach with Charlie and some friends,' Alice said, glancing at me and rolling her eyes. 'We're still in Barcelona. We're staying for a while, remember? We're both working in a restaurant.' She paused. 'I'm not exactly sure.' Paused again. 'I know you are. We are too.'

The conversation carried on with Alice saying very little. She pushed her fingers into the sand, grabbed a handful and let the grains trickle away. I looked up to see Jimmy and Charlie approaching armed with hot dogs and beers.

I caught Alice's eye and jabbed a finger in their direction to alert her. She turned around. 'I've got to go. I'll speak to you later,' she said quickly. 'I will, I promise.'

'Who were you on the phone to?' Charlie demanded, passing Alice a hot dog. Charlie took a bite of her own and mustard squelched out on to her bikini bottoms. She rubbed at the stain with the corner of a towel. 'It wasn't Mum, was it?'

Alice shrugged.

'Oh my God, sis, *don't* speak to her, otherwise she'll convince you to come home early.' Charlie looked upset rather than angry.

'I just want you and I to enjoy ourselves without any hassle. Don't fuck it up.'

Alice flushed. 'Don't be such a kid. We can't ignore her. She's our *mum*.'

'Some mum she's been,' Charlie muttered.

◆ ◆ ◆

Later, we played cards and when the setting sun began to shoot flames into the sky, I decided to have a quick dip before we left.

'Last chance,' I said to Alice. 'At least stick your feet in. You can wash off the sand.' This time she nodded and my heart lifted a little.

At the shoreline, I could see Charlie had been right earlier. The seabed shelved sharply and I felt Alice hesitate. She let me take her hand – it felt good in mine – and we waded in, feet sinking in the soft sand. The water rose quickly and when it was chest height for Alice, I stopped. She swayed as the waves rolled gently towards the shore and her other hand shot out in panic, so I grabbed that too. 'Alright?'

She nodded, not quite looking at me.

It was my turn to be curious. 'How come you never learnt to swim?'

'Oh, you know, Mum wasn't one for taking us to clubs.'

After the things she'd told me earlier I wasn't surprised. 'Do you want to learn?'

'Are you offering to be my swim instructor?'

I laughed. 'Are you flirting with me, Alice?'

'Maybe,' she said, eyes still averted but a smile twitching her mouth.

Hope soared in my chest and we stood for a moment letting the warm water lap around us. Then I had an idea. 'Hey, how about trying to float on your back? It's pretty easy and feels really relaxing.'

She looked unsure for a moment.

'I'll hold on to you, okay?'

She nodded. 'What do I do?'

'I'm going to tip you backwards, then you need to spread your arms and legs wide—'

Alice giggled and threw her hand over her mouth, but not before I caught a flash of cheeky Charlie in her expression. I smiled. 'Like a *starfish*. To help you stay afloat.'

Slowly, I turned her on to her back, supporting her as she flailed around to get her balance. Panic flickered across her face. 'Starfish,' I reminded her.

She pushed her arms and legs outwards and I pinned my eyes to her face, giving her my best reassuring smile. I didn't want her to think this was some kind of cheap trick.

Alice closed her eyes. Her hair fanned out around her and a smile played across her mouth as she floated. She looked so peaceful, so happy, and I felt the urge to lean down and kiss her. Carefully, I removed my hand from beneath her back so she could do this alone. Her eyes sprang open, alarmed, but I gave her the thumbs-up and she smiled and closed them again.

I could have watched Alice for the rest of the afternoon and late into the evening until the sea turned inky black. But, instead, I flipped on to my back and floated next to her. The water muffled the sounds above and I stared up at the smudges of orange and red streaking the sky, Matt's whisper tickling my ear. *Don't screw this up.* The waves rocked us closer, our fingertips grazed one another, and I took a chance, reaching out and curling my fingers through hers.

As we floated, I felt something peaceful settle over me for the first time in years.

I turned to look at Alice and found her watching me. She tugged my hand and, carefully, I stood back up, pulling her with me.

Alice's green eyes glowed against her honey skin, her eyelashes dark and glossy with water. 'How old was Matt when he died?' she asked, gripping my hands. I sensed this time she was doing it for me rather than herself.

I liked that she'd said his name. It made my brother – *Matt* – feel important, remembered, not forgotten. My gaze drifted beyond her towards the ball of fire slowly sinking into the horizon. 'Same age as me now. He would have been twenty-six. On the sixteenth of June.'

Alice's eyes widened. 'Oh, wow,' she breathed. 'We share a birthday.'

And in that moment, I totally believed Matt was binding himself to me, showing me the way, and perhaps bringing Alice to me, like a gift.

I pulled her closer, drawing circles with my thumbs over her damp cheeks, down her face and to the corners of her sweet lips. I lowered my mouth to meet hers, and this time our kisses were for real, looping back where we'd started that day in the kitchen, and all thoughts of anything – except Alice, her mouth, her damp body pressing into mine – drifted towards the setting sun.

Chapter 29

ALICE

Now

'Come to mine for eight,' says Susie outside Perfecte at the end of the following week.

Once again, we're the ones locking up. Andy's been disappearing as soon as Mariana leaves her office, throwing instructions for me to do this and that in his absence. At first I assumed he had meetings, but I began to notice the pen-tapping and foot-twitching as the day crept on, the fifteen-minute pause after Mariana waved goodbye and then the bolt for the door. Though it isn't my place to ask questions. Susie's none the wiser either.

'Call me if you get lost,' she adds, hopping on her bike. 'And please don't bring anything. Xavier's got the food and wine covered. I feel really bad we've not invited you sooner.'

Susie's been caught up in her own life. I've not minded. I've been unexpectedly content in my own company. Last weekend, I'd got a map from the tourist information centre and walked for hours in the *Barri Gòtic*, emerging into a small plaza here and there, often with a pretty church at the heart, a sculptural fountain – and always a cafe.

As I'd come into one of the squares, the warm scent of melted chocolate and sweet oranges had tickled my nose and tingled my taste buds. A waiter outside the cafe took a little bow as I passed and gestured for me to sit down. I'd automatically smiled, shaking my head, and continued on.

But then I'd stopped. What was the rush? I had nowhere to be. The emptiness of my day felt both liberating and intimidating, so I'd turned back and spoken in halting Catalan to order orange juice – *suc de taronia* – thick hot chocolate and crispy churros for dipping, and was rewarded with a welcoming smile.

My life here had begun to click into place.

I have a spring in my step as I wave goodbye to Susie and head back to my apartment to get changed. After shrugging off my initial reservations about moving in, I'd boldly taken the big bedroom with the four-poster and balcony, pushing aside foolish memories that this was once Andy's room. Jimmy's company downstairs is a lovely bonus and the familiarity of my surroundings has been a fast track to helping me settle in. I haven't had to worry about lying to Susie and Xavier either. Of course Jimmy and I know each other – he's my landlord.

After a cold drink on the balcony, where I watch the world go by and practise a few more Catalan phrases, I get ready to go out. Soon, I'm heading back down, and I catch Jimmy coming inside with a tray that teeters with dirty crockery, a waiter at his heels rattling off a drinks order.

'Darling,' he says, eyeing up my green maxi dress. 'Looking good. Off on a date?'

'Hardly.' I laugh. 'Let me help.' I reach out and take the tray from him.

'Thanks.' He goes behind the bar and as I head towards the kitchen, he suddenly spins around. 'Wait!'

I turn in surprise.

He smiles. 'Don't worry, leave that here. You don't want to ruin your dress.'

I'm bemused. 'It's no problem. I've got it.'

Jimmy skids out from behind the bar and slides between me and the kitchen door. 'Please?' he says, half-wrestling the tray out of my hands.

I let go and laugh. 'You're being very weird.'

His eyes dart this way and that. 'Off you go then. Have a nice evening.'

'Let me get the door for you.' Before he can protest, I nudge past him and push it open.

For a second, my head spins. It's as if by walking in here, I've stepped back in time.

Andy?

He's at the work bench clutching a yellow pepper, eyes wide, as though he thinks I'm a time traveller too, and this is the first time he's laid eyes on me in ten years.

We're back to where we started.

My brain rushes to catch up.

My gaze sweeps across the same wooden work bench, the hanging pots, the time Andy accidentally clipped my head with one, his cute concern that got me thinking it would be a good idea to kiss him . . .

A high-tech fan oscillates in my direction, blasting an Arctic chill that snaps me to my senses. 'What are you doing in here?' I stutter.

Jimmy sidles past and dumps the tray next to the sink. Andy shoots him laser eyes but says nothing.

'Alice just walked in,' says Jimmy with a shrug. 'So *I'll* just walk back out.' He disappears and leaves us eyeing each other warily like a pair of Janet's cats.

My head tries to piece together the old Andy with the new Andy, stood at the work bench, knife in hand, slicing vegetables – *as I taught him*. A jumble of fluttery feelings eddy together that feel as though they could manifest into hysterics – or sobs.

I have to get out of here. Now.

I hurry back out through the bar and into the sunshine, trying to steady my breath. Jimmy catches me before I leave. 'You told Andy I tried to stop you going in there, right?'

'What?' I'm still dazed.

'He doesn't want Mariana to know what he's up to. Don't say anything.'

By the time I'm close to Susie and Xavier's apartment, my heart rate has returned to normal and I have the urge to call Mum. All the feelings and memories I've carefully packed away are beginning to spill out.

'Hello?' Mum sounds bored, which suggests she's answered her phone without looking to see who's calling.

'It's me.'

'I know it's you, petal.'

I guess she's watching one of the soaps and I should be grateful she's distracted by the TV and not telling me she's lonely. But her disinterest makes me feel cut off, let loose, and I need something solid to cling on to. 'Is Charlie there?' I say.

'Why are you phoning me if you want to speak to her?'

'I don't, I was just asking – just checking everything's okay with you both.'

'Uh-huh.'

Why don't I feel relieved? Mum's fine. She's absorbed in her programmes. She's been fed. Nothing bad has happened. Charlie's done what she needs to do.

A thought sneaks in. *Mum doesn't need me.*

I swallow. Not true.

'You paid the credit card bill, didn't you?' I say.

'What? Yes, I told you. Ages ago.'

'And everything's . . . okay with your finances now?'

She lets out an impatient sigh. 'Alice, everything's just fine. Just the same as it was when I spoke to you this afternoon.'

The financial pressure is off. That's one reason I don't *have* to be in Barcelona anymore. I could go home . . . so why hasn't she asked me?

I recall Josep's sneer: *What do you know about running a school?* Mariana's response: *It is a trial. Nothing has been decided yet.*

If I went back now, how far would I have come?

I force a smile in the hope it lightens my voice. 'I'm going to my friend Susie's for dinner – a girl from work. She's lovely, really sweet.'

'Spanish, is she? You won't be able to understand her.'

The phone crackles and loses signal for a moment as the street narrows between the tall buildings, their stone facades grim and unyielding. I pass someone's home with pretty lace curtains at the window; a cat on the sill licks its paw. Up ahead, washing flips and dances along the balconies in the breeze like colourful bunting.

'Are you still there?' says Mum. 'I can't hear you. And, anyway, I've got to go. I've just got to the good bit in this episode.'

'Mum—'

But she's gone.

Outside the heavy wooden door to Susie and Xavier's apartment, I push away my worries and focus on the evening ahead. Susie buzzes me in and I climb the stone staircase. At her door, she welcomes me with a hug. She's wearing wide-legged trousers and a red top, which should clash with her auburn hair but she looks gorgeous.

I go through to an open-plan room with a tiny kitchen at one end, and a dining table made with planks of wood fixed to black metal legs. The living room overlooks the street where a fat sofa takes up most of the space and Susie's colourful vases and pots fill floor-to-ceiling shelves. Open doors let a breeze in from the balcony and the building opposite is close enough for me to see an elderly couple eating dinner at their window.

Xavier greets me with kisses to both cheeks. Like Mariana's father, he's a short man with broad shoulders but he wears a cheerful smile, which I'd immediately warmed to when I first met him.

'Welcome,' he says.

'*Bona vespre*, Alice.' Mariana materialises from behind me. She's wearing an off-the-shoulder top, which reveals gleaming bronzed skin. My maxi dress now feels more like an outfit a nun would choose.

'Hi, hello, *bon vespre*,' I mumble, surprised to find her here.

She air-kisses my cheeks, leaving a trail of sweet perfume, then the buzzer goes again. Xavier presses a glass of Cava into my hand and apologises for not inviting me over before, explaining he's been away on a course.

'Xavier is back next week and will help you build a website for Perfecte London,' adds Mariana.

I'm about to reply but my breath catches as Andy bounds through the door.

Chapter 30

ALICE

Now

Mariana's gaze lands momentarily on mine. I feel a stab of guilt as though she thinks Andy and I came here together but we're trying to pretend that we didn't. It doesn't help to know that this might have been a possibility if he'd told me he was cooking at the cafe, that he'd been invited – instead of keeping me in the dark.

He has no reason to answer to me.

'Sorry I'm late,' he mutters.

Mariana's tilts her head like a tiny, pretty bird, but he won't catch her eye, nor mine, nor anyone's. Instead, he strides over to the small breakfast bar and pours Cava into a glass so fast that it froths up and over the rim.

'Damn,' he exclaims, searching around for a cloth.

'*Cap problema*,' says Xavier, mopping up the spill. 'It's the weekend now, relaxing times, and we need to welcome our new friend and colleague. So, like the English say, cheers! *Salut!*'

We lift our glasses and Andy gives me a tiny smile. My insides twirl for a moment, still hooked on the shock of seeing him in the kitchen earlier. But I remind myself he's silently asking me to be part of his conspiracy – against his wife.

Mariana turns the conversation to work and, after a short while, Susie invites us to sit down and eat. I'm seated opposite Mariana and Andy, with Susie and Xavier at either end. It feels a bit uncomfortable, like all eyes are on me.

'The food looks lovely,' I say. Xavier's laid tapas out down the middle of the table so we can share delicate fried fish, garlic prawns, stuffed glossy red peppers, fat green olives, slices of cold meats and cheese. 'Who's the cook?'

'Xavier, of course.' Mariana laughs. 'His food is *estima* in my family.'

We begin to eat and I'm quiet as I savour each mouthful, considering the delicate balance of textures and flavours that send my taste buds into overdrive. I sense Andy watching me as I ask Xavier where he buys the ingredients, how he prepares the food, the optimum cooking temperature.

'You should be a chef,' I say, without thinking. 'This food is sensational.'

Andy begins to cough and Mariana thumps him a touch too hard on the back. 'I'm fine,' he splutters.

'A chef is a play job,' Mariana says, waving her hand so her bangles sing and catch the light. 'My cousin's computer work is essential for Perfecte.'

Xavier's dark eyebrows knit together and nobody says anything. I pop a juicy olive into my mouth. 'These are incredible.' I pick up the bowl and offer them around.

Andy takes them. 'Thanks,' he says, looking steadily back at me so that I fidget in my seat. For the olives? Or for staying quiet about his moonlighting? I'm curious. Why was he there? Though it explains why he's been skiving off work.

Mariana's eyes dart between us and then she lets out a shrill laugh. 'Andrew is a hopeless cook,' she says, squeezing his hand with pink fingernails that are studded with tiny gems. 'Unless you like an English roast dinner with fatty beef and lumps of potato.'

Andy snatches his hand away. Susie and Xavier exchange glances.

Mariana sounds critical, reminding me of Charlie, and out of habit, I jump on the defensive. 'Not *everyone* likes roast dinner in England. I make Spanish paella sometimes. I love Andy's—' I stop as I catch his eyes widen.

I've always been a crap liar and I hate this subterfuge. I'm tempted to stand up and blow open our stupid 'secret' – even though three of us in the room already know the truth. I'd have some sympathy if Mariana, Andy's *wife*, was none the wiser, but she knows everything.

I imagine saying, *Susie, Xavier, you should know Andy and I were an item once upon a time, but he'd rather pretend it never happened. But that's okay, I'd rather pretend it didn't happen, too.*

My throat aches a little. Seeing him in the kitchen today reminds me that isn't true.

'So, Alice, what does Andy think about your food events?' Mariana's eyes dart between us, face aglow.

'Food events?' says Xavier. 'What is this?'

I look at Andy but he's peeling more meat and cheese off the plate and sticking it straight into his mouth.

'Oh, it's not so much events as street food,' I begin. I explain how the demand for my Cornish pasties led to the idea of sitting and sharing food after class with students who love it as much as me. How impressed I'd been about the curry, which inspired me to book pop-up food vans to come to the school so we could try meals from around the world.

'What is a Cornish pasty?' says Xavier, bemused.

I go into a detailed explanation and notice Mariana's eyes glaze over.

'Getting the pastry right is what sets the best apart,' says Andy.

'And the crimp,' I add. 'It's not a Cornish pasty without a proper crimp.' We smile at one another.

Mariana focuses her gaze back on me. She curls her fingers around Andy's arm. 'See, these food events are a good idea, no?'

Andy tugs his arm away and there's an awkward pause.

Susie's face brightens. 'What do you cook at home, Alice?'

'Spaghetti bolognaise,' I reply. 'Sausage and mash, fish and chips.' I realise I'm recalling mum's weekly meal plan and come to a stop. I'm boring myself. 'It would be nice to make other things but my mum's fussy.'

'You live at home?' Mariana looks horrified. 'What happened to you?'

I'm puzzled. 'Nothing's *happened* to me. I've never left home.'

'But you're . . .' She waves her hand at me. 'How *old* are you?'

I try to laugh but it comes out like a squeak. 'It's nothing to do with my age. I care for my mum, she's . . . well, she has limited mobility. She has to use sticks to get around.'

Mariana leans forward. 'And you work as well?'

Her face is alert and I realise I need to be careful. I don't want her thinking I'm unable to cope with Mum's needs as well as the demands of running Perfecte London – though it's something I *am* worrying about. 'Yes,' I say firmly. 'Work is important to me and I love being here. I'm learning so much.'

Mariana sits back. 'Good. I'm glad you like my company and you like my city. And maybe you will find a handsome Catalan man to take home with you.' She gives Andy's arm another squeeze and a muscle flexes in his jaw.

'You're such a good person, Alice. As much as I love my parents, I couldn't *wait* to leave home,' says Susie.

Xavier nods. 'You have a big heart.'

For some reason a lump lodges in my throat and I swallow down a large mouthful of wine. I don't feel like I have a good heart. Being here, eating lovely food, drinking beautiful wine, *in Barcelona*. It feels dreamy, free – and selfish.

Poor Mum's stuck at home without me. *But tonight she didn't ask me to come back.*

Mariana begins to talk to Xavier about one of their cousins who's just had a baby and she wrinkles her nose. Andy stands to clear the empty plates. I help, waving away Susie's protests, and follow him over to the kitchen. At the sink, we have our backs to the others and I rinse off the plates while he stacks the dishwasher.

A wave of familiarity makes my throat burn again.

'Thanks,' he mutters, near enough for his breath to goosebump my skin. I pick up the scent of something clear, fresh and outdoorsy that reminds me of the sea.

I nod and turn back to the table. Mariana's eyes bore into mine. I don't want to be a pawn in their marriage. I don't want to pretend Andy and I – and Jimmy – don't know each other. Yes, I'm here to do a job, but I also want to spend time with Susie and Xavier. I don't want to be watching what I say in front of them. I'm going to have to put Andy straight tomorrow.

'Alice,' says Xavier. 'Barcelona is a city with *menjar fantàstic* – wonderful food. You must come with us to La Cova. It is one of our favourite places to experience what clever chefs are making here.'

I smile. 'Thanks, I'd like that.'

Andy's face unexpectedly lights up. 'What about a table at Graffiti?' he exclaims. 'Did you speak to the proprietor?'

'You know this place?' Xavier looks doubtful.

'Alice was staying at the hostel next door.'

I hold up my hands. 'Sorry. After my luggage got delivered to Cafè Vermell, I moved straight into the apartment as I had

176

everything with me. I never went back to the hostel, so I didn't get the chance to arrange anything.'

'Ah, never mind,' says Andy. 'La Cova is a cool place, too, but it's got popular and it's really hard to get a table.'

'We're on the waiting list,' Xavier adds.

'Maybe I will come this time,' says Mariana, swirling her wine then taking a sip.

'Really?' Andy snaps. 'You've never been bothered before.'

I'm taken aback by his tone. Susie raises her eyebrows at Xavier and they move over to the kitchen to prepare dessert.

'Maybe I am bothered now,' Mariana replies, eyes on me again.

I meet her gaze. She needs to know I have *no* interest in married men.

Chapter 31

Alice

Now

The following morning I'm up early to go to La Boqueria, the food market on La Rambla, before it gets too busy. Xavier's tapas last night has inspired me to play around with some recipes.

Jimmy's already in the bar, frowning at some paperwork, and I wonder if this has something to do with why Andy is helping out.

'Everything alright?' I say, touching his shoulder.

He jumps. 'Jesus, don't creep up on me like that.'

His face is pale and there are dark imprints beneath his eyes. 'You look like shit.'

'Thanks for nothing.' He cracks a small smile and rubs a hand over his buzz cut. 'I'm knackered.'

I hesitate. 'Is Andy in the kitchen today?' It still feels strange.

'No, he's at a family celebration. Though I have no idea why he's gone. It's not as if he—' He clamps his mouth shut. 'Anyway.'

A warm feeling spreads across my chest as an idea springs to mind. 'Would you like me to help? I mean, cook for you today?'

Jimmy's face lights up. 'Would you? That'd be amazing!' He hugs me hard. 'You sure?'

I'm beaming. 'I'd *love* to! Free rein, right? I can cook what I want? I was on my way to the market anyway.'

'Darling, you can do whatever you like.'

I go to leave and then stop at the door. 'Jimmy?'

He looks up.

'Why's Andy working here?'

Worry creases his forehead. 'Didn't he tell you at Susie and Xavier's last night?'

'I thought he wanted to keep it a secret from Mariana,' I respond snippily.

'I didn't think she . . .' Jimmy's eyes glaze over in thought. 'Well, yes, I guess he doesn't want Susie and Xavier to know either,' he murmurs. Then he brightens up. 'Juliana's usually the cook but she's not well at the moment, and my other chef is away, so he's helping out.'

'Oh, I'm sorry to hear that.'

Jimmy waves me away. 'She'll be fine once they get her medication sorted out. It's something to do with her thyroid, so she's exhausted all the time. Then, of course, the twins are a handful, I'm running this place . . . Thank God her parents live close by – they're a fantastic help.' His trademark grin is back. 'I'd have been stuck without Andy. He's a great guy – but don't tell him I said that!'

I head off to the market and as I go from stall to stall, picking out seafood, a ring of chorizo, shiny aubergines, garlic, I ponder what Jimmy said. Andy's a great guy? He hasn't *always* been a great guy.

Has he?

Soon I'm back in the kitchen with two bulging bags and I get to work. By afternoon, my experimental recipes have paid off as I plate up the last portions of grilled paprika scallops and chorizo, aubergine crisps with garlic aioli and Sofia's fail-safe paella. When

Mum calls me at 4.15 p.m. while I'm washing up, I realise I've not thought about her, or home, all day.

Joy bubbles out of my mouth before she's had a chance to speak. 'I've had the best day! I've been making tapas for a cafe in one of the squares.'

Mum's silent. 'I don't understand,' she says eventually. 'I thought you were working at the language school. To help Janet out. To get yourself a better job back here.' She pauses. 'Is this about money? Are you working two jobs because you're still worrying about my credit card? We talked about this yesterday. It's all sorted now.'

I'm about to explain but she moves the conversation on, telling me how she's persuaded Charlie to take all her online purchases out of her wardrobe and bring them downstairs. Mum's selling the lot on eBay apparently.

'You're not cross, are you?' she says.

I go over and sit on the stool by the fan to cool myself down. I've been trying for years to get Mum to stop frittering away her money on stuff she doesn't need or want. If this means she can earn something back *and* change her spending habits, then I'm all for it.

'No, not at all, it sounds like a great plan,' I say.

'We've been really busy,' she says. 'Charlie's got an idea for a business, too, so that's what we're going to do next.'

My ears prick up. 'What kind of business?' I say slowly.

Mum laughs. 'Perfume!'

◆ ◆ ◆

The phone call takes the shine off my earlier excitement, and I try – and fail – to speak to Charlie half a dozen times over the weekend in between cooking for Jimmy again. I'm anxious to find out what she's got planned. She's no clue how to run a business.

When I arrive at work on Monday, Mariana tells me Andy's away on business but doesn't elaborate. She directs me to Xavier's office and he helps me start to build Perfecte London's website. I've assumed Andy's working at Cafè Vermell but when I get back later, the kitchen is closed. I offer my help to Jimmy again, but he refuses, telling me I can't risk blowing my job at Perfecte by spreading myself too thin.

I'm disappointed. My weekend cooking has ignited a flame of passion I thought had been long extinguished, so I spend the evening experimenting in my own kitchen instead.

Towards the end of the week, I come into work and see Mariana's office is empty. My heart unexpectedly flickers at the sight of Andy back at his desk. I hover in the doorway, suddenly awkward after time apart. I clear my throat to get his attention.

He looks up. 'Hey.'

'You've returned.'

He leans back in his chair. 'Seems that way.'

'Good trip?'

He hides a smile. 'Possibly.'

'Did you go to London?'

He looks puzzled. 'No, why would I?' Then his expression clears. 'Oh. That. No, no, I didn't.'

That?

He eyes me in the doorway. 'Are you coming in? Or going somewhere?'

I run my hand over my hip, wondering if I've cinched in my belt too tight. I touch my shirt to make sure I've not accidentally left a button undone. And as I stride purposefully to my desk to hide my unease, my phone begins to chime and vibrate. Charlie's name flashes on the screen. 'Thank fuck,' I mutter, and Andy raises an eyebrow.

'Where the hell have you been, Charlie?' I hiss down the phone.

'Chill, I've been busy. Didn't you get my messages?'

'Didn't you get mine?' I retort. 'To *phone* me?'

'What do you think I'm doing now?'

I push my hands through my hair and catch Andy smirking, eyes still on his computer screen. I turn my back on him.

'I've got some news,' Charlie says brightly.

'That'll have to wait,' I snap. 'I need to talk to you first.'

'Be my guest,' she replies cheerfully.

'What's this business venture with Mum?'

'The perfume? Oh, it's nothing. Just something to keep her occupied.'

'And you didn't think to tell me?'

'There isn't much to say. Mum's selling her crap on eBay. She's been packaging everything up and then Delivery Leon comes along to collect it.' Charlie pauses. 'He's hot if you're into curly brown hair and a cherubic face.'

I roll my eyes. 'And? The perfume?'

'Well, I don't know, I need to look into it. I just threw the idea out there to keep her interested. Once all her shit has been sold I don't want her flopping back in front of the telly.'

'Well, yes, but—'

'Did you know she had four foot spas and a whole collection of really ugly dog ornaments? I don't know why you've let her buy these things.'

I grit my teeth. 'It's not up to me. It's her money.'

'Precisely, so if she wants to sell perfume, leave her be.'

The red credit card bill flashes into my mind. 'I don't want you to encourage her to spend.'

'So you think if you're not here, this thing is going to go tits up? I'm not a complete fuckwit, sis.' She sighs. 'Trust me, I'll keep an eye on her.'

But we both know what Charlie says and what she does aren't always the same thing. 'I've got to get back to work,' I say.

'Before you go, since you didn't ask, the reason I've been busy this week is because I've been prepping to pop the question.'

My mind is still on Mum and I'm slow to react. 'Pop the question,' I murmur, then I realise what she's talking about. '*What?* Who? You're—'

'Engaged!' Charlie yells loud enough for Andy to look up and smile.

I bolt upright. 'To Sarah? But you've only been together for . . .'

'Eighteen months.'

'No way! You can't count the breaks.'

'Ah, whatever. You should be congratulating me.'

I shake my head. I hope this is just another one of Charlie's impulsive decisions that fizzles into nothing. 'Congratulations.' My voice is flat.

'Wow, sis, don't sound so *excited*. I'm allowed to have a happy ending, you know?'

She's right and I don't want our conversation to turn spiky again. 'Sorry . . . Have you set a date yet?' I hold my breath.

'Yes. In a month.'

'*A month?*' I shriek and Andy laughs quietly.

'Relax! We're in love, there was a cancellation at the registry office – why wait? But I'm having my hen do in Barcelona the week before and I want you to organise it.'

My mouth is opening and closing but nothing is coming out.

'You still there?'

I nod, then remember to answer her. 'Yes, of course I will,' I say faintly. 'Congratulations, Charlie.'

'Aw, thanks, sis. Right, I'll let you go. Speak soon.'

I slump back into my chair and blow out my cheeks. Andy and I exchange a look and I throw him a small smile. 'Charlie's got engaged.'

'And that's not a good thing?'

'She can't commit to anything. She job-hops, doesn't think twice about moving in with her latest fling, then when she screws up, she's back home again. Sarah's lovely but I just don't know if Charlie really means to see it through. It's not fair on the poor woman.'

Andy shrugs. 'Sarah must know what she's letting herself in for. Perhaps it's best to leave them to it.'

I look at him in surprise. 'I guess. I'm just worried she's going to walk out and leave my mum.' I think back to my recent argument with Charlie, which, in our usual style, we've moved on from without mentioning again. 'She thinks Mum's more capable than she is. They rub each other up the wrong way.'

'Perhaps they'll find their way back to one another while you're gone,' he says. 'Things can often look different when you step back into a familiar situation after time apart.'

Andy's words seem to linger and I wonder if there really is a veil of sadness in his eyes. Perhaps he's not talking about Mum and Charlie after all – but us.

Chapter 32

ALICE

Now

Later that evening, I'm out on my balcony, dinner on my lap, glancing at the activity in the square below as I scroll through my phone for food inspiration. I've gone down a rabbit hole, discovering all kinds of regional delicacies in Spain – coastal Asturias for seafood, suckling pig in Castilla-Leon, fish stew with crayfish from Melilla. My twenty-year-old self would have dived into an Interrail food tour in this country alone. I still would now.

I realise I'm shovelling in my food without any thought – like Mum. Satisfaction from eating isn't hitting the spot tonight, and I know better. I should be sat at the table, my focus on what I see, taste and touch. Sharing food with loved ones. These rituals are the essence of the greatest culinary experiences.

I sigh. I'm missing the camaraderie of my students. Susie's out with family. Jimmy's too busy to pin down. I'm half-wishing Mariana had invited me to dinner again with her and Andy.

Only half.

I glance down at the bustle below. Could I go out on my own?

Although I've wandered around the old town during the day – with a map – striking out at night feels daunting. But then I remember the times when Andy and I explored, when I'd thought he knew where he was going, but he'd been making it up all along. We always found our way back home.

Home?

Before I change my mind, I jump up. In the kitchen, I glance around at the mess, feeling the pull to scrub everything clean like I usually do before I relax. But I'm not at home. I can break a habit.

I leave my city map on the table. I'm going out alone.

I stroll through the plaza, enjoying the warm evening air, and slip down the first street I see. Though I've eaten, reading about Spain's vast and varied food scene has pricked my taste buds, and my nervous energy about getting lost is rapidly turning to excitement at what I might find.

My route takes me past shops, open late and selling leather sandals, sweets and colourful glassware to wandering tourists. I chance another turn, down a smaller street and where the stone flags are worn slippery with age. It's cool and quiet, and I pass a couple of small bars with only one or two tables outside where chattering locals sip beer and eat tapas.

I carry on until a shop set in the stone walls of the tall buildings catches my eye. Cheeses of varying shapes and sizes are artfully arranged in the window but there are no labels, suggesting customers who come here know what they're buying. Bumped up tight to the building is a tiny *bodega*, doubling as a bar. Through the open door, I see dozens of wine bottles fill the walls and the buzz of life and laughter rolls out.

I smile. Cheese and wine. *Perfecte*.

I go into the cheese shop first. Although my language skills still aren't great, I'm getting better and only need to use my phone to translate some of the more difficult words. I glance at the food notes I'd made earlier and ask for a nutty mahon from Menorca, a lemony Galician tetilla, a rich olive roncal – and soon my plate is full.

The seller ushers me over to the *bodega* where I'm welcomed by a young waiter with a handsome smile. I glance around at the tables crammed next to one another, and up over the shelves of bottles that go on and on until they reach the ceiling. It's like a library of wine. There's even a ladder leaning against one of them to access the bottles out of reach.

As the waiter gestures for me to sit down, a familiar face at the neighbouring table is grinning at me. 'Fancy seeing you here,' says Andy.

I squeak out a surprised laugh. 'Of all places,' I say, squeezing past to sit down. Our tables are so close we look like we're sat together.

'Got enough cheese there,' he says, pointing at my plate.

I look down and pop a piece into my mouth. 'Probably not.'

He smiles again. 'So you're not sharing?'

I look over at the empty chair opposite him. Perhaps Mariana is in the loo. 'I might.'

The waiter appears with the wine menu. Andy rattles off something to him, and I detect he's speaking Spanish this time. I'm momentarily surprised, but I shouldn't be. He co-owns a language school. He's lived here for long enough. And as Mariana keeps reminding me, he is *intelligent*.

Banter flies between the two men for a moment and then the waiter grins at me. Andy slides his gaze my way. 'Red, white or rosé?' he murmurs.

I notice his glass is empty – and there isn't another one on the table. I look at the pages and pages of wine in the menu and back up at the bottles. 'Oh, I don't know, what do you recommend?'

Andy twiddles his empty glass. 'Do you want me to order for you?'

I nod. 'Do you and Mariana want one?' I gesture to the empty chair.

His brow furrows. 'It's just me.'

I don't have time to process what this might mean as he's giving the waiter our order. As the man leaves, I say to Andy, 'Do you know him?'

'Kind of. Only from coming in here so often.'

'Looks like I chose well.'

'How did you hear about this place?' he says curiously. 'It's mainly locals that come here.'

'Are you calling me a tourist? And there was me starting to feel right at home in Barcelona. Don't kill my dream.' I'm quipping, but I realise there's a solid truth in what I say. 'Just lucky, I guess. I went for a wander and here I am.'

Andy throws me a smile. 'A *wander*? You got brave, then?'

Our eyes lock for a moment as the past shimmers to the surface. I look away, nibble a piece of cheese. 'Didn't even need a map,' I shoot back.

Andy laughs quietly. 'Very brave.' He looks at my plate. 'You made some good choices there,' he murmurs.

I nudge the cheese closer to him. 'Help me eat it. I've got way too much. Which one's your favourite?'

The waiter returns with a bottle of Tempranillo, which Andy tells me is a type of Rioja. We enjoy the fruitiness of the red wine while nibbling the cheese, discussing the layers of flavours we can taste, and I note happiness radiating from Andy's face. Soon it's time to leave and we make our way back through the old town without really thinking, and before long, we're at the entrance to Plaça Reial. I've kind of forgotten I'm with Andy-from-work as it feels like I'm with *Andy*.

188

Senyor Cortez-Hall. The thought snaps me back to my senses.

'Did Jimmy tell you I cooked for him at the weekend?' I say, stopping. The shops are closed now and we're the only ones on the street.

'Did you?' He looks surprised.

'I offered. I really enjoyed myself.'

His face lights up again. 'It's a good feeling, right?'

'Jimmy told me his wife's ill and you're helping out.'

He flashes me a grin. 'Perhaps we should join forces?'

For the first time that evening, an uncomfortable silence falls between us. 'I don't understand,' I say eventually. 'Why are you being so secretive? When Mariana said you were on business this week, I wondered if you'd told her you were helping Jimmy out, but clearly you weren't as the kitchen was closed.'

Andy studies me for a moment and I think he's going to tell me something but instead his gaze drifts away.

I fiddle with my bag. 'I don't want to keep pretending,' I continue. 'I like Susie and Xavier. But it's hard work making sure I don't slip up and say something connected to living here before. I need to tell them before it gets out of hand.'

Still, he won't look at me.

'Why don't you want anyone to know about our past? You're so . . . exasperating.'

His eyes fall back on mine and he laughs softly. 'Exasperating?'

'Yes! Being back in the kitchen reminded me how much I'd loved working there, and I want to be able to talk about it. Does it matter that we were . . .' I struggle to say the words but press on before I lose my nerve. 'Look, I get that you're embarrassed about me, embarrassed you and I had a *thing* once . . .' A blush colours my cheeks. 'But it's not like Mariana doesn't know, so can't you just . . . get over it? *And* – I barely pause for breath – 'I'm *not* playing piggy-in-the-middle in your marriage anymore. Why can't you tell Mariana you're helping your friend in his time of need? I'm sure she'd understand.'

Andy appraises me. My pulse quickens as his eyes roam over my face, my mouth, and then he reaches out and I think he's going to stroke my cheek. Instead, he plucks something from my hair. 'Fluff,' he says lightly.

My face pinks again and he angles himself away from me, arms folded.

'I'm divorcing Mariana.' His tone is flat. A muscle flares in his jaw. 'You're not in the middle of anything. We've been separated for ages, for nearly a year, but not many people know.'

I stare at him. 'But . . . she . . . you . . .'

'She's clingy,' he says, glancing back at me. 'She's thinks I'm going to change my mind, but she knows it's over.'

Shock prickles my scalp.

He rolls back on his heels. 'She likes to keep up appearances. It's all a front. *Senyor i senyora Cortez-Hall* is the heart of the Perfecte brand.' He sighs. 'Trying to divorce my business partner has got messy and complicated – like her decision to bring you on board without telling me. She made me promise to keep our past a secret from Susie and Xavier. It's a family thing. The cousins love to tease and gossip – and more importantly she doesn't want her father to find out. She idolises him.'

My mind races to keep up, flashing over the past few weeks, thinking about what I've seen and heard: meeting Josep, Mariana's need to please him – *Andy is divorcing her?*

'She didn't have to buy Janet's business and bring me here,' I say, bewildered.

Andy shrugs. 'Riverside is thriving. She's really hooked by your food events.' He tosses me a smile. 'When Mariana catches the scent of success, nothing will stand in her way. She makes a plan and sticks to it. You can see why people knowing you and I had a past is a problem, can't you?'

My mind goes back to that day, ten years ago, when Charlie told me what she saw. A scene that tore through my life, leaving everything I trusted in tatters. Had that always been part of the plan?

Andy's backing away. 'See you tomorrow,' he says.

'Wait,' I say, catching his arm. 'Why didn't you tell me you were getting divorced?' Then immediately, I regret asking and snatch my hand back.

His eyes fix mine. 'Why would it matter to you?' It's a challenge and the fluttery feeling returns, forcing me to look away.

For a moment, we're silent again but there's something else I need to ask before he goes. 'Was your business trip to do with the divorce?'

He looks up at the narrow gap between the buildings where a slice of night sky has turned inky blue. He fiddles with the Gemini pendant. 'Yes – and no.'

'And you think you're *not* exasperating?'

He grins and looks so much like the old Andy that I can't help but smile back.

'Oh, and one other thing,' he says, before leaving. 'I've never been embarrassed of you – or of us – ever.'

Chapter 33

ANDY

Ten years ago

Kissing in the sea that day had blown my mind and held the promise of so much more. But the world had conspired against Alice and I for a while longer. Enric had come out of hospital earlier than expected and my mum asked me to move into his apartment for a few days to help with his recuperation.

Early one morning, I was rushing back to meet Alice at the cafe so we could go to La Boqueria together when I came through a small square that I'd forgotten all about. My eye caught a man beneath an orange tree unpacking farm produce from his truck. An idea began to form, but I didn't have time to linger, and with one last glance, I broke into a jog.

'Where's the fire?' said Alice as I fell through the cafe door, breathless. She'd pulled her hair into a loose ponytail and wore a sundress with narrow straps, revealing sun-kissed shoulders.

I wiped my hand across my forehead. 'I've just seen a guy setting up a stall in one of the squares and he's selling a load of fruit and vegetables. He had a ton of artichokes and I was thinking perhaps we should buy some? Do something with them today?'

Alice smiled – a full beam that made me glow inside. She tucked her arm through mine. 'Check you out, chef extraordinaire. You didn't even know what an artichoke was a month ago.' She leant towards me – close enough that I caught the scent of her hair – and she sniffed. 'No time to shower today?'

'Hey, I *ran* here so we wouldn't miss the best pickings.'

'And I appreciate it,' she said, laughing. 'So what recipe have you got in mind?'

'Me? No idea. They just looked good. You tell me – you're the expert.'

Alice laughed again. 'I can't say artichokes are my speciality. But I'm sure we'll come up with a plan.'

We.

Our day on the beach had shifted us to a new place. Being able to tell someone, tell *Alice*, that Matt had died – without downing a bottle of whisky afterwards – had loosened something in me. And Alice? Perhaps she felt more relaxed in my company because she knew how much I respected her job.

I hoped the change wasn't all in me.

We hadn't got far across the square when we spotted Mariana striding in our direction wearing a cerise pink skirt suit. 'Hello, friends,' she said, smiling. 'My *busy* friends.'

Alice returned her smile. 'I know, we've been caught up with the cafe. I'm sorry I've not made it to your class yet.'

Mariana's laugh tinkled. '*Cap problema*, life happens.' She glanced at me. 'Andrew, what is your excuse? Surely you have to eat? In fact, I was coming to find you. To invite you to lunch today, for our lesson.' She threw Alice a dazzling smile. 'Will you let him go? I know you are a strong woman in the kitchen. You need Andy. But I need him too.'

I shifted, uncomfortable, for some reason.

Alice smiled and held up her hands. 'I'm not his keeper.'

'So?' Mariana's gaze swivelled back to me. 'I collect you later?'

I glanced at my watch, my thoughts on the market in the square. 'I'm not sure,' I said, beginning to edge away. 'Sorry, but Alice and I have to be somewhere.' Mariana's smile slipped and I felt bad for coming across rude. 'Tomorrow?' I suggested, but then I remembered we had the day off – and I had plans – *big* plans. 'Actually, the day after tomorrow is better. Check with Sofia, but that should be fine.'

Mariana's eyes skimmed over us and she flicked her hair. 'Ah, I see, this is a special time. *Cita*, no?'

Heat warmed my cheeks and I caught Alice throwing me a quizzical look. 'Ah . . . yes.'

'I understand,' she said, nodding. 'Have a good time. I will see you then at 1 p.m.' She turned and tottered away.

'What was all that about?' Alice asked bemused. '*Cita?*'

I tugged my pendant. 'She thinks we're on a date,' I muttered.

'So this isn't just a regular market trip?' she said teasingly. 'An early morning date. I like it. In which case, I'd better be on my best behaviour.' And she slid her hand into mine and we headed off.

◆ ◆ ◆

Soon Alice and I were stepping out of the shadows of the street into the sunny square. A small chapel stood to our right, and a pair of benches flanked a small fountain where water poured from the mouth of an anguished angel. I pointed to the orange tree where several people were already gathered around the farmer's truck.

'Welcome to Plaça del Taronger,' I announced. 'Orange Tree Square.'

We joined the queue and before long we were being served, with Alice explaining we cooked for Cafè Vermell. I smiled. Me – cooking?

Not a chef, that would be a stretch. But yes, Alice's passion had got under my skin somehow and I couldn't wait to get back in the kitchen.

Alice selected four large artichokes. The man tried to get her to buy more, but she shook her head, explaining in broken Catalan with the help of her tatty phrasebook that the restaurant was small and we didn't need many.

I wanted to help, but the words got muddled in my head and wouldn't line up properly. Instead I said, 'How do we cook *les carxofes?*'

Alice glanced at me.

'In oven, or in pan, but the best is with grill with garlic.' The seller picked up a fennel and took a deep sniff. 'And you have this, too. You make salad with orange, onion' – he began filling Alice's basket – 'olive oil, olives.'

We paid and he beamed, revealing a gap where his front tooth had been. 'You cook, you sell, you return,' he said, adding two fat peaches to our purchases. 'Free.'

'How often are you here?' I asked.

'All days.'

As we turned to leave, a rainbow of ceramics spread out on a blanket caught my eye. We went over to take a closer look. A woman in a headscarf with a big smile looked up from where she was sat on a stool reading. I crouched down and picked up a coaster swirled with sea blues and streaks of sunset orange. 'This reminds me of our day at the beach,' I said to Alice.

She examined the piece carefully. 'It's lovely. The sea was so warm, wasn't it?'

Our eyes lingered for a moment but I caught a flicker of wariness that told me she didn't fully trust me yet. Did she want me to be the one to move things along? Or should I let her lead the way?

But Ibiza called. I was days from leaving – and she knew it.

I put the coaster back and thanked the woman.

We moved away and as we made our way to the cafe, Alice asked, 'How's Enric today?'

'Recovering well. I'm moving back in tonight.'

For some reason, my announcement felt loaded with meaning. Alice's gaze skittered over mine then she broke the tension with a laugh. 'Do you want me to say I've missed you?' she said, punching me lightly on the arm. 'Because I won't. You'll be gone by the weekend with no memory of who I am after a few nights out.'

I looped my fingers through hers. 'I won't ever forget you, Alice Taylor.'

We walked on in silence while I tried to work out what she was thinking. I could stay on at Cafè Vermell for a while, I had no fixed agenda, but I didn't want to suffocate whatever this was between us before it had even begun. We worked together, we lived together, we weren't sleeping together – yet. Did she want that? I knew I did.

Alice pulled the peaches out of the basket and handed me one. 'These look amazing, don't they?' she said.

She took a large bite. Juice dribbled down her chin and on to her dress. Of course, she had her eyes closed, concentrating on the taste and texture, and I watched, mesmerised, as pleasure fanned out across her face.

'Your dress,' I said, weakly – perhaps she didn't care.

'This is the most gorgeous thing I've ever eaten,' she murmured, wiping her mouth with the back of her hand.

You are the most gorgeous woman I've ever met.

'Go on, try yours.'

I bit into my peach, savouring the soft, pulpy sweetness and she watched, eyes dancing. I wondered if she was thinking what I was thinking. My gaze dropped to her lips, shiny with juice, and her tongue darted out to lick them clean. She smiled and reached up to wipe the residue from my mouth.

I took a chance, capturing her hand, kissing her fingers, sucking the juice from each one, then moving on to her lips where it no longer mattered that our mouths were sweet and sticky, because Alice was kissing me, I was kissing her, and I didn't want it to stop.

Eventually, she pulled away. 'Date over,' she whispered shakily. 'We need to get back.'

I didn't know how I was going to make it through the rest of the day.

Chapter 34

ANDY

Ten years ago

As the morning turned to afternoon, I made secret plans for our day off, but I needed to find a way of asking Alice out without ruining the surprise. After work, I caught her before she disappeared into her room and invited her to have a beer on my balcony later.

I held my breath while I waited for her to answer.

She beamed. 'Yes, I'd like that.'

Once she closed the door, I fist-bumped the air and wasted no time showering and changing. I grabbed a couple of beers from the fridge and called out to her as I went back to my room. 'I'm ready when you are.'

Stupid. The last thing I wanted was her to think I was luring her in for sex.

Alice appeared at my door holding beers and with wet hair that left dark patches on her sundress. She came inside and I watched her gaze travel up to the antique chandelier and drop back to the four-poster bed. I'd left my damp towel on the sheets, clean but still tangled from this morning, and on the chair clothes spilled out of the holdall I'd taken to Uncle Enric's.

'Sorry about the mess,' I said sheepishly.

Alice smiled. 'You should see Charlie's side of the room.' She handed me a bottle.

'Looks like we're having a party,' I exclaimed, gesturing to the two beers I'd put down on my bedside table. Her eyes combed over the bed again and landed back on mine. 'Sorry, I didn't mean—' I muttered and sloped outside.

We sat down at the bistro table and I rolled the cool bottle over my warm face. I wrestled over how I was going to ask Alice to come out with me tomorrow afternoon – *on a date* – but before I had a chance to say anything, her phone began blasting out the gospel choir. She sighed and stared at the screen for a moment before saying hello.

I stood up and went over to the railings. I wanted to ask, *Is this a holiday fling? Something more?* I needed to know. I couldn't go to Ibiza without finding out.

Down below, an older couple emerged from a door that led up to apartments overlooking the plaza. They had a puppy with them. The man tucked the woman's arm firmly in his and they strode out, laughing as their tiny dog danced around on its lead and let out high, excited barks.

'I set up a direct debit – why did you cancel it?' Alice was saying behind me. Her voice had taken on the same even tone as earlier when my mum had been flapping about some missing ingredients.

'They'd have sent you a reminder,' she continued. 'You should have opened the letter . . . The best thing to do is call tomorrow morning and ask if you can pay over the phone.'

It felt intrusive to be listening in so I turned and gestured to Alice that I was going inside.

She nodded and rolled her eyes.

I sat on the edge of my bed and took another swig of beer, wishing she'd hurry up as I wanted to say what I needed to say before I bottled it.

Alice appeared and I jumped up. 'Sorry about that,' she said.

'No problem. What's going on?'

She released a breath that sounded like a hiss. 'My mum is so incapable! Of *anything*,' she exploded, stomping around the room and startling me. 'I thought going away would mean she'd finally sort herself out, but she keeps finding ways to . . .' She stopped and covered her face with her hand. 'Never mind, it's boring.'

I pulled her into a hug. 'Not boring,' I said. 'It's good to get things out in the open sometimes.' I bent my head and grazed my lips over hers.

To my surprise, Alice reached up and pushed her fingers roughly through my hair, crushing me to her and kissing me hard. Thrilled, I pressed myself against her body, curling my hands around her bum, feeling her breasts soft against my chest. We fell into a crazed kissing frenzy, touching and stroking each other for what seemed like an eternity, and dizzy with wanting her, I almost tipped her back on to my bed . . .

No.

I dragged myself back to reality and pulled away, sucking in short, sharp breaths. Alice stared back at me, dazed, and I grabbed both her hands. I wanted her to know I *really* wanted this, I really did, but after what she'd been through with her cheating boyfriend, she needed to be the one to take the lead, not me. 'Hey,' I said softly.

She threw me an odd smile and tugged her hands free, brushing her hair flat and straightening her dress. 'It's okay,' she said in a strained voice, backing away. 'I understand. It's not a good idea, what with you leaving so soon.'

Before I had a chance to reply, she'd darted from the room, leaving me staring at the closing door.

What the hell? I threw myself on to the bed and stared up at the chandelier. I thumped the mattress. Had I read the signals right? I felt like I'd done something wrong.

My face crumpled as I felt a sharp stab of longing for my brother. He'd know what to do. But I'd *never ever* know what he might say.

My thoughts spiralled back to that night. After Matt had said he'd think about DJ-ing at my mate's party, I'd pushed into that crack of hope and kept asking.

And asking.

Eventually, I'd worn him down.

The evening had rolled around. Jimmy and I – the tallest in our group – swaggered into the newsagent's near the party, pretending to be eighteen, to buy vodka, rum and beers for us and the huddle waiting outside. We heard the music thumping before we reached the house. Delighted, we pushed ourselves through the throng of kids mashed together in the hallway and into the living room where Matt was at the decks.

I kept my face passive but pride and elation swirled my insides. Then the beats ramped up, the room exploded with dancing bodies and I grinned at Jimmy, tempted to fist-pump the air and shout, *That's my brother!* But I didn't. I stood to the side, acting cool, watching Matt listening to the music through his headphones, nodding to the beats, fiddling with the decks, until he looked up and saw us.

I grinned when he pointed his finger in our direction and I glanced around to see if my mates had noticed. Some of the kids looked over, eyes already fuzzy with booze, and then I saw her, a gorgeous brunette, pushing her hands through her hair, swinging her hips, a smile playing on her mouth, brave enough to dance alone.

Now, my chest ached. I *missed* my brother.

Chapter 35

ALICE

Now

On the weekend, I'm up early and sitting on the balcony with a coffee and a pastry I've been experimenting with. For a first attempt, it isn't bad. It's edible, at least. I'll take the rest down to Jimmy shortly.

Below, the square is beginning to wake. Waiters unstack chairs and throw tablecloths over tables, and I spot Andy emerge through one of the archways. He calls out greetings in a rattle of Catalan to the workers as he passes and laughter bounces between them. I can't help but smile. I'm beginning to realise the sparkle of the old Andy is still in him after all.

And he's divorcing Mariana.

My heart trips over. How come I didn't work it out? I'd noticed the tension between them now and then, but I'd been too busy focusing on their touch, how they looked at one another. I'd assumed Andy's stiff response was his dislike for public displays of affection. His need to maintain a professional stance. But as I think back, I see Mariana had been the instigator, not Andy.

Married, separated or divorced – as Andy pointed out, why does it matter to me?

It's all a front.

I ignore the flutter in my stomach. I don't want to think about it, and I shake any further thoughts aside by busying myself with getting ready. Soon I come down to the bar where Andy's chatting to Jimmy, but they fall silent as I approach.

'If you're talking about me, I'm not listening,' I say, wafting my plate of pastries close enough for the scent to work its magic.

Jimmy laughs. 'You think you matter that much to me, darling? I'm a married man.'

I swat him. 'Don't be mean, especially as I've brought you these.' I offer the plate and he grabs one and takes a generous bite. Andy does the same. 'They're not perfect, but not bad for a first try,' I add.

'You made them?' says Jimmy. 'These are *good*. We need coffee.'

'Not for me, I've had one. I'm off to La Boqueria. I've got some recipes to try out.'

'See?' Jimmy says to Andy with a satisfied smile. 'Told you.'

I place my hands on my hips and eyeball them both, causing a lazy smile to build on Andy's face. 'I *knew* you were talking about me,' I say.

'Just ask her,' Jimmy says. 'She's not going to say no.'

Andy drums his fingers on the bar. 'Do you want to help me in the kitchen today?' His voice is light and silly, reminding me again of the old Andy and not the rigid man I've been working with these last few weeks.

'*Help* you?' I can't help but laugh.

'Told you she wasn't interested,' he says to Jimmy.

'Did I say that?' I protest. 'I was just amused by your choice of words. Didn't *you* used to help *me*?'

'Uh-oh,' says Jimmy, shaking his head. 'Don't get all competitive on me. Just get your arses in the kitchen and make some decent food I can serve customers. Teamwork, you know?'

Andy and I lock eyes. I swear a current of excitement darts between us as the past springs back to life. I can see him standing at the hob, the flash of the flame as it licks the pan, the sizzle of garlic hitting butter, its mouth-watering scent mingling with the spice of chorizo, the heat of chilli.

'Come to the market with me?' I say.

Before long we're crossing the plaza and heading towards La Boqueria. 'What makes you think I wouldn't want to cook with you?' I say curiously.

'Yesterday you looked horrified when I suggested the idea.'

'Did I?' I let out a surprised laugh. *Uncomfortable, perhaps? Flattered? Yes. Nervous? Definitely.* 'Just a bit taken aback. After all, I thought this was your big secret. What's Mariana going to say when she finds out we're both working at Café Vermell?'

Andy's silent as we cross over La Rambla. Tourist stalls line the paved pedestrianised area, which runs down the middle of the wide boulevard, and they're beginning to open up. They're crammed with postcards and football tops, Catalan and Spanish flags, and all the other overpriced gifts tourists seem to fall for. Mum would love it. I must remember to buy her something before I go home. Perhaps another magnet for the fridge.

At the entrance to La Boqueria, Andy stops. 'Mariana doesn't have to know if nobody says anything,' he says meaningfully. 'I want to keep this one thing to myself. I don't want her interfering or sabotaging something I enjoy doing.'

His honesty startles me. 'Sounds like you've had a rough time with her,' I say.

He rolls back on his heels and looks up at the sky. 'You don't know the half of it,' he mutters. Then he shakes his head as if to shake the cloud away. 'Enough of that. I've got an idea. Do you remember the guy who used to sell farm produce from the back of his truck?'

He searches my face for recognition. I must be doing a good job of looking blank when in truth the memories feel fresh and more painful than I expect. 'At Plaça del Taronger? The square with the orange tree?' he adds. 'There's a big market on Saturdays. We should go there instead.'

Neither of us have mentioned the coaster that sits on his desk in plain view. Perhaps he thinks I haven't noticed. I wonder if he's remembering the artisan sat under the orange tree, her work spread out on a blanket – then, later, how I went back alone to buy the coaster for him. To show him that day on the beach meant something to me too.

I nod and Andy breaks into a warm smile that tightens my chest. 'I remember,' I squeak.

And it seems that's all I need to say.

I follow Andy through the winding streets towards the market. I thought I might have forgotten the way, but it seems at every corner something snags a memory and reminds me to take the next left or right. We fall into an easy conversation on the safe subject of Barcelona restaurants. Andy enthuses about places I should visit, which only the locals know about. He tells me more about La Cova, set in a cavernous cellar beneath the streets, which has won awards for its cured meats.

As we come into the square, it's apparent a lot has changed since I was last here. Market stalls with blue-and-white striped awnings circle the orange tree and a bustling crowd nudge one another to get closer to the wares and haggle with sellers.

Andy leads the way and moves easily through the throng, throwing banter to stallholders he has clearly known for a while. I'm envious of his language skills and vow to put more time into my Catalan language learning app. Mariana had laughed when I enquired about lessons, telling me it was unnecessary for a job in London. I didn't dare ask about an employee discount and there's no way I can afford their polished prices.

Andy and I walk around, selecting our favourite cheeses: a wedge of manchego, the nutty mahon and a smoked one from the north, which he says tastes amazing. Sellers hand-slice meat and scoop juicy olives from large vats of brine. Idly, I wonder if the artisan is still here and, as we move on from the produce towards stalls that sell art, jewellery and clothes, I'm delighted when I catch sight of a colourful display of ceramics. I draw nearer to take a closer look.

'Alice, this way!' Andy calls, pointing back to where we've just come. 'There's a stall that does amazing churros and they sell out quick.'

'You go, I'll catch up.' He frowns as I turn away and when I approach the stall, there's something familiar – *recently* familiar – about the style of the vases and bowls on display that confuses me. I look up.

Susie's grinning at me.

I stare, dumbfounded. She's wearing an orange striped scarf to tie back her hair – and something clicks into place.

'Remember me?' she says, roaring with laughter.

She's the artisan from a decade ago? I recall her wearing a headscarf and now I come to think about it, her Scottish accent. 'You look different . . .' I splutter, working hard to pretend this has nothing to do with my first visit all those years ago and everything to do with my surprise at seeing her here now instead of at work. 'I didn't know you had a stall,' I say lamely. 'You never said.'

'Oh, you know, the boss might not like me having two jobs so I don't shout about it.' She winks at Andy, who's appeared by my side. 'And I don't mean you.'

'Mariana isn't the boss,' he mutters. 'It's a joint business.'

Susie's still grinning. 'Just so you know, your secret is safe with me,' she says.

I glance at Andy but he's picked up a turquoise vase and turns it over in his hand.

'Come on! It's *fine*, all fine,' she insists, tapping her nose.

My head scrambles as I try to work out what she means. Is she talking about Andy and I being here together? Or is this something to do with Cafè Vermell? Or does she remember me buying the coaster? I stay quiet. It's up to Andy to ask.

Susie laughs. 'I'm not blind! I spotted Andy's coaster on his desk years ago when I first started working at Perfecte and he told me it was a gift from his ex.'

I feel myself start to blush.

'Mariana overheard and she was the one that brought up your name,' she says. 'Don't you remember, Andy? Alice's name flew out of her mouth like a dragon breathing fire!'

This is excruciating. I can't look at him.

'To be honest, I don't remember you coming to the stall, but your name got lodged in here.' She taps her temple. 'Then when you turned up for the job and things were a bit awkward between the three of you, I began to wonder if you were *that* Alice. Then at ours, at dinner, Xavier and I were pretty certain.'

Andy's still silent and I'm beginning to get annoyed. Is he really going to keep up the pretence? I'm about to blurt it all out when he finally opens his mouth.

'What do you mean?' he says, glancing at me. 'What happened at dinner?'

Susie laughs again. 'Mariana's eyes followed Alice around all evening. Honestly, she's so possessive.'

Then, just like that, the pressure of holding everything together finally dissolves into relief and I collapse into giggles. Even Andy breaks into a small smile.

'So what brings you two here today? Planning a romantic meal?' she says slyly, pointing at our bags.

Susie's words stab the light-hearted bubble. Andy turns ashen and I suddenly realise she doesn't know about the divorce, although this seems incredible – and I see what she sees.

Andy and I out together, like a couple *having an affair*.

I feel sick. I'm not that kind of woman and I don't want Susie to jump to conclusions. I glance at Andy who still hasn't opened his mouth and if he doesn't soon, I will. I'll say she's got this wrong, he's not married anymore and we're helping Jimmy out by cooking at Cafè Vermell. I elbow him and the jolt brings him back to his senses.

'You should know, Mariana and I are divorcing,' he finally says. 'We've been separated for a while.'

'Uh-huh.' Susie nods. 'It wasn't hard to guess. I think it's the worst-kept secret in the family.'

Surprise floods colour back into his face. 'Really?'

'Don't worry, I'm not going to confirm the rumours. I know what the oldies are like.' She shudders.

Andy relaxes, and he turns to me and smiles. He looks happier and lighter than I've seen him since I arrived and now the secrets are out in the open, I should be, too.

But I don't. His steady gaze stirs up old feelings – is cooking together today such a good idea after all?

Chapter 36

ALICE

Now

Andy's animated as we walk back to the cafe while I'm still absorbing that Susie's figured things out already. I'd been surprised when he launched into telling her how we met and that we used to work together at Cafè Vermell. He wasted no time explaining what we were doing today, showing her the produce and talking about the meals he'd planned. She was delighted and swore to say nothing to Mariana.

We come into the kitchen and dump the bags on the work bench. A wave of memories bring back the awkward feelings again, but Andy doesn't notice. He darts around, putting things away and getting things out. I hold back, amused by his enthusiasm and happy to let him take the lead because this time it feels like *his* kitchen, not mine. As he shows me how he wants the ingredients prepared, we talk a little, mostly about what we're doing and the ideas he has for next time.

Next time?

'This reminds me of cooking with my grandma,' I say as he gets me to tenderise the calamari in lemon juice and expresses the importance of using iced water to make tempura batter.

'You calling me old and cranky? Or wise and controlling?' he shoots back.

I smile. 'You're a good teacher,' I say, but so he should be. 'Do you remember? My grandma taught me how to cook. I learnt everything from her. Yes, she *was* controlling and wise, and old and cranky, but I still enjoyed her company.'

'So you're enjoying my company?' Andy's eyes dance with glee.

I laugh as I grab a tomato and a knife. 'I mean, it's been a long time since I've been around someone with so much passion.'

'Oh, yes?' He raises his eyebrow mischievously.

Old Andy.

This time I'm flustered because I can't think of a quick enough retort.

He must think he's gone too far. 'Sorry,' he says, his face becoming serious. 'Do you miss her?'

'Oh.' I put down the knife. 'It was a long time ago.'

He appraises me as if he's waiting for me to say something more. I don't want him to ask again why I didn't take up the restaurant apprenticeship, why I became a TESOL teacher instead. I don't want to admit: *I had no choice.*

Andy nods and moves away to the fridge. My thoughts jump to his own grief. My loss was in no way measurable to his. 'So . . .' I struggle to find the words to ask him how he's coping. I think back to what he told me all those years ago, how I'd left him soon after, my promise to return, but when . . . and then . . .

Pain and guilt choke my throat.

I can't ask. I *won't* ask.

Because it means I'll have to tell him what happened.

A terrifying thud shudders in my head, a flash of confusion, and I blink fast to force the memories away. I've become an expert at this over the years. Pushing them down deep enough so that they can almost be forgotten – almost.

'What happened to your mum?' Andy asks curiously. 'I mean, you said she needs sticks, that her mobility isn't good?'

My heart leaps in panic. It's like he can read my mind. I spin away and stand by the fan to let the cool air rush over my face. 'Yes.' What more can I say?

'So?'

His insistence prickles. What's it got to do with him?

Everything.

My mind scrabbles for a convincing answer. 'She had an accident. She broke her hip,' I say quickly. It's the truth – some of it. I fly back to the work bench and push a smile on to my face. Andy's staring at me, but I carry on slicing the tomatoes. 'I was surprised you told Susie that we're cooking for Jimmy,' I say, flipping the conversation.

Andy shrugs and takes the bowl of batter to the hob. 'She understands the workings of Mariana's family better than I thought,' he says eventually.

'Meaning?' I slide the tomatoes on to a plate.

Andy sighs. 'Neither of them gossiped about our separation even though they'd guessed. I can trust they won't say anything and stir up trouble with Mariana, and I knew they'd be pleased for me. Like you said, it's a good feeling to share what we love with people who care.'

I'm glad he's got his back to me because my cheeks go warm. Am I included in his joy?

'I can't believe her family don't know you're divorcing,' I carry on.

211

Andy drops the battered calamari into the pan and the oil spits. 'Marriage is for life in their eyes, especially for the older generation.' Flames leap up from the hob and he slams the frying pan around to crisp them. 'It's all about appearances for Mariana, remember? At Perfecte and in her personal life.'

I take a handful of rocket, a snip of fresh herbs, and tuck them in around the tomatoes with wafer-thin slices of manchego and a scattering of black olives.

'Why do you go along with it? I mean, why can't you demand she tells them?'

Andy lifts the calamari out. 'You make me sound like a pushover.'

I snort. 'That's not what I mean.'

'You don't understand, you don't know Mariana like I do. The best way to get what I want is to keep her on my side.'

Mum. I'm surprised when I realise I *do* understand what he's saying, but before I can tell him, he's turned away again.

'Can you take that to table four?' he says over his shoulder.

As I carry the plates outside, I wonder what else he wants from Mariana.

By mid-afternoon, there's a queue standing in the sunshine waiting for a table, and I zip in and out, serving meals as quickly as I can. In the pause between customers finishing and new ones sitting down, I go over to the fan to cool my sticky face – grateful for the industrial-sized thing that does a far better job than the one Enric had years before.

Andy makes the *croquetes de pernil*, ready for me to dip into egg and coat in breadcrumbs so he can fry them. He also asks me to cut potatoes into small cubes for his *patatas bravas*.

I keep the skin on. 'You're right, they do taste better,' I say, and we both smile at the memory.

Our afternoon is rushed and exhilarating and I don't hear my phone ring from where it's tucked in my bag, nor the second or third time. It's not until Andy and I are washing up later that the sound of the gospel choir bursting into song finally registers.

My hands are in soapy water and I glance at the clock. It's nearly 6 p.m. *Shit.*

Andy retrieves my phone and puts it on speaker.

'Sorry, sorry, I didn't realise the time,' I gabble.

Andy gives me a sideways glance.

'Where have you been? It's nearly teatime and you *said* we'd talk at 3.15 p.m. every day. My heart's been pounding all afternoon. I thought I was going to have a heart attack. I could barely swallow my biscuits. I thought something awful had happened to you.'

Guilt wrenches my stomach. 'I've been busy cooking at the cafe. Time ran away with me. Remember I said the other day I was helping a friend?'

'I don't understand! What's happened to the teaching job?'

'I'm still at Perfecte. It's just something I'm doing on my day off.'

Mum sounds shaky. 'We talked about this. I told you not to worry about money. You don't need to do two jobs. You'll get exhausted, you'll get ill and then you'll be no good to me or anyone.'

I glance at Andy but he's squatted down to tidy up the mess of trays and bowls on the bottom shelf of the work bench.

'It's not about money. I'm helping because I want to.'

'Who's your friend?' Mum's voice becomes suspicious. 'Is it a man?'

Andy snickers quietly.

'A boyfriend?'

Heat creeps into my cheeks. 'There's nothing for you to worry about.'

'That's such a relief,' she gasps. 'I know I said you needed to get a boyfriend, but I didn't mean all the way over there. You'll never come home and I can't be having that.'

Andy snorts and a tray clatters on to the floor.

I remember I'm still on speakerphone and pull my hands out of the water and wipe them with a tea towel. I switch the call to my ear. I don't need Andy to hear about my private life. *What private life?*

'How is it going selling your things on eBay?' I say.

Mum perks up. 'I'm doing ever so well. I've sold nearly everything. It really helped that it was all brand new and still in its packaging. I'm using the money to stock up on perfume.'

My stomach lurches. 'How much stock?' My thoughts fall back to the red credit card bill. 'Where's it from?'

'Stop worrying!' she snaps. 'I'm not a moron.'

'Sorry,' I murmur. 'What does Charlie think?'

'I wouldn't know. She's hardly here now she's got engaged.'

I should be there for her, but I'm here, having *fun* at Café Vermell.

With Andy.

After we say goodbye, I wipe down the surfaces, take off my apron and place it on the door hook.

'Your mum's missing you, then?' says Andy eventually. He's leaning back on the work bench, arms folded, and my eyes graze over his biceps.

'Yes.'

But is she?

'Do you talk to her at the same time every day?' He looks incredulous.

214

I nod, knowing it sounds like a crazy thing to do, but my responsibility to Mum, to Charlie, feels like something knitted into my DNA. No one will ever fully comprehend what it means to me.

'That's exhausting.'

'It's easier to keep Mum on my side,' I say, tilting my chin and repeating his words back to him.

A faint smile traces his face.

'I can't help it, I worry,' I say. 'Our relationship has always been complicated. I don't expect people to understand.'

Andy's eyes stay glued on me for a few more moments. Then he pushes himself away from the bench and heads towards the door. 'Especially when you've never bothered trying to explain,' he mutters.

And I find myself alone, staring, as the door swings shut behind him.

Chapter 37

Alice

Now

By a small miracle, Mariana is in meetings most afternoons the following week and Andy encourages me to skive off and go with him to Cafè Vermell. I don't need asking twice.

We spend the mornings discussing recipe ideas in low voices, pushing each other to be more creative: a twist of chilli, the tang of lemon, saltiness enlivened with honey. Andy tells me about the places he knows hidden in the depths of the old town, where throughout the week we pick up freshly caught sardines, the plumpest olives I've ever seen, and visit a shop that only sells cured meats. Along with our work commitments, it's chaotic, energising – and a little risky. By the afternoons, we're buzzing to get started.

Still, I worry Mariana's going to find out. Working at Cafè Vermell is like a pleasant dream. I'll be waking up soon. I'll be heading home. Back to Mum. Back to Janet. Back to help Mariana put her plan in place to open Perfecte London.

Towards the end of the week, I'm tapping my pen on my note-pad and staring out at the Sagrada Família towers, trying to decide what to do with the baby green peppers I'd bought that morning. The weeks are rushing by. Charlie and her friends will be here next weekend for her hen do. What with work and the cafe I've barely had a moment to come up with a plan.

Susie flies through the door and breaks my train of thought. 'Guess what?' she says breathlessly. 'Xavier's got a table for two at La Cova tonight. Someone cancelled and his name's at the top of the waiting list!'

Andy grins. 'You're joking? That's brilliant!' He pulls a sad face. 'But I can't pretend I'm not supremely jealous.'

Susie laughs. 'Well, that's good to hear because the table is yours.'

His face flashes surprise. 'Surely you've got nothing more important to do tonight than go to the best restaurant in the *entire* city?'

She shakes her head. 'I know, it's tragic, but we can't.' She grins. 'So?'

'You sure you don't want to change your plans?' he presses.

Susie sighs. 'Can't you just say thank you? Look . . . we just can't. Tonight is a mega clash with something important. It's something we've both been waiting ages to do.'

Andy opens his mouth but she holds up her hand. 'Don't ask! I'll tell you everything once I can. So . . . that table for two is yours if you want it.'

'Perhaps I'll be able to sneak out a doggy bag,' he suggests.

'Can't see that happening – there are never any leftovers when you're around.' Susie laughs again. 'Oh, Alice, you're going to love La Cova. I want you to report back and tell us everything you ate in teeny tiny detail – and take photos!'

'Me?' I say, glancing at Andy. 'Oh no, he'll take Jimmy. One of us needs to be at the cafe to cook.'

Susie glances at Andy. 'Well . . . I'll leave you both to sort it out.'

After she's gone, Andy turns to me, face alight. 'Jimmy won't be able to come because he'll need to help Juliana with the kids,' he says quickly. 'He's really grateful for our time. He'll totally understand why we can't be there tonight.'

I don't know what to say.

His smile falters. 'You don't want to come?'

While I try to work out if he's asking me, a passionate foodie, to join him in an amazing culinary experience, or if he's asking me out, something shifts between us. A flicker of *what if* zips through my body, culminating in a spike of desire.

Andy clears his throat. 'I mean, *will* you come with me? I'd like you to.'

I swallow and nod.

Back at my apartment later, I put on a dress in a tropical print I'd bought on impulse at a market after work one evening. I'm about to begin straightening my hair but when I stand in front of the mirror, I see the warmth of the evening has started to dry it into loose waves. I like the look and decide to leave it.

I'm ready a little early, so I go out to my balcony with a glass of wine to quell the nerves that jump around my insides. The sun's dropping away behind the tall buildings, casting parts of the square in shadow and leaving a balmy warmth behind. I lean on the railings and soak up the activity. An elderly couple shuffle arm in arm towards a door to one of the apartment buildings, a tiny dog on a lead prancing ahead of them. By the fountain, a busker begins to strum his guitar. His voice is soft and lilting and draws a passing couple closer, who slide their arms around one another as they listen.

It's the perfect evening for romance.

Is that what my night with Andy is about?

Soon, it's time to leave and as I cross the cafe terrace, Jimmy lets out a sharp wolf whistle, causing customers to turn and smile. 'Have a great time!' he calls. 'Don't do anything I wouldn't do!'

I cringe – and feel pleased all at the same time.

Jimmy thinks it's a date, so it must be.

◆ ◆ ◆

La Cova is on a street off a street within the maze of the old town and not far from my apartment. I make my way down the dimly lit staircase in flat gold leather sandals, wondering if Andy prefers the heels Mariana wears.

It's all a front.

It's like the words have uncorked all the feelings I've been trying to ignore, and now, here I am, on a date-not-date with Andy, about to eat fabulous food with him.

I take a deep breath and walk into the small, dark cellar room, where the tables are lit by candlelight and throw shadows up slick, stony black walls. I shiver a little in the cool temperatures, wishing I'd remembered to bring a jacket.

Andy rises from one of the tables in the far corner to make himself known. He's smiling and I'm suddenly warm all over.

'Hey,' he says, leaning down to kiss me on both cheeks. It's different from his brisk work greeting. He takes his time, lips connecting with my skin, his fresh, outdoorsy scent tingling my senses and jump-starting the flicker I'd felt earlier.

Despite the intimacy of the room, the restaurant hums with chatter and laughter, and chilled music thrums in the background. I'm not used to eating in places like this and I'm relieved to see the waiters wear jeans.

Andy's upbeat and excitable as we lean close to the candles to read what's on offer, and my tension melts away. After a brief pause, we look up and at the same time say, 'Shall we get the tasting menu?'

We laugh, but then his gaze lingers, and I slide my eyes away and down to the wine list. 'White or red? Or rosé?' For the first time in a long time, I'm not worrying about money. What with Jimmy's kindness to let me have the apartment rent-free, and my round-the-clock work hours, I've not had time to spend very much.

'We could pair the food with the wine?' Andy suggests.

I fade out for a moment, thinking about Charlie at the pub jabbering as she pours me my vodka and cranberry juice and throws in a bag of salt and vinegar crisps for free. Now, I'm sitting in Barcelona's most sought-after restaurant, discussing tasting menus and wine pairing.

With Andy.

'What's funny?' He looks bemused and I realise I'm chuckling and he's waiting for an answer.

I shake away my thoughts. 'Eating in a place like this isn't my usual style. Wine pairing sounds good.'

He laughs. 'This is a rare occasion for me, too.' He looks at me curiously. 'Where would you usually go out and eat?'

'I don't really. There's Mum to think about, I'm careful with my money . . .' I trail off. I don't want him to think I'm a lost cause and I can feel the conversation tipping into territory I'd rather not think about. I want to concentrate on the moment. On now. Before I'm thrust back to reality at home.

Before long, our first course arrives: wafer-thin slices of beef carpaccio tenderised in lime juice, which melt on my tongue. We talk a little about Perfecte. Andy tells me how Mariana's doting father helped her get started with her first language school and funded the expansion to their location now. Over the years, she's taken high risks with great success.

'She's ambitious,' he says. 'Ruthless sometimes, but her drive has got us where we are and I'm thankful for that.'

He looks at me thoughtfully but I fiddle with my cutlery. His admiration for Mariana reminds me how important success had been to him when we first met. Then I think he's going to say something else, but the waiter arrives with our next course. Potato foam infused with truffles and topped with a coil of delicate ibérico ham fashioned into a flower. I remember this is the place that has won awards for its cured meats.

'Impressive,' I say. 'Looks too beautiful to eat.'

'Untouched beauty is wasted,' he says, inspecting the flower from all angles. 'If you don't delve into its heart, you might not find its exquisite centre.'

Although he's talking about the food, his words skitter over my skin and I shiver. Carefully, he uncoils the petals and out pops a plump green olive.

We both laugh.

Throughout the meal, Andy and I ooh and ahh over the flavours, and I snatch glances at him when he isn't looking. I take in the casual black polo shirt that emphasises his shoulders and clings to his biceps, his brother's Gemini pendant at his throat.

The sight of it sets off flutters of nerves and I speak quickly before I talk myself out of what needs to be said. 'The night you told me what happened to Matt,' I blurt. 'It was a huge thing. You were brave enough to tell me and I'm sorry I left you so quickly.'

Andy looks at me in surprise.

I look down into the candle flame. 'I thought about how hard it must have been to say how you felt, and I didn't acknowledge your feelings . . .' The words become wedged.

I don't tell him I had always planned to come back.

But he'd broken my heart.

A slow smile creeps into his face. 'I think you acknowledged how I felt that night, in a very meaningful and very *unforgettable* way.'

My face burns at the memory and I clasp my hands so he can't see them shaking. His eyes don't leave mine and he slides his open palm across the table. Slowly, I reach out, our fingers touch and then he curls mine tightly into his.

'I was young and self-centred, so of course I wanted you to stay. One night was never going to be enough.' He flashes me a smile and then his face sobers. 'But I knew I had to wait.'

But you didn't wait.

Just at that moment, the waiter strolls over with our next course – miniature portions of paella decorated with slivers of crispy chorizo. We release hands and carry on eating, our conversation turning back to the food, and as further courses arrive, and we drink more wine, the tension drains away. Soon, we're talking about Charlie's hen do the following weekend and my lack of preparation. We brainstorm ideas and by the end of the evening, I have everything planned.

'Thanks, Andy,' I say as we climb the stairs to leave, sated with food and buzzing from the wine. 'You saved me. Charlie would have gone ballistic if I hadn't sorted anything out.'

Outside, the humidity cloaks me like a warm, welcome balm and suddenly I feel awkward about how to say goodbye. 'Which direction are you heading?'

'Home is this way,' he replies.

Home?

It's a front.

An unwelcome thought pops into my head. Is he still sharing a bed with Mariana?

'I'll walk you back,' he says.

'You don't need to,' I reply, sounding more cheerful than I feel. 'I'll get a taxi.'

He steps towards me and I assume he's going to peck my cheeks to say goodbye the Spanish way. Instead, sadness traces his eyes and he touches my face. I inhale sharply and his gaze lingers. Then he grazes his mouth over mine, sending a ripple of desire through me and I reach up and wrap my arms around his neck. Our kisses deepen, and at the touch of his tongue, I press myself against him, desperate to feel the heat of his body through the thin fabric of my dress.

'*Aneu a un hotel!*' someone yells as they roar past on a moped.

Andy jumps away and I snap back to reality, embarrassed that we've been caught snogging in the street like teenagers.

We eye each other warily. 'I have to go,' I say, rubbing the shiver on my arms that has nothing to do with being cold.

Andy stuffs his hands in his pockets and nods. And, before I can say anything else, he's spun around and walked away.

Chapter 38

ANDY

Ten years ago

'Would you like to go to Park Güell with me today?' Alice asked as she came into the apartment kitchen the following morning. My tea caught in my throat, making me cough and she thumped me on the back. 'I didn't realise my suggestion would cause such a stir,' she said drily, handing me a glass of water. 'I was only thinking you might be at a loose end.'

After the way she'd flown from my room last night I hadn't got a chance to ask her out.

Now *she* was asking *me*.

The trouble was my morning plans didn't include her. They *couldn't* include her. But I needed to tread carefully so I didn't screw this up.

Alice flushed at my silence and flicked her hand. 'No worries, it was just a thought. Have you got a lesson with Mariana?'

Her voice sounded light but she fastened her gaze on mine. I wanted to be honest, but I'd kill the surprise. Perhaps I should just tell her what I was doing? But I was already wondering if my idea was a bad one. What if it all went wrong?

I shook my head. But I'd been silent for too long and Alice's eyes narrowed as if she didn't believe me. She swept out of the room. 'Another time,' she called.

I jumped up and followed. 'I'd like to come, I really would. It's just I've got to go over to Enric's this morning and . . .' I grappled to remember how I was going to ask her last night but the words had disappeared.

Alice paused at her bedroom door, her back to me.

'Later? Dinner?' I blurted. I did a quick mental calculation. 'I'll meet you outside Park Güell, say, four o'clock?'

'There's no need,' she replied, her hand on the handle. 'I'm quite happy to go on my own.'

The golden opportunity was slipping away. I reached out to touch her shoulder, but I changed my mind and pulled away. Alice turned and my insides caught when I saw the wariness in her eyes.

'Meet me at four?' I repeated. 'Please?'

A smile twitched her mouth. 'Are you begging me, Andy?' she said softly.

'Honestly, it'll be worth the wait.' I cringed. I was making a big deal about something that might be a total flop.

Alice's gaze rolled over me. 'I suppose you know the park better than me. See you then.'

Soon I was throwing myself down the stairs and into the kitchen where my mum was at the stove. 'I need to have the paella ready earlier,' I jabbered. 'I've told Alice I'm going to meet her outside Park Güell at four.'

My mum's face lit up. '*Cap problema, fill*, we have time. Tell Enric you can't stay long, you're needed here.'

I flew over to my uncle's and helped with some chores, and in return he handed me a bag of meat from his cousin's farm in Valencia. Before long, I was back at Cafè Vermell. 'So let's begin,' said my mum. 'I have started the *brou*.' She pointed to a pan of chicken bones simmering on the hob. 'The broth and the *sofregit* are the magic that need our nurture to draw together the flavours.'

She pulled rabbit and chicken from the bag and laid them on a chopping board. I was relieved to see Enric's cousin had already prepared the meat and I wasn't having a lesson in butchery this morning too.

'Cut into small pieces,' she said. 'They will caramelise and bring out the flavour.' She placed a large paella pan on the hob and poured in a generous slug of oil.

I worked quickly and chucked in the meat, pushing it around to release the juices until they browned. Next, I gathered ingredients for the *sofregit* – saffron, paprika, tomatoes, onions.

'You like Alice, no?' my mum said. 'What is special about her?'

'*Mum.*'

'Come on, *fill*,' she said, waving a wooden spoon at me. 'There's no shame in falling in love. It is good to have these feelings.'

I snorted. 'I'm not in love. Jesus, I've not known her long.'

'Ah, but when you know, you know.'

'You mean like you and Dad?' I shot back. I didn't mean to sound sarcastic and I felt bad when she flinched.

She showed me how to grate the tomatoes. 'Yes. It was like that at the beginning. But things change. They do sometimes.'

I carried on preparing the vegetables. 'How about garlic? Rosemary?' I suggested.

My mum looked at me in surprise. 'They are optional, and since this is your paella, not mine, they must go in.'

I put the *sofrito* together in the pan and soon my mum was gesturing for me to tip the meat back in, add the beans, rice, the *brou*, and the paella began to simmer away. I stared into the pan, thinking back to the night Matt died, how my dad had flipped out, a vein bulging in his temple as he pointed his finger at me and shouted, 'It's your fault!'

'Your father loves you,' my mum said quietly. 'He will see you anytime.'

'He has a funny way of showing it,' I muttered. 'We don't even know where he is.'

'I can contact Auntie Sue. She will be able to help.' She sighed. 'I know you're hurting, *fill*. We are all hurting, but don't let what happened to your brother cloud what you do. Life is too short – we agree on that?'

I nodded, thinking about Alice. What was special about her? I couldn't think. I just knew that when I was with her, I felt good – things felt right.

'Is it ready?' I said, suddenly impatient to leave.

I went to stir the paella but my mum grabbed my hand. 'Oh no,' she said, laughing. 'We cannot rush this – no stirring. We need to let the rice at the bottom become sticky and crispy. This is the *socarrat* and where the true flavour lies. It is the best part, the heart of the paella.' She patted my cheek. 'Sometimes it is good to take our time, yes? To let things build, to grow – and also to heal.'

Her eyes glazed over and I squeezed her shoulder because I knew she was thinking about Matt, her *fill català*. She placed her hand over mine and we stood there lost in thought. Alice filled my mind again. Perhaps she needed time. To let things build and grow between us.

But I didn't have time – did I?

'Thank you for helping me with Enric. It means a lot,' my mum said.

Her eyes were moist. For some stupid reason, this was the first time I'd thought about my uncle being *her* brother. The operation had probably saved his life. I'd been part of his recovery. I hugged her and felt her body begin to shake as the tears came. I'd not done this enough over the years, but I was doing it now, and that *was* enough.

Eventually she pulled back. 'I think we will be fine with the girls after you and Jimmy leave,' she said, wiping her eyes. 'Enric said you go to Ibiza this weekend?'

She went over to the pan and dug a spoon in. I held my breath as she took a mouthful. Slowly, a smile crept into her face and her eyes began to glisten. 'Oh, *fill*, this is very good. You have done well – very well.' She sighed. 'I am not sending you away, but I know you are desperate to go, yes?' She smiled knowingly. 'Or maybe not?'

I felt the weight of the spoon in my hand, familiar now. The rich scent of tomatoes, garlic, paprika and rosemary billowing up from the pan, tingling my taste buds and unfurling my eagerness to see Alice and her joy when I presented her with the food. Did she want me to stay?

I had no idea.

Chapter 39

ANDY

Ten years ago

Soon, I was jumping on the metro that would take me through the city up to Park Güell. The paella was packed in a box inside a thermal bag, which had zero romance about it, but I hadn't really thought that through when I'd made the plan with Alice earlier. I strode up the steep hill and, as the familiar fairy-like architecture came into view, my heart began to race. I scanned the crowds that milled about the entrance for a glimpse of Alice, but I couldn't see her.

'Hi, stranger.'

I spun around at the tap on my shoulder and Alice's smile flooded me with pleasure.

She glanced at my bag. 'What's that?'

I tucked it behind my back. 'It's a surprise. You'll have to wait.' She tried to hide her smile but I saw it and felt another swell of happiness.

We made our way over to the kiosk and I asked for two tickets.

'Ja heu reservat?' said the lady behind the glass. 'You have booked?'

I glanced at Alice. 'No.'

'Sorry, no tickets. Come back tomorrow.'

Alice's face fell. 'Really?'

The lady shrugged again. 'Book in advance.'

We moved away. 'Bloody hell,' I said. I looked up the sweeping steps, decorated in colourful mosaics, and to the columns supporting a curved viewing platform. Visitors gathered around the edge, admiring the panorama of the city.

It was the perfect spot for a paella picnic.

I sighed. 'Come on, I'll be more organised next time.' I tugged Alice away.

'Organised?' she replied, arching an eyebrow.

Suddenly the paella box banging away in the bag began to seem like a really, really bad idea. We walked quickly back down the hill while I desperately tried to work out another plan.

'Andy, what's the rush?' Alice put her hand on my arm to stop me. 'Are you going to tell me what's in the bag?'

'Paella,' I muttered.

Her eyes lit up. 'Sofia's paella?'

I looked down at my feet. 'My paella,' I mumbled. 'Mum helped me earlier.'

'*Your* paella?' She looked amused. 'Well, we must eat this. Right now.' We were standing outside a shop selling ice-creams and she plonked herself down at one of the tables. 'Come on, sit.'

I clocked the seller eyeing us. 'I'd better get some ice-creams. What flavour would you like?'

'Strawberry, vanilla and chocolate,' she said, counting them off on her fingers.

I laughed. 'Neapolitan, then.' I went to the window and rattled off our orders in Catalan. This seemed to put the seller at ease as he said nothing when I pulled the paella out of the bag. Thankfully, the food was still warm. I handed Alice a fork. 'Go on then, tell me your worst.'

'Hang on, what's all this about you not speaking Catalan?' she said, waving the fork in the direction of the window. 'You said you'd forgotten! Are you telling me you've been letting me struggle on with my phrasebook all this time? And you could've helped me out?'

She was laughing and I threw her a small, confused smile. 'I don't know what's going on. I grew up speaking Catalan at home. Matt and I shared a room and we used to yabber late into the evening, driving my mum mad because I was young and needed my sleep, and driving my dad mad because he didn't have a clue what we were on about.'

'A secret code,' she said.

I nodded – I liked that she understood straight away.

'Then after Matt—' I sighed. 'The harder I searched for the words, the more they floated away.' I looked back at the shop. 'I don't know what happened just then. I guess I spoke without thinking.'

Alice dug into the food and said nothing for a full minute while she ate. 'I can't believe you made this without me,' she said eventually. 'It's so unfair.'

I scanned her face. 'Don't you like it?'

She laughed. 'It's amazing! I'm just jealous you had a lesson from the pro and I wasn't there.'

'Perhaps I'll have to teach you.' I was flirting but I meant what I said.

Her face softened. 'I'd like that.' She shut her eyes for a moment. 'But it's not *exactly* like Sofia's,' she murmured to herself. 'What's different about this?'

'It's Valencian paella,' I said eagerly. 'No fish or shellfish.'

'Mmm, yes, but there's something else to it.'

I watched her emotions play out across her face: pleasure, curiosity, delight. A heat of happiness radiated across my chest.

'Garlic and rosemary!'

I laughed. 'Spot on.'

'What did Sofia think about that?' she said mischievously 'Or did you sneak it in when she wasn't looking?'

I smiled, remembering my mum's surprise. 'She wasn't expecting me to have my own ideas. I'm in her good books.'

We carried on eating, passing the box back and forth because I hadn't thought about bringing anything as obvious as plates.

'We should offer the ice-cream guy some,' said Alice, gesturing to the seller. 'To say thank you for letting us sit here.'

I went over and asked for an empty ice-cream cup and he handed it to me suspiciously. Then his eyes lit up when he saw what I was doing. Alice watched the man eat, her face alert, waiting for his reaction. I smiled. I didn't care what he thought; I'd already impressed the most important judge.

Alice.

'*Increíble*,' the man said, smacking his lips. '*On puc comprar més?*'

'He wants to know where he can buy more,' I translated for Alice.

She laughed. 'He's the chef!' she said, pointing to me. 'Come and find him at Cafè Vermell, Plaça Reial.'

Sometime later, we got up to leave. 'Finally, your promise comes true,' Alice teased.

'What promise?' I was puzzled.

'You said you'd take me exploring around the Barri Gòtic and now you can.'

'Got a map?' I threw back with a grin.

Her brow creased. 'No . . . It was easy to get here, one straight line on the metro. You know your way around, don't you?'

I laughed. 'Just kidding, we don't need a map – but for future reference, the gothic quarter is only one part of the *ciutat vella* – the old city. There are other districts too – El Raval, El Born and La Barceloneta.'

'You training to be a tour guide?' she said, laughing. 'Not that I'm complaining. I hate not knowing where I'm going.'

We hopped back on the metro with Alice telling me how she only felt truly comfortable travelling when she'd planned her route or had a map. So when we got off the train earlier than she expected at Plaça de Catalunya, she looked a little surprised.

'We're not really exploring if we know exactly where we are,' I said, squeezing her hand.

We crossed over the boulevard and ducked down a side street into the fringes of the old town. It was an area I didn't recognise but I didn't say anything to Alice. We ambled for a while, passing through small squares and admiring old churches, while Alice's words simmered in my head. *He's the chef.* To my surprise, something that had been needling me for a while rushed to the surface. 'I don't know if I'm good enough.'

Alice didn't miss a beat. 'To be a chef? Or a DJ?'

I liked that her thoughts were vibrating with my own. 'A DJ.'

'I don't think that can be true. Otherwise, you'd have settled for DJ-ing cheesy disco music. You know, like in Club Barça. Not heading off to hit the big time in Ibiza.'

Her response smacked sense into me. Not that she would know it. If I was really serious about becoming an ace DJ like Matt, I needed to keep practising. I should have been racing out of the kitchen every night to play the decks in any club that would have me – including Club Barça. Matt had worked like a demon to get experience. His determination had paid off. That's why he'd been invited to Ibiza all those years ago.

What had I done? Nothing.

'I'm only going because of Matt,' I said quietly. 'I found his contacts a few months ago and when I quit my job, it seemed like a good idea. I mean, maybe these people won't be there anymore. It was a while ago, but I feel like I should give it a shot.'

Alice scanned my face. 'You want to make your brother proud?'

Of course I did, but there was more, much more. Guilt ballooned big and suffocating inside my chest, containing words that I wouldn't ever be able to say out loud.

I *owed* him.

His life.

'Crazy. I can't make a dead person proud,' I muttered, trying to breathe through the tightness.

Alice squeezed my fingers and said nothing – but everything.

I inhaled deeply and blew out. 'Success is everything, right?'

She shrugged. 'Not for me. What even *is* success?'

My brother. Hotshot DJ. Wannabe music lawyer.

He never had the chance to find out.

I pushed the memories back down and switched up the conversation. 'How's your mum?'

'Oh, she's . . .' Alice wheeled her hand. 'You don't need to hear me whining on.'

'Why not? I've got time to kill on this walk.'

She nudged me. 'Very funny.'

Her gaze drifted and I waited for her to carry on. Evening was creeping in, casting the narrow streets in shadow. A small dog yapped through the railings of a balcony as we passed below and next door a woman was unpegging her washing. 'So?' I pressed. 'I can't hear any whining.'

A smile crossed Alice's lips, then she sighed. 'Mum's putting pressure on me to come home. She's squabbling with my grandma because she's complaining Mum's doing nothing to help out. I mean, she's always been hopeless but it's more noticeable without me there.'

'She's missing you.'

Alice huffed. 'Not sure she's *missing* me. She's missing me being the skivvy.'

'Have you said anything?'

'No, Mum's got a right old temper and sometimes I can't be bothered with the conflict. She's good at fighting battles. She's always got a comeback.'

'You learnt from the best, then.'

Alice flicked me. 'Oi, that's rude.'

'See?'

She stopped and held up her hands. 'You win.'

'You still got the last word.'

'Yes, I did, didn't I?'

We laughed and I whirled her into my arms and kissed her. When we finally extracted ourselves, Alice grinned and demanded we find ice-cream.

'You've already had ice-cream!' I said, laughing.

She made a face. 'It wasn't the best though, was it?'

We'd had a few mouthfuls and I'd left mine melting in the pot without really thinking about it. Perhaps my taste buds had finally woken up. 'So we're on the hunt for the best ice-cream in the city?'

She nodded. 'The best *vanilla* ice-cream and the best churros.'

'Together?' I was doubtful.

'Of course,' she replied, smiling. 'Just imagine dipping warm churros into the ice-cream and letting it melt a little so it coats the crispy outside.'

'You're supposed to dip churros in chocolate sauce.'

'So what? We don't have to do it the same as everyone else.'
She became thoughtful. 'Or we could shape the churros into small
pieces and mix it into the ice-cream, serve it like an Eton Mess
with berries.'

'Sprinkled in cinnamon,' I mused. 'Or cinnamon ice-cream?'
Alice brightened. 'Yes, I like it!'

She snuggled close and I put my arm around her. 'Sure you
can handle a late night?' I teased. 'It might take a while to find
perfection.'

Her eyes shone up at me. 'An all-nighter? Why not? We don't
have much time left.'

◆ ◆ ◆

Alice and I wandered, taking it in turns to choose which direction
to take. We sampled mouthfuls of churros and vanilla ice-cream at
every place we passed, but nothing hit the mark. Then as we came
into a more familiar part of the old town, a memory sparked. I
paused at a narrow opening between buildings. It was just about
wide enough for two people to walk through. I crossed my fingers.
'Come on.'

Puzzled, she followed and gasped as we emerged into the far
corner of the orange tree square.

'Plaça del Taronger! How did you know?' Alice turned a full
three-sixty. Mostly the square was in darkness, except for lights
woven through the tree branches, a small bar with a couple of old
guys outside and the glow from a kiosk. 'Is that . . . ice-cream?' she
said, pointing.

I nodded. 'Churros, too, I hope.'

Alice skipped over and called for me to hurry. For a moment,
she could have been me, a kid racing to choose my evening treat,

yelling over my shoulder at Matt because I was too impatient to queue.

Tonight, there was just Alice and me.

And I felt okay.

I caught up with her at the counter.

'I have a feeling this is going to be perfect,' she said, smiling.

'I do, too,' I said softly.

Hang on to her, bro.

Chapter 40

ALICE

Now

The following day, I find Andy and Mariana huddled in her office. They both look up as I pass the door and she waves. Andy's smile is distant. I don't want to think about what might have gone on between them after he returned home last night – divorce or not. Regret seems to be radiating off him in waves and hurt curls at the edges of my mood.

I settle down at my desk and open up the website I've nearly finished creating, thanks to Xavier's help. I should be pleased with my efforts, but the results leave me feeling flat.

Soon Susie appears with a bubbly smile and a tray of coffee, and heads into Mariana's office. She gestures enthusiastically at me to come through and as I reluctantly get up, I wonder why she's so excited.

Andy's gaze flits between her and me, and I wonder if he's thinking what I'm thinking. *Please don't ask us about La Cova last night in front of Mariana.*

Xavier appears, brows furrowed. Susie tucks her arm around his waist and hugs him close. 'We've got some news,' she says, breaking into a grin. 'Really big news!'

'You're pregnant,' says Mariana flatly. She wrinkles her pretty nose as though she's smelt something bad.

'Now that *would* be big news, but, no, we've still got plenty of time before babies.'

Mariana mutters something in Catalan.

'We've secured a lease to open a cafe and shop!' Susie's eyes shine. 'Xavier's going to cook and I'm going to sell my ceramics.'

Shock streaks across Andy's face and he battles to hide it.

'We've had our eye on an empty unit for ages,' Susie continues, 'but we couldn't track down the owner. We finally got to see it last night – that's why we couldn't go to La Cova. We've signed a lease – it's really going to happen!'

Mariana narrows her eyes. 'Are you telling me you are leaving us, Susie? *Both* of you? So Xavier can play at being a chef?'

Patches of red blotch Susie's cheeks. 'Yes, Mariana, that's right. We're sorry to go, but it's time for a change. This opportunity is really important to both of us. It's what we've always wanted to do.'

Susie's smile becomes strained and I'm annoyed with Mariana for making her feel awkward and apologetic instead of congratulating them.

'That's incredible,' I say, giving them both a quick hug. 'Well done. You must be absolutely over the moon.'

Xavier beams. 'It has been our dream for a long time. We did not think it would ever be possible.'

'There is no money in this,' Mariana says, bangles jangling as she waves her hands. 'You are *boig*, crazy, Xavier. You are a data man, you could be *ric*.'

He shrugs. 'Rich – and unhappy. This is what makes us happy.'

'Where's the building?' asks Andy.

Susie claps her hands. 'Plaça del Taronger! The square with the orange tree. It couldn't be more perfect, could it? I'll still see my regulars on market day, and hopefully they'll be won over by Xavier's cooking and come back with their friends.'

Andy's eyes glaze over for a moment, then he gives them a stiff nod. 'Congratulations.'

I'm baffled. I thought he'd be delighted for his friends, but perhaps he's sad to lose them from the business after all these years.

Mariana throws Xavier a smile that doesn't quite reach her eyes. 'And what does my *pare* say about this, sweet cousin? Have you told him yet?'

'What does it matter?' he retorts, and Susie squeezes his hand. 'I am not afraid of your father. He does not own my life.'

It's a bold statement with the unspoken suggestion *unlike you* hovering at its fringes. I think back to the day I met Josep. How flustered Mariana had been around him. How he'd shut her down. I find myself holding my breath as the atmosphere tilts – and feel a twinge of sympathy for her.

Mariana pales. Her pink blusher becomes two streaky lines on her cheeks. There's a hint of glassiness in her eyes, like she might cry.

'Okay, enough,' Andy snaps. 'Let's talk again later.'

Mariana sweeps out, ignoring us all. Susie huffs and Xavier whispers something to her before striding off as well. I drift back to my desk, feeling an odd mix of pity for Mariana and irritation that Andy stuck up for her. Given his friends' exciting announcement, shouldn't he be putting them first?

Susie follows us into Andy's office and closes the door. Her face is sunny again and I suspect this isn't the first time they've clashed with Mariana. 'Come on then, tell me about last night,' she demands.

Instinctively, I touch my mouth, thinking about Andy's kiss, but I catch him frowning and snap back to answering Susie's question. I tell her everything about our dinner experience and probe her about the new cafe-shop. Andy's silent and she throws him a puzzled look when she leaves, but says nothing.

It's like our kiss has extinguished Andy's enthusiasm for celebrating anything joyful.

I turn back to work. Mariana has left a pile of legal papers on my desk, which I've been putting off reading. I have no interest in this at all.

I get up and go over to the window to rest my eyes on the city view. I gaze at the beautiful old buildings that nestle among the new and watch the bustle of the boulevard below. I place my hand on the glass. Up here, in this box, I feel detached from the outside world. I have a craving to run into the sunshine and immerse myself in the chaos and energy and vibrancy that buzzes within the seams of the old town.

With a jolt, I realise I'm envious of Susie and Xavier's sparkling new chapter. My future back home with Mum in London seems dull by comparison. I'm unsure how I feel about working with Mariana in the long term. I still feel protective of my food events and the ideas I might roll out when I get back. It rankles that she's going to swoop in and tell me how to run them.

'Okay?' Andy says from behind me.

His closeness jump-starts the yearning that lingers from last night. But at the same time, it mingles with humiliation at how he chose to walk away. 'Just thinking about Susie and Xavier's exciting plans,' I say.

He nods and looks down at the people going about their daily business, not dwelling on regrets or feeling disappointed about their future. 'About last night,' he begins quietly.

Dread scuttles up my spine. I don't want to hear his apology. 'Oh, don't worry.' I stretch my mouth into a plastic smile. 'They say food is an aphrodisiac and along with all those glasses of wine we drank, mistakes happen!'

His eyes search for mine, but I can't look at him and plough on. 'I meant to say, before you left, thank you for taking me to the restaurant. I had a great time. It's an experience I won't ever forget.' This time my smile is softer, more genuine, but I'm aware my choice of words sounds like a farewell.

An experience I won't ever forget.

Do I see sadness flickering in his gaze? But then he nods and his mouth settles into a line. Behind us, Mariana suddenly appears back in the corridor and stares through the glazed wall. Her eyes taper to flinty slits and she flies through the door. 'I know you two have been sneaking out every afternoon,' she says shrilly, jabbing her finger at us both. 'We're running a business here, Alice, not a brothel. Do you want this job or not?'

My face smarts in embarrassment and panic makes me stutter. 'No, you're wrong, we're—'

'Shut up, Mariana. What I do is *my* business, not yours,' Andy yells. 'I'm sick of this! All of this! None of what's going on between you and I has anything to do with Alice!'

Mariana folds her arms. 'Is that right?'

Chapter 41

ALICE

Now

Charlie and her friends descend on Barcelona the following weekend, staying close by at a hotel in the square. I'm surprised at how
delighted I am to see her. We throw our arms around one another
and, in that instant, I know we're okay – the familiar pattern of
our fall-outs and make-ups was engraved in us years ago and we've
always bounced back.

I'm looking forward to unwinding as it's been a busy week.
After Mariana's accusation and threat to sack me, I threw my energy
into protecting my job at Perfecte. There's been no sneaking off to
Cafè Vermell, though Andy's gone AWOL again. Even Jimmy's
been vague, muttering something about a work thing.

'Oh my God, sis, this place looks *exactly* the same,' says Charlie
as she wanders around my apartment. I've managed to squirrel her
away from the others for a few hours so I can have her to myself.
'Is it weird being here again? Sleeping in *Andy's* room?'

Her wink makes me smile – we have a lot of catching up to do.

I wait until we're out on the balcony with a glass of wine.
'There's something I've not told you,' I say.

Charlie breaks into a grin. 'I knew it! This has got to be about a guy. Who is he? Have you got a hot Spanish lover? Tell me everything!'

'It's Andy.'

Her mouth falls open and I laugh. It's rare to catch Charlie out – and I like it.

'*The* Andy?' she says excitedly. 'The cute, cheeky guy with the sexy bod and messy blond hair? The guy you had great sex with?'

I laugh again. 'How would you know that?'

'You told me, remember?'

I shake my head. 'I don't think so.'

'You were doped up on lust, love – bloody *happy*, sis.'

'Like you were the relationship expert at eighteen,' I respond drily.

'You were seriously smitten. Shame he fucked things up.' She knocks back a gulp of wine. 'So go on, how did you hook up again?'

'We haven't. Not really.' Sadness twists my insides as I think about our mistake, his regret. I go back to the beginning and explain how we've been working together, Mariana, their divorce. How Andy and I have been cooking for Cafè Vermell. The kiss.

'So you're friends with benefits?' she says slyly. 'I like your Spanish style.'

I shake my head and sip my wine.

'No? Please don't tell me that's *it*? What a waste! He was one seriously hot guy – or has he gone fat and bald?'

I laugh lightly, a tingling feeling coming over me as I picture him. 'He still looks . . . great.'

'Bloody hell, sis. What's the problem?'

I twist my glass. 'I told you, we kissed – once – and that was it.'

'Don't tell me you went all coy on him!' Charlie screeches. 'What do you want? A frigging engagement ring?'

'We were standing in the street!'

'People do have sex outside,' she shoots back.

I smile and think how much I've missed Charlie's blunt humour. Did I really used to find her annoying?

'And?' She's on the edge of her chair. 'What happened after that?'

'Nothing. He walked off. I guess he thought, *That was a mistake.*'

'Perhaps you've become a shit kisser,' she offers with a grin. 'Not enough practice. So now what? What you going to do?'

I shrug. 'Nothing.'

Charlie's laugh is loud enough for a pigeon strutting along the railing to flap and take flight. 'Bloody hell, what's wrong with you? One rebuff and you're out? That's it? You're just going to give up?'

I shift uncomfortably. 'I think he made his feelings clear.'

'The guy has a lot going on! But, no matter, he *kissed* you.' She slugs wine into our glasses. 'You both were up for it, so why are you turning your back on him?'

'I don't know . . . Technically, he's still married, isn't he? And anyway, he walked away from me.'

Charlie looks exasperated, then she sighs and lowers her voice. 'You just told me he's been separated for nearly a year. Stop being scared, sis. You haven't got Mum or me to worry about while you're here. This is your time! Grab it with both hands – enjoy it, for fuck's sake. I mean, look at you!' She leans over and picks up a piece of my hair. 'Your hair looks so much better when you don't fry it with the straighteners. You look gorgeous.' She glances down at my leather gladiator sandals wrapped around my ankles. '*And* you're wearing fuck-me sandals.'

I swear she makes this stuff up.

'Stop overthinking,' she says. 'You've got nothing to lose.'

◆　◆　◆

Later, Charlie and I sip cocktails at the bar downstairs while we wait for the others to join us. Her foot jiggles; she's desperate for Jimmy to arrive.

'How are things with Mum?' I say. 'She said during the week that she didn't want to speak to me every afternoon any more.' Her announcement had stung a little, but I'd been so distracted with work I hadn't dwelt on it for long. I keep reminding myself it's because she's managing fine without me – which is a good thing.

'Thank fuck for that,' says Charlie. 'I've been nagging her for ages.'

'You *told* her not to call me?' I bristle.

'Chill, sis, it's for the best. She's fine and you don't need the pressure.'

I can't really dispute this because if I dig beneath the surface, I know it feels refreshing not to have the commitment.

Charlie sips her cocktail. 'Mum's loving life.'

'Really?'

'Yes, she buzzes around on her sticks now, answering the door to Leon, organising packaging and pick-ups for her perfume business. It's going well. She does stories and videos on Instagram and TikTok. She looks hilarious but it works – she's selling loads.'

I'm stunned into silence.

'And is she eating your vegan meals?' I say eventually, trying to get my head around this new version of Mum.

Charlie shakes her head. 'Nah, you were right, she didn't go for them. I've left her to make what she wants. She's not going to change her habits now.'

'You're not cooking for her?' My voice rises. 'What's she eating?'

'No idea, I don't keep tabs. She's a grown-up. She can work it out for herself.'

'But—'

Charlie presses her hand on mine. 'Stop worrying. Mum's fine. She likes having you around because you do stuff for her and she can't be arsed. You've done her a favour by leaving. It's forced her to be more independent.'

I snatch my hand away.

I'm still thinking about whether Mum really is more independent or if my sister is exaggerating when Jimmy walks into the bar. Charlie screams and runs over to him, leaping into his arms. He spins her around, laughing, and soon the three of us are chatting away while Charlie's friends arrive and Jimmy makes more cocktails. It feels like old times.

When the kitchen door opens a little later and Andy emerges, my breath catches. I had no idea he was here.

'Who is this *hot* guy?' Charlie shrieks, sliding off the bar stool and taking his face in her hands. She plants a smacker on both cheeks.

'Hot is the word,' he replies with a smile, fanning his face with his hand.

Perhaps it's the baggy T-shirt and shorts he's wearing that remind me of the old Andy. Maybe it's the way he pushes his hand through his hair, revealing tiny curls pressed around his temple from the heat. Or is it his mouth? When we'd kissed, my senses rushed back to that one night we'd spent together as though it had been yesterday – not ten years ago.

He walked away. He still lives with Mariana.

'Check him out, Alice!' Charlie says mischievously, running her hand through the air from Andy's head to his feet.

Now I'm the one feeling hot and flustered.

Andy laughs and scrapes his hand through his hair again. 'You haven't changed.'

'Why would I?' she says, spinning back to her cocktail. 'I love being me!'

We all laugh and as Andy retreats to the kitchen, I follow. 'You're back,' I say at the door. 'Do you need some help?'

His eyes roam over my green dress, dotted with tiny white flowers and slit high on one side. I hold myself taut as I wait for him to answer.

He sighs. 'No, I'm good, everything's under control. Go and enjoy yourself.'

I stare, my mood flattened as I wonder what I've done wrong.

Chapter 42

ALICE

Now

I push my blue thoughts away to focus on Charlie's celebrations. After we've eaten a satisfying round of Andy's tapas and consumed plenty of Cava, we stagger giddily out into the square. We're wearing matching pink satin jackets with a naked woman printed on the back – a rapper Charlie has the hots for, apparently – and we're already causing a stir.

I lead the way and head off down one of the streets that will take us to a rooftop bar. I don't bother shushing Charlie, who's belting out an ABBA song, her voice bouncing between the stone walls of the high buildings. As the hen, she has the honour of wearing the 'bride-to-be' sash, a feather boa and a curly pink wig with a nylon veil. To balance out her pansexual status, we've added an oversized penis tiara.

Charlie's taken a million selfies of us already and sent them to Sarah. I wonder what her fiancée is making of the spectacle. She's celebrating with a quiet meal at a pub near her mum's house in the countryside with a handful of old schoolfriends.

As we approach the door to the bar, the bouncer eyes us, arms folded. We're a rabble of pink satin and singing, and I hope he won't turn us away. Are we very British? Do Spanish women have hen parties like this? I can't imagine Mariana marched around the city in a fake wedding veil. I push the thought away. I don't want to think about her – or anything else that involves her marriage to Andy.

'Evening,' Charlie says, throwing her feather boa around the bouncer's neck and kissing him on both cheeks.

He laughs and we sweep past and squeeze into the lift, giggling as we exit at the top. We stomp past the tables, raising smiles from the other patrons, and a waiter ushers us to comfy seating with incredible views of the city away from everyone else.

Charlie bumps down on the sofa next to me. 'I love you,' she says, slurring a little.

'You look gorgeous.' I stroke the erect penis on her forehead.

She laughs. 'Sis, you're fun again! I *told* you Barcelona's good for you.'

We slump back into the cushions and I'm thinking we ought to drink water for a while if we're going to make it to Club Barça later to go dancing. Cocktails and Cava have made things hazy.

I slop water into two glasses. 'Drink this,' I say, shoving one in Charlie's hand and downing my own.

She takes a few noisy slurps and leans into me again. 'I'm having *such* a lovely time. I can't believe I'm getting married next week.'

'Me neither.' I'm still nervous about her decision and I shuffle around to face her. 'Are you sure it's the right thing to do? Is getting married to Sarah what you really want?' Tears spring into my sister's round green eyes and I squeeze her hand. 'It's not too late to back out,' I say. 'You know I'll support you.'

Charlie's mouth pinches shut. She scrubs at her eyes, leaving a smear of glittery black goo on her cheeks. 'Of *course* I want to marry Sarah – we love each other,' she says fiercely. 'It's you who's making me feel sad. You and your judgey ideas that I'm still the fucked-up little sister who doesn't have a clue about life. That it'd be impossible for me to fall in love and want to get married.'

I reel back from her, shocked.

Clumsily, Charlie pushes herself to standing, wobbling on her heels a little before grabbing the back of the sofa to steady herself. 'You need to stop babying me, Alice. You need to stop fussing over Mum. The world hasn't fallen apart with you gone. We're alright without you, so it's about time *you* grew up, not me.' She raises her hand to summon the waiter. 'Tequilas all round,' she yells.

I stare open-mouthed. Then rage thunders through me and I get up and march off to the toilets. How dare she speak to me like that in front of everyone? She says she's not a child, but she's behaving *exactly* like a child. Like she's always done.

I come out of the stall and find Charlie leaning against the sink. 'Sis, I don't want to fight, especially not this weekend,' she says. A ghost smile appears.

I begin to wash my hands. 'All I've ever done is look after you and now you're throwing everything back in my face,' I respond tartly.

She sighs. 'That's the point. You did everything for me – you still do! – and I'll forever be grateful. You were more of a parent than Mum ever was – and you still are.' She's silent for a moment. 'Mum had her problems, I see that now. But wasn't she brilliant at the fun stuff? I loved it when it was just the three of us and we'd have dance competitions in the living room with pizza take-out.'

I busy myself with drying my hands on a paper towel, but I'm beginning to soften.

'I wish she'd been fit enough to come here this weekend. She'd have loved it,' she adds wistfully.

'She'd have upstaged you,' I shoot back.

Charlie laughs quietly. 'I wouldn't have minded. God, she was so young when she had you and me. She didn't know how to look after herself, let alone us. Boarding school wasn't exactly a great start for her to learn to live in the real world.'

Her eyes burn into me. 'I'll never, ever forget what you've done for me, sis, but I'm a grown-up now, I can do things for myself. I hate that you never do anything for *yourself* because you're too busy worrying about me or running around after Mum. I get the two of you have a connection and she's demanding because she doesn't want to lose you, but this is your life, too.' She pokes a finger beneath her wig and scratches her scalp. It slips a little. She looks like a sad clown.

'I meant what I said earlier, about Barcelona being good for you. You *do* look different, and it's not just your hair and clothes – it's something else, something coming from within.' Charlie laughs. 'I sound quite intelligent, don't I?' Her face sobers again. 'You haven't got anyone but yourself to think about while you're here. Can't you find a way to keep your life like this? Make it all yours?' She leans her forehead on mine. 'I'm okay, sis, you can let me go.'

I squeeze my eyes tight to hold back the tears. I haven't wanted to let Charlie go. I've thrived on her bouncing in and out of my life with her dramas. Her life has given mine purpose.

We look at ourselves in the mirror. 'It's hard to take you seriously looking like that,' I say, tugging her wig straight and rearranging her veil and tiara. I dab at the smeared make-up with a wet tissue.

Charlie grins and her beautiful smile fills her face. I see a glimpse of myself in her. 'Ready?' she says. 'There's a tequila out there with your name on it.' She grasps my hand and a bolt of her energy fizzes through my body and lifts me up, making me feel light, giddy and hopeful for what's to come.

'Consider it Dutch courage,' she adds. 'For when we meet up with Andy and Jimmy later.'

◆ ◆ ◆

Our conga across the square to Club Barça would have drawn attention wherever we'd gone, but, along with our matching jackets, Charlie's pink wig and the penis tiara, the comedy is too much for some passers-by who laugh and take photos.

Charlie's at the helm, waving her feather boa; I'm holding on to her waist. At the door to the club, we laugh as the crowd parts to let us snake through to the dancefloor. Charlie breaks free and commands centre stage, her veil taking flight as she spins around. A chancer makes a grab for it. He tugs her towards him and they begin gyrating. I leave her be, closing my eyes and allowing myself to be drawn into the rhythmic throb of the music. I sway to the beat, feeling the bass vibrate my body, and as more people join the dancefloor and the crowd draws in, the tension of the past few weeks ebbs away.

After a while, I head to the bar to get a drink. I should have known Charlie would invite Jimmy and Andy along after work, but her announcement had still taken me by surprise. With alcohol-fuelled confidence, I scan the room, but I can't see them and I join the throng at the bar.

A man with dark eyes and curly eyelashes asks me if I'd like a drink. I'm wondering why he's assumed I'm English and then he mimics the conga, making me laugh. I'm about to say, 'Yes, why not?' when hands land on my shoulders.

I twist around and find myself jammed up against Andy. For a split second, I'm spun back in time and, without thinking, I kiss him.

His mouth is flat.

Heat flushes my already-hot face and I push him away, stumbling through the crowd until I reach outside. I scout around for somewhere quiet, but there's a queue of people waiting to go in, so I take off down a side street away from the square.

Almost immediately I stop and crumple to the ground. What was I thinking? Andy made it clear he didn't want me the first time. Nothing has changed. I lean back against the wall and the awfulness of realising I *want* him to want me cuts through me like a knife.

'Alice?'

I look up and there he is. But I don't want his pity. Working together is going to be humiliating enough. I will pack my bags and leave with Charlie tomorrow. Tell Mariana I've learnt enough and can finish anything else she needs me to do back in London.

Andy slides down next to me. 'Nice jacket. Pink suits you.'

I yank it off. This isn't funny anymore.

His eyes drop briefly to my dress, which reveals more of my cleavage than usual.

'I saw you dancing,' he says quietly.

'Yeah, well, you know me, I like to conga.'

He chuckles. 'I meant on the dancefloor. You had your eyes closed. You looked really . . . happy.'

I shoot him a sideways look and he fiddles with his pendant. 'Anyway,' he says, more brightly, 'I didn't have you down as a conga girl.'

I roll my eyes.

'Looks like a fun night.'

The stone wall feels cool against my bare shoulders and the fresh air sharpens the fuzz of alcohol. I exhale loudly. 'Sorry about just then. Too much tequila.'

He shifts a little so he can look at me. I catch a hint of his scent and butterflies take flight in my belly.

'No, *I'm* sorry . . . You caught me by surprise,' he says softly. 'Was it just the tequila?'

I shift my gaze away. 'Cocktails, Cava . . .' Humiliation washes over me. 'I'm not much of a drinker.'

'Do you feel okay? I mean, you don't feel sick or anything?'

I let out a small laugh. 'No.' Though my stomach rolls for much bigger reasons. I scrunch up my eyes and feel the honesty of alcohol insisting I answer his question properly. Charlie's echo comes back – what have I got to lose? 'I kissed you because, for a moment, we felt like us . . . from before,' I say.

Andy smiles sadly. 'I know what you mean.' His eyes don't leave mine as if he's weighing up what to say next. 'I think we're even.'

I frown. 'What do you mean?'

'I kissed you and walked away. You kissed me and ran away.' He pauses. 'Perhaps running off makes you a tiny bit meaner than me.'

I smile, but what he says is a reminder there are other things I need to ask. 'Have you been avoiding me? You haven't been in work and you wouldn't let me help you in the kitchen earlier.'

He looks surprised. 'I wanted you to enjoy Charlie's hen party. Plus – your dress. It's lovely – you look lovely.' His eyes linger on me for a moment. 'I've been doing something for work. But I can't tell you about it just yet.'

I store away his flattery for later. Right now, I'm indignant he's still got secrets. 'And there's something else,' I add, feeling tequila-brave again.

He looks amused. 'Okay?'

'Why are you still living with Mariana? If you're getting divorced?'

He's puzzled.

'Outside La Cova, you said you were going home.'

His face clears. 'Her house is huge! Well, it's her father's house, not hers, not ours even, and I don't live *with* her – I'm in the garden annexe.' He puffs out his cheeks. 'Our lives are completely separate. Remember, it's been nearly a year. I'm just waiting for her to sign the divorce papers and . . . some other paperwork she's holding out on.'

My brain is working hard to take everything in. It's like the final wall between us has come crumbling down. But now I'm nervous around this new empty space we could step into.

Andy shuffles closer to me, and my heart pounds with a painful mix of fear and longing. 'I'm sorry for walking away from you,' he whispers, his breath tickling my skin, his scent firing my senses. 'I promise I won't do it again.'

He cups my face and kisses me in the shadows of the buildings where there isn't anyone scooting past on a moped to break the moment, and nobody is running away. I don't know how long we stay entwined on the hard stony flags but I know my bum starts to go numb and Andy pulls me to my feet, smiling.

Our hands stay locked together and we wander further into the darkness of the old town, weaving this way and that. Andy's insistent he knows where he's going. Finally, we reach a familiar part of town where a narrow passage cuts through the tall buildings – and I smile.

We walk through to Plaça del Taronger and like all those years before, lights weave through the branches of the orange tree and water burbles from the angel fountain by the chapel. I think about the ceramic coaster I bought Andy, the farmer and the peaches, the building we see that will soon become Susie and Xavier's cafe-shop.

'It seemed like the right place to come,' he says.

We settle on a bench outside a bar with a handful of locals drinking inside. Andy orders a beer, I ask for sparkling water, and as we talk, he never lets go of my hand. I don't want him to either.

I smile, thinking that if I was Charlie, I'd have dragged him off to bed by now.

'What's funny?' he says, brushing his mouth over mine once again.

Andy's touch flares a longing in me that's become hot, fierce and hard to ignore. I don't reply, but tug him to his feet.

This time we fly back along the streets, laughing, and soon we spill back into the plaza where music still booms from the club. I remember Charlie and the others don't know I've gone, so I send her a quick text to say I'm safe at home.

Home?

I look across the square at my balcony and realise this really *does* feel like home. Andy catches my eye and we become giddy again as he chases me over to the cafe and up the stairs to the door. He presses into me as I turn the key, and we fall inside and kiss all the way to my bedroom – his bedroom.

An unexpected rush of tears floods my eyes. I brush them away before Andy notices but it's too late. He kisses my damp eyelids, my cheeks, strokes his hand down my neck, dropping butterfly kisses along my collarbone. Then slowly, carefully, he lowers the straps on my dress and my breath catches.

I am melting.

Is it the same? Familiar but different. Andy fiddles with the zip and I giggle softly when it gets stuck and I have to help him out. My dress pools on the floor and I bask in his delight when he discovers I'm not wearing a bra. His eyes drink me in for a moment, then we're touching in the places we've been aching to touch, redis-covering old feelings and familiar sensations, until he picks me up and I wrap my legs around him, half-crazed with longing.

'Why did you really leave me?' he mutters into my hair. 'I thought you were coming back – but I never saw you again.'

Chapter 43

ANDY

Ten years ago

The run of hot days broke when the skies darkened and a tropical storm arrived one morning, thrashing rain into the plaza and sending people running for cover. Customers crammed into our red booth seating, laughing, the high drama of the sudden downpour creating an excitable atmosphere inside the bar.

Alice and I worked at high speed to get food out. Jimmy turned around drinks and my mum served tables, as Charlie had gone off for a few days to meet friends in Madrid. I regretted agreeing to the lunch lesson with Mariana. I wanted to stay close to Alice.

While I waited for Mariana to arrive, the sun came back out and a large group of students from Perfecte turned up. We pushed the outside tables together and while I dried the surfaces and chairs, I picked up a message from Mariana asking me to meet her at the school instead.

Mum spun into the kitchen, fretting we didn't have enough food to give them. Alice directed her in a quiet, even voice that soothed her ruffled edges. I offered to stay – I *wanted* to stay – but

Alice assured me everything was under control and they both shooed me away.

When I arrived at Perfecte, I was puzzled to find the door locked but as soon as I pressed the buzzer, I was let in. I climbed the stairs, hearing the muffled sound of the radio in the shop below but no chatter drifting down from students. At the top, I became aware of a dripping sound and turned the corner to see water coming through the ceiling and splashing into a metal bin.

Mariana was on the phone. '*No puc ensenyar fins que no es solucioni el problema,*' she said, her voice tight. Her eyes met mine; they glistened with emotion. '*No està bé per a l'escola. Per què no ho pots entens?*'

The words scrolled through my mind in English: *I can't teach until the problem is fixed. Why don't you understand?* She'd delivered the last line impatiently and now her face had drained of colour.

'*Ho sento. Ajuda'm, pare.*'

I'm sorry. Help me, Father.

She pulled the phone away and stared at the empty screen. Then her face collapsed and she burst into tears.

I gaped for a moment, unsure what to do, then I went over and patted her arm. To my surprise, she flung herself on me and sobbed into my shoulder, so I patted her back instead, remembering my mum doing the same when I was a child.

After what seemed like a long time, her tears became sniffles and she pulled away, wiping her hand across her face.

'What's going on?' I said. The water had eased a little but a stain was spreading and the plaster had already begun to bubble and break away.

'Sorry,' she said, sniffing, and disappeared momentarily into her office. She returned with some tissues and mopped her face. 'I don't know what to do,' she muttered and slumped against the wall. Barefoot, she looked less sure of herself.

'It's just a leak,' I replied. 'It can be fixed.'

She shook her head. 'The roof is broken – the whole building is *old*.' She slapped her hand on the wall. 'I *hate* this place.'

Her vehemence took me aback, but I kind of got what she meant. Okay, so the blue and white tiles, exposed beams and shuttered balcony doors might have a certain charm, but they needed some serious renovations.

'*Pare*,' she whispered, tears beginning to choke her voice again. 'He says to be a success I have to do this on my own.' She swallowed and then her eyes became fierce. 'I will show him I can do this. I will not give up.'

'The rain isn't your fault. Blimey, it was tropical. Your dad will repair the roof, won't he? Didn't you say he owned the building?'

Mariana's mouth pinched together. 'That may be. But he wants to know why I have let this happen.'

I frowned. 'Sorry, you've lost me.'

She scrubbed her face again with the tissue. 'He gave me this chance. Perfecte is *my* school so it is *my* responsibility to look after *his* building.' She sighed and her face softened. 'Will you help me, Andrew?'

I looked up at the ceiling. 'Okay, so let's call a builder.'

I stayed longer with Mariana than I meant to as she wanted me to hang around and make sure the tradesperson knew what they were doing. It wasn't quite the Catalan lesson I was expecting. But with a few translations from Mariana, and some gesturing for words about the roof that neither of us knew in English or Catalan, she was satisfied the guy could patch up the problem and return to do the repairs.

The streets were dry by the time Mariana and I walked back to the cafe. She linked her arm through mine and kept thanking me as though I'd fixed the roof myself. In return, for every thank you she gave me, I bobbed my head and replied, *cap problema*, making her laugh.

As we got closer, I spotted my mum and Alice out on the terrace with coffee. The rush of customers must be over – and I was starving. Alice was talking animatedly, hands gesturing, smile broad, fingers tugging her hair away from her face as the breeze caught it.

'When are you going to Ibiza, Andrew?' Mariana squeezed my arm.

My eyes stayed glued to Alice. I felt my chest expand as I absorbed her energy, her *passion* – and just like that I knew the answer. 'I'm not. I'm staying,' I said.

It was as though my words carried over to Alice. She glanced my way and saw me coming towards her and I grinned. But her face creased into a frown and I wondered if she hadn't seen us after all. I pulled away from Mariana and jogged over, the power of my decision propelling me forward.

'Sorry, there was a leak at the school,' I said. 'Mariana needed some help.'

My mum nodded. 'Yes, the students told us. Is it fixed?'

'For now.'

'Took a while,' said Alice lightly.

I leant closer to them. 'She was a bit upset,' I whispered.

'Has Andrew told you his news?' Mariana said, joining us. She threw us a dazzling smile. 'He is not going to Ibiza. He is staying.'

Chapter 44

ANDY

Ten years ago

Later that evening, I'd just finished getting changed and was out on my balcony cooling down from my shower when I heard a knock and Alice's voice call out as she opened my bedroom door. She came outside, glowing in a yellow dress, and I touched her hair and drew her into my arms.

'You smell gorgeous,' I muttered as the heat of her body mingled with my own. We stood for a moment, breathing each other in, but then Alice pulled away.

I frowned. 'Everything okay? Want to sit down?' I gestured towards one of the wrought-iron chairs. 'I'll get some wine.' I scooted into the kitchen and returned with a bottle, glasses and an ice bucket that I'd nicked from downstairs. For once I'd planned ahead. I was staying, not leaving – but what did Alice think?

Alice was leaning on the railings and staring into the square. As I opened the bottle, I tried to ignore the rolling sensation that hollowed out my belly. I passed her a glass and she ran her finger through the condensation.

'You know, I thought you'd have gone to Ibiza by now,' she began, eyes on the fountain. 'I imagined getting up one morning and finding you'd done a runner, leaving me to manage the kitchen on my own.' She turned to me and tried to smile.

I laughed quietly. 'I wouldn't just *go*.'

Without saying goodbye.

'But you shouldn't miss this big opportunity,' she insisted.

'You know what I'm like, I live for the moment,' I replied with a shrug. 'I'm not good at making plans.'

'No,' she replied softly. 'I've noticed.'

We fell silent for a moment and I waited for her to continue.

'How was your lesson today?' she said.

I relaxed a little. 'Well, it wasn't a lesson in the end. Though I had a mad conversation in Catalan with a builder about a leaky roof.'

Alice didn't smile. 'Oh?'

'Mariana was flapping. She'd phoned her dad but he wasn't very helpful.' I paused, remembering her desperation on the phone, the way she'd clung to me. 'He sounds like a difficult man. Not very caring.' I explained what Mariana had told me. That her father said she'd never be a success until she'd learnt to stand on her own two feet. 'So that's why I ended up helping her.'

Alice's gaze drifted back to the fountain and she gulped a mouthful of wine. 'You spoke to the builder in Catalan?'

I shrugged. 'Yes, the three of us discussed what needed doing. Not that I had a clue – I mean, I know nothing about roofs or leaks or the words in English, let alone Catalan.'

Alice's eyes fell on mine. 'Sounds like Mariana has been a great help to you.'

I was startled. 'Help?'

She nodded, and slowly I got an inkling of what might be on her mind. 'I don't think Mariana's *helped*,' I said slowly. 'I think it's

263

just timing. Being here, living here, remembering the past.' I held up my glass. 'Relaxing, perhaps.'

You.

Alice's eyes remained glued to me. 'You told her you were staying. That you're not going to Ibiza.' She looked down into her glass. 'You didn't tell me.'

Laughter bubbled up at the absurdity of this conversation. Thrilled *because she cared*. I reached out and stroked her hair. I didn't need Matt to whisper words of wisdom, or tell me what to do, because the answers were right here in front of me. 'I *am* staying, Alice,' I said, cupping her face and grazing my mouth over hers. 'For you. Not for anyone else.'

Alice and I stood on the balcony with our arms around one another, absorbing the activity in the square and chatting while we finished the wine. We smiled as we watched the neighbours attempting to coax their puppy to walk in a straight line. The husband held the treats too high and the dog bounced up to reach them, like his legs were made of springs. His wife told him off but did no better job herself, and by the time the couple had reached the fountain, they were both in stitches.

'Sweet,' Alice murmured.

I turned to face her and ran my hand beneath her hair, stroking it to one side and dropping kisses down her neck. Alice shivered. I tugged her over to the chairs and pulled her on to my lap. A million questions bunched up in my head but I didn't want to talk, I wanted to inhale her scent, kiss her mouth, taste her skin . . . pull her inside.

The gospel choir sung heartily from where Alice had left her phone on the table. She glanced over. 'I'm not answering it,' she said.

I dropped my mouth and kissed the space between her clavicle, feeling her pulse against my lips as her breath quickened.

The chorus soared again. 'For fuck's sake,' she muttered, picking up the mobile. For a moment, I thought she was going to answer it, but instead she switched it off.

'Poor Mum,' I whispered with a smile.

She grinned. 'That is *such* a relief. I don't know why I didn't do it earlier.'

I brushed my lips over her bare shoulder and ran my hands down her arms. She opened her mouth to say something. I laughed lightly. 'Now what?'

'Sorry, I was thinking what if Mum was calling because something has happened to Charlie?'

I burst out laughing. 'If something had happened, Charlie would be calling you, not your mum.'

She sighed. 'Perhaps I should have sent Jimmy to Madrid with her – you know, to keep an eye out.'

'So you've finally worked out he's not the enemy and you want him to be her bodyguard instead?'

'Charlie told me he was a rubbish kisser. No chemistry apparently.'

I let out a hoot of laughter. 'Is that right? Does he know?'

She nodded. 'Apparently he's been asking her to teach him. But she's having none of it.'

'That's my Jimmy,' I said, smiling. 'Anyway, Charlie's practically an adult. She's not your responsibility anymore.'

Alice sighed again. 'Old habits.'

My thoughts hopped to Matt. He'd been annoying, like most big brothers are, but he always had my back. I felt a pinch of longing. 'I liked Matt looking out for me,' I said quietly. 'He never let me down.'

I wished he had.

If he'd been an arsehole and refused to DJ at the party then . . . Alice stroked my face, her eyes overflowed with compassion and I felt a rush of memories gather to the surface, demanding to be told. I swallowed but no words came out. A rock had wedged itself in my throat, its sharp edges scraping the insides.

Alice brushed her lips over my mouth as if encouraging me on.

'I went to a party,' I croaked. 'I got home in the early hours, pissed up, to find my parents in a fucking mess, telling me Matt had gone.' Tears threatened to cut loose but I was determined to get to the end so I kept swallowing to dislodge the rock. 'My brother was killed by a drunk driver – and it was all my fault.'

I sobbed like a baby and Alice led me inside and we lay down on my bed. Her arms held me tight and I buried myself in her neck, until my breath became jagged and the scent of her body calmed me down.

Alice didn't ask why it was my fault – and there was no way I could tell her.

The heat that had been sparking between us began to flame again and she pressed her mouth against mine, the flick of her tongue spinning me into another orbit. She ran her hands under my T-shirt and dragged it over my head with an urgency that ramped up the thrill.

The next moment she sprang up and whipped off her dress. Before I had a chance to admire her gorgeous body, she'd slid off her bra and dived back down next to me. Her mouth was back on mine and I gasped as her hands reached down to unhook my belt and push my shorts away. I ran my finger around the lace band of her knickers and she trembled.

I fucking trembled.

But – wait.

'What's the matter?' she said, as I pulled back.

'You sure you're okay with this?'

She nodded and pressed herself against me. 'The other night, I thought you weren't interested . . .'

I held her tight and turned her on to her back, trailing kisses down the length of her body and into the hidden places I'd been desperate to explore.

At some point, the evening crept in through the open door, pushing shadows into the room and a warm breeze skated over the tangle of our bodies.

'Yes, Alice, I *am* interested,' I muttered as she lay sleeping in my arms.

I had been from the start.

I knew I always would be.

Chapter 45

ANDY

Ten years ago

In that moment when I began to wake, the sunlight warming my face, cool air filtering through the open balcony door, I was smiling. But when I opened my eyes and reached for Alice, there was a cold, empty space next to me.

She'd gone.

I sat up and glanced around. Perhaps she was on the balcony. 'Alice?'

Nothing. I looked over at the door. Shut – with purpose. Not the act of someone quietly slipping out to pop to the loo. My pulse began to pick up pace. Did Alice regret last night? The thought made me queasy.

I jumped up, hopping into shorts left crumpled on the floor and slung on the T-shirt. My heart battered unreasonably and the door handle felt clumsy in my hand as I wrenched it open, impatient to find her.

Even before I reached Alice's room, I could see what she was doing.

Packing.

It felt like a punch to my gut. My breath snatched away, a roll of nausea, and I must have made some kind of noise because Alice looked up.

Red rimmed her eyes and tears tumbled silently down her cheeks. She was shaking and gulping and I ran to her, pulling her close and holding her tight, so she knew I'd never let go.

For a moment, she felt rigid. But when I whispered, 'Tell me,' she loosened and unravelled. This time it was me pulling her down to sit on the bed, me murmuring soothing words, kissing the wetness from her cheeks, and as her tears slowly ebbed away, she drew in a shaky breath.

'My grandma died,' she said, eyes filling again.

'Oh, Alice.' I stroked her hair and pressed my forehead to hers, feeling a rush of frustration and sadness because I knew I couldn't make everything better.

'When I woke this morning, I had a flutter of panic about switching my phone off last night,' she began. 'Perhaps, I had a sixth sense . . .' Her voice trailed away and then she grabbed my hands, eyes wide. 'Mum had left me so many messages! She was frantic! I couldn't believe it when I called her back . . .' Her voice fell again and she stood and went over to the window. 'It just doesn't seem *real*.'

'I know.'

She spun around. 'Oh, Andy, of course . . .'

I went over to her and stroked her face. 'This isn't about me.'

'But—'

I silenced her with a kiss. 'Let me help you get organised,' I said, glancing around at the clothes spilling out of the open drawers and the half-packed rucksack on her bed.

She laughed weakly. 'You? Organised?'

I grinned. 'There's a first time for everything.'

♦ ♦ ♦

I helped Alice arrange her flight and pushed aside my own feelings about her leaving – I'd deal with those later. She told me her grandma had died sat in a chair while watching TV, and when her mum had found her yesterday evening she'd been hysterical. With Alice's phone going to voicemail, and Charlie not answering hers, their mum had banged on a neighbour's door and asked for help.

It sounded grim. The shock felt familiar.

'I still can't get hold of Charlie,' choked Alice, as I came back on to the balcony with cups of tea. 'Her phone is going to voicemail now. Do you think she's switched it off?'

I sat down next to her. 'She's probably run out of charge. Keep trying – she'll call you. She'll want to tell you what a fantastic time she's having with her mates.'

Alice nodded and blew on her tea. 'Oh, Mariana phoned you,' she muttered, pointing to my mobile on the table. 'I asked her if I could give you a message but she said it wasn't important.'

'She's probably got another DIY problem she needs fixing at the school,' I replied.

Alice watched me. 'She likes you,' she said bluntly.

I laughed awkwardly. 'No way! She's had a run of bad luck with that building apparently. The leak tipped her over the edge. She'd had enough.'

Silence fell between us. I longed to feel Alice's naked body against mine one more time before she left, but she was standing and telling me she needed to check she'd packed everything. It would have to wait.

At the airport, Alice stared blankly into her coffee and said very little. I held her hand and watched over her. Every now and then, she'd jolt back to the present and squeeze my fingers and say, 'Sorry,' before her mind slid away again.

270

I ached to bring the light back into her eyes.

When it was time to say goodbye, I held her in my arms and we kissed, but I felt the wire of tension running through her body, her desperation to leave already pulling us apart.

I wanted to say, *I'll come with you! This isn't our end, Alice, this is our beginning.*

But my throat felt raw. I couldn't layer on any pressure.

We'd had one night together. Just one. I felt guilty for wanting her for myself.

'I have to go,' she said, her eyes glassy. 'I'm sorry, I—'

I brushed my mouth over hers to tell her it didn't matter, even though it did. I sucked in a breath and unclipped my brother's necklace. 'I want you to have this.'

She gasped. 'I can't . . .'

I kissed her again. 'You can. I want you to. This necklace belongs with a Gemini.'

I fastened it around her neck. Her fingers reached up and she stroked the pendant. 'Thank you.' She flashed a small smile. 'I've got something for you, too. I slipped it into your bedside table early this morning after we . . . Before . . .' Her face clouded over again and she forced a smile. 'I'll be back as soon as I can.'

'Take as long as you need.'

I watched Alice leave until I could no longer see her and returned to the apartment. In my bedroom, it was as though time had stood still. I imagined Alice and I having coffee on the balcony, her taking me by the hand and pulling me back to bed . . .

I sighed and pulled open the bedside drawer. Inside was something square wrapped in yellow tissue paper. It felt a little weighty in my hand. I pulled off the wrapping and found a ceramic coaster streaked in blues and oranges, a stamp of an orange tree on the reverse and the artisan's initials. I read the note tucked inside.

'For the beach. For Orange Tree Square. For us.'

Chapter 46

ALICE

Now

In that moment when I begin to wake, with the sunlight warming my face, cool air filtering through the open balcony door, I'm smiling. But when I open my eyes and reach for Andy, there's a cold, empty space next to me.

He's gone.

I sit up, a flutter of panic beating my chest as I think back over the night before, wondering for a heart-stopping moment if everything that happened between us was all a dream.

Then the door bangs open and Andy strolls in with coffee and a bag of pastries. 'Hungry?' he says.

I laugh, feeling foolish – and happy.

He hasn't left, and I'm not going anywhere this time.

Shyly, I tug the sheet up around me. Andy grins and dumps the cups down on the bedside table, slopping coffee over the sides. He bounces on to the bed and slowly lowers the sheet, dropping his mouth to my neck, making a trail of butterfly kisses down my body until we're back where we started last night and the coffee has gone cold.

When we eventually make it out on to the balcony with our breakfast, I feel as though I'm floating, content and dazed with the heat of Andy's touch still burning my skin. I'm reminded of how Charlie had described me as 'doped up on lust'. I repeat the story to Andy and he laughs. Then I remember I've left his question unanswered from last night.

Why did you really leave me, Alice?

Can I tell him I was coming back? Can I say – but *you'd* already left *me*?

An oak tree looms up in my mind, the sound of splintering glass.

There is so much more to the truth than I'm willing to tell him.

I drift back to now. Andy's talking about Cafè Vermell and tells me Juliana's returning to work. There's no mistaking the disappointment in his voice, but I'm hopeful we might still be needed. 'We often have a queue,' I say. 'She might call on us when it's busy?'

'I don't know . . . The kitchen isn't really big enough for three people.'

We sip our coffee and I spy the elderly neighbours shuffling out of their apartment, being tugged along by their little dog, which seems as lively as the puppy it had been ten years ago. 'Are you back in the office tomorrow?'

Andy's thoughtful and I'm wondering if he's thinking what I'm thinking: can we still work together after – *this*?

'I guess so,' he says eventually.

I give him a playful nudge. 'I thought you'd be more excited about hanging out with me. Don't worry, I'm sure I can keep my hands to myself. I won't give Mariana any reason to hassle you again.'

Andy's still staring blankly into the square.

Doubt dampens my mood. I'm jumping ahead, assuming we have a future. I test the waters. 'Well, it won't be for long as I'll be leaving in a few weeks.'

My eyes search his face but my comment hangs and still he says nothing. Then he jumps up and hugs me tight, sending me into a spin of confusion and longing, and I let him pull me back inside where all thoughts of Perfecte, Cafè Vermell – going home – become blotted from my mind.

◆　◆　◆

Before I know it, the hen weekend is over and Charlie leaves on a high. Of course, she and Jimmy had gone crazy with delight when they realised Andy stayed over, and did a weird dance in the bar, making us laugh.

By the time Monday rolls around, Andy and I have already decided it's best not to come into work together. I arrive alone with the excitable imprint of him still running down the length of my body after he kissed me awake this morning.

As the lift doors open, he's there with Susie behind the reception desk and they're talking quietly. They look up as I step out and exchange a quick glance. I'm thrown for a moment, like I've barged into a private meeting, and I'm unsure how to greet him.

Susie makes it easy. 'Wow, I love your dress – you're glowing!' She races over and draws me into a hug. 'Andy told me,' she whispers into my ear. 'OMG!'

We pull apart, my cheeks rosy, and Andy gives me a knowing smile. 'Morning.'

'*Bon dia*,' I reply, joy bubbling up again as I bounce off down the corridor, past the classrooms, and fling open the door.

Through the glass wall of Andy's office, I see Mariana standing at the window on the phone with her back to me. I creep in and settle down at my desk.

'*Pare*,' she pleads. '*Ajuda'm*.'

My head snaps up at the sound of her voice. I have no idea what she's saying, but she's on the brink of tears and I eye the door, hoping I can slink back out without being seen.

'*Ja s'ha acabat, el nostre projecte de passió. Ell vol vendre.*' This time a sob chokes out of her and she stuffs her hand to her mouth, shoulders shaking. '*No es pot fer res.* Nothing,' she whispers.

Slowly, I rise up and shuffle out from behind my desk but Mariana must hear as she jerks around. Tears cut a path through her make-up and leave dark spots on the collar of her cerise blouse. I fumble in my bag for a packet of tissues and thrust them at her before leaving.

Out in the corridor, my thoughts tumble back to the time Andy told me how he'd found Mariana sobbing on the phone to her father when there'd been a leak in the old building. I think about Josep's dismissive attitude towards his daughter. Xavier accusing Mariana of fearing her father. *Pare.*

My heart squeezes in sympathy. Some of us have a bond with a parent that's unfathomable to outsiders – and unbreakable.

Some of the other Catalan words linger, too. *Vendre? Passió?* A distant memory from a school French lesson kicks in. *Vendre* – did that mean *sell* in Catalan too? And *passió? Passion? Love?*

My compassion evaporates. I don't want to think about what her conversation might mean.

'Alice,' Mariana calls after me. I turn and her bangles chime as she gestures for me to follow her through to her office. At her desk, she dabs at her face with a tissue, pulls mascara, blusher and a lipstick from her bag. 'Have you a mirror?' she asks.

I nod and pass her a small compact.

She peers closely at herself. 'Do you love your father?' she says abruptly.

I weigh up what I want to say, watching her wipe away smudges from beneath her eyes. She blinks a little, unscrews the mascara. 'I don't know my father,' I say eventually.

Mariana pauses with the wand in her hand. 'Oh. Why is this?'

'My mum was young. I've never known him.'

Her eyes travel over my striped orange and yellow dress that I've not been brave enough to wear to work before. 'And this is not a problem for you?'

I shake my head. 'No. My mum has always been enough, more than enough, and I had my grandma for a long time too.'

Mariana holds up the mirror and begins to coat her curly lashes. 'You are a free woman,' she mutters. 'No father, no control.'

I think about dancing in the club on Saturday night, how my worries had melted away, my delicious weekend entwined in Andy's arms. Yet also the weirdness I feel now Mum's demands have stopped. My anxiety simmering beneath the surface. 'My mum isn't easy,' I offer.

She flips open the blusher. 'Oh, yes. You are her prisoner.'

I let out a bark of laughter. 'Hardly!'

Mariana shrugs. 'You have never left home. Until they are old, or die, the parents tell us what to do.'

I edge towards the door, wishing, for once, to be distracted by work.

'Are you going out later?' she says, gesturing towards my dress.

I look down and pluck the material. 'Oh no, I just fancied a change. I've had this for ages.'

'I like it,' she says. 'You look pretty.' She circles blusher on to her cheeks then snaps the mirror shut and hands it back to me.

After her accusation the other day, I wonder why she's being nice. Then I realise this is code for me to stay quiet. She doesn't want anyone to know about the call with her father – or her tears.

Mariana treats me to a dazzling smile. 'So now it is time for you to study the lessons,' she says. 'I want you to spend all days this week with the students, observing the teachers, reading their lesson plans.'

I'm taken aback, even though her reasons for me doing this are valid. I get that it's important I understand what makes a good teacher and a great lesson because Perfecte London needs to be as *perfecte* as here. Mariana's first overseas school must be a success story – as who knows where it will lead to?

Still, I can't help thinking she's deliberately keeping Andy and I apart. Does she somehow know what happened between us this weekend?

'On Friday you will be ready to finish,' she adds.

I nod. 'Then would you like me to teach?'

Mariana's laugh tinkles. 'No! Not necessary. I mean, you will finish here at Perfecte.'

I look at her stupidly. 'But I've still got a few weeks of training left.'

Mariana beams again. 'You will be done! So you can go home early. Consider this a bonus. It's time to return to *Mama*, no? Your sister is getting married this weekend – your *mama* cannot be left alone after this, can she?'

My mouth goes dry. I'm not ready. I want to stay.

I want more time with Andy.

There's nothing I can say.

I slope off and the day crawls as I try to keep focused on the classes by scribbling notes, but I find myself drifting to recipes instead of thinking about lesson plans.

Conversely, the evenings fly. Andy and I are out every night eating in his favourite restaurants, where he's warmly welcomed by everyone. I worry that people will gossip. Mariana might find out. But he takes my hand, kisses me on the mouth and makes it very public that he's with me.

But for how long?

We have the weekend together in London for Charlie's wedding.

But then he'll be returning to Barcelona alone.

Andy says he'll try to convince Mariana to keep me on for longer but nothing changes and I can't beg her to stay. If she doesn't know something is going on between us, she might become suspicious. And if she knows already? Either way, I don't want to be the one to toss in the hand grenade that blows up their divorce proceedings, which Andy's been so careful to manage.

He's in a difficult situation.

But I can't shake the feeling he's choosing Mariana over me.

Chapter 47

ALICE

Now

On Wednesday evening, Andy and I decide to take the slow, steady climb up Montjuïc hill. We pause halfway to admire the city panorama from the sidelines of the Barcelona 1992 Olympic swimming pool. By the time we reach the summit, we're both starving.

We find a spot beneath the shade of a tree, facing the sparkling sea and looking down over Port Vell. Colourful shipping containers line up along the quay like tiny toys and a tanker glides slowly across the horizon. I unpack fat olives, a circle of soft *Arzúa-Ulloa* cheese, a pot of sweet *condonyat* – a quince jam – and break off hunks of crusty bread.

'I really don't want you to go back to London,' Andy says softly, looping his fingers through mine. 'I'm sorry I've not been able to find a way to sort this out yet.'

If he's talking about getting Mariana to keep me here longer, it isn't going to happen. I've already accepted that. He's told me so many times that she's stubborn and likes to get her own way. She's no reason to change her mind.

But does he mean he doesn't want me to leave *at all*?

I pop a fleshy olive into my mouth and let its tanginess tingle my tongue. This is a pointless conversation. I have to go back. Janet's counting on me. Mum will want me home once Charlie's gone.

Of course, there's one obvious answer. Andy could come to London with me. We could run the new school together.

But the idea is so big, and our relationship so new and so fragile, I can't ask him. Nor do I want any second of the time we have left to be ruined by misery. I keep my tone light. 'At least we've got this weekend together.'

Despite everything, I'm excited about going to Charlie's wedding – and bringing Andy with me.

'I suppose.' He hasn't touched the food yet. I spread cheese on to a piece of bread, add a dollop of the *condonyat* and pass it to him.

'Come on, eat,' I say.

We become quiet for a moment.

'How are you feeling now about Charlie getting married?' Andy says eventually.

I sigh. 'I'm okay. We talked a lot when she was here. I'm happy for her. She really loves Sarah.'

Our eyes slide together but I look away first.

Love? Amor?

The sandwich turns dry in my mouth and I swallow it down with some water. Andy's gaze is unnerving so I stand and brush the crumbs off my top. Before me, the sea is an endless ripple of blue that stretches into the distance, merging into the sky at a point so far away it's hard to know where one begins and the other ends.

I feel very small. 'It's a big world out there,' I say softly.

I hear Andy come up behind me. He sweeps my hair to the side and kisses the nape of my neck, sending a shiver of sadness and longing through me.

'And you found your way back to me,' he murmurs. I feel him drape a necklace around my neck and fix the clasp. 'This has always belonged to you.'

I touch the cool metal of the Gemini pendant and turn to him.

'You should have kept it the first time,' he says, trying to smile.

I shake my head a little. 'It wouldn't have been right.'

'But it might have given me hope.'

'Hope?'

'That you would change your mind.'

I step away a little. 'What do you mean? *You* didn't want *me*.'

Andy frowns. 'Of course I did. But you didn't take my calls. You didn't come back!'

I suck in a shaky breath, dimly aware the memories still hurt. 'Sorting out my grandma's affairs took longer than I thought,' I mutter, fiddling with the necklace. 'Then Charlie told me you'd gone to Ibiza.'

He's incredulous. 'Gone? What do you mean? I never even saw Charlie!'

My head buzzes as the past gathers itself and I turn back towards the view, clasping my arms around my body to keep myself upright.

After the shock of hearing about my grandma's death, I'd returned home to find Mum a wreck and Philippe, as usual, nowhere to be seen. A new neighbour – Janet – had moved in across the street and she'd been kind enough to hold the fort until my return, making tea and bringing meals over for Mum.

In the blur of grief and dealing with everything that needed to be done in the days that followed, I didn't have the energy or focus to talk to Andy properly. But I knew inside my heart, I was letting him down.

In the haze of memories, my mind drifts back to the day Andy and I had on the beach – the sun a burning ball on the horizon shooting flames into the darkening blue of the sky. Andy telling me his brother had died. Me, floating for the first time with his reassuring hand beneath my back.

He'd trusted me. I'd trusted him.

Our kiss.

Then, later, baring his soul the night he told me Matt had been killed by a drunk driver.

Making love.

Back then, I didn't have the strength to deal with what I was going through, what Mum was going through – *and* give myself to him.

A few days after I got back, Charlie burst through the front door and tossed her rucksack to the floor. 'Oh, sis, I'm so sorry – I lost my phone,' she'd said, rushing over. She folded me into a hug and then Mum joined us, and for the first time in years we held each other close.

That night, Charlie came into my room and sat down on the edge of my bed. 'I've got something I need to tell you,' she said, plucking the fabric of the duvet cover.

Dread crawled up my spine and pushed me upright.

'On my way back to Plaça Reial, I saw Andy,' she said slowly, sadness drawing creases in her face. She sucked in a breath and her expression hardened, making my stomach flutter. 'I saw him walking down the steps to the metro with Mariana.'

I was confused. 'So?'

'He had his rucksack, she had a suitcase.'

'You think . . . ?' I shook my head. 'No.'

Charlie sighed and nodded. 'Mariana likes him. I mean, *really* likes him. She goes on and on about him after she's had a few drinks.'

Now, Andy touches my shoulder and my mind spins back to the hilltop. My throat squeezes tight with tears. 'You went to Ibiza with her,' I finish shakily. 'With *Mariana.*'

Andy pales and his gaze shifts into the distance. Jealousy carves through me as I realise a part of me had hoped he might say I'd got everything wrong.

'I hoped it wasn't true,' I whisper. 'But Charlie insisted. She went back to Café Vermell and Jimmy told her Mariana had invited you to her cousin's apartment over there.'

Andy's face flushes and he grips my arms. 'Yes, but not in the way you think.' He releases me and I see him reach for Matt's pendant out of habit and his fingers touch air. 'She was going anyway, just for a few days, and suggested I come along and check out the DJ scene while you were away.'

'But you must have known she liked you!' I cry. 'Charlie said she'd told her enough times when they were out partying.'

He laughs bitterly. 'I didn't – I really didn't. I was besotted with *you*, Alice! I had no room for noticing, let alone *feeling*, anything for anyone else.' He rubs the back of his neck. 'When Mariana suggested the idea, my mum practically pushed me out the door. Things were going so well for us in the kitchen, she was confident I'd see Ibiza wasn't the place for me after all.' His eyes glisten. 'That was it. It was never a romantic trip away with Mariana.'

Andy balls his fists and stares at me. 'I don't understand,' he says, voice rising. 'Had you forgotten? I'd not long told you Matt had been *killed*. It was so, so hard to tell you. Yet you believed I'd go off with someone else? With Mariana!'

My heart crushes beneath the weight of my guilt.

He droops a little and his eyes go to the horizon. 'I'd given a piece of myself to you that night, Alice,' he says quietly. 'But it was like once you were back home, back with your mum, you became a different person. You wouldn't take my calls and when we finally spoke, you were so *cold* . . .' He laughs sadly. 'You slept with me and left. I felt like your pity fuck.'

Chapter 48

ALICE

Now

Shock spirals as the new reality sinks in. I imagine Andy turning Mariana down. The familiar hot flush of embarrassment when she realises she's taken things too far. His kind nature smoothing things over so there's no awkwardness around her cousin.

Then I think of Charlie telling me what she believed to be true, but wasn't true, and me, being so unsure of who I was, who Andy might still be, believed he'd moved on without me – and chosen her.

Sadness squeezes my heart.

Andy sighs. 'Now I see why you didn't return my calls,' he says quietly. 'I didn't know you thought . . .' He grinds his fist into his hand. 'But when we eventually spoke on the phone, why didn't you just ask me? I could have explained everything.' His breath hisses in frustration.

My eyes drift away from him and flickering images of the oak tree come into focus, my vomit on the grass.

'Alice?' Andy says.

I snap back to the present. 'Are you forgetting something? You told me it was over!' I'm still clinging to the last shreds of truth. The strands that have helped me cover the thick layers of guilt I've carried for all these years.

To shield me from the *real* reason that kept Andy and I apart.

His face contorts. 'You left me!'

'I was dealing with my grandma's death,' I respond stonily.

'That was *your mum's* responsibility,' he retorts. He thrusts his hand through his hair and lowers his voice. 'I was angry that you were running around doing everything, with no help from her and no energy left to talk to me. I felt like I was losing you to your mum, and you wouldn't ever come back. When I said we were over, it was a childish, stupid and impulsive thing to say. I wanted you to fight for me. I never expected you to *agree*.'

I close my eyes. The shattering of glass sounds, a bloodied hoof dangles through the shards. The branches of the oak tree bow untouched in the breeze.

I had no choice, Andy.

'Oh, Alice,' he says, burying his face in my hair. 'What a fuck-up.'

◆　◆　◆

We clutch hands all the way back to my apartment and I turn over everything Andy's told me. Could we have . . . ? Would we have . . . ? It's too heartbreaking to think about. We tumble into bed as soon as we come through the door, and slowly make love to savour every minute we have until we'll be apart again.

I don't know how we can make this work, but there's a niggle that keeps saying, why isn't he putting in more effort with Mariana to keep me here? Why hasn't he suggested moving to London to run the language school with me?

We're lying snuggled up together when the gospel choir starts its booming chorus from my phone on the table. I clock the time. It's late for Mum and I wonder if she's having a last-minute panic about the wedding arrangements – not that there's much to worry about. Charlie and Sarah have planned their reception at The Crown and they've hired caterers.

My hand hovers for a moment as I think about Andy's words earlier. *I felt like I was losing you to your mum.* Then I take the call. 'Everything alright?' I say cheerfully.

'Awful,' Mum sobs.

I sit up, alarmed. 'What's happened? Is Charlie okay?'

'She's moved out.'

I tense – couldn't she have waited a couple more days? – but I keep my cool. 'She's getting married. She wasn't going to stick around forever,' I say lightly. 'Anyway, she told me you two are getting on just fine.'

'That's not it,' she sniffs.

My skin prickles. 'What's happened? Is it your perfume business?'

'No,' she wails. 'That's going *fantastic*. It's Philippe. Your bloody sister has invited him to the wedding.'

'Philippe?' I repeat, stupidly. I get up and pull on Andy's T-shirt. I let out a hysterical laugh. 'You know Charlie, she likes a surprise.'

'I hate him.'

The line hums for a moment and I glance at Andy – tousled hair, toned chest, *God he's irresistible* – and throw him a sheepish smile.

'He is her dad and you loved him once,' I say, turning my attention back to Mum. 'Charlie wouldn't be here if you hadn't.'

'You're here and I never loved your father.'

This is true.

'I told Philippe a decade ago I wasn't carrying on with him anymore,' she says, her voice rising again. 'I should never have let it go on for so long. His poor wife.'

Poor Charlie, more like.

When we'd been kids, Philippe used to rock up with an armful of presents for her, but it was never enough to soften the blow before he whisked Mum away. Mum always came first. In return, she put her life on hold for him.

Put *us* on hold.

For me, the certainty of having no dad had always been the less painful option. 'Do you need me to come home? I can change my flight.'

I notice Andy's face turn incredulous. Slowly, he shakes his head.

'You don't need to do that,' Mum says wearily. 'You'll be here on Friday.'

Andy swings his legs around to the edge of the bed and sits with his back to me.

'You need support,' I insist. 'It's going to be a shock seeing him again.'

'I'm not completely useless!' her voice shrills. 'I don't need you sorting out my life.'

I'm taken aback. What's happened to her while I've been gone?

'Sorry,' she says grumpily. 'It would be nice to see you.'

I end the call and scout the room, thoughts flitting between when I can get a flight, packing and how I can keep the peace between her and Philippe at the wedding. What was Charlie *thinking*?

'You're leaving?' Andy says, over his shoulder. 'Just like that? Your mum calls and you go running?'

I look up, startled at his tone. 'What's that supposed to mean?'

His lips press together. 'We're flying back the day after tomorrow. Why can't she wait until then? Why can't *you*?' He turns away again. 'You're still the mother and she's still the child. Not much has changed in ten years.'

I squeeze my eyes shut. I don't want to fall out with him. I scoot over and curl into his warm, silky back and nuzzle my face into the earthy scent of his neck. 'I'm sorry I'm leaving you early,' I mumble, running my mouth over his skin.

He shivers.

'It's only an extra day or so,' I say, swinging around and straddling his lap.

He sucks in a sharp breath. 'Don't distract me,' he says hoarsely. 'I'm trying to be annoyed with you.'

But it's too late, I can feel his distraction pressing between my legs and I'm melting again. He gathers himself for a moment and cups my face. 'Do you still want me to come to the wedding with you?'

His grave expression makes me smile. 'Are you crazy?' I drop butterfly kisses over his worry lines. 'Of course – and, anyway, we've got no choice. Charlie's invited you and no one can say no to Charlie.'

Chapter 49

ALICE

Now

'Sis!' Charlie yells down the stairs. 'I need some help.'

I'm in the middle of frying bacon for Mum's sandwich – it's Saturday morning, after all, *and* Charlie's wedding day – and I'm running late because I had to pop to the corner shop. Charlie had refused to add bacon to Mum's online delivery, saying it was no good for her weight. Apparently, they don't bother with the meal routine pinned to the fridge anymore. I'm not sure what Mum thinks about this. Though today is not the day to get into an argument with Charlie about it.

'Is my breakfast ready yet?' Mum calls from her wingback chair in the living room. 'Smells delicious. I've not had a bacon sandwich since you left.'

The doorbell goes and I give the bacon another push around the pan. In the twenty-four hours since I've been home, I've discovered the cupboards and fridge are stocked full, Mum has a cleaner – and my homemade bread tastes awful compared to the freshly baked loaves in Barcelona.

'You getting that?' Mum shouts.

I fly over to the door and find a large bunch of flowers on the doorstep. I pick them up and hurry back to the kitchen to dunk them in water. It's one of those expensive bouquets wrapped in brown paper and tied with twine. Cerise-pink roses nestle among spiky blue thistles and silver greenery. Sarah's got good taste.

'Alice? Did you hear me?' Charlie shouts again.

'Coming!'

I put the bacon sandwich together with a generous glob of tomato sauce on the side and take it through to Mum with a fresh cup of tea.

I need to make time to help her into the dress we bought yesterday. I'd been surprised when she suggested we go to Marks and Spencer's. I can't remember the last time she'd wanted – been *able* – to visit an actual shop to buy clothes. Mum had paid for a taxi, hobbled into the store on her sticks, and I'd found her somewhere to sit. I'd offered to bring a selection of dresses to her, but she'd insisted on coming around with me. We'd taken it slowly, with rest breaks, and afterwards sat in the cafe and had lunch.

I scuttle upstairs to Charlie, darting into the bathroom first to wash my greasy hands. I need to shower soon because it won't be long before Andy arrives. The thought of seeing him sends me into a flutter of nerves and excitement. His plane got delayed last night, so he went straight to the hotel and hasn't had a chance to meet Mum yet.

Will she like him?

I hope so.

Charlie's standing in front of the mirror in her wedding dress. Like a proud parent, tears spring to my eyes. She looks angelic. Surprisingly, she's chosen a conventional ivory bridal gown that nips in at her waist and falls to her feet. The off-the-shoulder style reveals her daisy chain tattoo, which loops across her collar bone and sparkles in gold shimmer. I was expecting a crazy hair colour but she's stuck to her natural blonde and has tonged in curls. One side is pinned with a gold-gemmed comb and she's wearing a pearl-studded tiara.

'Can you do the zip?' she says, pointing to her back. I close the dress and she spins around, throwing her arms wide. 'What do you think?'

I swallow down tears and try to smile. 'You look gorgeous.'

Charlie's marriage marks the end of us. No more Charlie barging back into our home with a holdall when things haven't worked out with her latest partner. She'll be living with Sarah above the pub. I feel a pang of sadness but I'm ready to let her go.

'I'm going to miss having you around,' I say, squeezing her hands.

'I'm only going to be at the bottom of the road and, anyway, you won't. You'll be too busy running the new school and managing a long-distance thing with Andy.'

My face falls. I'd brought Charlie up to speed when I'd got back yesterday.

'Sis, promise you'll talk to him this weekend?' she urges. 'Get everything out in the open, tell him how you feel. Don't repeat the mistakes of last time.'

'What can I say? I want you to move to London? It's a bit selfish.'

'He's a partner in the business! It's not like you're asking him to give up his job.'

'And what if things don't work out with us? I'll have dragged him here for nothing.'

Charlie shrugs. 'He'll have made the choice himself.'

I don't know what to do. But in the here and now, I want to focus on Charlie and her special day – then I'll make some decisions.

'Have you told Mum about Andy yet?'

I smile a little. 'Not exactly . . .'

'Uh-oh.'

'I'm going to ambush her when he arrives. She'll have to be on her best behaviour and won't have time to make any judgements.'

Charlie nods. 'Probably a good thing. Her mood is going to be all over the place with Philippe coming.' She catches my eye. 'I know you think it's a bad idea, but he's my dad and this is my wedding, right? They can be civil for a day.'

I put my hand on her arm. 'Don't worry. I made sure Mum and I had a proper chat about it yesterday. Now she's got over the shock, I think she's almost looking forward to seeing him again.'

'I don't know what's worse,' says Charlie, smiling. 'You know, you won't believe this, sis, but I think I'm going to miss her when I move out. Fun Mum's starting to come back. We've had a good time while you've been away.'

'Have you?' I feel a bit miffed.

'Don't get offended, it's a good thing, right?'

I throw her a quick smile. 'I suppose.'

She goes to give me a hug and I hold up my hands. 'Hey, careful bride-lady, you don't want to crush your dress. You know, I can't believe you're ready early for once. Do you want some help taking it off until it's time to go?'

'Still telling me what to do, sis?' she responds lightly. 'I'll leave it on. I'm going in a minute to help Sarah get ready. She's crap with hair and make-up, so I said I'd do it for her.'

I'm about to say that she can't let Sarah see her in her dress yet, it's bad luck, she'll spoil the surprise, but I bite my lip. It's none of my business. It's only tradition and they want to do things their way.

Charlie isn't my responsibility anymore.

◆ ◆ ◆

Before long, Charlie's gone, I'm showered and dressed, and I've left my hair to dry naturally while I help Mum get ready. She huffs as she climbs the stairs, but I'm delighted to see she's moving faster than usual, and soon she's back in front of the TV, very much the glamorous mother-of-the-bride.

When the doorbell goes, my heart spins and I fling open the door, certain it's Andy.

'Hi, Alice.'

Philippe stands on the doorstep. He looks tanned and dapper in a charcoal pinstriped suit, a pink tie, and hair streaked grey that curls around his collar. He throws me a cautious smile.

I glance nervously at Mum. She's absorbed in one of her programmes.

'Who is it?' she calls, without looking around.

I gesture for him to come in – better to have the showdown now than at the wedding.

'It's . . . Philippe.'

'What?' Mum peers around the edge of her wingback chair. She fumbles for her sticks but knocks them sideways and I go to help. 'Don't fuss, I can do it,' she snaps.

Philippe hovers by the door, his eyes wandering over the open-plan room he hasn't seen before. Mum shuffles towards him and his face contorts momentarily.

'Dani, you look wonderful,' he says, recovering himself. He goes over and kisses her cheeks. Mum's lost some weight since I've been away. The floral dress flatters her shape and the colour brings out the green of her eyes. I'm pleased she let me do her hair and make-up as she really is looking her best.

I realise I'm holding my breath.

Mum straightens up and eyeballs Philippe. 'You're looking pretty good yourself,' she says. 'But there'll be no shenanigans – not today, not any day. Are you clear?'

Her voice wobbles and my heart breaks a little for her. Yesterday she'd reminded me that after the accident she'd told Philippe enough was enough, she wouldn't continue their on-off affair. It only occurs to me now that I distanced myself from Andy at the same time. We both pushed away the people we loved.

Love. There's that word again. Did I love Andy back then?

Do I love him *now*?

I'm about to close the door when I see Janet making her way across our drive so we can share a taxi to the registry office. She's wearing a slightly-too-big hat with a peacock feather that droops over one side and her shiny red clutch bag doesn't really go with her outfit.

'Hello, hello,' she says, coming inside. 'How's the bride? Nervous?' She spots Philippe, who's sat down next to Mum. They're talking quietly.

I explain that Charlie's already left and suddenly remember I've forgotten to give her the flowers that came earlier. I do the introductions and Philippe stands to greet Janet, but she waves him away. 'No need, you carry on.' She turns to me. 'So? Is your fancy man here yet?'

I blush. While I was running around yesterday doing chores, I'd had a rushed conversation with Janet, explaining how I'd finished all the work I needed to do in Barcelona and wouldn't be returning. I'd gabbled through the story of how Andy and I knew each other before, his soon-to-be divorce, and that we'd recently got back together.

In fairness, Janet took it all in her stride. She was delighted to hear my news and simply nodded when I said I was waiting to hear Mariana's next steps for her Perfecte London action plan.

The doorbell goes again and since I'm still standing here, I open it straight away.

This time it *is* Andy.

He breaks into a grin that zips excitable tingles through my body. For a split second neither of us moves, as if we've forgotten how to say hello. Then we step forward at the same time, brushing lips, and he pulls me into a warm embrace that makes me giggle.

'I guess this is Andy,' says Janet, laughing behind me. 'I'm Janet, I work with Alice,' she says by way of explanation.

'She's my *boss*,' I correct.

'Of course! Good to finally meet you.' Andy bends and kisses both her cheeks like a true European.

I tug him over towards Mum, who's still talking with Philippe, but they're smiling so things must be good. 'Can I interrupt for a moment?' Without waiting for an answer, my words continue to tumble out. 'This is Andy, we met in Barcelona, we work together and he's coming to the wedding with me.'

Mum's silent. Her eyes drop to our clutched hands and her gaze travels back up and over Andy. He's wearing a blue suit with a yellow tie in a shade that complements my honey-coloured dress. He looks divine.

'Hello, I'm Dani,' she says.

'Nice to meet you.'

Mum's eyes narrow and my breath tightens as I wonder what she's going to say. 'I remember you. I saw your photo on the website Alice showed me. You own the school with your *wife*, don't you?'

There's an uncomfortable silence. Philippe clears his throat. But before I can explain, Janet gets in there first. 'They're getting divorced, Dani,' she says wearily. 'Don't cause trouble where there is none.'

Andy shoots me a look. I'll tell him later that Janet knows this information is top secret.

Mum nods and glances at me. 'Does Charlie know Andy's coming with you?'

Andy and I exchange glances. 'Yes, she does, she invited him,' I say and explain how we all know each other.

Mum's eyes cloud over for a moment. 'I don't remember you mentioning Andy before.'

I look at him and squeeze his hand. 'Things didn't work out for us back then.'

Mum catches Philippe's eye and he smiles softly back at her. 'But you've worked things out now?' she says.

My cheeks redden. I have no idea what happens to us after this weekend. There's no job for me in Barcelona and I've made a commitment to Janet that I intend to keep.

Where does Andy fit into all this?

'Taxi's here!' Janet calls. 'How are you getting to the registry office, Philippe? We haven't got space for you.'

'It's okay, I'm driving.' He stands and holds out his arm to Mum. 'Want a lift, Dani?'

A sudden flash of when I last saw him hits me unexpectedly between the eyes. 'No!' I shout, without thinking.

Everyone looks at me.

'Don't be silly,' Mum tuts. She pushes herself out of the chair and loops her arm through his. 'Alright then, Philippe, but keep your hands to yourself.' They laugh and go over to the front door where he helps Mum into her jacket.

I'm shaking a little and reach for her walking sticks. 'Don't forget these.'

'I'll be fine, Philippe's here.'

I hover anxiously as Mum makes her way down the steps, holding the handrail. She may be more mobile and a little lighter than when I was last here, but I'm still nervous.

I turn back to collect my wrap and find Andy holding it out for me. He folds it around my shoulders. 'You look gorgeous,' he whispers, grazing his mouth over mine.

My body sings with pleasure and, for a moment, I forget about Mum leaving with Philippe. Andy brushes his hands down my waist and over my hips, sparking the tingles again. I close my eyes, my mind racing on to when we can be alone in his hotel room.

'We'd better go,' I say, reluctantly pulling away.

Andy's eyes shine. 'I've got some really good news to tell you later.'

'Tell me now,' I reply, bemused.

He shakes his head. 'There's too much to say.'

'Time to go!' Janet calls.

Andy hops off down the steps while I lock up. I turn around and catch sight of Mum sat in the passenger seat of Philippe's car – his yellow vintage sports car – as if this is a perfectly normal thing to do.

A vice tightens my chest.

It can't be. It's not possible.

'Mum!' I squeak. 'You need to come in the taxi with us.'

'What? I'm fine here, stop fretting,' she calls back through the open window. 'You can be really over the top sometimes, petal. It's not a long drive. I'll see you in a minute.'

I go hot, then cold. After what happened, I don't understand how she can get into Philippe's car – *the same car* – and allow him to drive her.

Philippe leans across. 'I'll drive carefully, I promise.'

I've got no choice but to climb into the back seat of the taxi with Janet.

'You okay?' says Andy, turning around in his seat.

I nod and we set off. I cling on to my seatbelt, aware that Janet's rambling on about how she set up Riverside. And even though it's a story Andy knows already from me, he's polite enough to listen and say nothing. As we pull up outside the registry office, the first thing I see is Philippe's car parked on double yellow lines – and I exhale. Up ahead, they're walking arm in arm towards the steps and the three of us follow.

Andy's hand is reassuringly warm in mine. 'What was that about earlier?' he whispers.

Despite everything moving slowly in the right direction for us, I won't ever be able to tell him. It's a weight I bear alone. 'Nothing,' I reply.

Just then a message pings. I stop and fumble in my bag to retrieve my phone, anxious it's last-minute nerves from Charlie and she needs some reassurance.

> Alice, did you get my pretty flowers? They are to say thank you for your hard work. Mariana x

I read the message again. The roses were for me? From Mariana? Another text appears.

> Has Andrew told you our news? Finally, after months of him demanding we must sell, I have decided to buy him out. This means my plans have changed and I must speak to Janet. Enjoy the wedding – with Andrew. Bona sort, good luck x.

My world tilts and through the dizziness, I see Janet and Andy up ahead, climbing the steps. At the top, Andy turns to wait for me and smiles.

Has Andrew told you?

No, he hasn't told me anything. He never told me he wanted to sell the business. That there is no Perfecte London now, and – as far as he was concerned – there never would be.

He knew all along.

Chapter 50

ALICE

Now

I let Andy take my hand because I want to pretend everything is just fine until I have the headspace to process the fact he *demanded* that Mariana sell the business – but failed to tell me. This must have been the mysterious last piece of paperwork he'd been waiting for her to sign. No wonder he's not been in the office very much. No wonder he's had no interest in Perfecte London – because my new job was never going to happen.

As the ceremonial music begins – Bruno Mars' 'Just the Way You Are' – I press mute on the gibbering mess in my head and glue my gaze on to Charlie. She looks radiant as she glides down the aisle alone, by choice, to where Sarah waits open-mouthed. She looks equally stunning in a white tailored suit and with gold threads braided through her blonde hair.

Mum fidgets beside me, looking at Charlie but glancing back to the door. Philippe's not reappeared after going off to park the car. I hope Charlie hasn't noticed he's missing.

Soon the happy couple are saying their vows and I slide my hand away from Andy on the pretence of getting a tissue from my bag. He'll think my watery eyes are for my sister, but I'm calm, content and happy for her – my emotional turmoil is because of him. As the newlyweds walk back up the aisle, Sarah throws me a glowing smile.

I'm not losing my sister, I'm gaining another, and my heart soars.

Mum takes my arm and we make our way to where the taxi waits to take us to the pub. Soon the driver drops us at the entrance to the footpath and I'm pleasantly surprised by how far she can walk. I listen to her grumbling about Philippe while Andy trails along behind with a chattering Janet.

I'm tempted to call over my shoulder: *This is why our relationship would never have worked. My life is here – with my mum. Your life is over there – and it's all about you.*

The Crown looks incredible. Charlie and Sarah have done the decorations themselves. A foliage archway woven with creamy white roses and fairy lights frames the double doors. Inside, the tables have been pushed together to form one long seating area, upon which jam jars overflow with red roses, eucalyptus and delicate white baby's breath. Above, the old beams are wrapped in greenery, baubles and twists of silver ribbon while a large glitterball hangs above the space cleared for the dancefloor.

'The room looks beautiful,' I say as we greet the couple at the door. 'You've done an amazing job.'

'I can't take the credit,' says Sarah. 'It was my *wife's* vision.'

They share a beaming smile.

'My *wife* is a great team player,' Charlie adds, shining eyes stuck on Sarah.

'Sorry I'm late,' a voice gasps behind us.

Charlie lets out a squeal. 'Dad!'

Philippe's at the door, hair mussed, tie askew, panting slightly. 'Oh, darling, I'm so sorry I missed the important bit. Damn car.'

Charlie shrugs but she's still smiling. 'You've missed a lot of important things in my life, but you're here now.'

Mum shoots him a dirty look. 'You always were unreliable.'

'It was the car, Dani!' he says, throwing up his hands. 'I wanted to be there, but I couldn't find anywhere to park and then the damn thing broke down again.' He tucks his hair behind his ears. 'I should have got rid of it years ago.'

His eyes land briefly on mine but I look away.

Sarah ushers us to sit down and I feel Andy's gaze boring into my back as he follows me. He's been seated next to Mum, and I've been placed opposite with Philippe. Throughout the wedding roast dinner meal they keep the conversation light and peppered with their tales of running the nightclub together when Charlie and I were kids.

Andy's quiet and shoots me troubled looks now and then, but I don't catch his eye. Instead, I let myself be pulled into Mum's stories, encouraging her and Philippe to tell more, because then I don't have to think, I don't have to talk, I don't have to decide what to say to Andy after we've eaten.

Mum reaches the punchline to a funny anecdote. Philippe roars with laughter and I allow myself a small smile. Her broad grin is all Charlie's. I'm reminded that this witty version of herself is who she used to be before the TV habits crept in, the eating routines and the online shopping – though her perfume business seems to have put a stop to that.

Once we've finished our apple pie and ice-cream, listened and laughed at the speeches, Charlie switches the wedding playlist into party mode. Guests don't need asking twice. There's practically a stampede to get to the dancefloor.

Philippe takes the opportunity to go over to Mum's side and Andy stands and offers him his seat. We stare at one another across the table. Hurt criss-crosses his face but I'm churning with my own pain and humiliation. How could he have led me on? Prepping me for a job in London that was never going to happen? Making me feel that what we had might go somewhere this time? He's on the rebound. No wonder he didn't object when Mariana asked me to leave.

He has plans – and they don't include me.

'Alice.' Janet's sidled through the throng of guests and she leans in close. 'Andy's not very forthcoming about Perfecte London, is he?' she whispers, glancing at him. 'I've asked lots of questions, but he's really non-committal. Is there something going on?'

Angry tears spring to my eyes. Andy's decision to sell isn't just about me, it's about Janet's livelihood, too. 'Best to talk to Mariana – it's not Andy's project.' I feel guilty that I don't have the guts to tell her the truth. Perhaps I didn't work hard enough. I didn't impress Mariana. I didn't prove to Andy that our school was worth investing in. That *I* was worth investing in. Not enough to change his mind.

Janet's attention is pulled away by another guest and Andy materialises by my side. 'Talk to me, Alice,' he says quietly.

Unhappiness fills his eyes and I know I can't keep running every time things get difficult between us. Then, just as I'm about to suggest we go outside to talk, I catch Mum shuffling to her feet and feel the familiar tug to rush over and help. She grasps Philippe's arm and they smile at one another, and I feel myself relax a little.

'Poor Dani, she's never been the same since that awful car accident.' A voice drifts over from the crowd milling around us. 'I don't know what Alice was thinking, driving her mum home from the funeral after she'd had a drink. Dani's lucky to be alive.'

Shock prickles my scalp. Andy's face becomes as still and white as marble. Fear floods my ears and becomes a throbbing drumbeat of guilt. I swallow the bile in my mouth, and reach for him.

Andy leaps back and blood rushes angrily into his face. He twists away from me and pushes himself through the people while I watch, helpless, as he disappears out the pub door.

It's the curl of his mouth that disturbs me the most. Repulsion.

I pull myself together and hurriedly go after him, nudging my way through the packed dancefloor. Charlie catches me as I pass. She throws her arms around me and tugs me into a dance. My arms and legs work mechanically for a moment, my eyes frantically on the door, and then I manage to extract myself and run after Andy, hoping I'm not too late.

Outside, night has fallen and the footpath back up to the street is in darkness except for the streetlamp at the top. Suddenly, Andy emerges from the shadows near me and my heart jump-starts. 'I . . .'

Now the moment is here, I have no words.

Everything he has heard is true.

'Oh, I see, *now* you're ready to talk? After ignoring me all day? Worrying your little secret was going to come out?'

I pull my wrap tight. 'That's not—'

'I've heard all I need to hear,' he says, in a voice as cold and brittle as ice. His face has shuttered down and the mask is back, reminding me how he'd looked on my first day when he told me not to take the job.

He told me not to take the job.

Why did he say that?

Something new creeps into my head, but Andy's talking again. 'You didn't think this revelation was important enough to *tell* me?'

His words whip around my body, cutting into my skin and leaving a burning trail that sears my insides. 'I'm sorry—' I whisper.

'Sorry?' His laugh is streaked with hatred. But before I can say anything else, he spirals around and vanishes back into the darkness. For a moment all I hear is the thud of his feet. The hammer of my heart.

At the top of the footpath, he appears beneath the lamplight and I seize my chance. 'I love you!'

Andy stops.

My heart lifts.

But then he breaks into a run and is gone.

Chapter 51

ALICE

Now

'Tell me about Barcelona,' says Janet, handing me a mug of tea.

I plonk myself down in one of her ratty armchairs.

I've heard nothing from Andy – he's not returned my calls or texts – and I'm certain he's flown home.

His silence booms inside my head.

'So?' Janet prompts.

I force a bright smile and start to ramble about how weird it had been working at Cafè Vermell again, that Jimmy ran the place now – cooking with Andy. Tears become trapped in my throat as I stutter on, recalling our trips to the market and how we'd brainstorm recipes together, then finally my voice peters out, strangled by the effort not to cry.

Janet looks at me strangely.

I've said nothing about Perfecte.

I clear my throat. The black cat eyes my lap from the floor and I flick my hand to ward it off. 'Sorry, went off on a tangent,' I mutter. 'So, back to the job, it's been . . .' What has it been like? Ploughing through paperwork. Admiring lessons. Feeling intimidated by Perfecte's slick set-up. Fearful I won't be able to handle my new job in London. '. . . difficult.'

Janet's still watching me. She's like one of the cats, waiting for her moment to pounce.

My stomach churns with the memory of Mariana's dismissal, her text, Andy's lie – *my* hideous untruth.

'Mariana emailed me,' Janet ventures cautiously, eyes darting over my face from behind her glasses. 'She told me she's bought Andy out of Perfecte.'

A tiny bit of relief seeps out. Janet already knows what's going on. 'I'm sorry. It seems like I messed up. Going to Barcelona was a complete waste of time.' I grip my mug. 'Andy always knew there was never going to be a job for me in London once he'd persuaded Mariana to buy him out.'

Janet frowns. One of the ginger cats springs on to the arm of her chair and rubs its face against her shoulder. The tabby on her lap hisses a warning and she tickles its ears in consolation. 'But *was* Barcelona a complete waste of time?'

'Yes!' I insist. 'I wanted to do everything I could to help Riverside. But here I am, I've come full circle. I'm back where I started.'

Janet sips her tea. 'It sounds like you've achieved much more than you expected while you were over there.'

I flush. 'If you're talking about Andy, then that was a mistake.'

She looks perplexed. 'Really? But at the wedding—'

'We had an argument,' I cut in. I pick at the loose threads on the chair arm mauled by the cats. 'For the record, I didn't let the cooking interfere with my work at Perfecte.'

Janet laughs. 'Oh, Alice, don't feel guilty. I didn't imagine for one minute that you did. You're very reliable and more loyal than is good for you. Sometimes.'

I frown. 'What do you mean?'

'I didn't ask you to go to Barcelona to save me,' she says. 'I encouraged you to go for *you*. You've always talked fondly of your time there and, wow, what a lovely coincidence that you ended up working with Andy again – and I don't mean at Perfecte.' Her gaze sharpens. 'There's more to Barcelona than the school, isn't there?'

I look down into my tea. She's given me the chipped mug with the kitten picture again. It occurs to me she considers this one mine. 'You're not angry that I let you down?'

Janet leans over to pat my knee and the tabby slides off her lap, landing on all fours. 'What makes you think that? In my eyes, Mariana's invitation was exactly what you needed. A chance to get away and try something new that was just for you. I guess in the back of my mind I'd hoped you'd stay. But I would've been happy for you to come back and run Perfecte London, too. Either way, you'd be winning.'

She sits back again and the black cat seizes the chance to claim her lap.

'But I'm losing! There's nothing for me back there and there's no new language school here.'

Janet cocks her head. 'What makes you think that? Mariana's only put her plans to buy Riverside on hold. She and her father need to sort out the legal stuff and her divorce with Andy.'

I jerk in surprise. 'Her father? He knows?'

'Knows what?' Janet tugs a tissue from her sleeve and uses it to clean her glasses.

'That they're divorcing?' I say slowly. 'Remember, I said? Mariana wanted to keep it a secret so the Perfecte brand would stay intact.'

I think about Andy's predicament. He couldn't tell me he wanted out, but he warned me not to come. What else could he do?

Janet puts her glasses back on. She strokes the cat and it rumbles into a purr. 'I'm retiring, Alice,' she says eventually. 'In the nicest possible way, what you choose to do makes no difference to me. You are welcome to carry on working at my school and if Mariana gives you the job and it feels right, then take it. But if you don't . . .'

'Retiring?' I scrabble to make sense of what she's saying.

'I'm moving to Cornwall,' she continues with a distant smile. 'I know this must be a shock. There's no rush. Have a think about it and let me know.'

Panic flutters as I fast-forward my future. I could slip back into my old job, make something of my food events, accept Mariana's offer when the sale goes through, or . . .

Realisation smacks me in the face.

I don't want to do it. I don't want to teach English anymore. I don't want to run a school.

But what am I going to do instead?

I leave Janet's and cross back over to Mum's, barely glancing at Philippe's cranky sports car parked in our drive. There's been a reconciliation of sorts. Apparently he's been a widower for a number of years and I suspect he might stick around this time.

Inside, the pair of them are in front of the TV, arguing with good humour about the correct answer to a game-show question. It's not one of Mum's usual programmes and I'm mildly surprised she's let him watch something different. I call out a greeting and wander into the kitchen, lost in thought as I put the kettle on.

'Cuppa, Philippe?' I call through to the living room.

He glances away from the TV. 'No, thanks, love.'

'Nor me,' Mum adds quickly.

I frown. 'You know it's three o'clock? Do you want something else?'

Philippe gives her a questioning look and she pinks and shakes her head. 'No biscuits, thanks, petal, I'm watching my weight.'

He reaches out and squeezes her hand. 'Don't take this the wrong way, Dani, but I'm liking you with curves.'

Mum turns red and she laughs nervously. 'You always were a sweet talker.'

I sit with them for a while and our conversation moves on to Charlie and Sarah's wedding and their honeymoon road trip across Europe.

'Thank God Charlie never learnt to drive,' I say. 'She'd be a nightmare on the German Autobahn without a speed limit. Is Sarah a good driver? I hope they got the car serviced before they left.'

'You're such a worrier,' Mum remarks.

Philippe throws me a sympathetic look. 'Now, now, Dani, it's perfectly understandable for Alice to be concerned.'

Mum looks puzzled. 'Why? She hasn't driven in years.'

'No need to, living in London,' I say quickly, feeling the horrors of yesterday bubbling up to the surface again. Mum's mobility may be improving, but I don't need Philippe reminding me how she got into this state.

He glances between us. 'Dani, I know it's early days for us, but we can't avoid talking about what happened. In fact, we should. Let's get things out in the open.'

I get up from the sofa and stand by the window.

'Oh, you mean the car crash,' Mum says flatly.

I suck in a painful breath.

We never talk about the past. I've made it my mission to do everything I can to make it up to Mum. I don't want her to have reason to drag my horrific mistake back into the light.

Philippe sounds startled. 'You're not upset, Dani?'

My legs go wobbly. My chest begins to close in.

'I don't want to spend time dwelling on it,' she replies.

Nobody says anything. My breath snags. I suck and exhale, suck and exhale.

'Alice?' Mum's voice sounds faint. 'Oh, petal,' she says, sensing my pain. 'Come over here. Come and sit down.'

I turn stiffly, placing one foot in front of the other, and drop back down on the sofa.

Philippe looks stricken. 'I'm sorry I did this to you, Alice,' he says quietly. 'I've only myself to blame.'

A distant ringing begins in my ears, like an alarm going off, mounting until it reaches a high-pitched shrill. 'No!' I cry. 'You've got it wrong!'

Mum and Philippe glance at one another, shocked.

I throw my hands over my face. I see the deer leap out from nowhere, the twist of the steering wheel, the car bumping on to the grass, the oak tree, the yank of the wheel again.

The thud.

Philippe's shaking his head. 'Alice, no—'

I jump up. 'It was *my* fault! I was drunk, I wasn't in control. It's my fault Mum can't walk properly, that she's had to use sticks for all these years.' The terrible truth cannonballs into the room and ricochets at a speed that forces me back on to the sofa again.

Mum's gone pale. 'Don't be silly. If anyone's to blame, it's me.' She struggles to her feet, brushing off Philippe's offer to help, and comes over to where I'm sat. She drops a kiss on the top of my head. 'Alice, the crash wasn't your fault.'

She glances at Philippe and there, sat in our living room, they tell me everything.

◆ ◆ ◆

Later – much later – after the shock subsides, I come back downstairs and go into the kitchen. Dazed at all I've heard, I comb through the cupboards to find inspiration and solace in preparing dinner. A bag of paella rice catches my eye. I'd forgotten I bought it the other day. Andy's mum's recipe is seared into my memory and I'm drawn to the comfort of eating something reassuring and familiar.

I pull the ingredients together, improvising here and there to replace the things I don't have, the new truth about the car accident slowly sinking in. Outside, the grey summer skies darken. Rain begins to lash the window and I feel a longing for sunshine, warmth – even the claustrophobic heat of Cafè Vermell's kitchen. I think back to wandering around the markets, the sun on my shoulders as I sought out the best cuts of meat, scooped olives from the barrel, sniffed the earthy countryside buried in the farmer's vegetables.

With Andy.

Canned TV laughter catapults me back into the kitchen. I shake the memories away because that's what they are – memories, not my life.

Soon, I'm calling Mum and Philippe to the table. She gets to her feet and Philippe springs to her side and she takes his arm. They walk slowly towards me, Mum laughing at something he says, her face radiant.

We sit down and I serve them. 'Well,' says Mum, pushing at the paella with her fork and glancing at Philippe.

'This smells incredible,' he says, and nudges her. 'Come on, Dani, give it a go. If you want to come to my place in the South of France, you're going to need to be more adventurous with food.'

'I can't eat anything with eyes,' she replies.

'There aren't any prawns, just chicken,' I say mildly.

Philippe holds out a forkful to her. 'Try mine,' he says.

Mum giggles and pinks, and I shake my head in amusement as she takes a bite. The romantic gesture does the trick as she's soon tucking in and sounding surprised that the meal tastes so good after all.

'Did you learn to cook this in Barcelona, Alice?' asks Philippe.

I nod and get a flash of Sofia showing me how to de-shell a prawn. Her hand dismissing the foolishness I'd felt for not knowing what to do. The cooking tricks I'd passed on to Andy. The recipe ideas he'd shared with me. I'd been a teacher *and* a student in the kitchen at Café Vermell.

An idea shimmers for a moment then disappears.

Philippe takes a few more mouthfuls. 'This is delicious. It's as good as eating at any of the restaurants I go to.'

I'm flattered and surprised by his pleasure. Appreciation for my cooking in my own home is an alien feeling. Yet, in Barcelona, the customers were generous with their compliments.

It's as though the Alice over there is someone else entirely.

My thoughts fall back to Susie and Xavier's new cafe-shop. I imagined Andy might have been envious of their plans, but now I see it's *me* who had those feelings. Then when Jimmy no longer needed us at Café Vermell, I was the one who felt a huge hole of disappointment.

I'm not sure I really know how Andy feels anymore – about anything.

Philippe's still nodding and smiling as he eats, and something inside me shifts.

I don't want to stay at Riverside. I don't want to work for Mariana at Perfecte London. I want to be in Barcelona. Doing something for me.

But first I must talk to Andy.

Chapter 52

ALICE

Now

After the plane lands in Barcelona, I set off on the train to the city, navigate the metro and ascend from the gloom into the Spanish sunshine. I barely notice the heat shimmering up from the boulevard as I slide into the shadows of the old town. I pass people clustered around tables drinking coffee, dunking churros into chocolate, licking ice-creams. Mopeds putter past. Someone's watering blooms of pink bougainvillea on their balcony. An old woman on a stool strokes a cat.

Alice, the crash wasn't your fault.

It's a mantra I've been chanting non-stop in my head since Mum told me. I need the reminder, but I'm already feeling lighter.

And I want to share *everything* with Andy.

Yesterday, Mum, Philippe and I had talked long into the evening. Mum told me after I left for Barcelona she'd become increasingly frustrated with her lack of mobility. She'd taken up Zumba, getting a taxi there and back a few times a week, but had been too embarrassed to tell Charlie or me. Next week, she's determined to walk there.

My heart leaps as I get closer to the square. I've had plenty of time to think about why I'm here but now that I am, my confidence wobbles. A familiar figure comes into view, waltzing towards me in loose pink trousers and a tight pink vest, a white chiffon kimono billowing out behind her.

Mariana.

I wait for her to reach me and feel an unexpected roll of pleasure when she breaks into a warm smile. 'Alice?' she says. 'What are you doing back here? I thought you had decided Perfecte wasn't for you?'

'I've got an idea about doing something else,' I say vaguely.

'Cooking at Cafè Vermell?' she shoots back.

I'm stunned for a moment but then I remember I don't have anything to feel guilty about.

'Is Andrew with you?' She looks past me as if he might have ducked out of sight into a doorway.

I stretch my mouth into something I hope resembles a smile. 'No, that didn't work out.'

'Oh?' She looks genuinely surprised.

'Thank you for the flowers and the opportunity you gave me at Perfecte,' I continue, stealing Janet's line from the other day. She was right. If I hadn't taken up Mariana's offer, I wouldn't be back in Barcelona now. About to put into action something completely new.

All for me.

'I got your email,' Mariana replies with a shrug. 'These things happen.'

'Janet says you're still hoping to buy Riverside?' I say.

She nods. 'After the divorce has gone through, we are rebranding Perfecte as a father and daughter team.' Her smile is bright but I catch wariness in her eyes.

I lower my voice. 'Will you be okay? I mean, how did your father react to the divorce?'

Mariana stares at me for a moment. 'Oh, *Pare* never liked Andrew,' she says briskly. 'In the end, he only cared about the brand and the money.'

Her eyes glaze over for a moment and I feel a pinch of sympathy for her.

Mariana's gaze snaps back to mine. '*Pare* did not want me to buy Perfecte from Andrew and break the brand, but Andrew is *tossut*, like a mule, and did not give up.' Her laugh tinkles. 'We were stuck until I told *Pare* we were divorcing. But I am not stupid – I also shared my idea for the new brand – *pare i filla* – and that made him a happy man.' Her smile dazzles. '*Pare* loves me too much to say no, so now we are *all* happy.'

Mariana tilts her head. 'You should know. Andrew never loved me the way he loves you,' she says eventually and shrugs. 'So now I am alone. But like you, I have new ideas. I am moving to London. I will find myself an English gentleman.'

We eye each other. '*Gràcies*, Alice,' she says, brushing her lips to each of my cheeks. '*Bona sort* – good luck.'

I stare after her as she walks away, white chiffon drifting behind her like a bridal veil. I make my way slowly towards the entrance of Plaça del Taronger, turning over everything she's said. It wasn't just Mariana who'd prevented Andy from moving on, her father had too.

Andrew never loved me the way he loves you.

As I step back into the sunshine, it's like the blinding light pushes sense back into my brain. *He thinks I'm a drink driver, that I nearly killed my mum.*

Alice, the accident wasn't your fault.

I pause to steady my breathing and take in the pretty chapel, the birds pecking the water around the angel fountain, the striped awnings of the market stalls surrounding the orange tree. My gaze lands on Susie and Xavier's new cafe-shop. It's easy to spot as they're both outside, standing on dust sheets, paint pots at their feet. Susie's carefully dabbing orange paint on to a mural of an orange tree while Xavier's squatting down and painting the door frame.

Susie must have a sixth sense because she looks around. 'Alice!' she shouts. 'You're back!'

I grin and go over to them.

'I was going to call you later. Are you okay? Did you see Mariana? She was just here. She came to tell us she's . . .' She bites her lip, worry etching her face.

'Bought Andy out?' I say.

She relaxes. 'You know? I can't believe she's going to set up Perfecte London herself. You must be really disappointed.'

Xavier puts a warm arm around me. 'I'm sorry, my cousin is a force.'

I laugh. 'Perfecte wouldn't be such a success without Mariana's determination and ambition, would it?'

They glance at one another. 'You're happy, then?' asks Susie cautiously.

'Everything's turned out for the best,' I reply. *Almost.*

I suspect Susie already knows things haven't worked out between Andy and I as she clocks the emotion in my voice and puts down the paintbrush. She wipes her hands on her paint-splattered jeans. 'Xav, I'm taking a break. Alice and I have some serious catching up to do.'

Before long, Susie's showing me around the building and bouncing through their plans to renovate the two halves. There'll be a few tables outside the simple takeaway, which will lead through to her shop where a huge window looks on to the square. Xavier calls out now and then to dispute some of her wilder ideas, but their banter is light and friendly.

Soon Susie and I are sitting on upturned crates in her empty shop, sipping espressos. I fill her in on Janet's retirement, Mum's new relationship, and how I've decided to leave and make a go of it here.

'Have you got a plan?' Susie asks. Her eyes light up as if she's got an idea of her own.

'Susie,' Xavier warns.

'Some people are so frustrating,' she mutters.

I'm too jumpy with nerves to dwell on their exchange and I blurt out what I've been wanting to say since I first walked through the door. 'I want to open a cookery school. I was hoping there might be some space for me to use your kitchen here.'

They both stare at me for a few beats longer than is comfortable. Then Susie springs back into life and shrieks. 'Oh my God, what an amazing idea! What can we do to help?'

Xavier beckons me over and pushes open a door that leads through to a miniscule kitchen. There's barely room for two people, let alone an entire class.

My heart sinks. 'Don't worry, I'll find somewhere else. Let me know if you hear of anywhere?'

Xavier shifts uncomfortably and I sense I ought to let them get on.

'I'd better go,' I say brightly. 'Would you like some help later? I can come back.'

Susie beams. 'If you're sure, that would be great!'

I tug my suitcase towards Plaça Reial. Now I've had to abandon plan A, my thoughts pull at the strings of plan B. Asking Jimmy for a job at Café Vermell with Juliana is not the solution I'm looking for, but it will buy me some time.

I'm hoping I might find Andy still there. Though perhaps he already has the money from the sale and has gone. Maybe he's as desperate to leave Barcelona as he was to leave Mariana. I think back to the periods when he wasn't in work, the 'business trips' he'd taken – what plans has he been making?

At Charlie's wedding, he'd told me he had good news. But I'd jumped to my own conclusions and left him no opportunity to explain.

Now I want to listen. I'm eager for him to be happy.

As I get closer to the plaza, my stomach begins to flutter at the thought of seeing him. I must tell him why I didn't confront him about Mariana ten years ago. That it was easier to believe what I'd heard than admit what I did to Mum.

What I *thought* I'd done.

Now I'm no longer afraid to tell my secrets, I want to throw everything up in the air to see if any fragments of our relationship can be salvaged and put back together.

I walk into the square and pass the elderly couple with their little dog. They greet me with big smiles and I'm chuffed they recognise me. They shuffle past, bodies curled together as though decades of whispered words, shared joy, love and friendship have bound them tight. At the fountain, acrobats backflip to the cheers of the crowd and chatter rolls out from the tables.

Then I'm outside Café Vermell.

My gaze travels up to my bedroom.

Our bedroom?

The shadows of our past selves live on in the balcony, snuggled together, watching the activity below. But it's too painful to linger and I drag my eyes away and catch Jimmy coming out to the terrace.

He looks startled. 'What are you doing here? I thought you were staying in London?' His trademark grin is missing and my heart sinks. What's Andy told him?

I force a smile and point at my suitcase. 'Can I move back in?'

Jimmy glances inside. I sense his hesitation and rush on before I lose my nerve. 'I'm sure you've heard the news about Perfecte London. I was wondering if you'd consider taking me on? Please?'

Jimmy rubs his hand over his buzz cut and glances up at the balcony. The doors must be open because the curtains billow out and one snags the edge of the chair. Is Andy still here? Has he seen me?

Jimmy must clock the hope in my face. 'Alice,' he says, touching my arm. 'Andy's gone. He's on his way to London.'

My heart's heavy.

Chapter 53

ALICE

Now

Jimmy tells me if we hurry, we might catch Andy on the way to the airport as he's not been gone long. He tucks my suitcase behind the bar and ushers me on to the back of his moped. Before I've had time to consider whether this is a good idea, we're off at hair-raising speed, weaving through the traffic and buzzing down the back streets to Barcelona Sants train station.

Jimmy pulls up outside. My mind is still whirling from the ride and the news that Andy's on his way to London. Why am I chasing after him? London is Andy's fresh start. Barcelona is mine. What more is there to say?

'Go on, then,' Jimmy urges.

Why is Andy going to London? His plans don't include me.

Alice, the crash wasn't your fault.

Whatever Andy's reasons, I need to say sorry. For hiding things, for not explaining things. Perhaps he'll think I'm mad to rake over the past and he'll have little interest, but telling the truth will make a difference to me. I've nothing left to lose. He needs to know how my life played out after the car accident. To hear me admit how fear, guilt, love and loyalty kept me from being honest with myself – and with him.

And that's why I allowed myself to believe he'd chosen Mariana over me. A cowardly move so I didn't have to tell him we were over.

I don't want to be that person anymore.

I climb off the bike and thank Jimmy, who nods and screeches away. Soon I'm boarding the train to the airport, walking up the aisles, glancing at the seats. I press the button to access the next carriage, my mouth dry, and move past a woman bouncing her baby on her lap, a teenager hunched over his phone, a cluster of older ladies talking animatedly in English.

Perhaps he's not on this train. Perhaps I'm too early – or too late?

I enter the next carriage, my blood pulsing – and there he is. He's staring out of the window, unshaven, his messy blond hair making my heart ache and reminding me of when we first met. For a moment, I see the old Andy stretched out across the seats in a black T-shirt and baggy shorts, the gold hoop earring, his cheeky grin.

His brother's Gemini pendant.

I touch the necklace at my throat. 'Is this seat taken?'

Andy looks up, startled. A flush stains his cheeks. 'Alice . . . What the . . . ?'

Tentatively, I lower myself down opposite him.

'How did you find me?' He's curious rather than angry and I feel a flicker of hope.

'Jimmy.'

The train lurches into motion and I know I don't have much time to get everything out before we arrive at the airport. I draw in a shaky breath and try to gather my tumble of thoughts to work out where to start.

Tears well but I swallow them down. 'Not long ago, you asked me why I left you – I mean, ten years ago,' I say quietly. 'I want to explain what happened.'

Andy sighs. 'You thought I'd gone off to Ibiza with Mariana.'

I nod. 'But there's more – much more.'

Alice, the crash wasn't your fault.

Chapter 54

ALICE

Ten years ago

I'd stood at the front of the crematorium and spoken about my grandma but it was hard to remember what I'd said. But I'd not forgotten Mum clutching my arm so hard she'd left red imprints on my arm, her sobbing soaking the thin fabric of my dress. During the wake, I'd floated, disembodied, around the room, making sure everyone had felt welcome – and ignored Andy's insistent phone calls. Like I had for the previous few days.

I didn't want to hear his lies – or his truth. I had nothing to say.

As the mourners began drifting home in the late afternoon, Mum thrust a glass of Prosecco in my hand. 'Drink, Alice. You're pale. It will help you relax.'

I'd been about to refuse but my phone chimed a message, the vibrations like the sound of my anxious heartbeat. I knocked back a gulp of wine and opened it.

Please phone me, Alice. I miss you xxxx

I touched his necklace, my breath tight.

'Drink up. Philippe's bringing the car around,' said Mum.

I downed the rest of my glass and followed her outside. Missed me? Was it a trick? He had no idea I knew he'd gone off with Mariana.

Philippe's yellow sports car slid into view and he got out. 'You okay to take your mum home?' he said to me. 'I've had one too many, really.'

'Me?' I replied, alarmed. 'No way, I've not driven for ages.'

'You'll be fine.' He glanced over to where my sister was making her way towards us in black spiked heels, wearing a man's suit. 'Charlie and I are going to the club for a few quiet ones before we open. We'll get a taxi.'

My jaw stiffened. 'Have you asked Mum? She might want to come with you.'

'Of course he has.' Mum sighed. 'Don't fuss. I'm tired. I just want to go home.' Philippe gave her a firm hug and murmured something into her ear that made her giggle.

My thoughts floated back to Andy.

I miss you.

Was Mariana a mistake?

Philippe handed me the keys. 'Thanks for helping.'

'I'm not driving,' I repeated.

Mum prodded me into the driver's side. 'Come on, you need the practice. You've hardly been behind the wheel since you passed your test. Now, say a big thank you to Philippe for lending us his car.' She slid into the low-slung passenger seat with practised ease.

I sank down and adjusted my position this way and that until I felt as comfortable as I could. I looked around for the SatNav, but then I remembered Philippe's car was too old.

'Can you direct me, Mum?' I started the engine, put the car in gear and slowly pulled away over the crunch of gravel.

'I hope you're going to drive faster than this,' she huffed.

'Give me a chance,' I muttered. 'You know the way home, right?'

'Yes,' she snapped.

We set off, joining the commuter traffic, with Mum chattering about the people she'd not seen in years. After the arm-clutching at the crematorium, she'd sprung back to life and spent the afternoon twirling the room and entertaining guests with her stories about my grandma.

'Oh! You should have taken a right back there,' she said, glancing at the map on her phone.

I sighed. The traffic in the opposite direction was crawling. I indicated to turn around and we joined the queue.

Mum's foot jigged. 'Can't you go any faster?' she said.

I looked at the solid line ahead. 'Seriously?'

She glanced at her phone again. 'Take this right, then,' she said. 'Then it's left after that.'

'I can't just—'

'Yes, you can!'

I indicated and forced my way across the traffic, heart fluttering. I made it through. It wasn't so bad. Perhaps there were some advantages to driving a fancy sports car – I appeared to command some kind of respect on the road.

'See? You did great.'

I glanced over at her; she was staring out the window. The effects of our emotional day had sunk her face a little. 'How are you feeling now?' I asked her.

'Odd,' she sighed. 'I can't believe she's gone.'

Tears welled in my eyes and I blinked them away. 'Me, neither.'

We carried on in silence, aching thoughts of Grandma and of Andy twirling around my head.

Andy misses me.

I wouldn't see my grandma again.

I felt a wave of certainty. I would phone him when I got home. I *must* phone him. Andy had told me Matt had been killed by a drunk driver. We'd – I gulped – *made love*. Then everything that had happened since . . . What if I'd got it wrong? I needed to hear what Andy had to say. Otherwise how would I know if we had a chance of moving on from this?

'Which left turn is it?' I said, suddenly desperate to get home.

'Sorry, petal?'

'The turning? Which road is it?'

Mum glanced at the map. 'It's this one. Oh, hang on, wait . . . It's the next one.'

'You sure?'

She nodded and had another look at her phone. 'Oh, petal! You've gone past it again.'

I clenched the steering wheel. 'Can't you turn on the voice navigation? We'll get there much quicker.'

'You keep distracting me,' she huffed. 'Philippe would have got me home by now.'

I found myself passing through the gates of Richmond Park. 'Is this right?' I said, glancing over at Mum again.

Her foot bounced furiously but she said nothing, too stubborn to admit she'd made another mistake.

'*Please* put the navigation on,' I said, smoothing my tone.

'I'm not turning around again and, anyway, it's not far now, see?' She waved her mobile at me. 'Do you think I want to make this journey any longer than it should be?'

Gently, I batted the phone away. 'Careful,' I murmured, keeping my eyes glued to the road. Up ahead, a herd of deer stood around a large oak tree, and the car in front had slowed down to look. 'I just didn't think we'd go this way.'

'If you don't believe me, look yourself.' Mum's voice had begun to rise and she pushed the phone in front of my face again.

'Hey!' I shoved it aside and took some deep breaths to stay calm. 'I believe you,' I said more softly.

'I'm not sure you do. You think I'm incapable of doing stuff for myself, don't you?'

Mum's words flew at me like knives and the awful thing was that I did – I did think that sometimes, but I'd never tell her.

'I can see it in your face,' she shrieked. 'You think you know it all now, don't you? Gallivanting around Europe, getting a job in Barcelona. You think you're a woman of the world and I'm totally clueless! You don't want to be back living here with me. I'm a burden to you!'

I looked over at her, stricken. 'That's not true!'

But it was – and I felt sick.

I turned my eyes back to the road and screamed as a deer leapt out from nowhere. I twisted the steering wheel, narrowly avoiding the creature, and we bumped on to the grass, scattering the herd, careering towards the oak tree, and I yanked the wheel again.

A thick thud sounded and, in a flash of confusion, a series of weighty thumps boomed against the car, shattering the windscreen. We slammed to a halt.

With eyes pinched shut, I stayed gripping the wheel, terrified to look into the hideous silence. Slowly, I cracked them open. The oak tree stood beside us untroubled and untouched, the branches swaying in the breeze. My forehead throbbed and I touched where it was most tender, but it wasn't bleeding. I turned to look at Mum – and screamed. A deer's hoof jutted through the shattered windscreen, inches from her petrified face. We watched the body slide off the bonnet in a slick of blood.

I wrenched open the door, fell to the grass and vomited. Then, scrabbling to my feet, I ran around to Mum's side. Her mouth opened and closed but no sound came out. My eyes dropped to where she was clutching the top of her leg, face white, breath coming in short, panicky rasps.

I dialled 999.

I could have killed Mum.

This single thought has haunted me for a decade.

Chapter 55

ALICE

Now

Andy grips the seat and stares at me. I sense the train slowing as it gets closer to the airport. But I'm still hanging on to the rest of the conversation I'd had with Mum and Philippe yesterday, and force myself to finish.

'Alice, you weren't drunk!' Mum exclaimed, sitting down next to me on the sofa. 'You had *one* glass of Prosecco. One. The crash was an accident. It wasn't your fault.'

'My car had dodgy brakes,' Philippe added. He leant forward. 'That's why your mum broke it off with me.' His eyes became wary as he looked at her. 'Dani, you know I had no idea? I'd never have lent Alice my car if I'd known.'

Mum nodded. 'I knew in my heart the crash was nobody's fault. But my broken hip gave me something powerful to blame you for, Philippe. So I wouldn't keep coming back. I hated being the other woman in your life, especially as I knew you loved me, but I couldn't carry on. Not with your wife being so sick.' She sighed. 'My injury was a painful reminder why we shouldn't be together. It kept me strong on the dark days when I was desperate to start things up with you again.'

I looked down at the carpet, my hands shaking, my mouth dry. I swallowed. 'But I was the one driving,' I repeated. 'That lady at the wedding, she knew I was drunk and crashed the car.'

Philippe gasped. 'No way! I would never have let you drive if I'd thought you'd had too much to drink!'

'Who told you that?' Mum said sharply. 'That is *not* true. You had *one* drink.'

'How do you remember?' I say, dazed. 'The day is such a blur . . .'

'Because you were breathalysed,' she shrills. 'It's the first thing they do with the driver after an accident.'

'I hit the deer. I broke your hip,' I murmur. 'You've not been able to walk properly since.'

Mum snatched up my hand. 'I was getting in a flap about the directions and waving my phone around! The deer got spooked by the car in front. Philippe's brakes were temperamental. How could the accident have been your fault? You did the right thing by swerving away from the tree.'

Hysteria surged through me. 'I killed a deer!' I shouted. 'I could have killed you!'

'Oh, God,' Philippe muttered. 'I'm so sorry. I should never have lent you my car.'

'Stop,' Mum said, holding up her hand. 'That's enough, both of you. Alice, the crash was an accident – it wasn't your fault, do you hear me? I encouraged you to drive. I got the directions wrong. We should never have ended up in Richmond Park.'

Mum squeezed my hand hard enough to crush my fingers. 'The most important thing is we're both still here. I won't have the pair of you shouldering the blame because I played a part in this, too. Remember the physio exercises I was given to do after the operation? Alice, you worked bloody hard to make me do them and I refused. I could have done a lot more to help myself, but I didn't.'

Mum's words slowly began to sink in.

So, if it wasn't my fault, then . . . ?

I jumped up. 'You've ruined my life,' I said, my voice low and dangerous. 'You've made me feel like I *owed* you, that I *had* to look after you, that there was no other way.'

Mum's gaze slid away.

I turned to Philippe. 'I gave up everything for her!' I shrieked. 'I thought all this—' I swept my arm over her. 'This, her immobility, was my fault! Drunk behind the wheel! Careless driving!' My heart split open and the tears rushed out. Blinded, I ran up the stairs, ignoring Mum's calls.

I threw myself on to my bed and sobbed into the duvet, feeling twenty all over again, horrified, heartbroken – stuck in a life I never wanted.

I don't know how long I lay like that. I must have fallen into an exhausted sleep as sometime later, Mum appeared at my door. I saw she'd made it up the stairs without a stick. Tears glistened in her eyes. 'I'm sorry, Alice,' she said. 'I am *truly* sorry.'

She came into my room and pointed at my chair. 'Can I sit down?'

I pushed myself up to sitting and nodded.

'You know, going to Barcelona was the best thing you could have done for me,' she began softly. 'I've relied on you too much and that wasn't right, or fair. I convinced myself you were happy working for Janet and living with me because, with Philippe gone, I was lonely.' She twisted her hands together. 'I lost motivation for life. I had an ache in me that no amount of food or shopping could fill, and when my longing for Philippe finally faded, it was too late. My habits had become a crutch.' Her eyes raked over me. '*You* became my crutch.'

She smiled sadly. 'I never meant to hold you back. I should have opened my eyes and asked you what you wanted from your life.' She came over and sat down on my bed. 'I had no idea you loved Barcelona as much as you do, but you glowed when you came through the door the other day, and then when I saw you with Andy, I could see there was something else, something special between you.'

She touched my face, eyes worried. 'What happened, petal? Where is he?'

Chapter 56

ANDY

Now

I feel like two people.

I'm the Andy who's fallen for Alice, listening to her story finally unfold. I'm absorbing her sorrow, naked and anguished, and her pain cuts me as deep as if it were my own.

Then I'm Andy, the kid, watching numbly from the sidelines, scared the people I love will leave and never come back.

The train pulls into the station and I stand and sling my bag on to my shoulder. I'm reminded of when Alice got up to leave with Charlie all those years ago, when I'd been too young and too unsure of myself to ask for her phone number.

'Come on,' I say. 'There are things I need to tell you, too.'

Startled, Alice jumps up and we get off, joining the flow of passengers into the terminal, though I've no idea where I'm going. All I know is I'm not parting ways with Alice until we've said everything that needs to be said.

Then . . . ?

We find ourselves in a cafe, where we buy crap coffee and sit down at a table strewn with sandwich wrappers and sticky with spilt Coke. Alice whips into action, scrubbing the surface with paper napkins and a squeeze of hand sanitiser from her bag. Her efficiency – and that she cares – tickles my mouth into a faint smile.

Alice sips her coffee and grimaces.

'What did you see in me?' I say. 'When we first met, I mean?' I'm aware her answer really matters.

She looks at me in surprise and then throws me a careful smile. 'You were cute, cheeky – and a little bit annoying,' she says. 'But mostly I knew you were kind and you had a big heart.'

We smile sadly at one another.

'Was I really *me*? I always felt as though I had to be "more Matt" – like that would somehow bring him back to life or keep the memory of him alive.' I try my coffee and make a face. 'I knew straight away Ibiza wasn't for me. And what with not being able to cope with the pressure of my finance job in London, I felt like I'd failed Matt yet again. In my mind, he would have smashed it being a DJ and gone on to be the best music lawyer in the business. Success had meant so much to him.' I drum my fingers on the table. 'It never occurred to me he might struggle or fail, or grow to regret his choices.'

I sigh. 'I couldn't even handle working at Café Vermell without you. I didn't know who I was or what I wanted anymore.'

I pour sugar into my coffee but it still tastes like piss. Something occurs to me. A memory of Alice's strangled voice on the phone that day. How I'd chosen not to hear her anguish – only rejection. 'You called me after the accident, didn't you?'

Alice's face crumples but she swallows hard and nods. 'At the hospital, with Mum's injuries, knowing I'd had a drink . . .' She draws in a wobbly breath. 'I knew nothing you could say, or that I could say to you, would take away the horror of what I'd done. You were devastated by your brother's death . . . and all I could think about was how I'd nearly killed my mum. I didn't want you to despise me as much as I despised myself.'

Alice fades for a moment. The party scene flashes across my mind. Me, a kid, standing outside the house. My eyes glued to the pretty brunette, pleading with Matt to drive the other girl home. Winning him round again. Thinking about myself. Not thinking about the most important person in my life – my brother.

'Even if you'd said you wanted to be with me, I couldn't,' Alice whispers. 'I had to stay and look after Mum. You had a chance with Mariana, so I went along with the break-up.'

She'd posted back Matt's necklace. Saying everything without telling me anything.

My throat burns as the enormity of the past settles in. Matt's death. The car accident. The unfolding of my life with Mariana. Alice's loyalty to her mum. What if I'd swallowed my pride that day and told her I loved her? Instead of giving in to my bruised ego and saying we were over, when all I'd wanted was to hear her reassurance.

I'm still stirring my coffee, although the sugar granules are long dissolved. 'Mariana was besotted with me and she fed my ego,' I say. 'I leapt at the chance of forming a business partnership with her because I thought she was the path for me to become like Matt. They had the same ethos. Mariana believes success is everything.' I fiddle with the sugar wrapper. 'She swept me into marriage. But in the end we were married to work, not each other.' I look up at Alice. 'It took a while for me to figure that out.'

Her eyes skate over my face; she nods.

'I had to make a choice. Stay married to Mariana and keep the business going – or get out of both.' I push the coffee away. 'She had a complete meltdown when I told her I was leaving and demanded I move into the annexe so we could keep up the charade.

335

It took her longer to admit our marriage was over. She kept insisting she loved me but eventually she accepted she loved Perfecte more.'

I swallow. 'It was such a relief. I'd been going to counselling to figure out why I'd let the marriage drag on for so long. Turns out I needed help to work through my grief, to understand I didn't need to be Matt, I—' I lock on to Alice. 'I just needed to be *me*.'

Her eyes swim with emotion. People jostle past to join the queue to pay, bags knock into our table and the babble of voices rises around us.

But there's more I need to tell her. 'Let's find somewhere quieter,' I say.

We weave through the tables, past the shops, the rows of seats crammed with travellers waiting for their flights and find a spot by the windows that look out on to the runway. There's nowhere to sit but there's also no one else here.

Alice clutches her bag. 'I'm sorry things didn't work out with Mariana,' she says.

I want to reach out and pull her to me. Breathe in her scent and go back to where we were. But I can't – not yet.

'Do you understand why I didn't want you to take the job?' I say. 'I wanted to sell and get out way before you came along. But Mariana hung in there, desperate to keep Perfecte together, and I had no idea if your job in London would ever materialise.'

Alice gives me a small smile. 'It doesn't matter. I'm not bothered.'

My eyes drift towards the window. I wonder why she's come back to Barcelona and what her plans might be. A plane turns off the runway and taxis towards one of the stands. I wonder if it's mine.

Alice follows my gaze.

'The car accident sounds terrible,' I say softly. 'It must have been awful carrying the blame for your mum's injury for so long.'

The plane comes to a standstill, so the passengers can disembark to begin their holidays, make new business deals, visit loved ones, start a new life.

'I get how painful guilt feels, how it can eat away at you, I really do.' I place my hand against the glass and feel the memories gathering – and start to tell Alice what happened the night Matt died.

Chapter 57

ANDY

Fifteen years ago

Once I'd laid eyes on the stunning brunette swaying to Matt's tunes, I'd sprung over, fuelled with the shot of confidence I'd got from being the DJ's brother.

She laughed as I popped up by her side. 'What's the hurry? Got somewhere to be?'

'Not now I've seen you, baby.' I smirked.

She rolled her eyes and turned her head away, and I scrabbled to rescue the situation. I pointed at Matt. 'DJ's good, isn't he? That's my brother.'

She looked scornful. 'As if.'

But I saw her glance at him and then back at me.

I seized the moment. 'Want a drink?' I held up the bag of booze.

'Depends what's on offer.'

I swallowed down my second cheesy line. 'Come on, I'll show you.' I went through to the kitchen, breath taut in the hope that she was following. Bright lights glared on to crisp packets, empty bottles and half-drunk paper cups of booze that lay strewn across the surfaces. A group were playing a drinking game at the table, downing neat spirits, and the thick scent of weed snuck in through the open back door.

I cleared a space by the sink, dumped the bag down – and turned around.

The brunette smiled. 'So?'

My stomach tipped over in excitement and I grinned. 'We need cups,' I said, glancing around.

'Do we?' She laughed.

I tried not to look at her tight cropped top, her bare navel with its piercing. Even making eye contact with her was sending me into a spin.

Before long, we were challenging each other to neck shots using the bottle top and at some point I moved on to beer. Then we were snogging in the corner and her hands were all over me. Reluctantly, I dragged myself away to take a piss. A couple were rammed up against each other in the downstairs cloakroom, so I ran upstairs in search of the bathroom. I hurried down the corridor, trying the closed doors as I went, finding a bedroom piled high with coats and another with a pair making out on the bed.

I heard the scream before I found the bathroom. Instinctively I threw myself at the door. It flew open and I stumbled in to find a guy with a greasy smile, pinning a girl to the wall with his body.

I didn't think. I smashed away his triumph with one punch. He stumbled backwards and tipped into the bath, floundering like an upturned turtle, surprised to see blood on his fingers as he wiped his nose.

I looked at the girl. 'Are you okay?' Her hands scrabbled at the wall behind her, eyes darting this way and that. I held up my palms. 'I'm not going to hurt you.'

Shaking, she scrubbed at tears and snot with the back of her hand, smearing mascara and red lipstick across her face. I glanced back at the boy in the bath. He was trying to haul himself up, so I turned the shower on full blast. He screamed as the cold water hit him.

'I'll get you home,' I said to the girl, though I had no idea who she was or where she lived.

She nodded and took my hand, but she was still trembling as we passed the bedroom with the coats so I grabbed one off the pile and draped it around her shoulders. Some of the lads saw me coming down the stairs with my arm around her and wolf-whistled.

'Ignore them,' I muttered. Then I noticed the music had changed – Matt must have finished his set. 'Has my brother gone?' I called to Jimmy, who'd appeared in the doorway.

He nodded and pointed outside. 'Just packing his stuff into the car.'

The girl and I headed out and came face to face with the brunette. She took one look at us huddled together and stormed off.

'Hey!' I called helplessly, eyes glued to her sassy hips and the angry swish of her hair as she disappeared back inside.

I looked over to my brother. 'Matt! Can you take this girl home?' I shouted, ushering her forward.

He laughed. 'I'm not a taxi service.'

The girl flinched and I put my hand on her arm. Then I remembered the brunette and took it away again. 'Please?' I called.

'No,' he retorted. 'I'm going to a club.'

I glanced back inside. The brunette might already be pressed up against another guy and I wanted that mouth of hers back on mine – with the possibility of more.

'Mate!' I called again. 'I owe you one?'

'It's fine,' the girl murmured. 'I can get myself home.'

But it wasn't fine.

Matt was looking over at us, frowning, and then he came closer. 'I know you, don't I?' he said, taking in the girl's shivers and

340

smudged make-up. 'You're Dave's sister. I met you at your parents' place in Montpellier that time.'

She nodded, clutching the jacket closed, tears pooling her eyes again.

Matt glanced at me and clapped me on the shoulder. 'I'll take her home,' he said. 'Look after yourself, bro. Don't do anything stupid and don't do anything I wouldn't do.'

Chapter 58

ANDY

Now

Alice's hand is warm on my back.

'I barely said thanks, let alone goodbye, because all I was thinking about was chasing after the brunette,' I say quietly. 'For years I thought if I hadn't begged Matt to take the girl home, the accident wouldn't have happened.'

Alice's hand finds mine. She says nothing but the pressure of her fingers is all I need. After what she's gone through with her mum, she understands my pain more than anyone.

'Matt got the girl safely home and, afterwards, his mate Dave couldn't thank me enough. But I didn't deserve his thanks, not when a drunk driver had slewed across the lights and into my brother's car . . .' My voice cracks. 'It still hurts.'

I fall silent. Passengers climb the steps to board the plane – are they saying sad farewells or are they excited for what's to come?

Nothing would ever take away the pain of losing my brother, but time had helped me claw myself out of the shock and form a cushion around the tragedy, find a way for me to live with it, to manage my sorrow.

'Counselling helped me understand I'm only hurting myself by hanging on to the blame and guilt,' I say. 'There's no way Matt would have wanted me to live like that.'

Alice pulls me to her and we hold each other tight. I inhale the scent that is her, feel her warmth and comfort moulding my body, and my tension begins to slip away.

As we pull apart, she glances up at the screen. My London flight flashes the last warning to board. Next to it are the departure times for the trains back to the city.

'Why did you come to Barcelona?' I ask her.

'Why are you going to London?' she replies.

'To find you,' I say, taking her face in my hands. I kiss her eyes, her cheeks, her lips. 'Where do you want to go?'

Alice's smile floods me with warmth. 'Anywhere – as long as I'm with you.'

Our kiss is tentative and tender. It speaks of something new and hopeful for us. Slowly, we clasp hands and make our way back to the city.

On the train, Alice cautiously tells me how she wants to open a cookery school in Barcelona, her excitement growing as she talks. Her idea is so clever, so perfect – so *obvious* – it's like she's flicked on a light switch and I'm no longer grappling around in the dark with my own plans.

I'm buzzing by the time we get off the train and laughing as I bat away Alice's persistent questions about where we're going. I tell her to be patient and promise I'll reveal all soon.

Before long, we reach the narrow opening that leads into Plaça del Taronger, but rather than spill out to the sunshine, I stop outside a wooden door. Alice eyes its rough, warped surface scarred with woodworm and age. 'What are we doing here?'

I kiss away her confusion and feel the tickle of her smile beneath mine. The key grinds as I turn it and I nudge hard at the door wedged in the swollen frame. We step into the gloom and the musty smell of time and decay envelops us. There are no windows in here so I use the torch on my phone to sweep the room, revealing a large space, empty except for an old industrial work bench thick with dust.

'Oh,' says Alice.

I laugh at her disappointment. 'It's okay. You're not supposed to be impressed. It's just a store room.'

A door to our right suddenly flies open and throws blinding light into the room. Susie and Xavier stand on the threshold and the sunshine of the square glows through the cafe behind them.

'Oh!' she says again.

'Surprise!' they shout, throwing their arms in the air.

Alice turns to me, her face a mix of pleasure and confusion. 'Come on,' she says, grinning. 'You *have* to tell me now.'

I can't contain my excitement any longer; everything has slotted into place. 'I've been wanting to open a restaurant for ages and although I've been searching all over for premises, something has always been missing. When Susie and Xavier showed me this room, I thought it would be ideal, but I've been struggling to commit to the project, it's never felt quite right.'

Alice glances around at the dust motes twirling in the sunlight.

I grab her hands and realise mine are shaking a little. I lock my gaze on to hers. 'I want this to be your new cookery school.'

Alice says nothing; she doesn't need to. She flings her arms around me and holds me tight.

Now I know what's been missing. Not something, *someone*.

Alice.

Epilogue

ALICE

Six months later

A breeze twirls through Plaça del Taronger, rustling the leaves on the orange tree and fluttering the awnings on the market stalls.

I peek out from the wooden door and catch Mum and Philippe admiring the stained-glass windows in the chapel. She holds his arm, not because she has to these days, but because she wants to. The weight has fallen off. She's a Zumba fanatic and she's found a fantastic yoga teacher – Philippe's neighbour at his house in the South of France, where they're spending winter. The classes are doing wonders for Mum's hip.

They glance over to El Taronger – The Orange Tree – Susie and Xavier's cafe-shop.

A banner hangs above the door. The four of us had wrestled with the wind early this morning to string it across the balconies of our two apartments. I look up at the sky. Clouds scud over blue and I hope we've tied it on firmly enough.

I hear familiar laughter and my eyes find Jimmy holding his daughter in his arms. Juliana has their son by the hand. He's bouncing up and down, demanding Xavier's ice-cream – and why not?

Customers can't get enough of his homemade flavours – the cinnamon vanilla with churro pieces is divine. Jimmy smiles and passes his daughter to his wife. He picks up his son and flies him through the air, sounding like an aeroplane. The boy giggles.

I see Janet turn and smile at the delightful sound, at Jimmy's sunny face, his wife stroking their daughter's head. Janet's first in line outside the door. She glances at her watch, waiting for Charlie and Sarah, I presume. The trio are sharing accommodation while they visit and it's only a five-minute walk away. So typical for Charlie to be late.

Though it's not time yet.

Susie and Xavier have been kind enough to stay closed this morning, just for us. Usually, the queue for Xavier's legendary tapas and ice-cream would be trailing across the square by now. Susie's trade rolls gently throughout the day, allowing her to chat to customers while she works – and, of course, insist they indulge in one of Xavier's tasty treats on their way out.

But today is no ordinary day.

As the chapel clock inches towards midday, people slowly gather, one eye on the time, another on the banner, their bags filled with tasty foodstuffs bought from the market.

A familiar whoop draws eyes towards Charlie, who's skidded into the square, pulling Sarah along with her. Janet tuts – and smiles. They're not late, they're *almost* late. Mum and Philippe stroll over to join them.

I pull back inside and go to the adjoining door to the cafe. Xavier's laying out tapas dishes on the takeaway counter for customers to try. Across the way, Susie's arranging jewellery on a green velvet cloth – delicate fruit and vegetable ceramics shaped into brooches, earrings and pendants.

I turn back, Andy's hand slips around my waist and we survey our work.

Light pours through huge squares of ceiling glass that frame the blue sky above. The original wood floor has been sanded and varnished while the walls glow fresh and white. A high shelf runs around the perimeter of the room stacked with pans, and below there are hobs and ovens. We've buffed up the industrial work bench. Its stainless-steel surface glistens along the middle of the room, where we've set up workstations for the students.

Enric and Sofia come over and she kisses her son's cheeks, then mine. She touches her fingers to her lips and grazes Matt's Gemini necklace around my neck. 'Your brother would be very proud of you,' she says to Andy, tears brimming. '*I* am very proud of you.'

'And so am I,' adds Enric, patting his shoulder.

Andy hugs his mum, but it's almost time, so with one last squeeze, they leave us be.

I release a long, slow breath. My dream is about to become real.

Our dream.

The chapel bells begin to chime and we look at each other. 'Ready?' we say in unison and laugh.

A gust of wind snaps the banner and the people waiting look up – *Obert al migdia! Escola de Cuina El Taronger i Visites Gastronòmiques.*

It's midday. The Orange Tree Cookery School is open. The Food Tours will begin.

ACKNOWLEDGEMENTS

A big thank you for choosing *Summer Ever After* among the sea of amazing books out there and taking the time to read it – there is no better feeling and I will always be grateful.

I began writing this book during the pandemic, a time when many of us talked about the weirdness of not being able to go out and socialise, and that got me thinking about those trapped by families or partners – lockdown or not. What did it mean to be in a controlling relationship? Why might it happen? Could what seems like controlling to one person feel like an expression of love to another? How might that change?

After setting my first book, *Worlds Apart*, in Auckland, I felt strongly I wanted *Summer Ever After* to be located somewhere abroad, too. Not just because we were living through a time when we couldn't travel, but because I am an *absolute* holiday fanatic (with a yearning for my backpacking years!).

I chose Barcelona because I love this city. With so many new destinations on my list, I'm not usually keen to revisit places, but coming back here time and again is always a delight. Who knows? Maybe I'll discover the 'real' Plaça del Taronger one day . . .

As a debut author in May 2023, this is my second published book – and also the second novel I've ever written. There's been a lot to learn and I owe massive thank yous to the team behind the scenes. First, my agent, Rufus Purdy at The Two Piers Literary Agency, you're fab to work with and a great editor. To Victoria Oundjian, my editor at Amazon Publishing's Lake Union, plus the army of editors who have questioned what my characters might say or do to help me whip this book into shape. Emma Rogers – once again, I love the cover!

Pippa Lewis – I love our regular chats about our books and the quiet time we share tapping away at cafes in Brighton and Hove. Lisa Fransson, it's lovely when you're able to join us. Anna Burtt, it's fantastic to remain a part of Brighton's West Hill Writers. Your writing retreats are brilliant for headspace and workspace to write, catch up with friends, make new writing friends and listen to industry talks. Jo Furniss, thanks for sharing your author experiences, your invaluable advice, as well as hosting Hove Writers on a Monday evening. Love these meet-ups – we're very lucky to have such a supportive writing network in Brighton and Hove.

Xanthe and Kenzie. You were young kids when I started this book and now you're firmly entrenched in your teens. I hope you get to travel the world one day and see there is more to life than what you know. Like Alice and Andy (and me meeting your dad!), perhaps you'll find the love of your life along the way, too??

Ian, without travel there would be no us. Thank you for listening to my imaginary characters and plot ramblings, and for holding together our family in the real world when I'm floundering in my writing world. You are my rock. You are my Ever After.

Loved *Summer Ever After*? Then turn the page to read the first chapter of Jane Crittenden's debut, *Worlds Apart*.

AMY

Now

He's here.

I don't feel a rush of excitement. Nor a surge of blissful happiness. No swell of pleasure, not even a tiny sigh of relief. Nothing good registers in my brain or my body to encourage me to connect with this man. Instead, sharpness twists my chest and I think, *why now?*

Only minutes before, Shannon and I had been belting out a song that was playing on the radio in my empty café. She'd held the broom handle like a microphone and I twirled around her in my scarlet dress, a purchase she'd convinced me to make a few weeks before. I was still humming as we carried on clearing away the aftermath of the party and when I stuck my head inside the glass display counter to sweep up the cake crumbs . . .

He said my name.

I straightened up. But not because his voice set my heart aflutter or because I noticed his English accent, but simply because somebody, some *stranger*, called my name. And, like with all the customers who had come into my café that day to join our celebrations, I said, 'Hello.'

Now I properly see the man who stands in front of me and the second twist to my chest is so painful it obliterates the smile I had ready for this new customer.

'Amy?' he repeats. 'Amy Curtis? It is you, isn't it?'

He looks incredulous. Energy sparks his voice and instinctively I step back, the high heel of a shoe I'm not used to wearing grinding into Shannon's foot. She mutters a swear word and I shift slightly, letting my gaze stray away from him. Behind, the tables parade the post-party carnage and tangles of pink balloons sag and nod in the sea breeze that drifts through the open door. The radio is still playing but I can't hear the music anymore.

Why now?

It already seems peculiar that, just this morning, I'd stood in this very spot, staring at the vacant tables and the glass display crammed with scones, sponges and cupcakes, voicing my doubts to Shannon that we'd sell it all. Then I'd unlocked the doors and the first group of customers trailed in, then the second, the third – and they kept coming, pouring in and jamming themselves on to the terrace outside. There were so many people that we got out our just-in-case fold-out chairs, and customers balanced cake and tea on their laps, spilling on to the beach with picnic blankets. Shannon and I had spun from customer to customer, smiling and laughing, and then – as with all great parties – it was suddenly over.

And he's here.

My eyes can't connect with his. They butterfly over him and land on the remains of the three-layer anniversary cake sitting on a table to his left. I'd baked a fruit cake for the bottom, carrot cake for the middle and then Victoria sponge, finishing the tiers with a coating of chocolate fudge. The *15 Years* I'd carefully iced to mark the occasion is now an unintelligible sticky scrawl, disappearing as fast as the years since I took over the café from Shannon's in-laws, when . . . *don't.*

I force myself to look at him. I recognise the tilt in the corners of his mouth. Not smiling, exactly, just *amused.* Then I lock on to eyes, hazel, just like . . . *don't* . . .

'It *is* you.' He grins and holds his arms wide as if he expects me to run around from behind the counter and jump into his embrace. 'I can't believe I found you.'

Found me?

He waves a folded newspaper and I catch a glimpse of my smiling face. 'I saw the article. I couldn't believe your café was just a few miles down the road from me.'

Down the road?

Shannon's still clutching the broom handle and suddenly springs back into life. 'See, Amy? I told you the whole of Auckland would know who you are now. How does it feel to be a celebrity?'

She squeezes my arm, tighter than is normal or natural, and laughs. The throaty sound usually makes me smile; it's shameless and loud with a hint of something naughty that always makes people glance in her direction as though they might witness something salacious. If anyone's a celebrity around here, it's Shannon, not me.

I glance at the identical newspaper article in a frame propped up by the till. Shannon had presented it to me just before the party ended. She'd let out a high-pitched wolf whistle to catch everyone's attention and gave an embarrassing speech about my achievements, which sounded like they belonged to someone else. In the photo, I'm wearing the same scarlet dress as I do now. I'm standing in the doorway of my café, holding a tray of red velvet cupcakes iced in creamy vanilla, my mouth stretched into a broad grin. Beneath the picture, five gold stars ring out. The critic described me as a 'Brit abroad with a genuine nostalgia for home'. Though, in truth, I've lived here for half my life.

'"Auckland's Best Baker",' Chris says, pointing the newspaper at me like a weapon. 'I knew you'd smash it one day, Ames.'

Ames. I flinch. The memory tears open the scar of all that's gone on before.

ABOUT THE AUTHOR

Jane is a homes and interiors journalist for magazines such as *25 Beautiful Homes*, *Good Homes* and *House Beautiful*, and finds writing about house projects the perfect excuse to meet people and ask (lots of) questions. She has had stints of living in Canada, Greece, Spain, Ghana and New Zealand. Nowadays, she lives with her husband, two teenagers and their labradoodle by the coast in Hove, where she enjoys the beach and can often be found in local cafés writing, reading – and giving in to the temptation of a homemade brownie.

Follow Jane on Instagram @janecrittenden and Twitter @crittenden_jane.

Follow the Author on Amazon

If you enjoyed this book, follow Jane Crittenden on Amazon to be notified when the author releases a new book!
To do this, please follow these instructions:

Desktop:

1) Search for the author's name on Amazon or in the Amazon App.
2) Click on the author's name to arrive on their Amazon page.
3) Click the 'Follow' button.

Mobile and Tablet:

1) Search for the author's name on Amazon or in the Amazon App.
2) Click on one of the author's books.
3) Click on the author's name to arrive on their Amazon page.
4) Click the 'Follow' button.

Kindle eReader and Kindle App:

If you enjoyed this book on a Kindle eReader or in the Kindle App, you will find the author 'Follow' button after the last page.